COLLECTED STORIES

Mary Lavin

COLLECTED
STORIES

*With an introduction
by V. S. Pritchett*

HOUGHTON MIFFLIN COMPANY BOSTON

1971

"Sunday Brings Sunday," "The Long Ago," "The Young Girls," "A Visit to the Cemetery," "A Tragedy," and "The Long Holidays" are here published for the first time in the United States. The other stories originally appeared in the following magazines: *The Atlantic, Cosmopolitan, Good Housekeeping, Harper's Bazaar, The New Yorker,* and *The Yale Review.*

First Printing c

International Standard Book Number: 0-395-12099-3
Library of Congress Catalog Card Number: 73-132790
Printed in the United States of America

For My Family

CONTENTS

INTRODUCTION

by V. S. Pritchett

IN THE WRITING of short stories the Russians and the Italians, the Slavonic Jews and the Irish are supreme. Tales come easily to their mouths. At first one puts this down to the longer survival of folk literature or a peasantry in these cultures. Village life is a continuous story to the villager. There is something in this, but when we see the writer of short stories excelling in the town or the city, we have to look to other reasons for the special achievement in the countries I have named. Frank O'Connor used to argue that the short story was a natural form of writing in anarchic societies where the weight and concern of a stable society had not deadened spontaneity, or in those countries where there is a long experience of loneliness and uprooting. A seductive theory, but it seems to me too general. There has been a good deal of anarchy in Italian life but Alberto Moravia offered me quite a different explanation of the Italian success in this genre. There had been only one great Italian novel in the nineteenth century, he said, because the Italians cannot bear to look at themselves in the mirror too long; a quick glance is all their vanity or sense of drama can bear. And what would one add about the Irish gift? There is the passion for talk, the love of theater, the unceasing *play* with the detail of ordinary life, the love of the changes and evasions of personality, and the instinct for the immediate. There is commonly, in Irish writing, a double vision: the power to present the surface of life rapidly, but as a covering for something else. I would guess that the making of the Irish short story writers is their extraordinary sense that what we call real life is a veil; in other words, their dramatic sense of uncertainty. It is present in their comedy and their seriousness.

It is often said that this sense of uncertainty has sprung from the conflicts of several cultures; and this seems true, particularly true, of the writers of the Anglo-Irish dispensation. But that has passed and the Irish writer stands on native grounds. Yet a great short story writer, like Mary Lavin, who is describing the most ordinary people in provincial Ireland and without the colonial eye for bizarre effects, still displays the double vision and its unanswerable questions. There are the people, set plainly before us, but gradually their emotional underground is revealed and is shown to possess a somber chaos and growing power. She is writing most of the time about people who appear to be living, at first, in a state of inertia, in the lethargy of country life: then we notice that they are smoldering and what her stories contain is the smoldering of a hidden life. Her short stories are as dense as novels and we shall gradually apprehend the essence of complete life histories — as we do, for example in the first novel-like act of a play by Ibsen — and they make the novel form irrelevant. They give a real and not a fancied view of Irish domestic life and it combines the moving with the frightening. She excels in the full portraiture of power-loving women, downtrodden women, lonely women, bickering country girls, puzzled priests and seedy shopkeepers who might pass as country types first of all, but who soon reveal a human depth of endurance or emotional tumult in their secret lives.

Take the story "At Sallygap." It is on the old Irish theme of saying goodbye, of leaving for a better life abroad. A weak young man who belongs to a band is off to Paris on the Dublin mail boat with his friends, but at the last moment cannot bear to leave his girl waving alone on the quay. He scrambles back down the gangway. His pals on the boat throw his violin to him. Farcically — but with what symbolism! — it smashes on a stanchion. There he is. The question of escape is over. Henceforth, he is the girl's prisoner and we shall see him turn into a meek dealer whose only freedom is to go to farms on the Dublin mountains to collect eggs every now and then. Up to Sallygap he goes and one day makes a mild but, for him, ecstatic gesture, by missing the bus and walking back home four hours late. Between those two incidents lies the terrifying interior history of two people whose marriage has gone dead. He is nothing; but the woman is tremendous as she sits waiting by the kitchen fire for his return. She despises her husband for having given up his freedom for her. She is bored by him. She has moved, in her life, from irritability to a longing for the rage she has seen expressed by other couples in the poor street where she lives:

> She sought in the throbbing pulse and rippling flux of anger the excitement she had unconsciously hoped to find in her marriage bed. But her angers, too, were sterile, breeding no response in Manny. He was the same always. It seemed that she would never believe this, and she tried from time to time to break the strength of his weakness, and she fought against his kindness as if it were her enemy. And so, in an obscure way, it was.
>
> What Annie wanted was the flaming face, the racing pulse, the temper that raised red weals on the skin, and the heat of bodies crushed together in rage. And this need of her nature had never been satisfied except vicariously, leaning over the shop counter listening to the whispered stories of other women; stories of obscene blows given in drunken lusts, stories of cunning and cupidity and flashes of anger and hate that rent the darkness in tenement hallways around the block when she and Manny had been in bed for hours.

She runs through her emotions:

> But, as the evening wore out and there was still no sign of him, she began to think better of him. She began to think that in his weak way he was defying her at last. Maybe he was getting his temper up with drink. He wasn't a drinking man, but there was always a first time for everything.
>
> A wild elation welled up inside her, waiting for a torrential release in shouting or screaming. She had battered in his patience at last. At last he was going to try to get even

with her. Well! She was ready. She went into the kitchen, leaving the door into the shop half open while she knotted her hair as tight as she could, and when she came back the pricking pain on her neck, where the hair was caught too tightly, gave her a foretaste of the fight she would have, and made her eyes glitter. She let the customers go without giving them their usual bit of chitchat. She put the shutters up before the time. Where was he? It was getting very late now for a timid man like Manny. And he had had no dinner. She lifted the saucer that was covering his plate on the range. She ought to let him get a bite of food into him before she started a row. But where was he?

Many of these stories describe country deaths and widowhood, the jealousies of young girls, the disappointments of courtship, the terrible aspects of lonely lives, the sly consolation of elderly love; the picture of Ireland is a somber one, relieved only by the mean comedy of country calculations and watchfulness. Why is it that these stories are not merely depressing? Simply because Miss Lavin is a great artist; we are excited by her sympathy, her acute knowledge of the heart, her truthfulness and, above all, by the controlled revelation of untidy, powerful emotion. She has a full temperament. The tales are mutinies of an observant mind, a record of unrepentant tumult where one did not know it could exist. The truck driver who bores everyone at home because he won't stop opinionating, only does so because his life is lonely and, in fact, his capacity for finding someone anywhere to talk to lands him in a dreadful situation in which his talk is a blessing; and all the time, unknowingly, he is showing us an Ireland we would never have guessed. Miss Lavin goes into the deepest human instincts and is likely to find the epical and cleansing in what could easily be left as trivially sad. Her opening story, "The Green Grave and the Black Grave," reads like a tale from the Gaelic; but it seems to me far more moving and richer in meaning than, say, Synge's *Riders to the Sea* and to have a subtler tragic force. The distinction it makes between the customs of love faced by death — for grief is a fundamental theme with her — is superbly managed. I cannot think of any Irish writer who has

gone so profoundly without fear into the Irish heart. This fearless-
ness makes her remarkable.

Where else have we read stories of this kind? Not in English or
American literature. The obvious suggestion is in the Russian of,
say, Leskov, Aksakov or Shchedrin; not of Turgenev or Tolstoy.
She has the same animal eye for everyday life, the same gift for
immersing herself in people and not sacrificing the formlessness of
their lives to the cleverness of a formal art. She feels too much to
be adroit, anecdotal or "outside." Another aspect, I think, relates
her to the Russians of the nineteenth century: women dominate her
stories and they are likely to be women who are lonely; for just as
in Russia the women became lonely and powerful because the manhood of their men was destroyed by political tyranny, so, in Ireland,
the departure of the men and the curious domestic belligerence, and
even separation, of the sexes has put a special burden on women.
Not that she is writing propaganda on their behalf. Far from it. Her
stories are not the quick glances we get in other writers; they are
long gazes into the hearts of her people.

COLLECTED STORIES

THE GREEN GRAVE AND THE BLACK GRAVE

IT WAS A BODY all right. It was hard to see in the dark, and the scaly black sea was heaving up between them and the place where they saw the thing floating. But it was a body all right.

"I knew it was a shout I heard," said the taller of the two tall men in the black boat that was out fishing for mackerel. He was Tadg Mor and he was the father of the less tall man, that was blacker in the hair than him and broader in the chest than him, but was called Tadg Og because he was son to him. *Mor* means "big" and *Og* means "son."

"I knew it was a shout I heard," said Tadg Mor.

"I knew it was a boat I saw and I dragging in the second net," said Tadg Og.

"I said the sound I heard was a kittiwake, crying in the dark."

"And I said the boat I saw was a black wave blown up on the wind."

"It was a shout all right."

"It was a boat all right."

"It was a body all right."

"But where is the black boat?" Tadg Og asked.

"It must be that the black boat capsized," said Tadg Mor, "and went down into the green sea."

"Whose boat was it, would you venture for to say?" Tadg Og asked, pulling stroke for stroke at the sea.

"I'd venture for to say it was the boat of Eamon Buidhe," said Tadg Mor, pulling with his oar against the sharp up-pointing waves of the scaly, scurvy sea. The tall men rowed hard toward the clumsy thing that tossed on the tips of the deft green waves.

"Eamon Buidhe Murnane!" said Tadg Mor, lifting clear his silver-dropping oar.

"Eamon Buidhe Murnane!" said Tadg Og lifting his clear, dripless, yellow oar.

It was a hard drag, dragging him over the arching sides of the boat. His clothes logged him down to the water and the jutting waves jottled him back against the boat. His yellow hair slipped from their fingers like floss, and the loose fibers of his island-spun clothes broke free from their grip. But they got him up over the edge of the boat, at the end of a black hour that was only lit by the whiteness of the breaking wave. They laid him down on the boards of the floor on their haul of glittering mackerel, and they spread the nets out over him. But the scales of the fish glittered up through the net and so, too, the eyes of Eamon Buidhe Murnane glittered up through the net. And the live glitter of the dead eyes put a strain on Tadg Mor and he turned the body over on its face among the fish; and when they had looked a time at the black corpse with yellow hair, set in the silver and opal casket of fishes, they turned the oar blades out again into the scurvy seas, and pulled toward the land.

"How did you know it was Eamon Buidhe Murnane, and we forty pointed waves away from him at the time of your naming his name?" Tadg Og asked Tadg Mor.

"Whenever it is a thing that a man is pulled under by the sea," said Tadg Mor, "think around in your mind until you think out which man of all the men it might be that would be the man most missed, and that man, that you think out in your mind, will be the man that will be cast up on the shingle."

"This is a man that will be missed mightily," said Tadg Og.

"He is a man that will be mightily bemoaned," said Tadg Mor.

"He is a man that will never be replaced."

"He is a man that will be prayed for bitterly and mightily."

"Many a night, forgetful, his wife will set out food for him," said Tadg Og.

"The Brightest and the Bravest!" said Tadg Mor. "Those are the words that will be read over him — the Brightest and the Bravest."

The boat rose up on the points of the waves and cleft down again between the points, and the oars of Tadg Mor and the oars of Tadg Og split the points of many waves.

"How is it the green sea always greeds after the Brightest and the Bravest?" Tadg Og asked Tadg Mor.

"And for the only sons?" Tadg Mor said.

"And the widows' sons?"

"And the men with one-year wives. The one-year wife that's getting this corpse tonight" — Tadg Mor pointed down with his eyes — "will have a black sorrow this night."

"And every night after this night," said Tadg Og, because he was a young man and knew about such things.

"It's a great thing that he was not dragged down to the green grave, and that is a thing will lighten the nights of the one-year wife," said Tadg Mor.

"It isn't many are saved out of the green grave," said Tadg Og.

"Mairtin Mor wasn't got," said Tadg Mor.

"And Muiris Fada wasn't got."

"Lorcan Og wasn't got."

"Ruairi Dubh wasn't got."

"It was three weeks and the best part of a night before the Frenchman with the leather coat was got, and five boats out looking for him."

"It was seven weeks before Maolshaughlin O'Dalaigh was got, and his eye sockets emptied by the gulls and the gannies."

"And by the waves. The waves are great people to lick out your eyeballs!" said Tadg Mor.

"It was a good thing, this man to be got," said Tadg Og, "and his eyes bright in his head."

"Like he was looking up at the sky!"

"Like he was thinking to smile next thing he'd do."

"He was a great man to smile, this man," said Tadg Mor. "He was ever and always smiling."

"He was a great man to laugh too," said Tadg Og. "He was ever and always laughing."

"Times he was laughing and times he was not laughing," said Tadg Mor.

"Times all men stop from laughing," said Tadg Og.

"Times I saw this man and he not laughing. Times I saw him and he putting out in the black boat looking back at the inland woman where she'd be standing on the shore and her hair weaving the wind, and there wouldn't be any laugh on his face those times."

"An island man should take an island wife," said Tadg Og.

"An inland woman should take an inland man."

"The inland woman that took this man had a dreadful dread on her of the sea and the boats that put out in it."

"Times I saw this woman from the inlands standing on the shore, from his putting out with the dry black boat to his coming back with the shivering silver-belly boat."

"He got it hard to go from her every night."

"He got it harder than iron to go from her if there was a streak of storm gold in the sky at time of putting out."

"An island man should not be held down to a woman from the silent inlands."

"It was love-talk and love-looks that held down this man," said Tadg Mor.

"The island women give love-words and love-talk too," said Tadg Og.

"But not the love-words and the love-looks of this woman," said Tadg Mor. "Times I saw her wetting her feet in the waves and wetting her fingers in the waves and you'd see she was a kind of lovering the waves so they'd bring him back to her. Times he told me himself she had a dreadful dread of the green grave. 'There dies as many men in the inlands as in the islands,' I said. 'Tell her that,' I said. 'I told her that,' said he.

" ' "But they get the black grave burial," she said. "They get the black grave burial in clay that's blessed by two priests and they get the speeding of the green sods thrown down on them by their kinsmen." 'Tell her there's no worms in the green grave,' I said to him. 'I did,' said he. 'What did she say to that?' said I. 'She said, "The bone waits for the bone," said he. 'What does she mean by that?' said I. 'She gave another saying as her meaning to that saying,' said he. 'She said, "There's no sorrow in death when two go down together into the one black grave. Clay binds closer than love," she said, "but the green grave binds nothing," she said. "The green grave scatters," she said. "The green grave is for sons," she said, "and for brothers," she said, "but the black grave is for lovers," she said, "and for husbands in the faithful clay under the jealous sods." ' "

"She must be a great woman to make sayings," said Tadg Og.

"She made great sayings for that man every hour of the day, and she stitching the nets for him on the step while he'd be salting fish or blading oars."

"She'll be glad us to have saved him from the salt green grave. It's a great wonder but he was dragged down before he was got."

"She is the kind of woman that always has great wonders happening round her," said Tadg Mor. "If she is a woman from the inlands itself, she has a great power in herself. She has a great power over the sea. Times — and she on the cliff shore and her hair weaving the wind, like I told you — I'd point my eyes through the wind across at where Eamon Buidhe would be in the waves back of me, and there wouldn't be as much as one white tongue of spite rising out of the waves around his boat, and my black boat would be splattered over every board of it with white sea-spittle."

"I heard tell of women like that. She took the fury out of the sea and burned it out to white salt in her own heart."

The talk about the inland woman who fought the seas in her heart was slow talk and heavy talk, and slow and heavy talk was fit talk as the scurvy waves crawled over one another, scale by scale, and brought the bitter boat back to the shore.

Sometimes a spiteful tongue of foam forked up in the dark by the side of the boat and reached for the netted corpse on the boards. When this happened Tadg Og picked up the loose end of the raggy net and lashed out with it at the sea.

"Get down, you scaly-belly serpent," he said, "and let the corpse dry out in his dead-clothes."

"Take heed to your words, Tadg Og," Tadg Mor would say. "We have the point to round yet. Take heed to your words!"

"Here's a man took heed to his words and that didn't save him," said Tadg Og. "Here was a man was always singing back song for song to the singing sea, and look at him now lying there."

They looked at him lying on his face under the brown web of the nets in his casket of fish scales, silver and opal. And as they looked, another venomous tongue of the sea licked up the side of the boat and strained in toward the body. Tadg Og beat at it with the raggy net.

"Keep your strength for the loud knocking you'll have to give on the wooden door," said Tadg Mor. And Tadg Og understood that he was the one would walk up the shingle and bring the death news to the one-year wife, who was so strange among the island women with her hair weaving the wind at evening and her white feet wetted in the sea by day.

"Is it not a thing that she'll be, likely, out on the shore?" he asked, in a bright hope, pointing his eyes to where the white edge of the shore-wash shone by its own light in the dark.

"Is there a storm tonight?" said Tadg Mor. "Is there a great wind tonight? Is there a rain spate? Are there any signs of danger on the sea?"

"No," said Tadg Og, "there are none of those things that you mention."

"I will tell you the reason you asked that question," said Tadg Mor. "You asked that question because that question is the answer that you'd like to get."

"It's a hard thing to bring news to a one-year wife and she one that has a dreadful dread of the sea," said Tadg Og.

"It's good news you're bringing to the one-year wife when you bring news that her man is got safe, to go down like any inlander into a black grave blessed by a priest and tramped down by the feet of his kinsmen on the sod."

"It's a queer thing him to be caught by the sea on a fine night with no wind blowing," said Tadg Og.

"On a fine night the women lie down to sleep, and if any woman has a power over the sea, with her white feet in the water and her black hair in the wind and a bright fire in her heart, the sea can only wait until that woman's spirit is out of her body, likely back home in the inlands, and then the sea serpent gives a slow turnover on his scales, one that you wouldn't heed to yourself, maybe, and you standing up with no hold on the oars; and before there's time for more than the first shout out of you the boat is logging down to the depths of the water. And all the time the woman that would have saved you, with her willing and wishing for you, is in the deep bed of a dark sleep, having no knowledge of the thing that has happened until she hears the loud-handed knocking of the neighbor on the door outside."

Tadg Og knocked with his knuckles on the sideboards of the boat.

"Louder than that," Tadg Mor said.

Tadg Og knocked another, louder knock on the boat side.

"Have you no more knowledge than that of how to knock at a door in the fastness of the night and the people inside the house buried in sleep and the corpse down on the shore getting covered with sand and the fish scales drying into him so tight that the finger-nails of the washing women will be broken and split peeling them off him? Have you no more knowledge than that of how to knock with your knucklebones?"

Tadg Mor gave a loud knocking on the wet seat of the boat.

"That is the knock of a man that you might say knows how to knock at a door, daytime or nighttime," he said, and he knocked again. And he knocked again, louder, if it could be that any knock could be louder than the first knock.

Tadg Og listened and then he spoke, not looking at Tadg Mor, but looking at the oar he was rolling in the water. "Two people knocking would make a loud knocking entirely," he said.

"One has to stay with the dead," said Tadg Mor.

Tadg Og drew a long stroke on the oar and he drew a long breath out of his lungs, and he took a long look at the nearing shore.

"What will I say," he asked, "when she comes to my knocking?"

"When she comes to the knocking, step back a bit from the door, so's she'll see the wet shining on you and smell the salt water off you, and say in a loud voice that the sea is queer and rough this night."

"She'll be down with her to the shore if that's what I say."

"Say then," said Tadg Mor, pulling in the oar to slow the boat a bit, "say there's news come in that a boat went down beyond the point."

"If I say that, she'll be down with her to the shore without waiting to hear more, and her hair flying and her white feet freezing on the shingle."

"If that is so," said Tadg Mor, "then you'll have to stand back bold from the door and call out loudly in the night, 'The Brightest and the Bravest!' "

"What will she say to that?"

"She'll say, 'God bless them!' "

"And what will I say to that?"

"You'll say, 'God rest them!' "

"And what will she say to that?"

"She'll say, 'Is it in the black grave or the green grave?' "

"And what will I say to that?"

"You say, 'God rest Eamon Buidhe, in the black grave in the holy ground, blessed by the priest and sodded by the people.' "

"And what will she say to that?"

"She'll say, likely, 'Bring him in to me, Tadg Og!' "

"And what will I say to that?"

"Whatever you say after that, let it be loud and raising echoes under the rafters, so she won't hear the sound of the corpse being dragged up on the shingle. And when he's lifted up on to the scoured table, let whatever you say be loud then too, so's she won't be listening for the sound of the water drabbling down off his clothes on the floor!"

There was only the noise of the oars then, till a shoaly sound stole in between the oar strokes. It was the shoaly sound of the pebbles dragged back from the shore by the tide.

A few strokes more and they beached, and stepped out among the sprawling waves and dragged the boat after them till it cleft its depth in the damp shingle.

"See that you give a loud knocking, Tadg Og," said Tadg Mor, and Tadg Og set his head against the darkness, and his feet were heard for a good time grinding down the shifting shingle as he made for the house of the one-year wife. The house was set in a shrifty sea-field, and his steps did not sound down to the shore once he got to the dune grass of the shrifty sea-field. But in another little while there was a sound of a fist knocking upon wood, stroke after stroke of a strong hand coming down on hard wood. Tadg Mor, waiting with the body in the boat, recalled to himself all the times he went knocking on the island doors bringing news to the women of the death of their men. But island wives were the daughters of island widows. The sea gave food. The sea gave death. Life or death, it was all one in the end. The sea never lost its scabs. The sea was there before the coming of man. Island women had that knowledge. But what knowledge of the sea and its place in the world since the begining of time had a woman from the inlands? No knowledge. An inland woman had no knowledge when the loud knocking came on her door in the night. Tadg Mor listened to the loud, hard knocking of his son Tadg Og on the door of the one-year wife of Eamon Buidhe that was lying in the silver casket of fishes on the floor of the boat, cleft fast in the shingle sand. The night was cold. The fish scales glittered even though it was dark. They glittered in the whiteness made by the breaking waves breaking on the shore. The sound of the sea was sadder than the sight of the yellow-haired corpse, but still Tadg Mor was gladder to be down on the shore than up in the dune grass knocking at the one-night widow's door.

The knocking sound of Tadg Og's knuckles on the wooden door was a human sound and it sounded good in the ears of Tadg Mor for a time; but, like all sounds that continue too long, it sounded soon to be as inhuman as the washing of the waves tiding in on the shingle. Tadg Mor put up his rounded palms to his mouth and shouted out to Tadg Og to come back to the boat. Tadg Og came back running over the shore, and the air was grained with sounds of sliding shingle.

"There's no one in the house where you were knocking," said Tadg Mor.

"I knocked louder on the door than you knocked on the boat boards," said Tadg Og.

"I heard how you knocked," said Tadg Mor; "you knocked well. But let you knock better when you go to the neighbor's house to find out where the one-night widow is from her own house this night."

"If I got no answer at one door is it likely I'll get an answer at another door?" said Tadg Og. "It was you yourself I heard to say one time that the man that knows how a thing is to be done is the man should do that thing when that thing is to be done."

"How is a man to get knowledge of how to do a thing if that man doesn't do that thing when that thing is to be done?" said Tadg Mor.

Tadg Og got into the boat again and they sat there in the dark. After four or maybe five waves had broken by their side, Tadg Og lifted the net and felt the clothes of Eamon Buidhe.

"The clothes are drying into him," he said.

"If I was to go up with you to the house of Seana Bhride, who would there be to watch the dead?" said Tadg Mor, and then Tadg Og knew that Tadg Mor was going with him and he had no need to put great heed on the answer he gave to him.

"Let the sea watch him," he said, putting a leg out over the boat after the wave went back with its fistful of little complaining pebbles.

"We must take him out of the boat first," said Tadg Mor. "Take hold of him there by the feet," he said as he rolled back the net, putting it over the oar with each roll so it would not ravel and knot.

They lifted Eamon Buidhe out of the boat and the mackerel slipped about their feet into the place where he had left his shape. They dragged him up a boat length from the sprawling waves, and they faced his feet to the shore, but when they saw that that left his head lower than his feet, because the shingle shelved greatly at that point, they faced him about again toward the waves that were clashing their sharp, pointy scales together and sending up spits of white spray in the air. The dead man glittered with the silver and verdigris scales of the mackerel that were clinging to his clothing over every part.

Tadg Mor went up the sliding shingle in front of Tadg Og, and Tadg Og put his feet in the shelves that were made in the shingle by Tadg Mor because the length of the step they took was the same length. The sea sounded in their ears as they went through the shingle, but by the time the first coarse dune grass scratched at their clothing the only sound they could hear was the sound of the other's breathing.

The first cottage that rose out blacker than the night in their path was the cottage where Tadg Og made the empty knocking. Tadg Mor stopped in front of the door as if he might be thinking of trying his hand at knocking, but he thought better of it and went on after

Tadg Og to the house that was next to that house, and that was the house of Seana Bhride, a woman that would know anything that eye or ear could know about those that lived within three islands of her. Tadg Mor hit the door of Seana Bhride's house with a knock of his knuckles, and although it was a less loud knock than the echo of the knock that came down to the shore when Tadg Og struck the first knock on the door of the wife of Eamon Buidhe, there was a foot to the floor before he could raise his knuckle off the wood for another knock.

A candle lit up and a shadow fell across the windowpane and a face came whitening at the door gap.

"You came to the wrong house this dark night," said Seana Bhride. "The sea took all the men was ever in this house twelve years ago and two months and seventeen days."

"It may be that we have no corpse for this house, but we came to the right house for all that," said Tadg Mor. "We came to this house for knowledge of the house across two sea-fields from this house, where we got no answer to our knocking with our knuckles."

"And I knocked with a stone up out of the ground, as well," said Tadg Og, coming closer.

The woman with the candle-flame blowing drew back into the dark.

"Is it for the inland woman, the one-year wife, you're bringing the corpse you have below in the boat this night?" she said.

"It is, God help us," said Tadg Mor.

"It is, God help us," said Tadg Og.

"The Brightest and the Bravest," said Tadg Mor.

"Is it a thing that you got no answer to your knocking?" said the old woman, bending out again with the blowing candle-flame.

"No answer," said Tadg Og, "and sturdy knocking."

"Knocking to be heard above the sound of the sea," said Tadg Mor.

"They sleep deep, the people from the inland?" said Tadg Og, asking a question.

"The people of the inland sleep deep in the cottage in the middle of the fields," said Seana Bhride, "but when they're rooted up and set down by the sea their spirit never passes out of hearing of the step on the shingle. It's a queer thing entirely that you got no answer to your knocking."

"We got no answer to our knocking," said Tadg Mor and Tadg Og, bringing their words together like two oars striking the one wave, one on this side of the boat and one on that.

"When the inland woman puts her face down on the feather pillow," said Seana Bhride, "that pillow is like the seashells children put against their ears, that pillow has in it the sad crying voices of the sea."

"Is it that you think she is from home this night?" said Tadg Mor.

"It must be a thing that she is," said the old woman.

"Is it back to her people in the inlands she'd be gone?" said Tadg Og, who had more than the curiosity of the one night in him.

"Step into the kitchen," said the old woman, "while I ask Bríd Og if she saw the wife of Eamon Buidhe go from her house this night."

While she went into the room that was back from the kitchen, Tadg Og put a foot inside the kitchen door, but Tadg Mor stayed looking down to the shore.

"If it is a thing the inland woman is from home this night, where will we put Eamon Buidhe, that we have below on the shore, with his face and no sheet on it, and his eyes and no lids drawn down tight over them, and the fish scales sticking to him faster than they stuck to the mackerels when they swam beyond the nets, blue and silver and green?"

"Listen to Bríd Og," said Tadg Og, and he stepped a bit farther into the kitchen of Seana Bhride.

"Bríd Og," the old woman asked, "is it a thing that the inland woman from two fields over went from her house this night?"

"It is a thing that she went," said Bríd Og.

Tadg Og spoke to Tadg Mor: "Bríd Og talks soft in the day, but she talks as soft as the sea in summer when she talks in the night in the dark."

"Listen to what she says," said Tadg Mor, coming in a step after Tadg Og.

"Is it that she went to her people in the inlands?" Seana Bhride asked.

"The wife of Eamon Buidhe never stirred a foot to her people in the inlands since the first day she came to the islands, in her blue dress with the beads," said the voice of Bríd Og.

"Where did she go then?" said the old woman. "If it is a thing that she didn't go to her people in the inlands?"

"Where else but where she said she'd go," said the voice of Bríd Og, "out in the boat with her one-year husband?"

There was sound of rusty springs creaking in the room where Bríd Og slept, back behind the kitchen, and her voice was clearer and stronger like as if she was sitting up in the bed looking out at the black sea and the white points rising in it, lit by the light of their own brightness.

"She said the sea would never drag Eamon Buidhe down to the green grave and leave her to lie lonely in the black grave on the shore, in the black clay that held tight, under the weighty sods. She said a man and woman should lie in the one grave. She said a night never passed without her heart being burnt out to a cold white salt. She said that this night, and every night after, she'd go out with Eamon in the black boat over the scabby back of the sea. She said if he got the green grave, she'd get the green grave too, and her arms would be stronger than the weeds of the sea, to bind them together forever. She said the island women never fought the sea. She said the sea needed taming and besting. She said there was a curse on the black clay for women that lay alone in it while their men washed to and fro in the caves of the sea. She said the black clay was all right for inland women. She said the black clay was all right for sisters and mothers. She said the black clay was all right for girls that died at seven years. But the green grave was the grave for wives, she said, and she went out in the black boat this night and she's going out every night after," said Bríd Og.

"Tell Bríd Og there will be no night after," said Tadg Mor.

"Let her sleep till day," said Tadg Og. "Time enough to tell her in the day," and he strained his eyes past the flutter-flame candle as the old woman came out from Bríd Og's room.

"You heard what she said?" said the old woman.

"It's a bad thing he was got," said Tadg Og.

"That's a thing was never said on this island before this night," said Tadg Mor.

"There was a fire on every point of the cliff shore to light home the men who were dragging for Mairtin Mor," the old woman said.

"And he never was got," said Tadg Mor.

"There was a shroud spun for Ruairi Dubh between the time of the putting-out of the island boats to look for him and their coming back with the empty news in the green daylight," said the old woman.

"Ruairi Dubh was never got."

"Mairtin Mor was never got."

"Lorcan Og was never got."

"Muiris Fada was never got."

"My four sons were never got," said the old woman.

"The father of Bríd Og was never got," said Tadg Og, and he was looking at the shut door of the room where Bríd Og was lying in the dark; the candle shadows were running their hands over that door.

"The father of Bríd Og was never got," said Tadg Og again, forgetting what he was saying.

"Of all the men that had yellow coffins standing up on their ends by the gable, and all the men that had brown shrouds hanging up on the wall with the iron nail eating out through the yarn, it had to be the one man that should have never been got that was got," said Tadg Og, opening the top half of the door and letting in the deeper sound of the tide.

"That is the way," said Tadg Mor.

"That is ever and always the way," said the old woman.

"The sea is stronger than any man," said Tadg Mor.

"The sea is stronger than any woman," said Tadg Og.

"The sea is stronger than women from the inland fields," said Tadg Mor, going to the door.

"The sea is stronger than talk of love," said Tadg Og, going out after him into the dark. It was so dark, he could not see where the window of Bríd Og's room was, but he was looking where it might be while he buttoned over his jacket.

Tadg Mor and Tadg Og went back to the shore, keeping their feet well on the shelving shingle, as they went toward the sprawling waves. The waves were up to the sea-break in the graywacke wall.

The boat was floating free. It was gone from the cleft in the shingle. And the body of Eamon Bui, that had glittered with fish scales of opal and silver and verdigris, was gone from the shore. It was gone from the black land that was scored crisscross with grave-cuts by spade and shovel. It was gone and would never be got. The men spoke together.

"Mairtin Mor wasn't got."

"Muiris Fada wasn't got."

"Lorcan Og wasn't got."

"Ruairi Dubh wasn't got."

"The four sons of Seana Bhride were never got."

"The father of Bríd Og wasn't got."

The men of the island were caught down in the sea by the tight weeds of the sea. They were held in the tendrils of the sea anemone and by the pricks of the sallow thorn, by the green sea-grasses and the green sea-reeds and the winding stems of the green sea-daffodil. But Eamon Buidhe Murnane would be held fast in the white arms of his one-year wife, who came from the inlands where women have no knowledge of the sea but only a knowledge of love.

AT SALLYGAP

THE BUS climbed up the hilly roads on its way, through the Dublin Mountains, to the town of Enniskerry. On either side the hedges were so high that the passengers had nothing more interesting to look at than each other, but after a short time the road became steeper and then the fields that had been hidden were bared to view, slanting smoothly downward to the edge of the distant city.

Dublin was all exposed. The passengers told each other they could see every inch of it. They could certainly see every church steeple and every tower. But, had they admitted as much, they would have said that the spires and steeples that rose up out of the blue pools of distance below looked little better than dark thistles rising up defiantly in a pale pasture.

The sea that half-circled this indistinct city seemed as gray and motionless as the air. Suddenly, however, it was seen that the five-o'clock mail boat, looking no bigger than a child's toy boat, was pushing aside the plastery waves and curving around the pier at Dunlaoghaire on its way to the shores of England.

"There she goes!" said Manny Ryan to the young man in the gray flannel suit who shared the bus seat with him. "The fastest little boat for her size in the whole of the British Isles."

"What time does it take her to do the crossing?" asked the young man.

"Two hours and five minutes," said Manny, and he took out a watch and stared at it. "It's three thirty-nine now. She's out about four minutes, I'd say. That leaves her right to the dot. She'll dock at Holyhead at exactly five forty."

"She's dipping a bit," said the young man. "I suppose she's taking back a big load after the Horse Show."

"That's right. I saw by the paper this morning she took two thousand people across yesterday evening."

"You take a great interest in things, I see."

"I do. That's quite right for you! I take a great interest indeed, but I have my reasons. I have my reasons."

Manny put his elbow up against the ledge of the window and turned on his side in the tight space of the seat, so that he was almost facing his companion, who, having no window ledge to lean upon, was forced to remain with his profile to Manny while they were talking.

"You wouldn't think, would you," said Manny, "just by looking at me, that I had my choice to sail out of Dublin on that little boat one day, and I turned it down? You wouldn't think that now, would you?"

"I don't know so much about that," said the young man, uncomfortably. "Many a man goes over to Holyhead, for one class of thing or another."

But it was clear by his voice that he found it hard to picture Manny, with his shiny black suit and his bowler hat, in any other city than the one he had lately left in the bus. So strong was his impression that Manny was — as he put it — a Dubliner-coming-and-going, that he hastened to hide his impression by asking what business Manny had in Holyhead, if it wasn't an impertinence? He forgot apparently that Manny had never actually gone there, but Manny forgot that too in his haste to correct the young man on another score altogether.

"Is it Holyhead?" he asked in disgust. "Who goes there but jobbers and journeymen?"

"London?" asked the young man, raising his eyebrows.

"Policemen and servant girls," Manny said impatiently.

"Was it to the other side altogether, sir?" said the young man, and the "sir" whistled through the wax in Manny's ears like the sweetest note of a harpsichord, touched with a clever quill.

"To the other side altogether is right," he said. "I was heading for Paris — gay Paree, as they call it over there — and I often wish to God I hadn't turned my back on the idea."

"Is it a thing you didn't go, sir?"

"Well, now, as to that question," said Manny, "I won't say yes and I won't say no, but I'll tell you this much; I had my chance of going. That's something, isn't it? That's more than most can say! Isn't it?"

"It is indeed. But if it's a thing that you didn't go, sir, might I make so bold as to ask the reason?"

"I'll tell you," said Manny, "but first I'll have to tell you why I was ever going at all."

He took out a sepia-colored photograph from an old wallet and he held it over to the young man, who looked at it, holding it close to his face because it was faded in places and in other places the glaze was cracked. But he made out quite clearly all the same a group of young men sitting stiffly on cane-back chairs, their legs rigid in pinstripe trousers, their hair plastered back with oil, and their hands folded self-consciously over the awkward contours of trombones, fiddles and brass cornets.

In the center of the group, turned up on its rim, was a big yellow drum wearing a banner across its face with the words MARY STREET BAND printed on it in large block letters.

"That was us," said Manny, "the Mary Street Band. We used to play for all the dances in the city, and we played for the half-hour interval as well in the Mary Street Theatre."

He leaned over.

"That was me," he said, pointing to a young man with a fiddle on his knee, a young man who resembled him as a son might resemble a father.

"I'd recognize you all right," said the stranger, looking up at Manny's face and down again at the photograph. Both faces had the same nervous thinness, the same pointed jaw, and the same cleft of weakness in the chin. Only the eyes were different. The eyes in the photograph were light in color, either from bad lighting on the part of the photographer or from youthful shallowness and immaturity in the sitter. The eyes of the older Manny were dark. They had a depth that might have come from sadness, but, wherever it came from, it was out of keeping with the cockiness of his striped city suiting and his bowler hat.

"There was a party of us — the few lads you see there at the back, and the one to the left of the drum — planning on getting out, going across to Paris and trying the dance halls over there — *palais*, they call them on the other side. We'd stuck together for three years, but these few lads I'm after pointing out to you got sick of playing to the Dublin jackeens. I got sick of them, too. They were always spitting, sucking oranges and catcalling up at the artistes. We heard tell it was different altogether across the water. Tell me this, were you ever in Paris, young fellow? 'Gay Paree,' I should be saying."

"No, I can't say that I was," said the young man.

"Man alive!" said Manny. "Sure that's the place for a young fellow like you. Clear out and go. That's my advice to you. Take it or leave it. That's my advice to you, although I don't know from Adam who you are or what you are. That's what I'd say to you if you were my own son. Cut and run for it."

Manny gave a deep sigh that went down the back of the lady in front, who shivered and drew her collar closer.

"Paris!" he said again, and sighed once more. "Paris, lit up all night as bright as the sun, with strings of lights pulling out of each other from one side of the street to the other, and fountains and bandstands every other yard along the way. The people go up and down linked, and singing, at any hour of the day or night, and the publicans — they have some other name on them over there, of course — are coming to the door every minute with aprons round their middle, like women, and sweeping the pavement outside the door and finishing off maybe by swilling a bucket of wine over it to wash it down."

"You seem to have a pretty good idea of it for a man who was never there!"

"I have a lot of post cards," said Manny, "and myself and the lads were never done talking about it before ever we decided on going at all. In the end we just packed up one night and said, 'Off with us!' There had been some bit of a row that night at the theater, and somehow or other an old dead cat got flung up on the stage. Did you ever hear the like of that for ignorance? 'Holy God,' we said, 'that's too much to take from any audience.'"

"All I can say is, it's no wonder you packed your bags!" said the young man.

"Is it now?" said Manny. "That's what I tell myself. My bags were all packed and strapped, and what was more, before very long they were halfway up the plank of that little boat you see pulling out there."

They looked out the bus window, down over the falling fields of the mountainside, to the sea and the vanishing boat.

"Is that right?" said the young man.

"That's right. My bags were on the gangplank and there was Annie below on the quay, with the tears in her eyes. That was the first time I gave a thought to her at all. Annie is my wife. At least she is now. She wasn't then. I gave one look at her standing there in the rain — it was raining at the time — with her handkerchief rolled up in her hand ready to wave as soon as the boat got going. The porters were pushing past her with their truckloads of trunks and hitting up against her. Did you ever notice how rough those fellows are? Well, with the rain and the porters and one thing and another, I got to pitying her, standing there. I got to thinking, do you know, of all the things we'd done together. Nothing bad, you know. Nothing to be ashamed of, if you understand, but still I didn't like to think of her standing watching me going off, maybe for good, and she thinking over the things I'd said to her one time or another. You know yourself, I suppose, the kind of thing you're apt to say to a girl, off and on?"

"I do," said the young man.

"You do? Well, in that case you'll understand how I felt seeing her standing there. I felt so bad I tried to get back for a few last words with her before the boat pulled out, but there were people coming up against me all the time and I was having to stand aside every other step I took and crush in against the rails to let them pass. And some of them were cranky devils, telling me to get to hell out of the way, to come if I was coming and go if I was going, and — for God Almighty's sake — to take my bloody bag out of the way. It was jabbing them in the legs without my noticing it, and as sure as I pulled it to one side it jabbed into someone on the other side. There was terrible confusion. You'd think, wouldn't you, that the officials would be able to put a stop to it? But I declare to God they were worse than the people that were traveling. There was one of them clicking tickets at the bottom of the gangway, and all he did was let a shout at me to say I was obstructing the passage. Obstructing!

" 'Come on up, Manny,' shouted the lads from up above on the deck.

" 'Goodbye, Manny,' Annie said in a little bit of a voice you'd hardly hear above the banging of cases and the screaming of the sea gulls."

"You didn't go down!"

"Down I went."

"And the boys?"

"They were staring like as if they were transfixed! They couldn't believe their eyes. They kept calling down to me from the deck above, but the wind was going the other way and we couldn't hear one word they were saying. Then the whistles began to blow, and the sailors began spitting on their hands and pulling at the ropes to let the plank up into the boat. The train was getting ready to go back to Westland Row. It was going to pull out any minute.

" 'I knew you'd come to your senses,' Annie said. 'Have you got your bag?'

"I held it up.

" 'Your fiddle?' she said.

"By God, if I hadn't left the fiddle above on the deck! Would you believe that? I started shouting up at the lads, and Timmy Coyne — that was the little fellow with the mustache sitting next me in the photo — Timmy put his hands up to his mouth like he was playing a bugle — it was the piano he played in the band, by the way — and he shouts out 'Wha-a-a — at?' like that, drawing it out so's we could hear it.

" 'The fiddle!' I shouted. But 'fiddle' isn't a word you can stretch out, you know. No matter how slow you say it, it's said and done in a minute. 'Fiddle.' Try it for yourself. 'Fiddle.' It's a funny sort of word, isn't it, when you say it over a few times like that? It sort of loses its meaning. Anyway, Timmy didn't hear me.

" 'Ca-a-a-n't — hea-ea-ear!' says he.

"A couple of people round about me began to shout up too. 'Fiddle.' 'Fiddle,' they shouted. The boat was pushing off from the pier. Suddenly one real game fellow that was after putting a fine

young girl on the boat, and after kissing her too in front of everyone, ups and pulls off his hat, and crooking it under his arm, like it
was a fiddle, he starts pulling his right hand back and forth across
it for all the world as if he was playing a real fiddle. Timmy takes
one look at him and down he ducks and starts rooting around on
the deck. The next minute he ups and rests the fiddle case on the
rails.

" 'Catch!' he shouts, and over comes the fiddle across the space of
water that was blinding white by this time with the foam from the
moving boat.

" 'It's into the water!' shouts someone.

" 'Not on your life!' shouts your man on the wharf, and he leaps
into the air to catch it. But you know how slippy them wooden
boards are with that green slimy stuff on them? You do? Well,
to make a long story short, down slips your man, and down comes
your fiddle on one of the iron stumps they tie the boat to, and fiddle
and case, and even the little bow, were smashed to smithereens
under my eyes. You should have heard the crowd laughing. I always say it's easy enough to rise a laugh when you're not doing it
for money!"

"What did Annie say?"

" 'It's the hand of God,' she said."

"What did you say?"

"Sure, what could I say? I just went over and gave a kick with
my foot to the bits of wood, and put them floating out on the water,
along with the potato peels and cabbage stalks that were just after
being flung out of a porthole."

Manny looked down at the gray feather of smoke on the horizon
that was all that now remained of the mail boat.

"Whenever I see that little boat," he said, "I get to thinking of the
sea and the way it was that day, with all the dirt lapping up and
down on it and the bits of the fiddle looking like bits of an old box.
Walking back to the train, we could see the bits of it floating along
on the water under us, through the big cracks in the boards. I
never can understand why it is they leave such big spaces between
those boards anyway. And just as we were going out the gate to the
platform, what did I see, down through the splits, but a bit of the

bow. And here's a curious thing for you! You could tell what it was the minute you looked at it, broken and all as it was. 'Oh, look!' you'd say if you happened to be passing along the pier, going for a walk and not knowing anything about me or the boys. 'Look!' you'd say to whoever was with you. 'Isn't that the bow of a fiddle?' "

"Did you ever hear from the boys again?" the young man asked.

"We changed our address," Manny said. "I heard they broke up after a bit. Maybe they wrote and we never got the letter. After we got married we went to live in King Street, over the shop. We opened a shop, you see, in King Street. You know King Street? Our shop is down past the Gaiety. The shop took up pretty near all our time on account of us knowing nothing about business. We never got a minute to ourselves. Look at today! I've been out since early morning trying to get to hear of someone that would deliver eggs to the door. That's what I'm doing now, too, going up here to Sallygap to see a man I was told about by one of the dealers in Moore Street. The dealer gets them from him twice a week, and I didn't see why he couldn't bring us in a couple of dozen at the same time. If he does, we'll put up a card on the window saying 'Fresh Eggs Daily.' The Dublin people go mad for a fresh egg. Did you ever notice that?"

The conductor came down the aisle and leaned in to Manny.

"We're coming near to Sallygap now," said the conductor.

"Is that right?" said Manny. "Give a touch to the bell, so, and get the driver to stop. Anywhere here will do nicely."

He turned to the young man confidentially. "I have to look for the place, you see."

"I hope you find it all right, sir."

"I hope so. Well, good day to you now. Don't forget the advice I gave you." Manny pointed with his thumb in the direction of the sea. Then he got off the bus and for the first time in years found himself on a country road alone.

The house he was looking for was easy enough to find. The farmer promised to send in the eggs twice a week, and three times if the orders got bigger. He wanted to know if Manny ever tried selling chickens or geese. Manny said his wife took care of the orders.

The farmer asked if he would mention the matter to his wife. Manny agreed to do so.

By that time Manny wanted a drink. He wasn't a drinking man, but he wanted a glass of beer, just then, to take the thirst off him. He remembered that they had passed a public house a while before he got off the bus. He started walking back toward it.

As he walked along he thought of the boys again. It was a long time since he had thought of them. The boat had put him in mind of them. And the young fellow he was sitting beside was just about the age he was himself in those days. That must be why he'd told him so much. He was a nice young fellow. Manny wondered who he was, and he wondered, just as idly, what hour he himself would get a bus going back to Dublin.

But it was nice, mind you, walking along the road. He didn't care if the bus was a bit slow in coming. It was not as if it was raining or cold. It was a nice evening. He'd often heard tell of young lads from Dublin coming up here on their bicycles on a fine evening, and leaving the bicycles inside a fence while they went walking in the heather. Just walking, mind you; just walking. He used to think it was a bit daft. Now that he was up here himself, he could see how a quiet sort of chap might like this class of thing. Manny looked at the hedges that were tangled with wild vetches, and he looked at an old apple tree crocheted over with gray lichen. He looked at the gleaming grass in the wet ditch, and at the flowers and flowering reeds that grew there. They all have names, I suppose, he thought. Could you beat that!

Walking along, he soon came to a cottage with dirty brown thatch from which streaks of rain had run down the wall, leaving yellow stripes on the lime. As he got near, a woman came to the door with a black pot and swilled out a slop of green water into the road, leaving a stench of cabbage in the air when she went in. It was a queer time to be cooking her cabbage, Manny thought, and then he chuckled. "For God's sake," he said out loud, "will you look at the old duck!"

A duck had flapped over from the other side of the road to see if the cabbage water made a pool big enough to swim in. "Will you just look at him!" Manny said, and, as the road was empty, he must have been talking to himself. And he was giving himself very superfluous advice, because he was staring at the duck as hard as he could. But as he stood there a geranium pot was taken down from inside one of the small windows of the cottage, and a face came close to the glass. "They don't like you stopping and staring, I suppose," he thought, and he moved along.

His thoughts for some time were on the smallness and darkness of the place. He wondered how people put up with living in a little poke like that, and the thought of his own rooms behind the shop in King Street seemed better to him than it had for a long time. After all, they had a range. They had gas. They had the use of the lavatory on the upper landing. He was pleased to think of all the many advantages he had over those people that peeped out at him. He used to feel that the rooms in King Street were terrible and that he was doomed to live in them all his life, while men no older than he went here and went there, and did this and did that, and some of them even went off to Paris. But at that moment he felt it was a fine thing after all to have a place of your own to keep things in, a place where you could lie down if you were sick or worn out. And it was within a stone's throw of the Pillar.

He didn't get out enough — that was the trouble. If he got out and about more he'd have the right attitude to the house, and maybe to the shop, too. No wonder he'd be sick of it; never leaving it except like this, to do a message. He should take an odd day off. Man! What was he talking about? He ought to take a week. He ought to run over to Paris and look up the boys. Then, as if aghast at the magnitude of his revolt, Manny gave himself an alternative. He should go over to Liverpool, anyway, for one of the weekend race meetings. With a bit of luck he might make his expenses, and that would shut Annie's mouth.

The public house came into view just then, and very opportunely, because Manny walked in with the confidence of one who contemplates a sojourn in distant lands.

He ordered his drink. There were two or three locals leaning against the counter, and a large man, obviously a commercial traveler, stood cleaning his spectacles and asking questions about the locality. The locals were looking sheepishly at their empty glasses that were draped with scum. The traveler gave orders for the glasses to be filled up again. He looked down the counter at Manny as if he would like to include him in the order, but there was a repelling air of independence about Manny, due perhaps to his bowler hat, which sat self-consciously upon the bar counter.

Manny listened to the talk at the other end of the bar. Once or twice the locals mistook the traveler's meaning, but Manny felt a warmth in his heart for them. Their dull-wittedness gave him a feeling of security. He felt a great dislike for the talkative traveler. He hoped that they would not be on the same bus going back to the city.

Just then the sound of a motor stole into the stillness outside. The bus was coming. Manny drank up, and put out his hand for his hat. Out of the corner of his eye he saw the traveler buttoning his overcoat. He heard his jocose farewells to the locals, who were already leaning back with greater ease against the counter.

Manny went toward the door. The traveler went toward the door. In the doorway they met.

"I see you are taking this bus, too," said the traveler. Manny had, of course, intended going back on that bus. He had no idea when there would be another one. But a great revulsion came over him at the thought of journeying back with the large, talkative man.

"I'm waiting for the next bus," he said, impulsively.

"I'm sorry!" said the traveler. "I should have been glad of your company. Good evening."

"Good evening," said Manny, and he stood back from the dust of the bus as it started up again.

When the dust had blown into the hedges, Manny stepped into the middle of the road and doggedly faced the way the bus had gone. He would probably be walking for a long time before another bus caught up with him, but he did not care. A rare recklessness possessed him and, when the night came down shortly over him, the feeling of recklessness strengthened. He walked along, looking from side to side, and in his heart the night's potent beauty was beginning to have effect. He felt confused. The dark hills and the pale sky and the city pricking out its shape upon the sea with starry lights filled him with strangely mingled feelings of sadness and joy. And when the sky flowered into a thousand stars of forget-me-not blue he was strangled by the need to know what had come over him, but having no other way to stem the tide of desolating joy within him, he ran down the road the way he used to run on the roads as a young lad. And as he ran he laughed out loud to think that he, Manny Ryan, was running along a country road in the dark, hardly knowing when he'd run into a hedge or a ditch.

Yesterday, if anyone had come to him and suggested that he'd do such a thing, he would have split his sides laughing. And tomorrow, if he were to try and persuade Annie to take a walk out in the country, she'd look at him as if he was daft. The Dublin people couldn't tell you the difference between a bush and a tree. Manny stood to recover his breath. That was a fact. All the Dublin people were good for was talking. They'd talk you out of your mind.

He thought of his wife with her yellow elbows coming through the black unraveled sleeve of her cardigan, as she leaned across the counter in the dismal shop, giving off old shaffoge with any shawley that came the way with an hour, or maybe two hours, to spare. He thought of the bars filled with his cronies talking about the state of the country for all they were fit, men that never saw more of it than you'd see from the top of a tram. He thought of the skitting young fellows and girls outside Whitefriar Street after late Mass on Sunday, and he thought of the old men standing at the pub ends of the streets, ringing themselves round with spits. He thought of the old women leaning against the jambs of their doorways, with white crockery milk jugs hanging out of their hands, forgotten in the squalor of their gossip. He thought of the children sitting among the trodden and rancid cabbage butts on the edge of the paths, repeating the gossip they had heard when they crouched, unheeded, under some counter. He thought of the young and the old, the men and the women and the pale frightened children, who were shuffling along kneelers in churches all over the city, waiting their turn to snuffle out their sins in the dark wooden confessionals.

It seemed as if the cool green light of day scarcely ever reached those people, and the breeze that blew into their streets came out from their own drafty houses thickened with the warm odor of boiling potatoes. The loathing he'd felt for the city, years before, when he first came to Dublin, stole over him again as it had come over him one night long ago in the little theater in Mary Street. Dublin jackeens! he thought.

"Dublin jackeens!" he said then out loud, the gibe coming forth from some dim corner in his mind where the memory of a buttercup field, and a cobbled yard pricked with grass, gave him the right to feel immunity from them. Once more he longed to get away from Dublin. But this time there was a difference. He wanted to get away from Dublin — yes — but not from Ireland. He didn't want to go away from Ireland, he thought, with anguish; not away from her yellow fields and not away from her emerald ditches; only to get away from the stuffy Dublin streets and people that walked them. Even to get away occasionally for an hour, like this, would satisfy him.

Wasn't it well, after all, he hadn't gone to Paris? Things turned out for the best in the end. If he had gone away he might never have come up here to Sallygap. And he would never have found out that peace was not a matter of one city or another, but a matter of hedges and fields and waddling ducks and a handful of stars. Cities were all alike. Paris was no better or no worse than Dublin when you looked into the matter clearly. Paris was a wicked place, by all accounts, even if they did have a rare time there at night, with the lights and the bandstands.

Who ever heard of the boys since they went? Where were they? God alone knew! They were playing, maybe, in some cellar done up with striped tablecloths, like in the pictures, with smoke cutting their guts, and women with big thighs and dresses torn open down to the waist sitting on their knees and cracking the strings of their sinews with the weight.

A sweat broke out on Manny, and he had to stand in the cold road to let the vision fade and the winds cool his burning face. He was damn glad he had stayed at home. What was the need in anybody going across seas when all a man had to do, if he got sick of himself, was take a bus and come up to a place like this? As long as a fellow could come up to a place like this, what was the need of going farther?

I'll come up here again, he thought, upon my word I will. He had found his real escape at last from the sordidness of the life he led, and perhaps in time the seed of sensitiveness that had lain sterile in his heart through his bleak and unnatural spring and summer might have had a rare and wonderful winter flowering. There are gentle souls who take nothing from their coarse rearing, and less from their chance schooling, but who yet retain a natural sensitivity, and sometimes it flowers, as Manny's did, in the hills.

"I'll come back again," he said out loud. "I'll come back again all right." He turned and took a last look at the hanging hills before he went round the last bend in the road, where the houses and shops of Rathfarnham would hide them from view.

With the first shops and the first beginnings of the city with its dazzling tramlines, its noises, and its shoving crowds, Manny felt the tiredness he had not felt in all the miles of rough road he had walked. His feet burned. His thighs felt heavy. His back was weighed down with a knapsack of weariness. He took a tram and sat on the edge of the only seat that was vacant, his light weight joggling with every motion, and the elbow and hipbone of a fat woman on the inside of the seat nudging him with the insistence of inadvertency. Smells of gas and oil sickened him. Broken lights strained his eyes. But most of all a dread of returning home came over him as he remembered that Annie had told him to hurry. The sharp notes of Annie's voice echoed sudden and loud in his ears, and it seemed impossible that he had forgotten what she said. He felt like a little boy who had blotted his copy, a little boy who had lost the change, a little boy creeping in under fear of the whip.

The fear of Annie's tongue hung over him all the way along the suburbs. When he reached home and saw the closed shutters of the shop, his hand was so stiff and cold that when he put it into the letter box he could hardly find the string by which the latch of the door could be pulled back from outside. His hand clattered the letter box for a long time before he found it. Then he pulled the string and the door opened. He went in and felt for the knob of the kitchen door. He didn't see that the door was wide open because the room was dark and the fire was only a powdering of hot gray ash. Then he saw a red glow in the dark and he realized the door

was open and Annie was sitting at the fire. Next minute his eyes
became used to the dark, and, the customary position of things sup-
plementing the eye, where it failed, enabled him to reach the fire
and sit down opposite her on the other side of the range. He said
nothing but sat watching her and wondering when she would
speak.

Annie did not speak. The truth was that she had been so excited
by his unusual absence that she was unfit for any emotion at his
eventual return.

Marriage had been an act of unselfishness on Manny's part. He
had married Annie because he had thought that was what would
make her happy, and he was content to give up his freedom for
that object. She, however, had not thought of marriage as anything
but a means of breaking the monotony. But she had found it a
greater monotony than the one she had fled from, and, unlike the
other, it had no anteroom of hope leading to something better.
Manny accepted her so complacently from the first day that he
bored her in a week with his monotonously kind manner. Soon she
began to show an artificial irritation at trifles in the hope of stirring
up a little excitement, but Manny was kinder and more gentle on
those occasions than he was before. Gradually her irritability and
petulance became more daring until they could scarcely be classed
as such venial sins. And soon, too, what had been slyly deliberate became involuntary, and the sour expression of her face hardened
into the mask of middle age. She sought in the throbbing pulse and
rippling flux of anger the excitement she had unconsciously hoped
to find in her marriage bed. But her angers, too, were sterile, breeding no response in Manny. He was the same always. It seemed
that she would never believe this, and she tried from time to time to
break the strength of his weakness, and she fought against his kindness as if it were her enemy. And so, in an obscure way, it was.

What Annie wanted was the flaming face, the racing pulse, the
temper that raised red weals on the skin, and the heat of bodies
crushed together in rage. And this need of her nature had never
been satisfied except vicariously, leaning over the shop counter
listening to the whispered stories of other women; stories of obscene
blows given in drunken lusts, stories of cunning and cupidity and

flashes of anger and hate that rent the darkness in tenement hall-
ways around the block when she and Manny had been in bed for
hours.

"Ah, woman dear," they'd said to her, "sure you know nothing at
all about life." And then, as if she were to be pitied, they'd rolled up
their sleeves indulgently and show her scalds and scabs. "Take a
look at that!" they'd say.

And sometimes, standing at the hall door in the dark at night after
the shop was long shut, she would hear a scream in some room high
up across the street or round the corner, followed maybe by children's voices sounding as if they were frightened out of their wits.
Or sometimes a neighbor would come down the street sobbing
loudly, linked on either side by her children, sobbing too and telling
her in high childish voices not to mind, not to mind. Not to mind
what, Annie wondered? Which of the incentive words and gestures
she had heard the neighbors tell about had provoked this woman to
hysteria? She used to draw back a bit into the doorway while they
were passing, and sometimes, her thin shoulder blades pressed against
the wall so they wouldn't see her spying on them, she might catch
a glimpse of Manny sitting in the kitchen with his stocking feet up
on the cooling range while he read the paper. Her eyes would
flicker with hatred and resentment, and she would have an impulse
to be revenged on him by going in a poking the range, to send
clouds of ashes over him till he'd have to get up and go out.

This evening, when he did not come back on time, she set her
mind on planning some taunt for him as he came through the shop.
If there were customers there, so much the better. One time she
wouldn't have risked a row before the customers, but she had soon
found it helped trade more than it hindered it, particularly when
Manny never answered back or made trouble. But, as the evening
wore out and there was still no sign of him, she began to think better of him. She began to think that in his weak way he was defying
her at last. Maybe he was getting his temper up with drink. He
wasn't a drinking man, but there was always a first time for everything.

A wild elation welled up inside her, waiting for a torrential release in shouting or screaming. She had battered in his patience at

last. At last he was going to try to get even with her. Well! She was ready. She went into the kitchen, leaving the door into the shop half open while she knotted her hair as tight as she could, and when she came back the pricking pain on her neck, where the hair was caught too tightly, gave her a foretaste of the fight she would have, and made her eyes glitter. She let the customers go without giving them their usual bit of chitchat. She put the shutters up before the time. Where was he? It was getting very late now for a timid man like Manny. And he had had no dinner. She lifted the saucer that was covering his plate on the range. She ought to let him get a bite of food into him before she started the row. But where was he?

She was on her way out to the door to look up the street when she saw the silhouette of the poorhouse hearse, the Black Maria, passing the door. Supposing he was gone for good? The little skunk! It would be just like him to go over the river wall, like a rat in the dark, and never be heard of again. She would be cheated in this like everything else. Then the blackness lifted a little in her heart and she began to consider other possibilities. Maybe he'd skipped off to better himself somewhere and give her a miss? Again anger throbbed in her breast, but it eased when she remembered that he wouldn't have any money. Thanks be to the Almighty — and to her own good sense — she hadn't given him the money for the eggs. She wondered if he'd got them. Had he gone for them at all?

One after another, then, pictures of horror came into her mind. She saw a sodden corpse, white and hideously swollen, being carried in across the shop, and dripping water from muddy clothes upon the thirsty wooden boards. She saw herself at the wake, moaning and rocking from side to side, with everyone pitying her.

He wasn't a bad sort, the poor fellow, always wanting to take her to the Gaiety when the opera was on. He wasn't to blame for being so weak. His hands always went dead when he was cold. His face got a terrible blue color in frosty weather. She thought about the peculiar habit he had of sleeping with his feet outside the bedclothes. And she began to feel uneasy about the past as well as about the future. She walked up and down the dark room, mauled by memories.

Once in a while she went into the street and looked up and down. She did that in an effort to anticipate the terror that she felt was coming nearer every minute, rounding each corner more rapidly than the one before. But the evening winds were cooling the air and breathing their clear sweet peace even into the city streets. The lights were lighted, but their rays were not yet drawn out from them because the day had still some brightness of its own. They kept their gold carefully folded inside their glass globes, against the hour when their light would be needed, and it seemed as if they had no other function than to decorate the streets with gilt stars. The trams too were lit up, and they sailed like gilded galleons down the evanescent evening blue. The noises of trucks and drays sounded singly in the stillness and seemed to say that they were going off as fast as they could, and that soon the city would be given over to cars and taxis traveling to gaudy cinemas and theaters pearled with lights.

The evening was so fair and so serene, so green and blue and gilt, that it threatened to rob her of all her dreads and drown her fears. It was better to sit by the whitening fire and imagine that the city outside was dark and vicious as she had often felt it to be, crossing it late on winter nights; a place of evil shadows, with police standing silently in the alleyways, and its shops shut down and barricaded with boards like coffin lids, and all the private houses fortified with battered ash cans lined up along the path, and, dreariest of all, the Green with its padlocked gates and its tree-high railings, through which you heard the agonies of a thousand cats wailing in the dark shrubberies.

She did not know which of her black forebodings she felt to be the more likely, but the ones that brought terror without robbing her entirely of the object of her terror were the ones that most appealed to her. And so she more or less expected a living Manny to be brought home to her; but one in whom some latent mutinous instinct had at last set up a twanging of chords that would echo throughout the rest of their lives and put reality into their relationship. She waited for his coming with more eagerness than when he was coming to court her.

But the instant she heard his footfall she knew he was the same

old Manny. He was all right. And he was sober. Her fears faded
out in widening ripples, leaving stillness and stagnation in her heart
once more. When he put his head inside the door she knew by his
hesitation and his apologetic cough that it was not even his own
pleasure had kept him out so late, much less a high-riding revolt.
She didn't even want to know what it was that kept him. She knew
it was some pale and weedy shoot from the anemia of his character,
and not a sudden bursting into leaf of unsuspected manliness.

She sat by the fire without moving.

At last Manny was driven to break the silence himself.

"Did you keep my dinner?" he asked timidly, going over to the
range, stooping his head as he went to avoid a slap of the wet
sheets and towels that hung across the kitchen on a piece of string.
He opened the door of the oven and looked in, bending down.
There was nothing there, and he shut the door quietly and stole a
look at Annie. She was sitting scratching her head, with a hairpin
she had pulled out of the tight knot of hair on her neck. When she
had finished scratching she stood up.

"Get up out of that!" she ordered tonelessly, and, pulling a damp
cloth off the line over his head, she took a hot plate from the top
of the stove and went over to a pile of rubbish in the corner of the
room. "Light the gas," she said, pulling out a square of brown paper
from the pile of rubbish and setting the plate down upon it on the
table.

The nauseous smell of gas roamed around the room in streamers
that soon ran together into one thick odor. The green light took
away the only dignity the room had — its darkness. Manny sat
down to the dinner set on the brown paper. It was a plate of meat
flanked on two sides by tallow-yellow potatoes and a mound of
cabbage that still held the shape of the fork that patted it. Meat,
potato and cabbage were all stuck fast to the plate. And around
the rim of it the gravy was crusted into a brown paper doily.

"It looks good," Manny said appeasingly, "and it smells good."

"It smelled better four hours ago," said Annie, cleaning a knife
with her fingers and putting it down beside the plate.

Manny wondered if this reference to keeping the dinner hot was
intended as an opening for him to say where he had been, and what

had kept him, but when he looked at her he decided on saying nothing.

He ate his dinner in silence and tried as best he could to keep the food in his mouth from making noise, but the sounds of chewing seemed so loud in his own ears that after a few mouthfuls he began to swallow down the coarse lumps of beef unchewed. Soon the silence became so terrible he could eat no more. He pushed aside his plate and sat staring at the ring of grease it left on the absorbent brown paper. Suddenly he thought of the paper he had used the night before his wedding to get grease off his sleeve. In those days he used to read in bed and he'd get his clothes all candle grease, because he humped up his clothes to raise the candlestick higher beside the bed. That was a long time ago, but the past had been coming back into his mind all day. He used to hear his mother say that you relived all your life in your mind before you died, but he hated all those ignorant old superstitions. Yet the silence in the kitchen was enough to make a man go mad.

He turned around in the chair and deliberately drew down the lash of her rage. "I went up to Sallygap to get the eggs, but I missed the bus and walked home."

"From Sallygap?"

He had expected a vicious answer. He looked at her. She was picking her teeth with a bit of the brown paper she tore off the table.

"Gets in your teeth, doesn't it?" he said in a fainthearted hope that there was not going to be any row.

"Are you finished?" she asked.

He looked at his plate.

"Finished," he said. "All except my tea. I'll wet the tea myself if you like."

"The tea is on the pot," she said, and as he poured the spluttering water into the teapot she got up and went over to the dresser and took down a cup and saucer. She put them on the table.

The cup had not been washed since it had last been used. There was a sandy sediment of moist sugar in the bottom of it, and down the outside were yellow streaks of tea.

"This cup is a bit dirty," he said, moving over to the sink.

"It's your own dirt, then," she said to him. "It was you who had it last."

He stood irresolute, and then he said he'd like a clean cup.

"There's a quarter pound of sugar in the bottom of that cup," she said, and then she snapped another question at him suddenly with some apparent relevancy in her own mind. "What did you do with the return ticket?"

He rooted in his pockets and took out the half-ticket. She snapped it up and looked at it closely, and then she stuck it down in a jug that was hanging by its handle on the nail of the dresser.

"Is he going to send the eggs?"

"Every Monday and Friday."

"Give me that cup." She went over to the sink, where she ran the cold tap on it. She clattered it back on the saucer; wet. Cold drops splashed onto his hot hands from her wet hands. She stood looking down at him.

"It's a queer thing when a man disgusts to himself!" she said.

Her eyes were greener than ever. They used to remind him of the sea at Howth, where they went walking while they were courting. They were the same color still, but now they reminded him suddenly of the green water under the landing stage at Dunlaoghaire. And as the sticky sea had that day been flecked with splinters of a broken fiddle, Annie's eyes above him now were flecked with malevolence.

Ever since their first quarrel, he'd been afraid of her sharp tongue. But it had been the fear of a timid soul. Now, looking up into her eyes, his immature and childish fear fell from him, and instead of it there came into his heart a terrible adult fear; a fear that came from his instincts, from his blood. He thought of all the talk he had heard at different times in public houses, talk of morgues and murders, and he remembered what he had said to himself up at Sallygap about the people of Dublin; that they were ignorant people with clogged pools in their blood that clotted easily to unjust hate. They held their hate. He thought of Paris, with its flashing lights and its quick flashing hates and its quick flashing knives; its women with hands quick to slap a face at an effrontery, their red lips glossy with temper. And the dangers of Paris seemed suddenly fresh and vital compared with the dead anger in the sullen, malevolent eyes that were watching him. Desperately he thought of the hills, but the thought of them gave him no refuge. The happy hills were fading from his mind already. He would never seek a sanctuary among them again. For there was no sanctuary from hatred such as he saw in Annie's eyes, unless it came from behind some night, when a raised hatchet crashed down on his skull, or from a queer taste in the mouth followed by a twisting in the guts. She had him imprisoned forever in her hatred. His little fiddle had crashed on the pier the day he gave up all his dreams for her, and it had floated in splintered sticks on the dirty water. He thought of it for a moment and then he thought of nothing at all for a while, but just sat watching her as she went about the room.

Then suddenly he remembered that she had said something to him when she clattered down the wet cup on the saucer in front of him a little while before. He tried to think what it was she had said. He couldn't remember what it was.

But he remembered, distinctly, thinking at the time that whatever it was, it was true.

THE CEMETERY IN THE DEMESNE

"HE makes me sick," said the carter's sister-in-law. "He never stops talking. I don't know how you stick it, in the same room with him at night. He can't keep his mouth shut for five minutes. I can hear him down through the boards in the floor. I'd go mad listening to him if I didn't put my head under the bedclothes."

"I wouldn't mind you!" said the carter's wife, testily. "You're odd! You're queer! You'd want him to sew up his mouth and never say a word." She flicked a few crumbs from the table with a sweep of her elbow. "As for me, I like listening to him. He has something to say about everything."

"You don't need to tell me that," her sister said. "I never knew such a bag of wind."

"Let me tell you this then," said the carter's wife. "It's not a bad thing at all, to be able to talk at your ease on any subject. He's never lost for a word, no matter what he's talking about. And what is more, he can talk to any and everyone. The highest and the lowest are all one to him."

"You don't need to tell me that either," said her sister. "I know it well. A bag of meal would be as good as a wife to that man, any day, if it had ears on it to listen to his old talk and his old stories."

"I don't think words like that come well from you, Cissie," said the carter's wife, "when you're depending on him for every bit you eat, and for the roof over your head if it comes to that."

"Don't worry," Cissie said. "I pay well for everything I get by listening to him talking, every evening, till my eyes are dropping out of my head with sleep."

"No one asks you to stay up!"

"Don't I tell you I can't sleep in my bed at night with the sound of his voice coming down through the floor? How would it be, do you suppose, if I was inside there in my room, listening to him out here, with nothing but a bit of a partition between me and him?" She gave a thump to the partition of plywood that cut the room in two.

"You can't hear what he's saying, can you?" her sister asked, uneasily.

"I don't try! I put my head under the blankets, and, even than, it's like as if he was shouting in my ear!"

"I hope they don't hear him next door?" his wife said. "The walls are very thin. I must warn him."

"He won't take much notice of your warning, if I know him rightly," said his sister-in-law. "The bigger the audience the more he likes it. He'd stay up till morning if he thought the neighbors could hear him."

Just then there was a sound of feet on the floor overhead. A door opened and steps sounded on the stairs.

"Don't let him hear you criticizing him," said his wife, taking down the teapot from the dresser and shoving it into her sister's hand, while she herself took up a loaf of bread and began to slice it down rapidly with a knife that she wiped from time to time on her skirt, to free its jagged edge from the crumbs that clogged it.

"Are my boots polished?" the carter asked, but genially, as he took them up from the side of the range. "There's nothing like real leather for taking a decent shine," he said, turning amicably to his sister-in-law. "Most of the shoes they sell in the shops today are made out of some kind of cardboard. They're not putting real leather into the cheaper class of shoe nowadays. You can hardly tell the difference in the shop, but the first time you try to polish them you can tell the difference at once. The imitation leather won't take the shine." He sat down and began to put on the boots. "Of course, if you know where to go, and who you're dealing with, you can be sure of getting the worth of your money. I always get my boots at one particular shop. I never go anywhere else. The man I deal with knows that there is no use giving me anything but the purest of leather. And look at the difference!" He held up his left leg with his hand, and showed the boot, tightly laced on it. "Look at this!" he said, lifting the other foot, with the other boot on it, the laces streaming back on the floor. "Anyone with an eye in his head could see that was real leather." He bent down to lace the second boot, but before he had drawn the bootlace through the first eyelet, he looked up again. "What in the world would we do without leather?" he asked. "Did either of you women ever stop to think of all the uses leather is put to in this world? Did you ever stop to think about that?"

"Do you know the time it is?" his wife asked, shortly, and she avoided looking at her sister, because she knew that Cissie was sneering at them both. She knew it by the very way the other woman went over to the back of the kitchen door and took down her brother-in-law's coat, and held it out for him to get into it. But the carter didn't notice the sneer. He thrust his hands into the sleeves and went over to the table where his wife was pouring tea into a thermos flask and wrapping up slices of bread in a piece of brown paper.

"I tell the fellows down at the sheds that I have two wives to look after me, instead of one," he said. And, while he stuffed the flask and the brown paper parcel into his side pockets, he laughed at his little joke, and repeated parts of it. "That's right. I have two wives instead of one," he said, and going out the door he waved at the two unsmiling women who, when the door closed, went back to the table, and sat down, and began to pour out fresh tea into their stale cups, on top of the cold dregs of the breakfast tea.

As the carter went along to the garaging sheds he took out a piece of paper on which his directions for the day had been written the previous night by the foreman. He was directed to take the three-ton truck with a full load of gravel, and deliver it at a graveyard in the other end of the county. The directions were typed on office paper, but the foreman had written something on the back, with a short stub of pencil that wrote indistinctly. As far as the carter could make out it said that the graveyard was inside the walls of a gentleman's demesne.

That's a queer place for a graveyard, he thought to himself, as he reached the sheds, and found that the other trucks had drawn out. He was the last. His truck was loaded and ready. He started it up, and pulled out of the shed.

The day was gray, and what thin sunlight there was kept failing and disappearing as clouds blew over the sky. He thought about the long journey ahead, and he thought about the two women he had left in the house behind him. They'll have another cup of tea after I'm gone, he thought; and they'll sit there talking till it's time to bring the children to school. He envied their freedom and, gripping the steering wheel tighter, he stared at the blue tar road in front of him. He hated to think of the miles of flat Midland country that lay between him and his destination. And he hated the return journey over the same flat roads. Women have an easy time, he thought, going about the house at their own pace all day, and chatting with the tradesmen and messengers that come to the door. Not that he minded working — he gripped the wheel tighter — it was up to men to work and keep their women in comfort. Woman is the weaker sex. He wondered where he had heard that saying. It was a very true saying.

But as the truck traveled over the flat blue road, the carter began to feel that he might have had a better job than the one he had. It was no life for an able-bodied man, he thought, going along, mile after mile, all by yourself without a sinner to talk to, and doing nothing but keeping the truck in the middle of the road. It wasn't natural. No man should work alone, out of earshot of his fellow men. Man should work with man. It was a poor thing to have to spend the best part of the day with your mouth shut.

The carter had to do the journey inside a certain scheduled time, and it was not flexible enough to allow for many stops along the way. Once or twice, when he flashed by a filling station, he looked with envy at the mechanics standing talking by the pumps, but his truck was overhauled every night, and oiled, and filled with petrol, and there was seldom any occasion to stop at a garage. However, this morning, as he came near to a small town, about middle way in the journey, he began to notice a knocking noise in the engine. He'd better have it seen to, he thought, and he stopped at the next filling station. A big red-faced man stood at the door, with his hands in his pockets. There's no harm in caution, the carter thought. It doesn't pay to take risks.

"It doesn't pay to take risks," he said to the red-faced man when one of the mechanics had examined the engine and found there was nothing the matter except a loose nut that could be tightened in a second.

"You're quite right," said the garage proprietor. "If there were more people like yourself there would be less accidents."

"It's a risky job, driving a truck night and day," said the carter. "You never can tell when some fool will come round a corner on the wrong side of the road and send you into Eternity."

"That's right," said the red-faced man. "But you could meet your death on a straight piece of a road as quick as on a bend. A skid could send you flying over the ditch to your death."

"If a tire blew out while you were traveling against time, where were you?" the carter said, nodding in agreement.

"If it comes to that," said the garage proprietor, "life is all risk. You could drive that truck for forty years and in the end you could be killed by a slate falling off your own roof."

"That's a fact," said the carter. "I heard of a man who was a steeplejack and he met his end by eating sardines that were tainted from being too long in the tin."

"There you are!" said the garageman. "What did I tell you! Life is one long risk."

"I knew another man," said the carter, "and he was sitting by his own hearth when the leg of his trousers caught fire and he was burned to death, with his wife and children looking at him, not able to do anything for him."

The garageman threw up his hands in horror.

"You must hear queer things," he said, "in your journeys back and forth across the country. I often envy the lorries, when I see them flashing past here, at all times of the day and night. I think it's hard on a man to have to stay all day in the one spot."

"We see Life, all right," the carter said, and he patted the red enamel sides of the truck. There were two ways of looking at everything, he thought. "Of course," he said, turning back to the other man, "it isn't everyone that would profit by his experiences the way I do."

"I suppose not," the man said.

"There are some men," the carter said, "who have the same job as I have and I meet them off and on in the course of my job, and they haven't as much to say as a mule. You'd think they were never outside their own back doors. Would you believe that?"

"I would. Indeed I would," the garageman said, and he moved away as another car drew up at the curb.

"I'll be on my way," said the carter, and he swung up into the seat of his truck and, waving his hand, he let out the brake. He felt like singing. There was nothing like a bit of company. There was nothing like passing the time of day with another human being. Now ditches and hedges streamed by on either side, and their greenery brought him gladness, although he kept his eyes on the blue road and only glanced away from it to look at the battered signposts.

The demesne was now only a quarter of a mile away. The hedges and ditches were rich and deep from the dampness that remained under the trees, even in sunlight. He drove slowly and ventured to look around him at the country. Cissie and the wife would want to hear the layout of the land. They'd want to know what the countryside was like in the vicinity of the demesne. Women set great store by little things like that.

The demesne was on his left when he went around the next corner. The gate was high and there were spikes along the top of it. He blew the horn for the gatekeeper and then he sat and looked around him. The trees in the demesne were the best he ever saw. There was one tree and the branches of it stretched right across the roof of the gate lodge. He looked at the door of the lodge which was wide open, expecting every minute to see someone run out to open the gate, but the doorway remained empty, although he could see flames throbbing in the grate of the room within. He blew the horn again. Still no one came. At last he alighted from the truck and began to push back the heavy wings of the gate. They

were no sooner pushed open than they began to swing slowly back
again. He was looking around for a stone with which to keep them
open when a woman ran out of the house, pushing her hair back
with her hand as she ran. She caught the left wing of the gate and
flung it back without looking at him and without saying a word.

"Did you hear me blowing the horn?" the carter asked, looking
at her before he went back to the truck.

"I did," said the woman.

"It's a wonder you didn't come out sooner," said the carter.
"Every minute that I'm delayed counts against me on my pay sheet.
I have to do this journey in scheduled time. Do you know that?"

The woman was unlikely to offer an apology. The carter knew
this and he spoke more to himself than to her. Suddenly, however,
she pushed her hand through her hair again and gave the only
apology that can be expected from certain natures: an explanation.

"I have a sick child inside there," she said, nodding at the open
door. "I sit looking at him and I don't remember rightly where I
am. I don't think to get as much as a cup of tea for myself. You
could be talking to me, and I wouldn't think to answer you. You
could be shouting in my ear, and I wouldn't think to raise my head
and look at you. Isn't that a terrible thing?"

"What is the matter with the child?" said the carter.

"I don't know," said the woman. "Nobody knows. It just lies
looking up at me, and doesn't ask to move. I'm afraid it's done for!"
She spoke with that calm and curious acceptance of misfortune that
is found only among peasants, and that passes among those who do
not understand them, for callousness and indifference.

"Did you get the doctor?" said the carter, with the city man's
urgency to act, to do something, to throw up some bulwark between him and an impending doom.

"I got the district nurse to look at him," said the woman. "The
doctor wouldn't come out all this way from town just to look at a
child no bigger than a cabbage."

"What did the nurse say? Did she do anything for the child?"

"She looked at him. She took him up and she looked at him, but
she said there was nothing she could do. She said I'd better start
getting him ready for the road."

"Is she a capable woman?" the carter asked anxiously, taking off his cap and scratching his head in perplexity.

The woman looked at him without comprehension. After a minute or two she remembered that he had said something about the nurse.

"The nurse is every bit as good as the doctor," she said. "It's the opinion of many people around these parts that she's better than the doctor. There are people around these parts who would sooner see the nurse called in to them than the doctor, any day. And there are other people that would sooner get a bottle from the vet than from either the nurse or the doctor!"

"How old is the child?" the carter asked.

"Would you like to see him?" said the woman.

"I'll just bring the truck inside the demesne," said the man, and he ran out the gate, and got into the truck and drove it inside, but when he looked the woman had gone into the lodge again. The lodge was single-storied, but it was as high as a two-storied house. The walls were made of stone, and the windows were mullioned. There was a crest over the high pointed arch of the door but it had been obscured by green cushions of lichen, as well as by Time, which had altered the spelling of many of the words. The lodge had been built at the same time as the main house, and it had been decorated in keeping with it, and not with the habits and possessions of the people who would inhabit it.

The carter went to the dark doorway.

"Come in," the woman's voice said.

The room was dark. The mullioned windows that looked so well from without, let in so little and so frail a light that at first the carter thought there were no windows at all in the room, and he moved toward the shadowy light of the fire, expecting to find the child in a cradle before it. But the child was in a corner of the room, directly under the thin pointed window, and its pallor was made greater by the elongated shafts of white light that fell across its face.

"How do you think he looks?" the woman asked, staring down at the wax doll in the cradle.

The carter thought at first that the child was already dead, but at the sound of the voices it opened its eyes and looked up with a straight stare that excluded mother and stranger alike, and yet had

some definite object on which it focused with all the intensity of
which it was capable. The eyes were dark, and unlike the eyes of a
child.

"Do you ever lift it up?" the carter asked.

"Oh, yes," said the woman, and stooping down she lifted the
child up at once and dandled it halfheartedly for a few minutes.
But as the heavy head fell from side to side on the weak neck she
dandled it less eagerly and wrapped her arms closer around it.

"It's as light as a feather," she said, then, with a flash of pride in
her voice.

She tossed the child up and down once more. "It's the lightest
child I ever came across for its age," she said.

The carter held out his arms.

"Would it come to me?" he asked.

"Is it this child?" The woman wiped the child's face with a
corner of her dress, and laid it into the carter's arms. "This child
would go to anyone. He's not a bit shy. He wouldn't act strange
with anyone. Isn't that a great thing? I hate children that cry and
make a fuss the minute a stranger looks at them. This is the bravest
child I ever saw. I've seen a great many children in my time, and I
never saw a child that could equal this one in making up to strangers. It never struggles. It never cries. It's not the least bit afraid.
The greatest stranger that ever was could take up this child and it
wouldn't pass the least remarks on him no more than if it was his
father. There's a child in a house down the road from here, the
third house from the crossroads — you'll pass it on your way out,
I'll point it out to you, you can see it through the trees — and in
that house, as I was saying, there is a child that's two weeks older
than this one, and as strong as a young bull, and yet that child
wouldn't let a stranger touch it without struggling and raising the
roof with screams. If you want to look at it you have to stand behind the cot, because the very first minute it catches sight of a
strange face it begins to bang its fists on the rails of the cot, and
kick off the blankets and scream till it's as red as a turkey cock.
Isn't that a horrid disposition for a child? What way will it grow
up, I wonder, when it's ugly-tempered like that, and it only a young
child? That's what I say to my husband. Do you know, I hate go-

ing over near that house. Would you believe that? And I'll tell you another thing. When I have to go over there I'm always glad to get back to this little creature that's as good as gold, and never cries or kicks, or turns from one side to another from the time you lay him down till you pick him up. He's afraid of nothing. The other day there was a wasp walking over his face and he never took the least notice of it, but just lay there looking up at me till I chased it away. He's a remarkable child. That has to be admitted. The day and the night are all one to him. He'll lie as quiet in the darkest room as he will out under the brightest sun that ever shone. He's afraid of nothing." She leaned over and wiped the child's mouth again, with the corner of her dress, as he lay in the carter's arms. "See! No matter what you do to him he doesn't cry. He has a lovely disposition. He wouldn't be afraid in a graveyard, as the saying is." She pushed the thin hair back from the frail white temple where the veins showed as if under glass. "He's a little angel."

"Ah, well, it's the best that are taken," said the carter, and he put the child back in her arms.

"He might get over it yet," said the woman dully, as she took the child and rocked it from side to side, as one might soothe and comfort a frightened or disturbed child.

"He might," said the carter. "I have heard of cases where children worse than that got better, and were as good as ever they were."

"I heard of cases like that myself," said the woman. "I heard of children that were as good as boxed up for the clay, when they took a change for the better and never looked back once at the way they were going!"

"I can believe that," said the carter. "Children that begin weakly are often the strongest at the finish. Many a bad start had a good end." As he said this he made his way reluctantly toward the door. "I'd better be getting on with my work," he said. "I have a load of gravel to deliver."

"Are you delivering it at the Big House?" said the woman, coming after him to the door.

"No," said the carter. "I understand there is a cemetery here?"

The woman nodded her head.

"I have instructions to deposit the gravel at the gate of the cemetery," the carter said. "It appears they are going to put a new path across it from one end to the other."

"It's about time they thought of doing something to that cemetery," said the woman. "It's a disgrace to the parish. Just because it's inside the walls of a gentleman's demesne no one ever thinks to pull up a weed, much less lay down a decent path for the funerals to travel over on a wet day."

"It's a queer place for a cemetery, isn't it?" said the carter.

"There's hardly ever anyone put down in it now," said the woman. "There's a new cemetery in the village. Once in a great while some old woman that has outlasted her time is brought in here to be put down with the rest of her family. But there's not many left now to go down there. When they put down one old woman that lives beyond at the crossroads, and another old one that lives in the next parish, but who belongs here by rights, they'll close up that graveyard altogether, and no one will ever go near it. That's my opinion. The weeds will eat into the stones."

"How far up the drive is it?"

"It's one third of the way up the drive. You'll have to watch out for the pathway with both your eyes, because it's all grown over with nettles and dandelions, and the branches of the trees touch the ground."

"It must be an awkward place to get into?" said the carter, as he started the engine of the truck.

"It's an awkward place to be put down in," said the woman, coming over to the side of the truck. "If the river is flooded the open grave gets filled up with water, and they have to lower the coffin down into the water. The people have to stand back, it goes in with such a splash. But the chief mourners don't like to stand back in case it would look like slighting the dead. They stand there as the coffin is pushed over the edge, and they get the muddy water all over them. Your heart would break just to look at the poor creatures, coming out this gate on their way home after it's all over, and their good mourning clothes, that came straight out of the shop, all covered with dirt, and their shoes sopping wet."

The woman rocked the child to and fro as she spoke, and the

carter nodded and let in the clutch. She stood back a few paces as the truck began to move, and she looked at the child to see what it made of the noise and the bright red enamel of the truck. It was staring straight in front of it and it was impossible to tell what it saw and what it did not see. "You're a little angel," said its mother, rocking it again as she went into the house.

The carter went slowly up the drive. "This must be the path," he thought, as he came to a slight thinning in the shrubs along the drive. He got out and pushed aside the laurels. There was a gap there all right, and there was the remains of a path, but it was grown over with grass and nettles and great clusters of dock weed. He went up the pathway a few yards and when he came to a slight rise in the ground, in the distance he could see the slow river, clogged with reeds and stifled with the overhanging branches of ash trees. Down in a hollow near the river, he could see the irregular grassy mounds of the graveyard. There were small rough stones strewn about, covered with moss and patches of lichen. There were five or six headstones still standing but they were tottering this way and that, like human figures that had been scattered suddenly and indiscriminately by a great gust of wind.

"I'll go in and have a look at the place," he said to himself, and he broke a way still further through the laurel, but the strange, damp odors of the undergrowth assailed him: pungent dock leaves, decaying elder flowers, the smell of rotten beech leaves. He stood irresolute. Then there was a stir in the wet leaves near his feet, and two gleaming jet-black eyes were fixed on him for an instant, as a small living creature darted through the weeds.

"A rabbit!" said the carter. But he knew it was a rat. "I'd better unload the truck first," he told himself, and he went back to the driveway.

It didn't take long to unloose the tailboard of the truck and let the gravel rattle out in a heap on the grass, but when it was fastened again, and the chains secured, the carter took out his watch and looked at it. "It's getting late," he said, "I'd better not delay. I'll probably be down here again sometime," and he backed the truck into the laurels to turn it. The low branches of the trees and the branches of the laurel slapped its sides, and the back wheel caught in a rut between the drive and the grass bank, but at last the truck was turned and he started back to the gateway.

The gate had been closed. The carter had to blow the horn again. This time the woman came running out so fast he thought the child must have taken a turn for the better. She grabbed the iron gates with both hands and swung them back against the stone piers with such great energy that they trembled for a time with the impact.

"Is the child any better?" the carter asked.

"No," said the woman, "but I had some good news. The postboy has just been here and he left me a letter from my mother."

The carter shut off the engine and leaned out to hear better.

"My mother told me to wrap the child up in warm clothes and take it down to the priest and ask him to read a gospel over it! She said the priest would make a lot of excuses, but that he couldn't refuse. She said I wasn't to listen to any excuses or arguments, and I was not to go away until he read the gospel. She said that anyone who has a gospel read over him will get better and be as well as ever he was!" She pushed her hair off her tanned face, and the carter was surprised at the fine white texture of the skin on her forehead where the thick hair had lain. After the damp and lonely graveyard, with its rotten smells and foul weeds, he would have liked to linger in the warmth of this woman's company. Slight as it was, he clung to the small human relationship she represented. He was grateful to her for intruding her intimate talk upon the unnatural loneliness of the countryside. Above all he was grateful to her for giving him what he wanted most of all, a chance to break his own silence. He stepped down from the truck.

"I have heard of such a thing as a gospel being read over a person," he said, "but it is a very unusual thing. I thought it was more usual to touch the sick person with a relic. Have you got a relic?"

"No," said the woman.

"Has anyone in the village got one?"

"I never heard tell of one."

"That's too bad," said the carter, "because it would be more suitable than getting a gospel read. Getting a gospel read is a very serious step to take, specially in the case of so young a child."

"I suppose so," said the woman dully.

"The priests don't like being asked to do it, you know."

"But they can't refuse!" A timid defiance brightened her cheeks.

"They can't refuse," said the carter, "but that is why they don't like being asked to do it. They want people to realize what a serious step it is. Don't you see?"

The woman did not see.

"I'd think they ought to be glad of a chance to use their influence to cure people," she said.

The carter said nothing for a few minutes. He was pondering her words.

"I suppose they can't cure everyone," he said at last, "or there would be no sick people in the world at all."

"Wouldn't it be a good thing?" said the woman simply.

For a moment the carter was taken aback. Then he looked at the woman with a stern expression on his face.

"If there were no sick people there would be no dead people, and if there were no dead people it would be a queer world."

"Why?" said the woman.

The carter was about to show annoyance, but on second thoughts he controlled himself and showed only a small trace of exasperation, by the slow way he spaced every word.

"The world would get overcrowded," he said. "There would be people being born all the time, and none of them dying. Oh, it wouldn't do at all. It wouldn't do at all." He looked very sternly at the woman.

"That's true," she said. "I never thought of it that way." Then suddenly she put her head to one side. "Did you hear a cry?" she asked, turning back urgently to the doorway.

The carter followed her. They went into the dark lodge. The child was all right. He seemed to be sleeping.

"Poor little mite," said the mother. "Isn't it terrible to see it lying there not able to say what's wrong with it?"

"God knows," said the carter, "but it might be all for the best if it was taken."

"That's what I say to myself, over and over again, when I'm going about the house, doing my work."

"The world is full of wickedness," said the carter.

"I know that," said the woman.

"A man in my position sees Life, you know."

"Yes, to be sure," said the woman.

"And do you know something, there were many times that I thought to myself that it might be no harm not to be born at all! Life is harder on a man than it is on a woman. I'm always telling that to my wife. Women know nothing at all about the evils of the world. They know nothing about its wickedness."

"I often heard my husband say the same thing."

"I don't doubt of that," said the carter, "but of course in my job a man sees more of Life in one day than most men see in a lifetime. In my job you see Life, and you see it at its worst." He looked down at the child. "Yes indeed, it might be the best thing that ever happened to this helpless little creature, if he was taken now, before he has time to find out the suffering and evil of the world."

"The poor little mite," said the woman. She leaned in across the cot and took down a letter from the windowsill. "Here's the letter I got from my mother," she said, and in the instant of taking up the letter and looking at it she forgot all they had said in the last few minutes. "I wonder what the priest would say to me if I only just asked him if he'd consider it was wrong to read a gospel over him?"

The carter sat down on the edge of a chair. "No man can be expected to know exactly what another man will say," he said. "You know that yourself, ma'am, as well as I do, but just the same I'd venture to give it as my opinion that the priest would say the same thing that I have just said to you myself. It's a very serious step."

"But he couldn't refuse? My mother said he couldn't refuse!"

"He couldn't refuse. That's true. But it's my opinion that he'd advise you to leave well enough alone!"

The carter uttered the last four words in such a low and ominous tone of voice that the woman, who had been abstractedly reading the letter again, looked up with a fright.

"What do you mean by that?"

"He might try to warn you of the cost!"

"What cost? The priest wouldn't take any money!"

"I didn't mean money."

The woman did not understand.

"Wouldn't I give anything to save the poor mite," she said, but she looked uneasy.

The carter shook his head.

"You may say that now," he said, "but how do you know that you will always feel the same way?"

"I don't know what you're talking about."

"Well," said the carter, "it seems to me I heard tell it wasn't lucky to have a gospel read over anyone. Them that are to go, are to go, and that is all there is to it. It's my opinion that if there is any interference in their going, by the reading of gospels or the like, some other blow is sure to fall on the family as a consequence."

"I never heard that," said the woman slowly, considering his words. Then she looked up swiftly. "What other blow could fall on us?" she asked, and then she thrust her own words aside. "And what if one did fall? Could it be worse than losing the child?" She pondered for another instant, this time over her own words. "Wouldn't I gladly suffer anything," she said, "rather than have this poor child taken away without having a taste of life?"

The carter grew more engrossed in the conversation.

"You might be ready to suffer anything," he said, "but who knows where the cross might fall!" To emphasize his words he threw out his hand and pointed to the cot. "Who knows but it might be the child itself that would suffer in after years. It might live to regret the day that it was made to prolong its unwilling life in this vale of tears!"

The mother looked at him with her fierce eyes, and then she turned them on the cot. Then she caught up the child and held it closer to her. It made no sound, but the carter saw that it had opened its strange dark eyes and was staring at him.

"Now that I bring the subject to my mind," he said, "I seem to remember hearing a story about a woman that had a gospel read over a young child one time, and from the minute the priest walked out the door — and I believe he was very upset, with the sweat rolling off him, they said — the child looked up and began to take a turn for the better. It never once looked back. It got stronger every day, and brighter in the cheeks, and freer in the limbs, till it was the grandest child you could ask to see."

While he described the other child, the carter looked critically at the pale child before him, as if he was prompted in his words by the great comparison between them. For instance, as his eyes fell on the pale floss of hair on the sick child, he broke off in the middle of another sentence to say that the child he was speaking about had a great head of black curls.

"He had the grandest head of black curls you ever saw on a human being and it never changed in spite of all he went through afterwards, and even on the day that they carried him in and laid him on the dirty counter of the public house, his hair was the most remarkable thing about him. The people that were staring in through the splits in the shutters were all agreed that he had the most beautiful head of hair they ever saw. 'Isn't it a shocking tragedy?' they said to one another, 'and look at the lovely head of hair he had.'"

"What happened to him?" The woman pressed her own child so tightly against her bosom that it made a faint sound of protest, and there was a trickle of moisture from its mouth.

"I was telling the end before the beginning," the carter said. "My wife is always complaining that that is a great habit with me! Well, I've spoiled the story now, I suppose, but you can piece it together for yourself. The child lived, and grew to be a fine limb of a boy, too fine, you might say, because he seemed to be thriving at the expense of the rest of the family. From the day he recovered there was a shadow of misfortune over every one of them. First a sheep died . . ."

"I wouldn't mind a sheep," the woman said impulsively.

"Oh, these people didn't mind the sheep either," said the carter. "As a matter of fact I don't think they connected it with the reading of the gospel at all. Even when another sheep died, they didn't connect the two things. And even when the cow was found dead in the ditch, they didn't connect that with the gospel either, although by this time the people all around the countryside were beginning to whisper and gossip about them. But after the cow died, worse things happened every day. Misfortunes began to fall on that family as fast as the leaves fall off the trees, until one day, without giving them time to save as much as a plate off the dresser, the house took fire and went up in flames like a barrel of oil. It was burnt to a cinder before their very eyes!"

"God between us and all harm!" said the woman. Then a spark of defiance lit in her eye. "I suppose it was a thatched house?" she said cunningly and she looked up at the high ceiling over them. "I hate this lodge," she said, then with great intensity, "I wouldn't care if it burned down this very minute. It's as damp as a vault. On a wet day the water streams down the walls just as if there was someone up on the roof pouring it down through the slates, but there's no danger of it taking fire. That's one good thing about it!" Defiance was now gleaming brightly in her face.

The carter felt an obscure resentment.

"Misfortune comes in different forms," he said sharply. "To everyone according to his needs, you might say."

"What happened the young lad in the end?"

The carter stared through the doorway at the bright trees outside.

"There's no use cataloguing the misfortune that came on the poor creatures," he said, "and on the children that weren't even born at the time that the gospel was read in the house, but it was the young fellow himself that got the worst fate of all."

"What happened him?"

"Well, ma'am, you know as well as I do, that there are some things that can happen a young man that are too terrible to be told among decent people? Isn't that the case? Well, it was the case with this young man anyway, and you saw the end he got, stabbed in the back in a drunken brawl and laid out on the counter of a public house for a coroner's inquest."

"God help us all," said the woman, and she laid the child back in the cot again. "It's a wonder my mother didn't warn me that bad luck might come of the cure?"

"There are some people," said the carter, "and they can't look ahead. Sufficient for the day is their motto. Let tomorrow take care of itself, they say."

"My mother is an old woman," said the lodgekeeper's wife, with a trace of apology in her voice.

"Old people have strange notions," said the carter, relenting somewhat.

"They put a lot of faith in prayers and relics," said the woman, disparagingly.

"Oh, prayer is all right," said the carter hastily. "I have nothing against prayer. I never go to bed myself without kneeling down for five minutes beside my bed, if it's only counting the flies on the wall I am, but I wouldn't care to have anything to do with gospels. Relics and gospels are unnatural, that's the way I look on it. I'm a great believer in Nature. Trust in Nature I always say, and Nature won't fail you."

"The nurse said something like that too," said the woman. "She said you'd never know the minute the child would take a change for the better."

"What did I tell you?" said the man, and he stood up. "Don't be talked into anything unnatural. That's my advice. But please yourself, of course. Please yourself." He went over to the door and stepped outside. Still he was reluctant to go. "I suppose you couldn't tell me the meaning of this inscription over the door?" he said, looking upwards.

"I heard what it meant one time, but I forget it," said the woman. "If my husband was here he could tell you. He got a scholar to figure it out and write it down for him."

"I suppose a scholar would only have to stand out a bit from it and he could rhyme off the meaning without any trouble, as clear as if he was reading from a newspaper? Isn't learning a great thing? The people nowadays don't put the value they ought on learning. The old people knew what could be accomplished by learning. The old people . . ."

The woman raised her head, and held it to one side again.

"Did you hear a noise?" she said. "I thought I heard the child cry?" She went back into the house.

"I'd better be on my way," said the carter, and when she didn't come back he got into the truck and drove out the gate.

Outside the gate he alighted again and closed the heavy gate and fastened the padlock by putting his arm through the bars. The woman still didn't come out.

"God help us all," said the carter as he drove away, and he thought how interested his wife and Cissie would be when he went home that night, and took off his boots, and related all that had happened. He drove faster as he thought of the pleasures of his own fireside.

The trees and hedges were casting dark shadows. Day was failing. High in the summits of the trees, among the green leaves, the last gold birds of sunlight were fluttering their wings. The carter kept his eyes on the road. And all the way along he was planning the words that he would use when he told the day's story to the two women at home, and, as he thought about it, the day's events fell into place and formed a picture — the still, white child and the damp graveyard, and the furtive rat and the rainy funerals, and the fierce blue eyes of the lodgekeeper's wife.

All the way along the darkening road, and afterwards when he was walking back from the sheds (after putting up the truck) the carter thought about the child, and the rats, and the water-logged graves. And suddenly he began to set more value on life than he had ever set on it before. Life is a great thing, he said to himself. There's no avoiding death, but there's no use in taking needless risks. Not that I hold with reading gospels over people, he said. You cannot prolong life beyond its normal course.

At the door of his own house the carter paused and rested for a few minutes. He felt more tired than he had ever felt, and yet he had often made longer journeys. He didn't feel much like talking when he went in and hung up his coat on the peg inside the door.

"How did you get on today?" his wife asked.

"All right."

"Anything strange?"

"No."

"Did you meet anyone interesting?"

"No."

"You don't seem to be in a very good humor?"

"I'm all right," the carter said. "There's nothing wrong with me."

When he had eaten his supper, he sat down by the fire.

"I'm trying to remember something," he said. "I'm trying to remember the name of a woman you told me about one time, who had a gospel read over her son and who never had a day's luck afterwards. What was her name?"

"I don't know who you're talking about," said his wife.

"Of course you do. It was you that told me the story in the first place. Some woman that you knew long ago had a gospel read over a child and the child got better, but the family had one misfortune after another until in the end the boy himself was stabbed in the back when he was only twenty years old."

"I never told you any such thing. I never heard of anyone that had a gospel read over a child."

"You're a stupid woman," said the carter. "You must remember it. First the sheep died, and then the cow died, and in the end the boy himself died. Don't you remember he was laid out on the counter of a public house?"

"I never told you a story like that. Maybe Cissie told it to you. Did you, Cissie?"

"I did not," said Cissie flatly. "I don't know what you're talking about. What does it mean, getting a gospel read over a person? I never heard of such a thing." She looked at her sister.

"It was never done where we came from," said the carter's wife.

"Where did I hear it so?" said the carter, "if I didn't hear it from one or other of you women."

"Maybe you heard it down at the sheds from one of the other men?" his wife suggested.

"I often told you before," said the carter crossly, "that those fellows haven't got a word to throw to a dog."

"Maybe you read it in a book," said his sister-in-law, looking back viciously at his wife, as she went out of the room, because she was always saying that it would be an ease to them all if he could be persuaded to read at night when he came home. It would keep him quiet. He'd sit still and not be going from one room to another, all the time, never shutting his mouth.

"She knows I never read a book," the carter said indignantly.

"Maybe you made it up," said his wife, giggling, and she pulled a lock of his hair playfully.

"Leave me alone," the carter said, roughly, pulling away from her. "And for God's sake stop talking nonsense. How could I make up a long story like that, if there wasn't some truth in it? If that's your idea of a joke it's not mine," he said. "I often heard women get queer ideas! I'm going to bed!"

"What ails him?" Cissie said, coming into the room.

"I don't know," said his wife. "He kicked off his boots and wouldn't say a word to me. He's gone to bed." The tears came into her eyes. "He didn't even say good night!"

"That's nothing to cry about," said Cissie. "You should be glad. We'll have a bit of peace. We can get something done." She stood looking around the room, as if she had never been in it before. Then she ran over to the cupboard in the corner and threw back the flaps of the door. "We can play checkers," she said, and began to take down the black and white checkerboard and the counters that were as new and glossy as the day they were bought, ten years before.

The carter's wife dried her eyes in the sleeve of her blouse.

"I'll have the black counters," she said, "if you have no objection."

"No objection at all," said Cissie, and she began to lay them out, whistling as she did so, and beating time to the whistling by tapping her feet on the floor.

The carter's wife blew her nose, and wiped her cheeks with the palms of her hands. They had been streaked with her tears. Then she looked at Cissie.

"You look very pretty tonight, Cissie," she said. "I never saw you with such a good color."

"I never felt better," Cissie said. "Where will you sit? In the armchair or here?"

"Any chair at all."

"I think you'd be more comfortable in the armchair," Cissie said. "And I'll give you the first move."

"I almost forget how to play," said the carter's wife, as she made the first move.

"It doesn't look as if you had forgotten," said Cissie, making a counter move. "Your move!" she called then, more impersonally, and continued to call it out gaily, as the pattern of the counters altered with the course of the play and the clock ticked loudly, and a big bluebottle, that had been closed into the room when the windows were shut, flew here and there and every now and then hit off the white porcelain lampshade.

Upstairs, lying in bed, the carter thought about the woman with the white forehead and the dying child. He wondered if the child was dead, and when he went to sleep he dreamt of an open grave filled with water, and when he looked at the mud-splashed mourners he saw they were rats dressed up as humans and they looked at him with the same still stare as the dying child. He woke up and leaned out of bed, with his elbow supported on a chest of drawers. There was a sound of rain falling in heavy drops on the tin roof of a shed. He shivered and looked around the room to see if there were extra blankets, and drew one over himself.

Next morning his wife shook him by the shoulder.

"Here's your tea," she said.

He sat up in bed and took the cup in his hand.

"Is it raining?" he asked.

"No," said his wife.

"I'm glad of that much itself," said the carter, preparing to get up.

"I don't see what difference it makes to you whether it's raining or shining," said his wife. "You're under cover all day long, but I have to leave the children to school and call for them again in the afternoon. Last Wednesday it poured all day and I got sopping wet. I came home and changed my clothes, but just when they were dried it was time to go out again and bring the children home."

"Is my breakfast ready?" said the carter. "Go downstairs and don't be delaying me. I can't dress and talk at the same time."

His wife looked at him and bit her lip.

"What's wrong with you now?" said Cissie, when she saw her coming downstairs drying her eyes.

"He cut me short," said the carter's wife. "He said he couldn't dress and talk at the same time."

"It's the first obstacle that was ever put to his tongue if that's the case," said Cissie. "Stop your crying and have some sense. If I know him he'll make up for his silence when he comes down. He'll be talking with his mouth full and spitting crumbs all over the table-cloth."

"You're very unkind, Cissie," said his wife. "That only happened on one occasion when he was excited over something."

"Once is enough!" said Cissie. "Ugh!"

"Don't let him hear you criticizing him!" said his wife as his foot sounded on the stairs.

"Are my boots polished?" the carter asked, coming into the room. He put them on. "Is my lunch ready?" he said, and he took up the parcel of bread and butter.

"Where are you going today?" said his wife.

"How do I know until I go down to the yard and get my directions? Don't ask foolish questions!" said the carter. "Women are always asking foolish questions. I never knew a woman yet that was happy with her mouth shut! It's talk, talk, talk, all the time. Why don't you shut up once in a while!"

He went out and banged the door. The sun was up now, and the sky was as blue as a woman's eye. The carter looked upwards and began to whistle as he went along, but after a few minutes he saw that there was a mist rising up from the moist earth under his feet.

In the house behind him the women stood at the window looking out.

"What is he kicking the ground for?" said Cissie, as they saw him kick the clay on the path.

"There's something wrong with him," his wife said.

And three evenings later she said the same thing. She was polishing his boots by the range while her sister was putting up the checkerboard and closing the doors of the cupboard.

"He didn't have two words to throw to a dog tonight," her sister said. "It gave me the creeps to see him sitting there saying nothing before he went to bed."

"He hardly opened his mouth six times since in the last week," said his wife. "And I hate to see him going off to his bed at nine o'clock; a man that liked to stay talking till the daylight came in the window."

"I don't hear him talking after you go to bed either," said Cissie.

"He's asleep when I go upstairs," said his wife. "Or he lets on to be."

"There's something wrong with him all right," said Cissie. "There's something on his mind."

The wife sat down on the edge of a chair, grateful for a chance to talk about the situation.

"There must be," she said, and she pondered this possibility in silence, looking down at the floor. Then she looked up again. "Or maybe it's something he ate?"

SUNDAY BRINGS SUNDAY

"PRAYER is an efficacious thing," said the curate with the white face, and, as he glanced up at the wet windows of the cold out-parish church, the light caught on the glass of his spectacles and made them shine like two flat disks of green that gave the startling impression his eye sockets were vacant, or filled only with a pale watery fluid. "Prayer, as I have said before, is an efficacious thing. It is a good thing for all of us to go down on our knees and humble ourselves by prayer."

He paused and the congregation shuffled their feet in the silence made by the pause. The curate looked down again from the windows and fixed his eye on the knob of the door at the end of the small cement chapel. "It is the duty of all of us to pray." He swung the white tassel of his stole around in a slow arc. "We should all of us try to cultivate the habit of prayer. Every man and woman should be aware of the power of prayer. The heads of houses should be aware of the power of prayer. Fathers and mothers should give an example to their children in this matter. The heads of houses should not be ashamed to be seen by those under them kneeling down at the appointed times and saying a few devout prayers. They should not be ashamed to be seen on their knees by their children, or their friends, or by those in their charge, servants and employees and the like. When the Angelus rings they should make the sign of the cross openly and not be ashamed, and, when convenient, they should go down on their knees. It is a common thing, especially in towns and cities, but sometimes indeed in country places like this as well, for people to be ashamed to be seen kneeling down A thing like that is a great mistake. I hope no one here listening to me today would be in danger of making that great mistake." He looked away from the knob of the outer door and fixed his eyes on the knob of the door that led up to the organ loft.

"Prayer is an efficacious means of obtaining favors for ourselves and those belonging to us. But we should not pray for favors only. We should pray at all times and without waiting to be in trouble. The man or woman who never takes the time to kneel down and say a prayer when he is in good health, with everything going well, cannot expect God to fly to his assistance the minute that man, or that woman, as the case may be, throws himself down in time of need to implore God's help. Yet, how often we find that man, or that woman, when he, or she, is in trouble of one kind or another, as, for instance, the sickness of a valuable beast or some such animal, or the sickness of a child or of some person very dear to them, how often we find that man, or that woman complaining that God will not come to his or her assistance? How often that man or that woman expects God to be ready and waiting to cure that beast or that child, as the case may be, just because that person has thrown himself down in time of need to ask for help, forgetting that when he was in good health, with everything going the way he wanted, he never took time out of the long day and night to offer up one prayer for any purpose whatsoever." The curate looked up again, and again his eye sockets filled with the white reflection of the vacant sky.

"There are a great many people in this parish and what I am saying here today does not apply to them, although few of us are perfect, and that is not what I wish to convey either, you understand — God is grateful to those people, mostly old people and pious women — and let us hope they never slip out of their pious practices. It is to the people who have slipped out of this pious practice that I wish to speak here today, and speak very seriously. So if there are any such people here, mostly growing young people and men, who used at one time never to pass the church without raising their hats and saying a prayer for themselves, or for those belonging to them, or for the dead of the parish, but who through vanity or shame or some other worldly temptation, have fallen away from this habit, all I can say to them is that they ought to repair this state of affairs before it is too late and they are deprived, perhaps forever, of the chance to do so. It is to those people I would like to say a few words this morning, but I will not keep you long because it is a very wet morning and many of you, I know, have come a long distance to this church this morning." The rain struck the windowpane once more as if to corroborate the curate's words.

"Just a few words, then, to those who may have slipped out of the habit of saying their morning and evening prayers or the habit of saying the Angelus or offering up a few words to God at any of the other times that Holy Mother Church ordains to be a suitable time for prayer. I will ask those people if it is a thing that they think they will be on this earth forever? Because if that is what those people think, they are, as we all know, greatly mistaken. And when these people are on their deathbeds, as we all of us will one day be, great and small, rich and poor, the highest and the lowest, they will say then, when it is too late, 'If only I had not abandoned the habit of prayer!' They will be sorry in that hour that they went their own way, willful, and not caring whether they were acting in accordance with the right ideas or not. Then they will be regretful. Then they will be remorseful. Ah, it is then they will lament that they did not continue in the practice laid down by the Church as the most efficacious means of ensuring that we do not stray from the state of sanctifying grace. On that day those people will present a very sorry sight indeed to the eyes of the beholders who will stand back, helpless, and watch him, or her, as the case may be, turning over and over in the pains of death and calling out, with pitiful voices, that they wished they had not given up the efficacious habits they had been taught to believe in when they were innocent children going to school.

"It is a very pitiful scene that I paint for you, and one which I hope none of you will ever have the extreme sadness to witness. But I ask you to turn these things over in your mind, and if there are any of you who have dropped, unconsciously it may be, into the habit of getting into bed at night, on a cold night perhaps, or after a hard day's work, without first kneeling down for a few minutes to thank God for having safely passed another day, then let that person be resolved from this day forward not to let such a thing occur again. I ask you to turn over in your mind whether it is better to get down on your knees for three minutes or to spend an eternity in the dark pit of damnation, lit only by the flames of hell; those flames that never quench. It is a terrible thought, but one which it is helpful to keep constantly before us."

The curate had been knotting and unknotting the cord that tied his stole, but now, by giving it a sharp tug and tying it into a tight knot he gave the congregation a hint that the sermon was near its end.

"That will be all that I will say on this matter for this morning, but remember that prayer is an efficacious thing and that it is the duty of all those who have young people under their care, whether of either sex, to see that those young people are given a good example in this matter. Next Sunday I will say a few words about the different kinds of prayer and the different times that it is meet for us to pray."

The curate swung back to the altar. The Mass continued. The tassels on his stole soon were still.

Outside the rain could be heard falling with a hard sound on the corrugated roof of the shed where the priest kept his car on wet days and days of dnagerous frost. And the wind at moments came and pushed against the thin panes of cheap green glass as if it would crash its way through, drenching the shivering congregation with a shower of broken glass. Inside, the altar boys answered the responses in shrill voices that sounded bleak and undeveloped, and the gray color of their badly laundered surplices gave them a dreary appearance as they huddled together chattering the Latin verses without comprehension of their meaning. The candle flames gesticulated uneasily. And a smell of rubber came up between the pews from the raincoats of the schoolchildren. And from the woolen shawls of the women and the felt caps of the men there came that strange cold stench that rises off a hairy sheepdog coming in with wet fur.

The Mass ended. Before the priest left the altar he knelt on one knee at the foot of the altar and called out loudly:

"A prayer for the eternal salvation of all deceased members of this parish, and this congregation:
"O God Who . . ."
The congregation repeated after him:
"O God Who . . ."
"Through the infinite merits . . ."
"Through the infinite merits . . ."
"Of Thine only . . ."
"Of Thine only . . ."
"Beloved Son . . ."
"Beloved Son . . ."
When the prayer had dragged a weary centipedal way from beginning to end, the priest and the servers rose and went toward a small door to the left of the altar. Before they reached it, this door, that led into the vestry, was opened from inside by a woman in black with a few sticks of kindling wood in her hand. She was not so much seen perhaps, as known to be there, by the rest of the congregation. As the people filed out of the cold church, above the heavy trudging of their feet on the wooden boards and flagstones that marked the graves of former priests of the parish, from the vestry there could be heard the thin, finely drawn, but insistent sounds of hot fat spitting on a pan.

Once outside, the congregation went quickly toward the gate. The altar boys were flinging wide the wooden doors of the shed where the priest's car was kept and kicking away a brick from the back wheel to let the car slip out of the shed in readiness for the curate when he had finished his breakfast. A few men were stooping down with bright red faces to pump the tires of bicycles. And some people were already across the road, banging at the door of the local shop to get their week's provisions. Horses and ponies were being led out from the stables behind the shop and the idle shafts of traps and pony carts were being lifted from the wayside grass. The few motorcars that were there were being turned in the gateway of the chapel with the help of becks and nods and hand waving from the young fellows who were taking up a stand under the wall that they would have sat up on had it been fine.

The people moved like actors in a play, actors who have rehearsed

their lines and gestures so often that they could go through them in
their sleep, but who have long ago lost all understanding of the play's
significance. And, huddled in a corner of the chapel yard, under a
dripping tree, like an old woman of the chorus, whose part, even in
the fresh beginnings of the play, was to create an antique sense of
weariness and an antique sense of sorrow, there was a half-crazed
hag who kept crying out in a cracked, wailing voice:

"Sunday brings Sunday! Listen to an old woman. Let you listen
to an old woman. Sunday brings Sunday, as ever was and as ever
is!"

Mona raised up her bicycle from the wet grass by the side-chapel
wall and a shower of drops fell back into the grass from the shining
spokes and gleaming handlebars. She wheeled it over the yard and
leaned it against the ivy on the front wall of the chapel while she
beat her red hands together to warm them. The blood soon tingled
back into her fingers and she blew her breath on them to ease the
tingle. Then she went over to a piece of slate that had been lifted off
the roof a good while back by a big wind, and she stamped her feet
on this a few times till they tingled too. It was a lovely feeling; the
ready blood coursing back into her numb limbs.

By now the last stragglers were streaming out of the chapel yard
through the narrow gate. And after them the old mad hag went
strealing, with her dress slopping down, torn, into the wet and
mud.

"Sunday brings Sunday!" she kept saying. "Sunday brings Sunday. It's wet today. It will be fine tomorrow. It's winter now. It
will be summer on another day. Sunday brings Sunday."

Mad Mary seldom went into the chapel. She stayed around the
yard picking up bits of fallen twigs. Sometimes she spent the Mass
time tearing up handfuls of grass and cleaning the spokes of the
wheels on the priest's car. Very very rarely, she went inside the door
and then you could hear her, over the chilly voices of the servers,
and even over the curate's reading of the framed prayers on either
side of the tabernacle, as she talked to herself. Over and over, she
could be heard saying her private litany. What she meant no one
troubled to ask, because everyone put some meaning or other into
the words for himself and left it at that.

"Sunday brings Sunday! Sunday brings Sunday!"

It sounded like one of those sayings that are true no matter what way you take them.

When Mona got the feeling back properly into her fingers she went out of the yard; one of the last. There was a slope down the center path and the rains had made it steeper by washing runnels in the gravel. She went out the gate freewheeling. But just as she got to the granite piers and was turning into the road, one of the young men who were standing under the chapel wall put out his foot in front of the bicycle and she had to swerve over suddenly. The bicycle skidded and she crashed into a big laburnum bush that showered down its rains on her and drenched her face and hands with icy drops. But she held tight to the handlebars and steered the bicycle back to the center of the road again.

As she went off down the road, then, with cheeks red from shame, and red from health, and red from the gentle thrashing of the rain, she could hear the young fellows laughing behind her and she wished, she wished like anything, that she was sixteen.

When she got to be sixteen they wouldn't take liberties, Mona knew. They wouldn't as much as turn around then, when she rode out of the chapel yard. They'd keep facing to the wall, and scuffling the ground, and shoving each other, and wrestling. And if one of them got caught stealing a look at her legs when she'd be getting up on the bike, he'd have to say "How' you?" real respectful, and give her a beck of his cap.

It would be a great thing to be sixteen and getting looks from the fellows under their caps. The minute a girl went into service the fellows all quit treating her like a child and began looking to go walking out with her.

Mona wondered which of all the young lads that hadn't any steady girls would be the first to say "How' you" to her, and look to go walking out with her? Sometimes when she was in the kitchen at home, doing her sums on winter nights, or starching her pinafore for school, she heard voices outside on the dark road, voices that rang clearer if the night was frosty. You'd know by the ring of the voices that the people they belonged to were having great times for themselves. Other nights, walking along the road by herself, on a message perhaps, or just walking, she'd hear giggling inside a gate and she'd have to step out faster and not let on she heard anything. Fellows and girls couldn't stick having kids around, spying on them. That was what she'd been told anyway. But in a few months now, she'd be leaving school and then the fellows outside the chapel would give over their codding, and treat her proper. They'd say "How' you?" They'd beck their caps. They'd act respectful.

It didn't seem that there could be anything in the world as wonderful as hearing one of the fellows saying "How' you?" and seeing him becking his cap. Next to the crackly voice of the chapel-yard hag saying "Sunday brings Sunday," she kept hearing in her ears all the way home "how' you?" and "how' you?" Soon there wasn't one fellow in the whole village that Mona hadn't imagined stepping out a piece from the others and saying the first how' you to her. And when her mind ran out of fellows she began making up fellows she had never seen anywhere, and they were forwarder far than the ordinary real fellows that she knew in becking their caps and saying how' you. The people streaming out of the chapel would all be gaping at her, and the chapel-yard hag would be strealing after them and saying that Sunday brings Sunday.

Mona loved hearing the old hag giving out her crazy talk. She loved hearing her shouting out that Sunday brought Sunday, because that was just what Mona wanted. She wanted the Sundays to come on faster and faster. She wanted the time to pass. The days of the week were all more or less the same. They weren't easy to mark off from one another. There were the same things to be done on every one of them. But Sunday was different. Some Sundays were sunny. Some were rainy. There was a frost some Sundays and other Sundays the leaves were lashed about with the wind. If she was put to it, Mona could tell you what it was like on every single Sunday, back as far as you'd like to go. But who could remember what it was like on a Monday or a Wednesday? Mona couldn't tell you what it was like last Friday, let alone Wednesday or Monday.

On Sundays you could feel the year was traveling. You could know there was a big stir on the year when you sat listening to the sermons of the curate because the curate kept close to the season of the year in the words he gave out to the people during Mass. Mona loved sitting up for the sermon and listening to every word. She kept thinking how far they had got since the Sunday before, and she kept thinking how far more they'd have got by the next Sunday. In November there were sermons about the souls of the dead. Mona, listening to the curate's words about the departed dead, could almost see them writhing out from under their gravestones in the churchyard and circling up through the skies, past the green glass windows of the chapel, like slow curls of smoke from a fire that wasn't drawing well.

In December there were sermons about Ember days and fasting and the blue star over Bethlehem. In January there was Lent coming toward them, and then in no time it was the month of May and the curate was telling them about the beneficial practice of keeping a May altar in the home, and putting wildflowers in front of it if you didn't have any better. Devotions like that were what kept the faith alive, he said, and many a poor exile was saved on his deathbed by thinking of the simple faith of the people at home with their May altars always decorated to the best of their ability.

That was the sermon Mona liked best. That was one she remembered word for word from the last time it was given out. Didn't she herself always have the best altar in the village and the other scholars from the school came in to see it when they were passing home. Last year the curate heard about it from the teacher, and he made Mona stand up and he gave her a picture to put in her prayer book. That day Mona took a short cut home across the field where Kineelys kept the bull, so she'd get home quicker to tell her mother. Her mother was very proud, and the next Sunday, coming out from Mass, her mother and Mrs. Kineely had a long talk about it.

"The priest had a touch of a cold on him, this morning, I thought," said Mrs. Kineely.

"He's a lovely man, isn't he?" said Mona's mother.

"I hear he gave your Mona a holy picture for her prayer book when he was over in the schoolhouse?"

"He did," said Mona's mother. "He's a nice man."

"He takes a great interest in everything," said Mrs. Kineely. "But he's not strong. I'm afraid he's delicate, the poor man. But no wonder."

"No wonder indeed," said her mother. "It's a hard life they have, up out of their beds till one o'clock in the day without as much as a cup of tea inside their lips."

"Yes, and when they do get their bit of breakfast, think of them having to be victimized by eating it in that poke-hole of a sacristy with Nonny Kane's dirty cooking!"

"I don't like to think of it, and that's the truth."

"I don't understand why they have the like of Nonny Kane cooking for the priest in the first place. I wouldn't eat bit or bite in that one's house if I was to be without crust or crumb for forty days and forty nights. And that's the truth for you."

"I can believe it. It's a wonder to me he has her at all, but I suppose he couldn't very well pass over her and she living next door to the chapel."

"She's all right in her own way, I suppose, but I'll tell you what it is, I wouldn't trust her to lay out the best penny she had for a piece of bacon. Would you?"

"I wouldn't. I wouldn't trust her an inch. Isn't it terrible? I declare to God if I was cooking for the priest I'd be up the best part of the night skinning the bacon and rinsing out the kettle."

"I know you would. There's no need to tell anyone that. All Nonny Kane does is slap it up to him any old way. I didn't care much for the smell of the rashers she was frying for him this morning, did you?"

"Now that you mention it, I did not. Maybe I'm over particular, but I thought to myself that they didn't smell the way I'd like them to smell."

"You're not over particular in the least. And when it comes to cooking for the priest it would be a hard thing to be over particular, no matter how particular you were. If they don't deserve the best, I'd like to know who does?"

"The poor man! I declare to God, I often felt like asking him to step across the road to my place and have a cup of tea out of a teapot that wouldn't be rinsed out twice but three times or maybe four."

"I often heard my Mona say just that very thing," said Mona's mother.

"Your Mona is very fond of him. She's a good girl, that one is."

"You should see the altar she has up!" Mona's mother said.

"That's because of what the priest said about altars the last Sunday but one, I suppose?"

"Why else? Why else?" said her mother. "That girl drinks in every word the priest utters. She's a good girl, even if I am her mother and say it myself. Do you know what it is, Mrs. Kineely? I believe in my heart that if the priest told that girl of mine to cut off her right hand she'd do it without thinking another thought."

"You don't need to tell me. I'd know that by the way she sits looking up at him every Sunday."

"She is a good biddable child. There's no saying against it."

"She'll be getting a good job, one of these days. Isn't she near the age to be leaving off school?"

"This coming summer," said Mona's mother, and then she looked around her and drew her coat tighter across her chest. She leaned a little nearer to Mrs. Kineely. "I wouldn't want to say too much, you understand, Mrs. Kineely," she whispered, "but we have reason to hope that there's a position ready and waiting for her the minute she leaves off school, and not too far from where we're standing this minute either, if you understand me?"

Mrs. Kineely nodded her head.

"If that's the case," she said, "she's only getting what she deserves, a nice good biddable little girl like she is!"

"I hope you understand, Mrs. Kineely," said Mona's mother anxiously, "about my not being able to mention any names. The whole thing hasn't gone any further than the exchanging of winks, if you know what I mean?"

"I know what you mean, of course. What's the use of letting too much of your business out and about? I respect you for keeping your affairs to yourself, not that I don't understand perfectly well the party you're making reference to, and I'm glad to think the little girl is doing so well for herself. That party will give her the right training."

"That's what I say," said Mona's mother, "but isn't it a wonder they're taking her at all and she not trained in any way?"

"It's no wonder at all. Aren't they getting a fine strong little girl, and willing and clean? And wasn't the last girl this party took in a fully trained girl and yet I hear she was always upsetting his instruments and all the world knows there's a strict law in that house — and always was as long as I can remember — against anyone going next nor near the surgery, let alone touching his instruments."

"Mona is the very girl they want so, if that's the case, because a better girl to do what she's told I never met, if I do say it and I her own mother. That girl never did a pennyworth of harm to a living soul unless it was for want of knowing there was any harm in what she was doing."

"You may be sure too this certain party we were mentioning a while back is well informed on that score. And she's a lucky girl the same girl is! They'll give her a training up at that house will stand to her all the days of her life. Would you mind telling me how it came about?"

"I'll be glad to tell you, Mrs. Kineely. You're a good friend to Mona, and I'm sure she'd be glad for you to know! She was coming out the yard of the school a week or so back and there was this party's car coming down the road . . ."

The story Mona's mother told Mrs. Kineely was accurate in every word, but her knowledge of the story was mainly due to her own industry in putting the right questions to Mona who was inclined to put no heed at all on the incident at the time it occurred and who even forgot to tell her mother about it at all for several days.

"Why didn't you tell me this before?" her mother had said.

"I forgot."

"I don't see how you could forget a thing like that," her mother said, looking at her sharply. "You're quick enough to run in off the road with every little tittle-tattle that's said to you by people of no importance. Why didn't you tell me this before?"

"I put no pass on it."

"You put no pass on it? What do you put pass on, so, if you didn't put pass on this? Let me tell you, miss, it's about time you put pass on the proper things. What did they say to you? Tell me that?"

"They said nothing, Mother."

"Is it a fool I have for a daughter! They didn't drive up in their motorcar just to look at you, did they?"

"They asked me my name."

"I hope you gave your full name?"

"I said 'Mona'!"

"What did they say?"

"They said 'Mona what?' "

"And what did you say?"

"I said 'Mona Clane.' "

"You should have said your confirmation name: Mona Bernadette Clane. But never mind. What did they say then?"

"They asked me what class I was in."

"What did you say?"

"I said I was in the sixth class."

"How do they know what that means? You should have said you were in the last class in the school. But what harm! He's an educated man, I suppose he'll have an idea what you meant. What else did they say?"

"They asked how my father was."

"And what did you say?"

"I said he was all right."

"What business had you to say the like of that? What kind of a girl are you? Wasn't it you yourself put the plaster on his back last week?"

"But the plaster was only because he was stiff after shearing the sheep."

"No matter what it was for, you had no business to say he was well and he going around with his back nearly burnt off him with a plaster. And let me tell you another thing, a man isn't well if he has to have a plaster put on him after shearing the few sheep we have out there in the pen. What else did they say?"

"They didn't say any more."

"Did *she* say anything?"

"She asked who washed the pinafore I had on me."

"I hope you said you did it yourself?"

"But it was you, Mother!"

Her mother jerked her shoulders with impatience. "Ah well!" she said then, resignedly. "I suppose it can't be helped now. Never mind. What else did she say?"

"She asked me why my hair was cut short. Why did she ask me a thing like that?"

"She was afraid of ringworm. What did you say?"

"I said nothing."

"Why didn't you say it took up too much time combing and brushing it?"

"*He* said that!"

"Who?"

"The doctor."

"I thought you said they didn't say anything else?"

"They didn't ask any more questions, but when I said nothing about why my hair was cut short he took a look at me and he laughed. 'It takes up too much time, I suppose, brushing and combing it,' he said. 'It's pretty hair, healthy and thick.'"

"What did she say to that?"

"She said she hoped I washed it often."

"What did you say to that?"

"I said nothing."

"What did she say then?"

"She didn't say anything else to me."

"Did she say anything to him that you could catch?"

"She said, 'That's all, I think' to him, and he said 'Goodbye.'"

"Did she say goodbye?"

"She sort of smiled."

"How did he say goodbye?"

"He said 'Goodbye, Mona. You're a good girl. Stand back now from the splatters.'"

"Did he say anything else?"

"He said to tell my father he'd look in on him some day during the coming month."

"He said that?"

"Yes, Mother."

"What kind of a girl are you? Why didn't you tell me that in the first place and not be putting me to all these rounds?"

Mona's mother ran over to the half-door leading out into the yard and she called out to Mona's father who was rolling a cartwheel across the cobbles.

"Come in, will you," she said, "when you know I want you. What kind of a man are you?"

Mona's father rested the wheel up against the house.

"That wheel is warped," he said. "I'll have to tighten the spokes. Say what you have to say and let me get on with my business."

"What I have to say is more your business than what you're doing," his wife said. "I want to let you know you may be expecting the doctor to drop in on you one of these days to talk about getting Mona into service with his wife."

"How do you know?" Mona's father asked.

"He didn't say anything about that, Mother," Mona cried.

"Will you let me talk, both of you!" said the mother, and she turned to the father. "Don't hold out for too much money," she said, "because she's not trained, but don't let her go too easy either, because she's a good girl and very biddable." She turned to Mona, "Run up the street, Mona, like a good girl and repeat all you're after saying to me to your Aunt Brigid. But tell her not to let on to a soul, and tell her not to mention names on any account. Tell her the whole thing hasn't gone beyond a wink in the dark yet. But tell her we're in hopes. And then come back as quick as you can and tell me everything she says to you. Don't make any reply if you meet anyone asking you any questions. Say you don't know to everything anyone asks you. Run off now, like a good girl."

Mona ran up the street, and as she ran by the chapel she went inside for a minute and knelt on the floor near the holy water font. She said a prayer for the souls of those poor sinners that the curate said were to be found walking the streets of the cities of the world with not one to say a prayer for them. Mona thought that sermon was the saddest sermon she'd ever heard, and she never let a day pass without praying for the poor sinners who were walking around the world with their sins heavy on them. The curate had spoken so sadly about them, looking up at the green glass windows and telling how Holy Mother Church made a special point of emphasizing the need on the part of the faithful to pray for all those who, through weakness or ignorance, had the misfortune to give up the protection of the sacraments.

Mona did not know what those cities of sin were like, but she felt that whatever they were like it was a good thing not to be in them. It was a good thing to be walking along lanes and cart roads between the safe mearings of hedge and ditch. On those roads and in those lanes no greater harm could come to you than a prick from a bramble. Even the ditches were shallow.

The ditches were shallow and there were yellow flowers growing in them, and the hedges were bloomy with rose, when the doctor's car drew up to the house and it was arranged that Mona would go into service as soon as she left off school. But school didn't break up till the middle of July and there was a long month to go.

Every evening all through that June, Mona heard the voices of the fellows and girls who were working at the haymaking by moonlight and they seemed to be having great larks together. Late in the night, too, when she was in bed, she could hear their voices still, out beyond the haggard, out beyond the paddock, down on the road leading to the mill valley. And the voices were as insistent as the scent of the hay coming in through the small square window. She could neither see the hay whose fragrance was so sweet, nor guess at the identity of those whose laughing voices made her lean up sleepily on her elbow to listen.

Outside in the hay-scented moonlight the wind was weaving the gray ghosts of the future; but weaving the ghosts of the glad hours only. In her big bed, that filled the room so the door didn't open the whole way, and the chest of drawers had to be put sideways, Mona lay impatiently whittling away at the hickory stick of her childhood. She had no heed for the hours ahead that she must have vaguely known would be filled with the noises of dirty wash sousing and gray slop spilling, coal hods clattering and the noiseless run of wet wood splinters into the soft wet palms of your hands. But Sunday brings Sunday, and so the time came along at last for Mona to scrub her cheeks and get up on her bicycle and go away to service with the doctor's wife. She scrubbed her cheeks till they shone as bright as a polished apple, and she put her suitcase over the handlebars of the bicycle and went off down the road. It was two miles by the main road and only a mile and a bit by the cross-country road, but it was all ruts and it took longer going by it. She had to sleep in. But she had Wednesdays free, and Sunday evenings free as well. It was much better than most jobs. All this her mother kept telling her as she was getting up on the bicycle. But she wasn't half listening. What did she care as long as she was through with school, and out on her own?

Mona went home the first Wednesday. And the Sunday after that, on her way into the chapel, she got a chance to whisper to her mother that she'd be home that evening too if the weather kept up.

The weather kept up, but Mona didn't get home. Just as she was going out of the chapel-yard after Mass the doctor and his wife stopped to talk to her father and she stood waiting for them, back a bit from the car because she didn't want to get in till she was told. The fellows were sitting on the wall. They were shoving and codding with themselves. But Jimmy Carney was standing a bit off from the others, and Mona just happened to look at him. Jimmy got a bit red. He drove his hands into his pockets and then he pulled them out again, and then he got redder still, and she saw he didn't have any cap on. But just as she was thinking that, he gave a beck to the yellow forelock that was hanging down over his eye. She could just barely hear him saying "how' you" in a slumpy sort of way, but she knew by the sort of a smile he gave, after saying it, that she was making no mistake. The next thing he'd be looking to go out walking with her! She knew! She knew! It was just like she thought it would be!

And sure enough, that afternoon, there he was, waiting in the laurels when she came freewheeling down the doctor's driveway. And he had a new cap on, one with a stiff peak on it and the button shut like a city fellow's cap.

They left her bicycle in the laurels.

It was sort of awkward at first walking linked, but she got used to it after a bit.

"I mustn't forget to get the bicycle, going back," she said.

"It's all right," said Jimmy, "the laurels are thick."

There wasn't much to say. But soon the moon came out and then the silence wasn't so bad because anything they said seemed to stay echoing in the air for a long while after they stopped saying it. And other sounds from over the fields, the sound of a dog yelping and of cans being got ready for milking, and, once, the sound of a train, all served to fill in the silences just as good as if they were talking. But no one could say they were laughing or having great times. You could hardly expect it, perhaps, the first night. But Mona kept thinking of the laughing she used to hear on the roads at haymaking times when she was lying in her bed. It might be better another night, she thought.

But it was the same the next time. And the next. She and Jimmy never had much to laugh about, not when they were alone anyhow. If they caught up with other fellows and girls walking in the gray shadows of the trees that the moon threw down across the roads, the others began nudging and laughing and then Jimmy began nudging her and she began laughing and they had pretty good times then. It was getting late in the year and the smell of the honeysuckle was heavier than the smell of the hay in June had been when she used to sit up in bed and hug her knees and wish like anything that she was sixteen and out at service. And there had been something mysterious about the scent of the hay, and the scent of the honeysuckle was sickly and strong. Mona knew before the honeysuckle faded that the laughing she used to hear was the laughing of threes and fours, and that when a fellow and girl were walking along alone, or sitting on a gate, they didn't feel much like laughing. There wasn't much to laugh at. And they didn't have much to talk about if it came to that. Once you stopped talking it was hard to get started again. It was all very heavy, the talk and the air, and even when the scent of the honeysuckle was gone there was a strong heavy smell from the leaves that were beginning to turn yellow, and in the ditches the fallen leaves sent up a stifling odor that you'd kind of have to like, all the same. So Mona thought anyway. You wouldn't know what Jimmy was thinking, unless he told you. And he didn't tell things much.

Would it be nicer, and kind of fresher, when spring came, or, better still, when the summer came? There'd be good times at the haymaking. That was one thing, anyway. She was sorry she'd missed it this year. She had only missed it by so little. She could remember the way the fresh hay scent came in through the window, and with it the sounds of the voices in the valley. She remembered the way the window sash spread out its pale shadow on the floor, the shadow twice as big as the window itself. She remembered it all the time she was walking with Jimmy that late summertime and she remembered it more than ever when the evenings began to get chilly and they started going into Ruane's hayrick out of the cold. The first thing she thought of every time they plumped down on the hay and put the scent of it waving up through the air was the nights long ago when she was longing for this; having a fellow treating her proper and the other fellows having to give over their tittering at her as if she was of no account.

But in Ruane's the dark shadow of the hanger fell across the hay-rick and the close hay had a stronger smell than the hay had when it lay drying out in the fields. They didn't have anything to laugh at there. There was only their two selves. They didn't have much to say, either, and Jimmy's voice wasn't clear or gay like the voices she used to hear long ago. Jimmy's voice was thick like as if he had a cold. And he didn't have a cold. His voice was always thick when they were in Ruane's hayrick, lying down on the hay and pressing out its hidden odors with their weight.

No matter how bright the moon shone out, no matter how deeply the tree shadows stained the pale blue road in the moonlight, no matter how brilliantly red Mona scrubbed her glossy cheeks, the evenings were not what she had expected, and it was always stuffy and odorous in the hayrick back of Ruane's, and Jimmy's voice always got thick, and his hands got sweated and clumsy the minute they began tricking or pushing each other about, the minute, that is to say, they began to have any fun at all.

When the real winter set in, Mona was sorry, in one way, but in another way she was glad. It was all one, though, anyway, whether she was sorry or not because her mistress wouldn't let her out after dark.

"I wouldn't be responsible!" the doctor's wife said to her husband. "I hope she won't mind, she's such a child! I'll have a talk with her. She's so innocent."

"Is she giving satisfaction?" the doctor asked.

"She's excellent," said his wife, "for her age and her lack of training. She's willing and able. She's a good little girl."

"She never went near the surgery, that's one thing," said the doctor. "I could tell in a second."

"Even if you couldn't tell, I could reassure you. She is so obedient. She does everything I say and just the right way. It's such a relief. I hope she won't be discouraged about not getting out during the coming months. There will be a stretch in the light after January. I hope she won't mind. But I couldn't be responsible."

"She won't mind," said the doctor, confidently, "if you have a little talk with her."

Mona didn't mind. It was put so nicely. The mistress came right down and sat on the edge of the table.

"I couldn't be responsible for you, Mona," she said. "I'd feel as responsible as if you were my own child. You're very young. You're very inexperienced. You have no idea of the dangers. That's why I'm speaking to you so frankly. I couldn't be responsible for you these dark nights coming back along the road. Think of the byroads! Think of the tinkers! The dark laurels! The avenue! Everything! Write to your mother or tell her next time you're over. She'll understand, I'm sure. And you'll find plenty to do here. There's a gramophone in the attic. You can take it down, and I think there's a pack of cards in the drawer of that table." She pulled out the drawer, and while she rooted among the cutlery she said that the winter wouldn't last very long. "A few short months and it's over," she said. "And there's knitting. I forgot there was knitting. You knit, don't you?"

So Mona only saw Jimmy on Sundays going into Mass and coming out. He was always sitting on the wall with the other fellows, but if ever he got a chance while the doctor was heating up the engine he'd edge over along the wall till he got near enough to say how' you. If he didn't get a chance for that, he always got a chance to wink. It was a great break in the week, anyway, because the six of spades and the three of diamonds were missing out of the pack of cards, and the only records she found for the old gramophone were some songs in a foreign language. Sunday made a great break. And the year was traveling.

"Sunday brings Sunday." You could hear the old chapel-hag. No matter how much of a racket the doctor's car made and no matter how loud the doctor was talking, Mona could always hear the old chapel-hag. It was a great comfort to her, just like it always was. It made her think the summer was coming in long leaps, from one Sunday to another; traveling tirelessly. Soon it would be warmer and the evenings would be bright again. She and Jimmy would be out in the gray moonlight at haymaking.

Or maybe she'd be out with a different fellow; one that would be twice as nice as Jimmy! Poor Jimmy wasn't bad. He was all right in himself, but she'd like a fellow more well up. She'd like if some other fellow came and said how' you to her some Sunday when Jimmy was codding with the other fellows on the wall, and if the new fellow came up the drive of the doctor's ahead of Jimmy she'd dodge in by the laurels and give Jimmy the slip and go off with the other fellow.

Jimmy was slow. He was all right, but he was slow. He was the first fellow that ever said how' you to her and he told her the last time she saw him that he wanted her to stick with him no matter what happened. But he wasn't well up. He wouldn't know how to act if anything queer happened. His voice thickened up and his hands sweated.

And the night the dreadful thing did happen, in the hayrick, back of Ruane's, he got up and ran out of the haggard and when he came back he had his hands in his pocket like he was trying to let on he knew everything, and that it was all right. But the minute he saw her sitting on the hay he flung himself down on his face and started to cry. It was awful. When she shook him and asked him if it was any harm what they did, he said how did he know. And he said how could it be any harm when lots of fellows did it. But he went on lying on his face all the same and she had to shake him with both hands.

"And what about girls? Is it any harm for them?"

"I don't know about girls," he said. "I never went with any till you."

"But how could the fellows do it without girls?" she asked, but his head was smothered up in the hay so she had to say it louder.

"Quit yelling, will you? Do you want to be heard in the house?"

"They often heard us before!"

"That was different!" he said.

"How was it different?"

"I don't know."

That was true for him. He didn't know anything. She didn't know herself, but you'd expect a fellow would know. It was his fault. If it was any harm it was his fault. Poor Jimmy. She was kind of sorry for him. Even if it was his fault he didn't have to be

so scared about it. As long as you didn't mean to do any harm it
was all right. Wasn't it?

The sweat came out on him when she asked him that. It came out
in white drops on his white face. She thought of the great white
faces of her father's sheep when they were penned up waiting their
turn for the shearing. The eyes of the sheep used to be dark and
dreadful in their white faces and that was the way Jimmy looked in
the dark hayrick; white with big pools of frightened eyes like as if
something dreadful was going to happen and he didn't know rightly
what it was. He was no good in any kind of trouble. He was twice
as scared as she was.

"You're leaving your cap after you, Jimmy," she had to say. She
had to put it into his hands. His hands were cold as ice. A minute
before that they had been as hot as hot.

If only in the summery time that was leaping in long leaps from
Sunday to Sunday, she could meet a fellow with nice hands, a
fellow so full of life he'd be always laughing and wanting to go
dancing two towns away, she'd never give another thought to
Jimmy. Then when there'd be no darkness anywhere on the roads
but the darkness from the great tree shadows, they'd walk along
linked and laughing. Even when winter came again and they had
to shelter in Ruane's hayrick — or maybe they'd go to another
hayrick, one that would be bigger; one that would be nicer and
brighter — she wouldn't have any need to be scared as long as the
fellow knew a bit more than Jimmy. Jimmy was slow. Jimmy was
stupid.

As Sunday brought Sunday Mona longed more and more for the
summer, and the more Sundays that passed the more she longed for
some other fellow besides Jimmy to give her a beck of his cap and
link her off, down the road before everyone, and leave Jimmy
gawking.

The thought of Jimmy was a hot thick thought, and even in the
chapel where everything was so cold, the stone floor and the cheap
green glass, the thought of Jimmy was hot and clammy. Even when
the curate with the light glinting off his glasses started reading out
the list of the confraternity guilds that were to go to confession the
next Saturday, even when a vicious wind scourged the window-

panes with a scatter of rain, she thought about Jimmy, and she felt sort of sick.

One Sunday her hands got so cold her fingers swelled up and when she tried to see herself in the brass pole that held up a green silk banner on the end of the pew she could see that her cheeks were white and she wished they'd redden up like they used to when she was at school. If only she could have a cup of hot tea, right then, she might feel better. Her cheeks would flush up a bit; for a while, anyway.

She'd give anything for a cup of hot tea! She wondered what would happen if she got so cold that she had to stand up and go out of the chapel to stamp her feet on the broken slate in the yard? Would everyone stare? Would her mother give out about it the next time she went home? And going back in the car would the doctor be asking what was the matter?

There was nothing the matter, only that she couldn't warm up. She couldn't warm up no matter what she did. For about a week now, or maybe two, maybe three, she hadn't taken any stock of how long it was, the cold kept her awake half the night, and in the morning the cold floor and the cold wind coming in between the sashes of the window made her head reel and she felt queer all over, ever until she let a cup of strong hot tea down her throat.

If only she could have a cup of tea now. She looked up at the cold white marble altar and a shiver went through her, under her shoulder blades. Her shoulders ached. She wanted to sit up, but it wasn't the time to sit up yet.

When the time to sit up came around at last, and the curate turned about to give the sermon, Mona felt better. But when he looked up at the windows and the white rain-sodden light glittered on his glasses, for the first time in her life Mona didn't heed what he said, and the long sermon with its Latin words fell heavily on the air with the falling force of dead things.

It was hard to sit up straight. It was easier to listen when she slumped down and shut her eyes.

"It is an efficacious thing," the curate said, "to kneel down on your knees for a few minutes out of the twenty-four hours that go to make up a day and say a few prayers in order not to let it be said that you passed the day in the pursuit of your own interests regardless of the higher things that should occupy the minds of all those Christians who are worthy to be called by the name. I know that the people of this parish are, for the most part, good-living people who say their prayers regularly, but there are a great many sinners in other parts of the world, not so much in our own country I am thankful to be able to say, but in other pagan places, who have abandoned the habit of prayer. It is easy for us to see how great a mistake this is for such people because it is by prayer that we avoid sin. It is a very pious practice for those who have themselves received the grace necessary for living a good holy life, occasionally to say a prayer for those who have not of themselves had the wisdom necessary to pray for the grace to avoid temptation. As I have said, it is by prayer that we obtain the grace to avoid sin."

Mona looked up. She'd heard the last sentence. She sat up straighter. Her back didn't ache so bad. She wasn't shivering so bad. It is by prayer that we avoid sin. Well! She said her prayers every night. She never missed a night. She never went by the chapel without going in to say a prayer. She wore a medal all the time; she wore it in bed even. And every time she heard the medal knocking off the sink or the coal bucket she said an ejaculation.

She looked up at the curate. He knew everything, she supposed. He knew everything that was right and everything that was wrong. He had to know everything on account of hearing confessions. She never said anything to him in confession about Jimmy and what happened. It wasn't any harm. You couldn't do any harm if you didn't mean to do any harm. Or could you? And how could you tell him, anyway? What way would she say it?

If he'd only say something from the altar about what was wrong and what was right! If he'd only say something about kissing and that kind of thing. But he didn't. How would he say it, anyway? It would sound queer. Still if he only just gave people a hint. All he said was that company-keeping wasn't right. But anyone could see that was only talk. Didn't everyone keep company? Wasn't her own father always talking about the time he and her mother were company-keeping? Weren't the old people always laughing till their sides split whenever there was a sermon on company-keeping? "Where would he be himself," they said, "if there was no such thing as courting?" And her Uncle Mathew that was the wisest man in their parts, and that was a schoolmaster in his young days, said to herself one day last winter: "Mona," he said. "Aren't you Mona? You are. I knew it. Very well then, Mona, let me tell you this, there's been courting and there's been company-keeping since the first blackbird sat on the first bush and let the first shout of a song out of him! Remember that, my girl." Every fellow and girl in the parish were company-keeping, no matter what the priest said. "Have you got a boy yet?" the old ones were always asking a girl. The blacksmith was always coming to the door of the forge when the children were coming home from school, and it was always the one word with him. "Did anyone get to steal a kiss off you yet?" And the men that were waiting for their horses to be shod would roar out laughing and some of them might let on to be going to make a run at you. "I hate that old blacksmith," Mona said to her mother.

"It isn't right to say you hate anyone," her mother said, "let alone a fine upright man like James Farrelly, a man that never did an ounce of harm in his life." And he *was* a good man. She knew that now. He was head of his guild. He was always in the back of the chapel, praying out loud, and wasn't a bit ashamed when people turned around and stared at him.

Company-keeping was no harm. The priest meant something else. Why couldn't he speak out more particular? Why couldn't he say out straight what was wrong and what was not? Why couldn't he? If he only gave an idea; only an idea. He should give people some idea.

Suddenly Mona's shoulders ached worse than when she first sat up. Her feet were freezing. The cold was awful. She was a terrible wicked girl, thinking bad of the priest. It wasn't his fault. How could he talk about such things in the chapel? It might be a sin to talk about them in the chapel. Sin was a queer thing. She never thought about it before. But now she did. Now she remembered what the priest said one time about the dark sinners that were walking in the sad streets of bright cities with their sins creeping black behind them. What kind of sins, she wondered?

She had to close her eyes. The people knelt down but she stayed
sitting up. She kept her eyes closed tight, because the light from the
cold green glass of the windows scalded them. The starched white
soutane of the curate scalded them.

Jimmy said it was all right. He said every fellow did it, some
time or another. That's what he said. And Jimmy never told a lie.
That was one thing certain. Jimmy had a medal pinned on the inside of his trouser pocket. And one day in the graveyard when he
stood on a wreath and broke the glass he cried, sitting on the curb
of a tombstone and then he took a shilling and he buried it under the
grave. Jimmy was good. He said what they did was all right. But
when he said it his voice was all caught up with phlegm and when
he put his head down in the hay she could hear him snuffling.

Maybe they oughtn't to have done it? But they didn't do it on
purpose. They were only pushing and shoving and having fun.

Again a scatter of rain struck the windowpanes and the cold voice
of the curate struck through her stifling thoughts.

"It is the duty of parents and teachers to instruct children and
servants and all those entrusted to their care."

In the pew behind her she could hear the wintry moaning of the
hag, who had come in out of the rain.

"Sunday brings Sunday."

Mona felt a great fear rising slowly in her heart when she thought
of the way the priest's voice every Sunday, and the voice of the
hag, and the voices of the fellows calling how' you from the wall
were lashing on the year till it galloped, taking seven steps at a time.
If she kept on feeling this queer way she would have no choice
but to get up and go down the aisle and out of the chapel. And
outside it would be colder. What would she do outside? If she
cycled home to her own house she mightn't get back in time and
she might miss the doctor's car. And anyway there was next Sunday to face. If she felt worse today than she did last Sunday she
might be worse again next week. And there'd be so many questions,
she'd sooner die than face them. And Jimmy across the aisle in the
men's side of the chapel would be sweating and rubbing his lips together if he saw her go out. He'd be scared. And people would see
him. And it would all be talked over later on, in the chapel yard

when the people were straggling out from Mass. The old hag might even have something to say, in a cracked voice for all to hear. She couldn't go out. That was all there was to it. She'd have to bear it. Mona clenched her hands together. She'd bear it. And she'd pray as hard as she could that nothing would happen to her. She'd light as many candles as she could out of what was left of her pay after some was sent home to her father. She might, maybe, skip a week of sending money home and put such a blaze of candles all over the candelabra that the smoke of them would go up like the souls of the dead went up out of the tombstones. Prayer was an efficacious thing, the priest said. By prayer we avoid sin. She always did what the priest said. Her mother often told people that her Mona would cut off her right hand if the priest told her to do it. That was right. She'd cut off her right hand. She'd do it that minute, if it was any good. She'd do anything if only it would be that there was nothing the matter with her. She'd pray and pray and pray that in the lovely summertime she'd have red cheeks again.

"Sunday brings Sunday." If there was anything the matter she'd soon find out. The priest was still talking and the light was glinting still off his glasses. It wasn't his fault that Jimmy didn't know anything about anything any more than she did. It wasn't. Sure it wasn't? And anyway, it wasn't right to blame anyone for anything they didn't mean to do; least of all a priest. He didn't know how easy things could happen. He didn't know anything about the like of her or Jimmy, only seeing them in school and giving them pictures to put in their prayer books.

"Sunday brings Sunday." Where was that voice? Was Mass over? Mona couldn't see well, but she could hear feet moving and she could hear the hag's voice shrilling in her ear. The feet were the feet of the year! The year was coming! The year was rushing up the rutty graveled yard. It was rushing in over the splintered wooden floor and grating on the flagstones where the dead priests of the parish were buried. It made a sound like the sound of a million feet, but it had only one blunt leg. She knew that. Ha! she knew that. She could see it even though she had her fists dug into her eyes. The year was a hobbled old hag! It was climbing over the pews. It was on top of her! It was skipping the Mondays and skipping the Thursdays and hopping from Sunday to Sunday. The Sundays were a lot of lice-eaten pews. It didn't take long to hop over them. It didn't take long to hobble along when you were an old hag on a Sunday stick.

Sunday stick!
Sunday stick?
Who said that?
Who said that.
Who was sick?
Who was sick.
Sunday stick?
Sunday stick.

It wasn't cold now. It was hot. Nothing was cold anymore. The wind beat a batter on the wooden door but every batter of the wind sent rings of heat up to her head. There was a scatter of pebbled rain on the windowpanes but no light glinted on the curate's glasses, because there was no light. The chapel was dark and getting darker and darker every minute. The darkness was like water and suddenly she was floating on it like the weeds that flowed on the ditches. But the ditches were cool and green, and she flowed in some dark water that was dirty and yellow and warm like hay.

THE LONG AGO

EVERYONE WAS KIND to Hallie. You'd be surprised at the number
of young people in the town who visited her, and went for walks
with her, and did little messages for her. But, although she was always gentle and courteous to them, and gave them tea when they
called at the house, there were only two people in the town whose
company Hallie really enjoyed. One was Ella Fallon, who used to
be Ella White, and the other was Dolly Feeney, who used to be
Dolly Frewen. Dolly and Ella and Hallie had all been girls together.
They had a great many memories in common, but their main bond
was that Dolly and Ella had been in Hallie's confidence in those
days, long ago, when they were all young girls, and Dolly and Ella
knew what other people believed to be only gossip, that if it had
not been for the intervention of a certain person Hallie too would
have been married, like themselves, and have a home of her own.
Dolly and Ella had read every note that had passed between Hallie
and Dominie Sinnot. They knew it was Dominie who had given
Hallie the gold brooch which she always wore, the brooch that had
the word "Dearest" written on it in seed pearls. And Dolly always
stoutly maintained that Dominie had once as good as told her, although not in so many words, that he would never marry any other
girl but Hallie.

Ah well, that was all long ago, and Dominie was only a law student at the time. He was young and innocent, and he did not realize
that an elderly man would hardly make an offer of partnership to a
penniless young solicitor unless there was more to the offer than
met the eye at first glance.

Hallie never blamed Dominie. When he married Jasper Kane's daughter Blossom, she felt he was inveigled into it. She understood. She forgave. Nevertheless she liked to think that there were two people, at least, who knew the whole story. She felt it was no injustice to Blossom that a small spark of the truth should be tended and kept alive, particularly when poor Dominie had lived for so short a time.

"I believe he would be alive today if he it was you married, Hallie!" said Dolly, one day.

Hallie could not permit such a thing to be said. But she felt a surge of affection for Dolly. Dolly knew. Dolly understood. And if a need should arise it would be a comfort to know there was someone to whom she could speak openly. Indeed, shortly after Dominie's death a serious situation did arise, but as things turned out there had been no need to speak of the matter to anyone. It was like this. Hallie felt that Dominie would have wished her to visit his grave. She was certain of it. In fact, for two or three nights after his death he had come to her in a dream, and it seemed to her that he was trying to give her some message; to say something to her. Hallie racked her brain, but she could not think what else Dominie could wish but that she should visit his grave. So she did. Every evening she slipped out to the cemetery, and knelt beside poor Dominie's mound for a few minutes. They were the happiest moments of her day. But even these moments were spoiled, because nine evenings out of ten Blossom appeared in her widow's weeds, and Hallie had to get up and move away, and pretend that she was visiting her own family grave. As if Blossom did not know, as well as everyone else, that Hallie's parents were buried in the old cemetery, and that, overcrowded, had long been closed to burials. No one ever went into it. It might have been a little difficult for Blossom too, but as events turned out the situation settled itself; for inside a short time Blossom encountered another difficulty and one drove out the other as fire drives out fire. Blossom got married again, and, unlike Dominie, her second husband was a big assertive fellow that would not let her out of his sight, but made her go everywhere with him, hanging on his arm. It was awkward to visit the grave of a first husband on the arm of a second, particularly when the cemetery gates were so narrow. Two people could not possibly pass through linked. So Blossom gave up going there to Dominie's grave. She ordered a first-class headstone to be erected, and left it at that. The grave was all Hallie's then. And Hallie soon had it a regular showpiece. The yew tree she planted back of the headstone did remarkably well. The box hedge around the border was not doing as well as it might perhaps, but if it did not thrive in the next year, Hallie intended to take it up, and try how a small privet hedge would do.

There had, of course, been one or two remarks made about Hallie's attentions to the grave. And some of them were carried back to Hallie. There had been a certain remark made by Old Jasper. That had been carried to her, too. But Hallie was above those things. And Dolly and Ella were a great support.

"Don't mind him, Hallie!" Dolly urged. "His conscience isn't too clear about the way you were treated."

Those were the kind of remarks that Hallie treasured.

The year that Hallie made the important decision of buying a plot for herself in the new cemetery, and that plot right beside the one in which Dominie was buried, people felt that she was getting eccentric. But Ella and Dolly understood.

"I know how you feel," Ella said. "If things had gone as they should, I know where your coffin would go; down into the same grave with him."

"I thought things over carefully," Hallie said, "and I would not have bought the plot if Blossom had stayed a widow."

Dolly and Ella felt bad when they talked over things together afterward.

"She doesn't seem to realize that Blossom will have to go down with Dominie anyway, whether she likes it or not, because a wife is buried with the first husband no matter how many times she marries."

"Don't tell her that!" Ella said. "Let her have what small comforts she can get."

Ella was always softer toward Hallie than Dolly, because, as far as these things can be known, it seemed that Ella was happier in her marriage than Dolly. Not that Dolly was dissatisfied. Sam Feeney was a man in a thousand. He was making his way in the town as well. He was buying up property hand over fist, and Dolly would have an easy life of it some day, although for the moment she had to keep pace with Sam's ideas about economy and thrift. Dolly's marriage had not been such a love match as that between Ella and Oliver; Dolly had married for more practical reasons. She'd felt the need of strong support. That was probably why it was such a terrible blow when Sam was brought down low with pneumonia, and putting up hardly any fight, was dead inside three days from the day he took to his bed.

Strange to say, it was to Hallie that Dolly turned. It was Hallie who held her together. It was she who made the funeral arrangements. No one would ever have imagined that an inexperienced spinster could have acted with such sympathy and understanding. Up in the bedroom, after the coffin had been got downstairs, Hallie put her arms around Dolly and persuaded her to control herself enough to go to the cemetery.

"Remember me!" Hallie said. "When Dominie died I had to stand on the outskirts of the crowd, like a stranger. It's different for you! You can stand at the edge of the grave and know that no one has a right to stand nearer to it."

Dolly recovered her composure at once. "Poor Hallie," she said, "I never fully realized all you must have suffered at that time." Her mind was taken off her own trouble for a few minutes. "Do you know, Hallie," she said, "I had forgotten it until this minute, but I remember distinctly when Dominie's coffin was going down into the grave, I saw Blossom looking across the grave at the man she is married to now! You remember he had only just come to the town. I am sure and certain she was wondering who he was at that very minute. There were tears on her face, but there was curiosity in her eyes." At the thought of Blossom's infidelity to Dominie, Dolly braced up wonderfully, and saw where her own duty lay. "Give me my hat," she said. "I mustn't keep the hearse waiting. Sam was always on time wherever he went. I won't delay him now."

Hallie was proud of the way Dolly behaved at Sam's grave, not giving as much as a glance to either side of her. She kept her eyes on the coffin until it was hidden under the last sod. People were more impressed by her silence than they would have been by any amount of sobbing and screaming.

Blossom's screams could have been heard a mile away when the first sod went down on Dominie's coffin, but going out the cemetery gates after the funeral Hallie had seen her nudging her sister to look at the mud on the tail of the priest's soutane.

Ella was astonished at Dolly's composure. "Oh, Dolly! I don't know how you kept up!" she said stupidly. "I'd have broken down. I'd have fallen into the grave if it was Oliver!" And then she had made things worse still. "God forbid that the like should happen," she said. That was tactless of Ella. Dolly and Hallie had exchanged glances. There are times when the silent heart grieves deepest, they seemed to say, each to the other.

After Sam's death Dolly and Hallie grew nearer. Ella was the odd one now.

It wasn't as if Dolly had much time. She had two children and they took up a good part of her time, and Sam's affairs had not been in as good an order as might have been expected or could have been wished. Dolly had several things to investigate. She was in and out of Old Jasper Kane's office several times a day. And there was talk of a lawsuit. Nevertheless, it was undeniable that she had more time to spare than formerly, and it became an almost regular thing for Hallie and herself to go for a walk along the mill path every evening after supper just as they used to do in the long ago, when they were girls with their hair in plaits.

No one could know what those walks meant to Hallie. The thought of them bore her up through the long day, in a house that was empty and dark and cold. For nothing she did, no fire she lit, no light she burned could bring back the warmth and brightness of the days when her parents were alive, and she was young; young! The sight of her faded face, and her faded hair, and her thin body that had dried up without giving out any of its sweetness, had been a bitter sight in her mirror for many a long day, but somehow it did not trouble her as much after she took up her old companionship with Dolly. The days went quicker when there was something she could look forward to in the evenings. True, she and Dolly, and Ella too, had occasionally taken a walk in the years that were gone,

but it was different altogether to look forward to them as a regular
thing; every evening. It was — Hallie told herself a thousand times
— just like long ago.

And as she and Dolly strolled along by the mill in the soft twilight it seemed sometimes to Hallie that they were indeed back in
the long ago. There they were, swaying lightly from side to side
as they walked along with arms linked, humming a tune together,
softly in part time. There were the evening skies, the same as ever,
darkening away to the east, with a gleam still in the branches of
the western trees. There were the bats striking through the dark
air in fits and starts. There was the sound of the mill pond; and there
by the dark river water was the same old sound of the cattle moving
noisily in the rushy bottoms. The same. The same. It was all
the same as long ago. And, inside, deep inside, under the changed
shape of their bodies, weren't they, she and Dolly, the same Hallie
and Dolly of long ago?

More and more of the past was dragged up and out of its golden
mist, as they walked and talked in the twilight.

"Do you remember the first day Ella put up her hair?"

"Do I? It fell down in church just as she was genuflecting outside her pew."

"I thought her cheeks would take fire."

There might be a short silence, then, as the images rose and pir-
ouetted and their minds were besieged by visions of Ella, thin as a
birch twig, with her toppling mass of pale hair, standing all confused in the aisle of the chapel, her cheeks flaming, not knowing
whether to stoop and pick up her hairpins or whether to get into the
pew as if nothing had happened and let her hair hang down her
back as it always did.

"Do I remember!" Softly, and timidly then, Hallie might venture
further into that misty past. "Do you remember the day you first
put up your own hair, Dolly?"

"Will I ever forget it." Dolly, might as well at that moment have
been staring into the spotted old mirror in her girlhood bedroom, a
mirror that reflected a saucy seventeen-year-old, her mouth filled
with hairpins and a pile of chestnut hair caught on top of her head,
to see how it looked, and the rest of her hair rambling down her

shoulder. But with a rich and generous impulse she repressed the vision. "I'll never forget the day that *you* put up your own hair, Hallie," she said. "And I know there was someone else who never forgot it either."

"Who?" breathed Hallie. Her heart fluttered. It seemed as if it was once again that day, oh! such a day, a Sunday! She'd let her hair loose from its braids and piled it up in a cloudy mass on the top of her head, but all the way down the street to the chapel, she had been so afraid that the same thing that happened to Ella might happen to her. And when she went into the chapel, although she had not turned her head to look in his direction, she knew that Dominie was kneeling just inside the door, where he could see her as she entered. And she knew that Dominie was staring at her. If *her* hair had fallen down then what would she have done? What would she have done!

"What would I have done, Dolly, if my hair had fallen down that day? Ella was able to console herself that Oliver wasn't in the chapel that day. He was down with a cold. How lucky she was! Think if he had been there! Think if he had seen her!"

"Oh, I don't suppose it would have mattered so much," Dolly said, a little impatiently. The practicality of experience was not altogether drowned in the misty vapors of these reminiscences. And in full knowledge of the intimacies of marriage, she could not always bring herself to feel again exactly as she felt long ago. She could talk about, think about, and recall, hour after hour, the emotions and dreams of long ago. But she could not experience them again and she even wished that Ella were with them. Ella and she had so many things in common. But Ella seldom got out in the evening. The children had to be put to bed, and after that she hardly wanted to come out. She would be too tired. Anyway that was the only hour she had alone with Oliver. Dolly sighed. She understood how it was that Ella did not come with them for their walks.

Hallie, for instance, never understood. How many times had she remarked on Ella's absence! "If only Ella was with us! It would be just like long ago. The three of us! Just the three of us! Do you remember the way she used to start singing as soon as we got out of sight of the town? She had such a lovely voice." Hallie could get quite censorious with Ella. "I think she ought to try and get out in the evenings if it were only for a few minutes; just for the change; just for the fresh air." She wouldn't listen to any excuses from Dolly. "You have your children, too," she said accusingly when Dolly explained that Ella had to put her children to bed.

"Girls are able to do a lot for themselves," Dolly said, "and my girls are older than Ella's little people."

"Why doesn't she come out after they are in bed?" Hallie asked.

"That's the only time she gets any privacy with Oliver," said Dolly, but she regretted having said it, because Hallie unlinked her, and stepped out more briskly.

"I should think she'd have seen enough of him in the last ten years," she said, in a chilly voice.

That annoyed Dolly. It was all she could do not to give her an answer. "What do you know about it!" she wanted to say, and to say it fiercely too, so that there would be no mistake as to her meaning. Hallie would see then, for once and for all, that there was a difference between a married woman and a spinster, and that even a widow was not the same as a woman who had never had a man in the house.

But as soon as these bitter words came into Dolly's mind she put them away. After all, it was mean to think of Hallie as an old maid. She had been prettier than any of them, and had a sweeter disposition even than Ella. And if Dominie Sinnot had not been the worthless weakling he was, Hallie would have been married sooner and younger than either herself or Ella. If it came to that, Hallie could have married someone else if she had not been so wrapped up in Dominie, even after he married Blossom. No! It wasn't fair to call her an old maid.

"Don't walk so fast, Hallie," she said, "my shoe is hurting me." She was trying to pretend that it was she who had lagged back, and not Hallie who had hurried ahead. "Isn't it chilly?" she said, as they drew abreast again, and she made this remark as an excuse for drawing Hallie's arm through her own once more. Deliberately she tried to feel critical of Ella. Ella should try to be more tactful! It was not very delicate to keep talking about Oliver all the time, considering poor Sam, and where *he* was, poor soul. Ella and Oliver might have been nearer to each other in age than she and Sam, but that didn't mean that there was any greater bond between them. As a matter of fact, love wasn't everything. But try as she might, Dolly could not help echoing Hallie's wish, and before they had gone another fifty yards the wish had broken out in the same words that Hallie had used. "If only Ella was here with us!"

"If only she was!" Hallie cried and so took up the refrain. "If only she was! It would be just like long ago! Wouldn't it?" And pressing Dolly's arm she urged her agreement. "Wouldn't it?" she demanded. "Wouldn't it be just like long ago?"

"It would," said Dolly, but unenthusiastically, because her impatience with Hallie had flooded back at Hallie's first words. Hallie was good and kind, and she would never forget her sympathy on the day of Sam's funeral, and it was good to have her company, and it was nice, too, to remember the time when they were young, but the truth of the matter was that there was something unalterably different in the way that she and Hallie looked at the past. To her — and to Ella, too, she felt sure — the past was a misty, dreamy land which was not altogether out of sight but which they knew they could never re-enter. But Hallie had never left it. It was the present which was dim and unreal to her. It was gray and uneventful, and counted for nothing compared with the glow of the days that were gone.

Dolly sighed. They had reached the crossroad; a point two miles outside the town. This was a point at which they usually turned back. Beyond this the road ran between tall trees, and was lonely and dark, and on the left of the road somewhere, they weren't quite sure where, a man had been done to death by thieves, or so they had always been told. One night Ella had insisted that they should go further. It had been a moonlight night, full of light and shadow.

"Oh, come on. Let's go down the ghosty road," Ella urged. "Come on."

But they wouldn't go. Hallie had a stone in her shoe, or so she said, and wouldn't go a step further. She, Dolly, had been scared, and said so.

"All right, go home!" Ella said. "I'll go by myself! It's too nice and bright to go indoors." And away she went, with her sprightly gait, down the lonely road lit up in the center where the moon played down through the branches of the trees, but dark and gloomy to either side where the thick black tree trunks were knit together by tangled undergrowths. On she went, firm and straight, and so brave! And there Hallie and Dolly had stood, feeling slightly foolish to think that Ella was two years younger than either of them, and yet had more spirit.

But a second after Ella had gone out of sight around the first bend in the road, they heard their names called, and there she was flying back to them, her feet flashing and her skirts held up in either hand.

"Run, run!" she cried as she caught up with them, but they only laughed and linked her safely between them again, because they knew that she had fancied her courage so great, her imagination had had to supply terrors equally as great.

Afterward, whenever they came to that crossroads they used to joke about that night. "How about going another few yards?" they used to say, just to rattle Ella. And even when Ella was not with them, they sometimes kept up the joke.

"If we had Ella here we might go a bit further down the road," Dolly might say as they reached the crossroads.

That was the kind of remark that Hallie valued; a remark that concentrated so much on the past in its essence.

"I often meant to ask her if she really saw anything that night; or if she only got a feeling of fright. What do you think?"

But again Dolly felt impatient. Was it not enough to try to recall, without trying to re-enter, the past? As a matter of fact, at that very moment she was thinking that there was something very pressing which she would have to ask Ella one of these days; it was a question about Sam's insurance money. Ella might be able to give her some advice. Ella could ask Oliver. Oliver might know.

"What are you thinking of, Dolly?" Hallie asked, breaking in just then on her thoughts, hoping in all probability to have some other incident of their youth dredged up into the present.

"I was just wondering if Oliver has his life insured," said Dolly, speaking out of her thoughts.

Hallie was disappointed. She turned her head aside and stared away over the moonlit fields. She wasn't interested.

However, if Hallie was not interested in what Dolly said that particular night, it was not many nights before she had reason to recall Dolly's words. "Dolly!" she cried, her eyes opened wide with awe, when she met Dolly coming down the street. "Wasn't it queer that you should speak of Oliver the other night?"

"Why?" said Dolly. "And what did I say, anyway?"

"Oh, don't you remember?" said Hallie, impatiently. "You were wondering if he had his life insured."

"Well? What was queer about that?"

"But haven't you heard?" cried Hallie. "He's ill."

Dolly had an unpleasant sensation that Hallie was overstraining the coincidence.

"Oh, I don't see anything queer about it," she said. "I suppose he has a cold. He's hardly likely to give anyone the benefit of his insurance."

Hallie drew an enormous breath. "Oh, but that's it," she said. "He is bad. It's not a cold. It's more than that. The doctor doesn't know what's the matter with him. Yes! he has the doctor — and a nurse. And there's talk of getting a night nurse."

"Oh, that's only talk!" Dolly said, impatiently. "Who told you all this?"

"It's not talk," said Hallie. "I heard it from Ella herself. She came to the door as I was passing. She's nearly out of her mind."

Dolly was reluctant to believe the worst. A guilty feeling came over her at the thought of the remark she had made about the insurance. She had only wanted to know for purposes of comparison. She was determined that Hallie must be wrong.

"Oh, I wouldn't mind Ella," she said. "Look at me. I was nearly out of my mind when Sam got ill!" She had no sooner mentioned poor Sam's name than she saw the look on Hallie's face. Her own face fell as she thought of where Sam had finished up. "Well," she said, crossly. "If he's bad we'd better go up there at once. Ella is no person for dealing with an emergency. Think of that houseful of children. Think of the turmoil. Oh! if anything should happen! Hurry! Hurry!" And she caught Hallie's arm and turned her around in the direction of Ella's house.

When they got to Ella's house Hallie and Dolly found that they were not the only ones who had thought it their duty to be there. It was Ella's mother who opened the door for them and as they were going into the parlor they had to stand aside to let Ella's sister pass out with a tray full of soiled cups and saucers. There were strange voices in the kitchen, too. While, in the parlor, there was a large crowd of neighbors and relatives. And in the middle of them all was Ella, sitting down in her own parlor like a visitor.

"Oh, Hallie! Oh, Dolly!" When she saw them Ella's face lit up, but several people urged her back into her chair as she tried to rise and meet them. She sat back at once, but she looked strained and white and as if she did not know where she was or what she was supposed to do. Someone else provided them with chairs. And a minute later Ella's sister, returning with a tray of steaming cups, proffered them tea and pressed upon them the information that Oliver's condition was serious. The crisis was expected any minute.

Hallie and Dolly felt frustrated. They had come down to help Ella; to take charge of the children; to see if everything was being done for Oliver, and instead of that they were treated like visitors. And all over the house they could hear other people charging themselves with the tasks they had intended to undertake.

"Is the doctor with him?" Dolly asked, reluctant to be put into the background.

"Oh, he's been up there since three o'clock," Ella's mother said. She looked at the clock and clicked her fingers together. "That reminds me, he must be brought down for something to eat." She turned away importantly, pausing only to whisper something to a cousin of Ella's sitting near the door, who promptly rose and followed her out of the parlor, closing the door.

"Can't we do something?" Dolly whispered to Hallie. "Did you say there was a nurse?"

"Ella said there was one," Hallie said, "but I don't know if she's a proper nurse."

"What do you mean by that?" Dolly asked.

"Well, Oliver's cousin is here," said Hallie, "and she has a nursing diploma."

"A nursing diploma!" Dolly exclaimed contemptuously, but she could say no more just then because a young girl put her head around the corner of the door.

"That's her! That's the nurse!" Hallie said and nudged her, and

Dolly saw that the girl undoubtedly wore a nurse's cap over her yellow curls, and that she was also wearing a white medical coat. But under the white coat a silk dress, with a flowery pattern showed with every turn she made. And her long legs were covered with thin stockings, and stuck into small fashionable shoes with high heels.

"Can I speak to you for a moment, please?" said the nurse, addressing the person nearest to her, who rose at once and followed her out into the hall. They also closed the door after them.

"I don't think much of her," Dolly whispered. "I think I'll ask Ella why she doesn't send down for the regular nurse."

But before she had time to rise from her seat the person who had gone out with the young nurse came back into the room. It was at once apparent what the nurse had wanted. The woman, who was, in fact, Ella's next-door neighbor, went over to Ella and whispered to her, and then to the women at either side of her, who at once began to assist Ella to rise. This assistance was given so copiously and so energetically that almost before Hallie and Dolly knew what was happening Ella had been led out of the room.

"The crisis!" Everyone had whispered the word at the same time, and the whisper ran around the parlor like a gust of wind. "The crisis!" Then the room that had been quiet and subdued became still more quiet. People still spoke to each other in whispers, but now they were no longer interested either in what they said or in what was being said to them. Everyone was straining to try to overhear the sounds from above. But where formerly there had been footsteps on the boards above, and an occasional voice, there was an almost absolute silence now.

The longer this silence lasted the deeper it became, until those who had occasion to move — to cross their legs, to open or shut their handbags — did so with such exaggerated care that their awkward movements took the place of conversation, and occupied the idle eyes of those who sat upon the chairs around the wall.

During this vigil, once, there was a widespread diversion when a child's voice was heard outside in the passage, asking a question in a shrill tone. Inside in the parlor several people started to their feet in dismay, when footsteps were heard hurrying down the passage, and the child's voice stopped in the middle of a word. Then the footsteps were heard again, hurrying away, but sounding heavier as if the child had been snatched up and carried out of earshot.

The stillness settled down again. Hallie and Dolly were weighted down with it, too. And it lay so heavily upon Dolly that her indignation could no more than smolder.

As for Hallie, she yielded to the silence. Wasn't she used to it? Her thoughts began to drift away one by one to their usual strolling ground: the past.

First she thought about Oliver. It was strange to think of him lying up there in his bed, with all those women whispering and tiptoeing around him. Even the small resentment she had always borne against him for being best man at Dominie's wedding began to wear away as she thought of him stretched out at the mercy of the unknown. After all, he could hardly have refused Dominie. He had nothing against Blossom either, she supposed. He would have been best man for Dominie no matter who Dominie married. Poor Oliver! Was he going to die? Did he know he was bad? Dominie, they said, didn't know he was dying. Even when they brought the priest to him he thought the priest had come on a friendly visit. And he was unconscious the day he was anointed.

Would it have made any difference, she wondered, if Dominie had known he was dying? Would he have sent her any message? Then a new thought entered her mind. Perhaps he had sent her a message! Perhaps Blossom had kept it from her! But at this point Hallie pulled herself up. He didn't know he was dying, she told herself impatiently. For it was by never putting the strain of incredulity upon it that she had kept intact through all the years the thin net of her romance. But he was thinking of me, she said to herself. I can be sure of that! And after that she gave herself over to imagining the scene in the room upstairs with Oliver lying helpless and speechless, but instead of Oliver it was Dominie. Indeed the young man who was that moment dying was, at one and the same time, Oliver and Dominie.

Did Oliver know that Ella was beside him? Hallie wondered. For all the world she would not wish unhappiness to Ella, but this much she could say, that if it should happen that Oliver did not know Ella, she, Hallie, would be able to understand Ella's feelings better than anyone else. After all, Sam had been aware of Dolly up to his last breath. His very last words had been about some insurance policy. But if Oliver were to die without speaking to Ella, it seemed to Hallie that she and Ella would have something in common with each other, something even Dolly could not understand.

All at once Hallie, just like Dolly a few nights before, felt a longing to talk to Ella. She and Ella had more in common than Dolly ever knew. After all they had both agreed at the time of Dolly's marriage that there had been something too practical about Dolly's choice. Dolly had picked out Sam. There had not been that inevitable attraction of nature to nature that there had been between Ella and Oliver, and between herself and Dominie. Why! Ella had always wanted to have lots of money and pretty clothes, but she never gave these a thought after she met Oliver. Hallie would never forget the day Ella told her she was going to be married.

"He's very poor, Hallie. I'll never have things nice, the way I planned."

"That doesn't matter," Hallie had replied.

Ella had pressed her hand. "I knew you'd say that. You see, Oliver and I are just like you and Dominie!"

Dolly had never said anything like that. How could she? There wasn't anything about Sam that would make anyone couple him with Dominie. No, it was Ella and Oliver who had been the most like Dominie and herself, and that was why it had hurt so bitterly, after Dominie had gone away, to have to stand in the chapel and smile, when Ella and Oliver were married.

That hurt had never been assuaged. It was strange, but even when she had been saying to Dolly that it would have been like long ago to have Ella with them on their walks she had to force herself to say it. It wouldn't! It wouldn't! Because wherever Ella went, the shadow of Oliver went too. For one thing Ella was always talking about him too. And it hurt. It hurt.

But now Oliver was ill and Hallie knew she mustn't bear resentment against him. He was ill, and maybe dying.

Just then there was a stir in the parlor. Someone had heard a sound in the room upstairs.

"The crisis!"

Once again the whisper ran around the room, and the next minute there was a sound of footsteps running down the stairs, not the tiptoe running of a few minutes previous, but the audible footsteps of someone who put speed before all else. Then footsteps ran up the hall and the door opened.

It was the young nurse again, but this time she did not direct her voice to any one person in particular but addressed the whole room. "The children?" she cried. "I thought they were here!" But when she saw they were not she withdrew her head, and shut the door with a loud slam. Everyone in the parlor exchanged glances.

"They want the children to say goodbye. He must be sinking fast."

"Oh, my poor Oliver." A woman who was only distantly related to him threw up her hands and burst into tears.

"Hush, hush!" cried several other women as they stood up and rushed over, not to silence her but to direct her grief into what they considered more suitable channels.

"He's not to be pitied," they cried. "He's going to a better world. But think of the poor young widow! Think of her! Poor Ella!"

And everyone in the room took up the name. "Poor Ella. Poor Ella. What in the world will she do now, with those young children and no father to look after them?"

"Poor Ella. Poor Ella. Where is she now? There should be someone with her. She shouldn't be let stay in the room till the end. Poor Ella. I'm sure she has no arrangements made. And the children! They should be sent out of the house. They'll be under everyone's feet!"

All, all were aware of the millions of things to be done. All, all were eager to undertake some of the tasks. For it was tantalizing to remain shut up in a front parlor, while, from all over the house, in kitchens and passages and in the upper rooms, there was such an outburst of activity. There were sounds of footsteps running along passages, running back and forth in rooms, running up and down stairs. There were heavy articles of furniture being dragged from place to place. There were things being dropped and things being knocked against the wall. All over the house there was the feeling that time was precious. Suspense had kept down all noise and activity. But now the suspense was over. Oliver was going. There could be no mistake about it, for apparently the death rattle had been heard in his throat. And not a minute must be wasted of the precious time that was left before death imposed necessity for absolute silence and decorum.

Soon Hallie found herself alone in the parlor. She felt no desire to go out into the tumult. She looked around her and began indifferently to gather up the cups and saucers that she found on tables and chairs, and to pile them on a tray, but she left the tray on the table and went to sit down at the glowing fire.

Oliver was really dying. Poor Ella. It was strange to think that they had all three of them been left alone within so short a time. Dominie was only three years dead. Sam was less than a year dead. And now Oliver. She sighed. In various ways the three of them had been preyed upon and devoured by the years that had once appeared to them, far off on the horizon, as bright birds laden with sweetness. The tears came into her eyes. She had been the first to see the bitter beak and claw hidden by that brilliant plumage. She thought of the seven bitter years of heartache that had had to be borne even before Dominie died. And after Dominie died it was still a long time before the others got any real inkling of what her grief had been.

But now they were all three of them alike in their losses as they had once been alike in their hopes and dreams. Never, never would she have admitted such a thing before this day, but in her heart she had always felt a resentment against the happiness that the other two had known and that she had missed. And now that happiness had deserted them too. Now they would know how she had suffered all those years. At least Ella knew. Somehow it had never given her as much satisfaction to have Dolly back with her again in the evenings as it would have done to have had Ella. There was always the suspicion that Dolly had not felt so deeply about Sam as she would like people to believe. But there was no mistaking the fact that Ella was in love with Oliver.

And that was why during their evening walks, when she and Dolly talked about when they were girls, it had secretly made her heart ache to think that Ella was cut off from them and their talk by the four walls of her house, by the needs of her children and by the demands that were made on her by Oliver, her husband.

Ella could never be interested for long in the past, because the present made such demands upon her. If they met in the daytime she was unable to delay for more than a word or two. "I must go home to get Oliver his tea!" Even the few words they sometimes had coming out of the chapel on Sundays were cut short as often as not by the sight of Oliver waiting impatiently outside the gate. "I must fly," Ella would cry. "I mustn't keep Oliver waiting. We're going for a little walk. This is the only chance we get of a breath of air."

And when Hallie and Dolly were walking by the mill path in the evening and wishing that Ella was with them, it had flashed into Hallie's mind that Ella had probably been there that morning in the sunlight with her husband.

Sometimes when walking along, dreaming and stargazing, and thinking that Dolly was perhaps putting her feet in the very footprints that they made when they were girls long ago, and that she herself might be stepping in the very footprints of Dominie, it would be all spoiled suddenly by the thought that instead of the invisible footprints of the past she was in all likelihood stepping into the actual footprints of Ella and Oliver.

But now Oliver's feet would never print the road again. In spite of the fact that she had never really liked him, Hallie felt sorry for him and the tears came into her eyes. But her thoughts returned to Ella. She would telll Ella about the way she tried to think she was walking in Dominie's footprints. Ella might like to try and think that, in the same way, she was walking in Oliver's footsteps.

A feeling of tenderness toward Ella welled up in Hallie as she sat there alone in Ella's parlor. Now Ella would be no better off than she herself. Ella too would be lonely and sad. And she would be glad to come out walking with Dolly and herself in the evenings.

Suddenly it seemed to Hallie that Oliver had always stood between her and her full satisfaction in the past. And now he was stepping out of the way. Ella would come out with them again in the evenings; just as she used to do when they were girls. It would be different, of course. The years had made their changes. But whereas a short time ago Ella had put the present before the past, now Hallie knew she would put the past before the present. They would talk about when they were young. They would think about that golden time. It would be almost as if at times they were back in it, with their hair down their backs, wandering along its roads of springtime and its eternally, leafy youth.

Just as the leafy boughs of springtime and youth were about to enclose her with the fragrance in the small stuffy parlor of Ella's house, Hallie was recalled to where she was by a piercing scream from the upper room.

"Ella!" Hallie sprang to her feet. She must go to her.

But before she had time to cross the room there were voices in the passage, and above the others she heard Dolly's voice distinctly.

"Take her into the parlor," Dolly said.

"Keep her there," said another voice.

"Don't let her back upstairs again," said yet another voice, and this time it seemed like the voice of the young nurse.

Then the door opened, and Dolly and Ella's mother and the distant cousin that had burst into tears all appeared in the doorway and Ella with them. And as Ella struggled they spoke to each other over her head, entirely disregarding her reactions.

"Keep her in here," the nurse urged. "Don't let her upstairs again. It's no place for her now. She should be made lie down. She should be made take a glass of brandy if it was only a sip to wet her lips." Carried on their surge, Ella was hurried into the center of the parlor, followed by several relatives and neighbors.

In the center of the room under the hanging lamp, Hallie stood uncertainly. She felt awkward. Everyone else had given assistance, while she had sat looking into the fire. She was dazed and disconcerted. But she was not the only one who was disconcerted. The women who pushed and led Ella thought they were showing her into an empty room. They were as surprised as Hallie, when they came upon her standing in the middle of the floor.

But to Ella it seemed the most natural thing in the world.

"Oh, Hallie!" she cried, and she threw out her arms, and where before she had hung back protestingly and struggled with Dolly and her mother, she now rushed forward.

"Oh, Hallie!" she cried. "Did you hear? He's dying. Oliver is dying. He's leaving me."

Hallie's arm flew out to enlace with the outflung arms of her friend. This was the way it had been in the past. This was the way they had flung themselves upon each other in the tempests of girlish grief.

"Oh, Hallie! Hallie, what will I do?" Ella cried, and clung to her with all her strength. It seemed as if she would listen, where she had been deaf to all that had been uttered in her hearing since the first dreadful moment when Oliver had taken ill. She would listen to Hallie. Whatever Hallie wanted her to do, she would do.

Behind her back the other women were making signs to Hallie. "Make her sit down." Dolly made the suggestion wordlessly by means of urgent gestures.

"Keep her distracted," said Oliver's cousin out loud, no doubt feeling justified in disregarding Ella because of the way Ella had buried her head on Hallie's shoulder.

Hallie looked up for an instant. They were all staring at her. She was the center of the room. They were all waiting to hear what she would say. And Ella too lifted her head and her swollen eyes seemed to be beseeching her for help.

"Oh, Hallie, Hallie!" Ella cried. "How will I live without him? What will I do? Tell me. Tell me."

Suddenly the room faded away and Hallie imagined over their heads the leafy trees of their youth and springtime.

"Don't feel so bad, Ella," she cried. "While you were all upstairs, I was sitting here thinking how lovely it would be when you, Dolly and I are all alone again, like we used to be. Like long ago."

But almost before she had time to finish the sentence something happened. First, Ella broke away from her, and then someone — it might have been Ella — gave her a violent push backward. And then all around her it seemed that people were talking all at the same time and all saying the same thing.

"Hush, Ella. Hush. She didn't mean it. She didn't know what she was saying."

And then the past that had flashed green around her was gone.

And she was standing in Ella's parlor under the lamp in the middle
of the room. And Ella was screaming worse than before and struggling with the women who were trying to make her sit down on the
sofa.

"Are you mad? Such a thing to say to her." Oliver's cousin
was crimson with rage.

Hallie felt dazed. She looked around for Dolly. But Dolly was
bending over Ella and when she looked up her eyes were narrow
with contempt.

"Were you out of your mind?" she said, calling out across the
room without caring who heard.

What had she said? Hallie's mind was confused. She looked at
Ella.

"Such a thing to say to me!" Ella said, and she began to scream
again.

"See what you've done!" Dolly cried, as the screams grew louder
and could not be silenced. "Let me talk to her," she said, pushing
the women aside again and, going over to Ella, she put her arm
around her, and bent down close to whisper something into her
ear. Ella stopped screaming.

Hallie stared. She had not heard what Dolly said, but her eyes
fastened on the hands of her friends as they clung to each other
with a tight clasp. And on their hands she saw their worn wedding
rings.

All at once she guessed what Dolly had said to Ella. And she
knew, also, what Dolly meant.

THE YOUNG GIRLS

THE PARTY was for Ena. She was twenty-one that day. But Emily, the younger sister, was allowed to invite a few friends of her own. She asked Nell and Ursula and Dolly.

Emily told her friends that she was going to wear a long dress, so Ursula and Dolly had long dresses specially made. Nell already had one.

Most of Ena's friends came down from town with her on the afternoon train. And although they did not see him till the end of the journey, when they all jumped out on the platform, Harry, the son of the house, had been on the same train too, with *his* friends. Harry was also a student, like Ena, but he was in his final year.

There was a great deal of laughing as the two groups met, and since it was a very fine day there was no problem about getting out to the house; they all set off gaily down the country road, between the flowery summer hedges. The loud voices and the tricking of the young people as they went along caused the farmers in the fields to leave off tossing hay for a minute to stare out over the hedges at them, and even to wave good-humoredly.

It was only six o'clock when they got to the house but that didn't matter. There were sandwiches laid out for them, and in any case the party had begun at the precise moment the two contingents met on the platform. The party was them, and they were the party.

It was different for Emily's friends. They did not come till eight o'clock because that was the time given on the invitation cards. By then there was such a din all over the lower part of the house they had to ring the bell several times. Even Emily herself, who was intermittently watching out for them, only heard them by the merest chance. They had almost despaired of getting in when she flew down the stairs and threw open the door.

"What kept you?" She was in a high state of excitement. "Take off your things," she commanded when they were barely inside, but her mother, who was passing through the hall just then, intervened briskly.

"They might like to go upstairs, Emily. They might like to tidy their hair. Not that it's necessary," she said hastily, as Ursula and Dolly blushed and their hands flew to their foreheads.

But Emily's mother had hurried away without looking at them. For some reason, that they earnestly hoped had nothing to do with them, she was frowning. Ursula and Dolly looked down uneasily at their new dresses. In the big oval mirror in the hall their dresses looked very odd flouncing out under their coats. The coats seemed as if they had shrunk. Nell was all right because she had a proper evening coat and under it only a frosty glint could be seen of her ice-blue taffeta.

"Mother didn't intend to get me a long dress for ages yet," said Dolly, ignoring Emily and turning for courage to Ursula and Nell.

"Oh, I wouldn't mind your mother," Nell said shortly. She looked around. "Where will we put our coats?" she asked in a businesslike voice.

"Oh, come upstairs first," said Emily. "I want to see your dresses properly. I won't get a chance when we start dancing. There's such a crush here."

And indeed that was so. As they hurried up the wide stairs, they glanced back over their shoulders at the party. It was in full swing all right. For a moment it was like looking at the hobby horses going around without you, and seeming as if they would never stop to let you get on.

At the top of the stairs Emily threw open the door of her room.

"You can leave your things on my bed," she said affably.

But the door of Ena's room was wide open and Emily's friends stared in with awe at the way the bed was piled high with coats and evening capes. Even the chairs were laden, and as for the floor, it

was littered with slippers and shoes and slipper boxes that had their
lids thrown back abandonedly. Most exciting of all, mists of powder
dimmed the mirrors, and particles of scented dust floated in the air,
particularly under the lamps.

"Would you like to leave your things in there?" asked Emily
anxiously, when she saw how hard it was for them to tear themselves
away from the door.

"Oh, no," they cried quickly, all together, and they hurried after
her into the other room.

It had given them a marvelous feeling of exhilaration to look into
Ena's room, but they wanted the security of being among familiar
things. At once they straightened their stockings and began to comb
their hair very vigorously.

"I always love this room, Emily," said Dolly, staring into the
mirror and smiling.

"I love looking at your books, Emily," Ursula said, as she pushed
to make place for her face, too, in the small oval of glass.

Nell stood to one side. She was waiting for the pool of the mirror to be completely empty before she bent and peered into it. And
while she waited she picked up a picture in a silver frame that stood
on a table by the bed.

"Emily, is this your brother Harry, when he was small?"

But Emily was scarcely listening. She was sitting on the side of
the bed with her hairbursh in her hand, and with it she stroked the
white crotchet counterpane in time to streamers of music that came
in through the open window and wavered in the air.

"Is this your brother Harry when he was small?" Nell asked again,
taking the frame over and sitting down beside Emily on the bed.

"No, that's me when I was small."

"Oh," said Nell, and she left the frame down on the bed. The mirror was free.

Dolly stood in the middle of the room.

"Do you think I ought to wear this flower in my hair?" she asked,
holding up a floppy silk poppy.

"I wouldn't — for one," Emily said scathingly, and she looked
for support to the others.

"I don't like it — for two," said Ursula.

Dolly pinned the poppy in her hair. "I don't much like it either," she said, "but mother said to bring it along in case I changed my mind!"

"I'll tell you what's wrong with it," said Nell. "It makes you look too young."

"What's wrong with that?" said Dolly. "Mother says we'll be old soon enough." She put her head to one side the better to consider the problem.

"Mothers always try to keep their children young-looking. I suppose it's to keep themselves from feeling old, but I'll tell you one thing — men don't like girls that look too young!"

Dolly's lips trembled. "What will I do? Will I wear it or will I not? Someone tell me."

"Don't wear it!" said Ursula.

"I wouldn't," said Emily.

"It's hideous," said Nell.

"Oh dear," Dolly sighed. "Mother bought it specially for this party. She'll be disappointed."

"Don't be silly — how will she know whether you wore it or not?" said Nell, but she couldn't have expected an answer because she shrugged her shoulders. "Please yourself, Dolly," she said, and as if to end the discussion she went over to the window.

Down on the terrace the colored lights were looped from yew tree to yew tree, and beyond that the ground sloped down to a lower, and lighted terrace.

"Come and see," said Nell. "There are people walking on the lower terrace. I can see their dresses gleaming in the dark."

They all ran over to the window and leaned out over the window-sash.

"Isn't it lovely?" said Ursula.

"It was awfully nice of you to ask us, Emily," said Dolly.

Nell said nothing, but her lips were moving silently.

"There are forty-seven lights," she said. "I've just counted them. There are more of the blue than any other color. I wonder why?" She turned to Emily. "I suppose Harry put them up?"

"No, the gardener put them up yesterday."

"Oh!" said Nell. She looked out again. "Some of them are crooked," she said.

For a few minutes they stood at the open window looking out at the harlequin lights that swayed indecisively, as the night wind gently lifted them and gently let them fall again. The sad sighing of the wind was more insistent than the violins in the room below. And as they stood there shyness stole over them again, and they felt a great reluctance to go downstairs at all. If only they could stay up here — forever.

Emily was the first to come away from the window.

"I suppose we should go down," she said uneasily. "Mother will be looking for me."

But Ursula darted over to the mirror again and peered urgently into it.

"I'll have to comb my hair again. Where is the comb? Did anybody see the comb?" she asked desperately, lifting the pots and jars, even the very smallest ones that could not possibly conceal it.

Dolly took up the poppy again.

"If I don't wear it in my hair, perhaps I could wear it in my belt?" she said.

"Oh bother." Nell frowned. "The buckle of my shoe is loose. Now we're in real trouble. I'll have to sew it on tighter."

"Show me!" Ursula cried. "Oh dear," she said. "I'll help you. Have you a needle and thread, Emily?"

They were all eager to postpone the dreadful moment of exposing themselves to the company down below.

But just then the clock on the landing struck the hour.

"Listen!" said Nell authoritatively, and she put up her finger for silence. "Nine o'clock."

"Nine o'clock!" Emily's eyes opened very wide. "Why, the evening is nearly over already." She said it as if she did not know whether to be sorry or glad.

But Nell, who had taken off her slipper, had it on again in a second. She sprang to her feet.

"Don't bother about the needle," she said. "It will stay on, I'm sure. We must go down at once. We should have gone long ago. It's a shame to have wasted so much time up here. Are you coming or are you not?" she demanded, looking coldly at Dolly who had tucked the flower in her belt. "How much longer are you going to delay, I'd like to know?"

The others too looked angrily at Dolly.

"Hurry up, Dolly," they said. Dolly dropped the flower on the dressing table.

"Hurry, hurry!" she said too.

And soon they were all four hurrying each other indiscriminately and pushing each other forward as they crowded out onto the landing. But there they came to a stand again and held back; one behind the other.

"Oh, why did I sit on the bed?" said Emily dolefully. "I'm sure my dress is all creased."

"Turn around till we see," Ursula said, but she had her own worries. "Are you shy, Emily?" she whispered.

Nell answered both questions.

"The creases won't be noticed when you're dancing, Emily," she said, "and anyway, the heat of the room will take them out." But to Ursula she was scathing. "Why should she be shy in her own house!"

"Oh, but it doesn't seem a bit like my own house tonight," Emily said. She was standing at the head of the stairs looking downward. There was no one in the hall underneath. The dancers were all in the drawing room. "We simply must go down through," she said, and she gave Ursula a push. But Ursula gave Dolly a push.

"You go first, Dolly!"

"For heaven's sake!" cried Nell. "You're acting like children." Picking up the hem of her dress she began to descend. There was disdain in her every step.

"Isn't Nell marvelous," said Emily.

"I wish I had her poise," said Ursula. "I'm so shy."

"What about me?" Emily cried.

"I don't think it matters really," said Dolly. "Mother says it's natural to be shy at our age, and anything that is natural is all right. She says blushing is attractive."

Halfway down the stairs Nell heard and looked back.

"Nonsense," she said. "Are you coming, or are you not?"

Slowly the others began to descend.

At the foot of the stairs Emily's mother met them. She was coming in from the garden.

"Something went wrong with the lights," she said vaguely, "but it was something simple," she added, smiling quickly. "Harry fixed it in a minute. They are pretty, don't you think?" But she spoke absent-mindedly. Then she saw Emily. "Where have you been?" she asked sharply. "Harry was looking for you. He needed someone to hold the ladder. Please stay around, Emily! There are things to be done. A party doesn't run by itself, you know!"

While she spoke, Emily's mother was catching back the large glossy leaves of a plant that might get in the way of the dancers coming out of the drawing room at that minute, the music having just ceased.

"Can I help?" Ursula asked politely.

"You can help by enjoying yourself, my dear," said Emily's mother. "Oh, here's Harry. Come here, young man! I have partners for you!"

Oh, how awful — Emily's friends drew back as if behind them they had shells in which to hide.

But the worst was over before it began.

"Hello, girls," Harry said. Nell was the only one whose name he could recall. "Hello, Nell," he said politely, but it was to the one nearest him he bowed. "May I have this dance?" he said to Dolly, and putting his arm around her waist he waltzed her away on the very first new note of the music.

The music had begun again so quickly that most of the couples were still on the floor and had not separated. They began to dance again without changing partners. Those who did, found new partners on the floor. No one came out into the hall. After a minute Ursula sat down on the bottom step of the stairs.

"Don't do that!" said Nell sharply. "It's fatal!" She frowned. But apparently not at Ursula. "Really, I can't stand her," she said, and the others knew she must mean Dolly. "She's always pushing herself forward."

"Did you like her dress?" Emily asked pacifically.

"It might be all right at a children's party," said Nell. "All those ruffles; all those bows. She has the worst taste in the world."

"It's not really her fault, I think. Her mother makes her wear them."

"Why does she listen to her mother! All mothers are the same. You have to disregard them. I always choose my own clothes."

Emily and Ursula immediately felt free to look their fill at the elegant ice-blue dress. It was so severe they looked down apprehensively at their own dresses which now, if not as bad as Dolly's, yet seemed as if they might have dispensed with some trimmings.

"Oh dear, I'm sure I look all wrong," Ursula said.

"Why Ursula, you look lovely."

"Are you sure? I'd much rather be told the truth!" Ursula cried, and in preparation for receiving it she looked very frightened and held out her skirt.

"But it's a beautiful dress," cried Emily.

"Yellow is always safe," said Nell.

"Mine is an old one," said Emily quickly. "It used to belong to Ena. Mother cut it down for me."

"You'd never know that," said Nell, "except for a certain style about it — Ena's clothes always have style about them."

At the mention of Ena they all turned and looked into the drawing room to try if they'd see her.

There she was! Dancing with a dark and handsome man! They were directly under the chandelier in the center of the room.

"I wish I had an older sister," said Ursula. "She looks wonderful tonight."

"Doesn't she?" Emily said proudly. "She's very popular too, isn't she?"

Nell was pensive. "I wonder what it's like to be as popular as that?"

The music had stopped again. At last! And people were coming out to sit on the stairs. Harry came out without Dolly.

"Can I have the next dance, Nell?" he asked.

"Where's Dolly?" Emily asked.

"Oh Dolly? I introduced her to Stephen Martin, a friend of mine. He's a medical student." As the girls stared he laughed. "He asked to be introduced," he said. "You girls will have to watch out. Dolly will be the belle of the ball!" He put his arm around Nell as the band started to tune up. "Let's ask them to play something slow," he said.

Ursula and Emily looked at each other.

"I wish someone would ask us," said Ursula.

"Oh, I don't," cried Emily. "I'm going into the kitchen to see if they're going to serve supper soon."

Ursula's face lit up. "Oh, can I come too?"

But just as they reached the swinging green-baize door of the stillroom, a voice called out and detained Ursula. It was Emily's mother again.

"Is that you, Ursula? There's someone I want you to meet." Emily's mother was accompanied by an elderly gentleman. "He is an old friend of your mother's, my dear. Be nice to him," she whispered, "he has a handsome son!"

The elderly man took Ursula's arm.

"Come and tell me about your mother. How is she, my dear?" he said. He guided her carefully through the dancers. "We must keep an eye out for my son," he said. "Where has he gone, I wonder? Where has he gone?" And as they made their way with difficulty through the thickening circles on the floor he kept saying the same thing over and over again. "Where has he gone? Where has he gone?"

At last they reached the other side of the room.

"Ah, there he is — the scamp!" he cried. "He's dancing, I see. We will just have to sit down and be patient. There is nothing else for it." He pulled out a chair. "Those pretty little feet will not complain, I'm sure," he said, looking at them. "You're danced off your feet, my dear, I know! A rest will do you no harm. You don't believe me, but wait — wait!" He sat down beside her. "Tell me all about your dear mother. Is she well? I'm sure she hasn't aged like me? And yet, I doubt if I'd know her now if she walked into this room. Can you imagine that! How is her hair? Is it the same? She had the most beautiful head of hair. Beautiful! Beautiful!" he said, and he began to tap his foot in time to the tune that was playing, a very very slow tune. "Beau-ti-ful," he sighed, beating time now with his hand as well. "Beau-ti-ful! Beau-ti-ful!"

It was about twelve o'clock when they first missed Dolly. Nell came over to them and asked if they'd seen her.

"I haven't seen her for ages," said Emily, conscience-stricken.

"Nor me," said Ursula. "Not since she went off that time with Harry!"

"Perhaps she is in the library?" said Emily. "There were lots of chairs put in there for people to sit and talk if they wanted."

"She isn't there," said Nell. "I was in there a few minutes ago with Harry and it was empty."

"Perhaps she's out on the terrace?"

"She couldn't be out there. There's no one out there now. The lights went wrong again. And anyway, it's got cold. They've shut the drawing room windows."

"You're *sure* she's not in the library?"

"Positive. But I suppose we could look again to satisfy you."

They looked in the library. They looked in every room downstairs except the kitchen.

"Perhaps she's helping your mother in the kitchen?"

"Is it Dolly?" Emily raised her eyebrows, not very kindly.

Anyway, there was Emily's mother over at the window, talking to Harry's former tutor.

"Where could she be?"

"I can't imagine!"

"Ah well, there is no use worrying about her," said Ursula. "She can't be far away."

But Nell looked at them with stern surprise.

"That's no attitude to take! She's our friend, for all her faults. We wouldn't want anything to happen to her."

"What could happen to her?"

"Oh Nell! What do you mean?"

"Well, you know how silly she is! Anything could happen!" Nell turned around and scanned the dancers.

"Who is she with, I wonder?"

Emily seemed to have got an inspiration. She too sifted the dancers with a quick glance.

"Where is that fellow who asked for an introduction to her? I don't see him anywhere either."

Nell pursed her lips. "As a matter of fact, that's what made me nervous in the first place," she said. "Harry told me that he hasn't a very good reputation. And then when I saw she wasn't dancing I thought I'd better give a look for her. I couldn't make out where she'd gone! I even looked on the terrace."

"You didn't go out on the terrace all alone, Nell?"

"Why not?"

"Oh Nell, you're wonderful!" The other two glanced out of the window. The terrace was indeed dark and lonely without the little colored lights.

"I wonder would she have gone down to the river," Nell said suddenly.

"Down to the river!" Ursula and Emily stared at Nell in amazed disbelief. "She'd be scared to death!" said Ursula, and at the thought she herself shuddered.

"Not if there was someone with her," Nell said quietly.

"Do you mean that medical student? But she only met him tonight for the first time."

"I know, but you must remember she's very innocent for her age."

Emily wrung her hands. "Oh, this is awful. Awful!"

"It's too bad it should happen at your party, Emily. I will say that," Nell said dismally. "Not that I'm surprised," she added. "I always felt that something dreadful would happen to her the way she smiles at everyone whether she knows them or not, and tosses her hair back every minute. To say nothing of the way she puts her head on one side like a bird when she looks at you! A girl like that is bound to get into a mess sooner or later."

"But surely it's not too late. Surely there's something we can do?"

"There's only one thing we can do and that's find her," said Ursula. "Do you think we ought to go out" — she faltered — "go down to the river?"

"Wait a minute," Nell's voice was peremptory. "We mustn't let people see us — or guess where we are going. A thing like this could damage her reputation, you know!" She paused. "Let's pretend we're too hot." She began to fan herself with her hand, delicately and prettily.

Ursula and Emily obediently waved their own hands backward

and forward in front of their faces once or twice, but very abstract-edly.

"That's enough, I'm sure," said Emily then. "Let's go."

"Wait a minute!" It was Ursula who held her back.

"What will we do if we find them?"

"Oh, there's no use planning things like that in advance," said Nell. "It depends upon the circumstances."

With a scared look at each other Ursula and Emily tried vainly to interpret those circumstances.

"Perhaps we ought to bring someone with us — someone older," Ursula suggested nervously, pausing on the threshold of the french doors.

"A nice friend you are," said Nell. "Come on."

It was chilly on the terrace. Clouds raced over the moon. The grass was wet too. And there was the sad moaning of the wind in the trees. They stood on the top terrace for a minute and looked down the grassy slopes to where the river ran. It ran so slow, and silently, they only knew how near it was when a water fowl beat the water with its wings.

"We'll have to be careful going down the steps. Some of them are loose, I think," said Nell. "Isn't that so, Emily?"

"It's not *that* I mind," said Emily. "It's the frogs. There are al-ways frogs down here."

They stopped again and shuddered.

"We can't put a frog before Dolly," Ursula said firmly, and she took another downward step.

"We must be careful of our dresses, though," said Nell.

"Hold up the hem," said Emily. "It would be a pity to spoil our appearance for such a goose."

"Goose isn't what I'd call her," Nell said grimly as they got to the terrace and started down the second flight of steps. "I sometimes wonder if she's as innocent as she makes out. Well, we'll soon see," she said ominously.

"Oh dear!" cried the others, and they paused.

"Won't it be very awkward if they are down here — for us, I mean?"

"That depends on how we find them. If they're kissing, or

anything, we won't go all the way over to them, but just cough loudly from a distance, and call out to Dolly — "

"Call out what?" Emily breathed, as if they'd come on the most insuperable obstacle of all.

"Anything at all!" Nell said. "The first lie that comes into our heads. For instance, we could say her mother was on the phone."

It was a much simpler plan than the others would, unaided, have arrived at.

"They won't be kissing, though," Ursula said confidently. "She wouldn't let him kiss her the first time she met him."

"Oh, wouldn't she! Dolly's soft enough for anything. Think of the way she's always making up to people, and begging their pardon for nothing at all. She has no sense of her own dignity. That kind of girl is usually ready for anything."

There was a short silence.

"Did you ever kiss anyone, Nell?" asked Ursula, balancing badly on a shaking stone as she spoke.

"Of course I did," said Nell, in a tone of voice that indicated contempt for the question. "But there's kissing and kissing. Kissing is nothing when you know what you're doing. And a lot" — she paused — "a lot depends on who you're kissing. But Dolly is such a fool she'd kiss anyone, I do believe, and never know the danger!"

Just then the wind stirred the ivy leaves that twined around the stone balustrade of the lower terrace. The moon went behind a cloud again. And on the river — now so near — a night fowl gave a secretive call.

The dangers of life seemed as vague as ever, but they seemed somehow nearer. Ursula caught at Emily's hand but Nell was relentless.

"Come on."

They went down the last flight, right down to the river level where the grass was tall and deep. They had to lift the hems of their dresses and hold them high as they made their way to the water edge and stepped up safely at last upon the slimy boat-slip.

"There's no sign of her down here," Emily said at last.

"They wouldn't be in the boat-house by any chance?" Ursula asked.

"The boat-house is always locked at night," Emily said quickly and, as she thought, tactfully.

But Nell was in no mood for tact.

"A good job if you ask me," she said. "Some men are frightfully fascinating, you know. They can cast a spell over a girl. I know a case where — "

But just then Ursula caught her by the arm.

"Shh," she said. "I thought I heard whispering."

It was only the whispers of the wind though, and the soft answers of leaf and branch.

"I've just thought of something awful," Emily said in a low voice. "Suppose they were down here and suppose they hid when they heard our voices. In the bushes!" She lowered her voice still more. "Suppose they heard every word we said. Suppose they're listening now!"

"Well, if that is the case," said Nell — and instead of lowering she raised her voice, loud and clear — "if that is the case I hope Dolly knows the contempt we have for her. For my part I'll never feel the same toward her again."

"Nor me!" said Emily, loud and clear.

"Nor me, nor me!" Ursula cried, as if it were a game they were playing. "Nor me! Nor me!"

They all fell silent and stood absolutely still. Because they were certain that there would be some reply. But there was no sound. And while they were standing there unspeaking the moon slipped out again and shone down brightly over them and over everything.

"It's lovely down here now — isn't it?" said Nell, more gently. "Look at that cypress reflected on the water. I wouldn't blame Dolly so much if it was like this all the time. But it isn't," she said firmly, as if calling herself to order.

At that very moment Ursula gave a thin scream.

"Something tipped against my leg!"

"You only imagined it," they said, but they drew closer together.

"I didn't. It was something wet and slimy."

There was a short terse silence and in it they both turned to Emily. It was her house. She ought to know what it was.

"I expect it was a frog," Emily said defiantly. "I warned you."

"Oh no!"

Ursula screamed. "Let's get out of here," she cried.

Nell didn't wait to scream. She sprang off the boat-slip and ran for her life through the sounding grasses.

"Hold up your dress, Nell," Emily shouted, but Nell didn't hear; Nell didn't care. So Emily too jumped down and took flight.

At the top of the first terrace they ventured to stand and get their breath.

"What about Dolly?"

"Don't mention her name to me." In the darkness Nell was trying to examine her dress. "That horrid girl. My dress is all wet, I can feel it, and it's all her fault. She's not worth the half of what we've gone through for her. She's — she's — she's vulgar! That's what she is! And as well as that it was mean of her in the first place to go sneaking off without a word to us. She probably thought we'd be jealous, the little fool! I'd love to slap her face."

"I don't blame you," Emily said. "So would I."

"Me too," said Ursula. "I've turned completely against her. My slippers are sopping wet."

"All our slippers are wet. They're probably spoiled for good — ruined. Well, let's go up back to the house anyway; we can see the damage then — we'll know the worst!"

In sight of the house, though, they stopped again. All the windows were brightly lit and the lawn was marked out in a trellis of light and shade.

"Doesn't the house look lovely?" Emily said irrepressibly. "And listen to the music. Oh, listen to the music!"

Walking for some reason on tippy-toes they crept up closer.

"Look at Ena!"

Ena was standing at the french door talking to one of her partners. Her silhouette was dark in spite of her white dress, but where the light from behind lay along her shoulders it gave the white satin a golden gloss.

"I'd love to be Ena," Ursula sighed.

Nell turned to her in surprise.

"I'd hate to be anyone but me," she said.

"Oh, it's all right for you," said Ursula, "but I'm so fat." Ursula looked depreciatingly down at her sash that could not possibly be tied any tighter.

"I'll tell you what," said Emily. "Let's go in by the side door. Then maybe we can sneak upstairs the back way and tidy ourselves."

As they passed around by the side of the house through the pantry window they saw Harry bending over a tub of ice cream and putting large spoonfuls of pink and green ice on tiny plates with mitered edges.

"Oh, look. Harry is dishing out the ices," said Nell, and when they went inside she ran over to the big mirror that hung on the wall of the passageway. "My hair is not tossed at all," she said, and she glanced along the passage to where the dancers could be seen standing around in the main hall eating ice cream carefully with paper spatulas. "I won't bother to go upstairs."

"Your slippers are wet through — don't forget," Ursula said, almost accusingly.

"Oh very well." Nell let herself be led up the backstairs. "Only don't let us talk any more about that creature," she warned. "I never knew anyone so tiresome. I never want to see her again. I promise you!"

The backstairs, like a tributary, ran into the same landing as the main stairway. And there they examined their slippers. Emily felt obscurely at fault.

"A wet towel might take away the green stains."

"Never!" said Nell. "Think of tennis shoes."

But they were all agreed that they could try. And in the bathroom they were able at least to pick off the green blades that were stuck to the soles. While they were there they combed out their hair again and washed their hands and pushed back their cuticles. Most energetically of all, they took out swan's-down powder puffs and beat their poor noses unmercifully.

Nell sat down sadly on the rim of the bath. "My dress is the only one that is badly stained. Oh, that terrible, terrible Dolly. Horrid girl. She has spoiled your party, Emily."

"I know that," Emily said, and she too sat sadly on the bath edge.

"Make room for me," said Ursula. "How I hate to think of her —

of *them*, I mean. To think that very probably at this minute they are kissing in the bushes."

"Mind you, it's not him I blame though," said Nell. "It's always the woman's fault."

Ursula looked down at her feet.

"Is he very fast?" she asked, and she turned to Emily. "I'm surprised at his being a friend of your brother."

"Don't be idiotic, Ursula," said Nell. "One can't be responsible for all of one's friends. Look at us and her! And Harry must make millions of friends. Anyway you can't judge men by our standards. They are not chaste by nature the way we are."

Sitting along the rim of the cold porcelain bath in their thin silk dresses, they felt exceptionally chaste indeed, and staring down at the tiles on the floor it seemed that even the music that only faintly reached them was nevertheless a travesty of their vague virginal antagonism to everything — oh, but everything — in the world.

Emily was the first to speak.

"I once saw our kitchen maid in the woods with a soldier. He was kissing her like anything."

They shuddered.

"And that," Nell said, "was in the daytime, I presume. Think what it would be like in the woods at this hour!" A shiver ran through her at the thought, and since they were sitting so close the shiver ran through the three of them.

"How can she be so cheap?" said Nell. "If she was even a bit older."

"I wish we were all a bit older," Emily said suddenly. "Life is a great responsibility, don't you think?"

"It's terrible," Ursula said. "I don't like to think about it at all — life, I mean."

But Nell suddenly stood up.

"The rim of that bath is cold. We shouldn't sit there. It's very bad to sit on anything cold."

Emily sprang up. "I heard that too!"

"But why?" Ursula asked, as she got to her feet after them.

"I don't know," said Nell, "but in any case we don't want to spend the whole night here, do we?"

"What will we do then?" asked Ursula. "About Dolly, I mean," she added hastily.

"What can we do?"

"Nothing, I suppose," said Emily, "unless you think we should tell Mother."

"Are you out of your mind?" Nell stared at her. "That's the last thing on earth to do. The only thing we can do for her now is try to save her reputation. We mustn't pretend we notice anything wrong. As a matter of fact we should go down at once — this very minute — in order to try and divert suspicion!"

The bathroom door was always a bit swollen from steam and they had to tug at it to get it open, but when it opened, from below a great burst of music gushed up like a geyser, and when at that moment the pianist ran his fingers over the treble, little jets of music flowed upward and played in the air like fountains.

Surprisingly it was Nell who suddenly held back. She glanced at the others with a frightened face.

"Isn't it queer? When you two wanted to come up here at first to tidy yourselves I didn't want to come at all. And now I don't want to go down. I'd just like to stay here looking down over the banister. I'd even like to be at home — at home in bed."

At once Emily and Ursula began to wish that they too were in bed. How nice it would be lying quietly in the dark. And for Emily it would be especially nice listening to the music downstairs.

"I wish — " said Emily, but her wish was not to be made known, for just then there was a voice in the hall below and as the three girls drew back in a huddle from the banisters there was a step on the stairs. Someone was coming up, two steps at a time.

"Oh, it's only Harry." Emily was so relieved.

"Oh no, not Harry." Nell flew to see and leaned right over the banister so far the others caught the ends of her sash to keep her from falling over.

But Harry was halfway up, and staring upward his eyes caught hers just as if they were playing a game of catch-catch.

"Nell!" Harry said. "I was looking for you. There was ice cream."

"Is it all gone?" Emily cried dolefully.

"Oh, are you and Ursula there too? Where have you been all evening?" he asked, but indifferently. "Come on, Nell," he said. "Let's go and see if there's any left."

In an instant Nell had run along the landing and swung around the big mahogany knob of the banister. She forgot to hold up the hem of her dress but the dress came safe because it belled out as she ran down the stairs. It bore her right into Harry's arms.

But just as the pair met the other two heard a tearing sound.

"He's stood on it. He's torn it," Emily and Ursula told each other aghast. "She'll be furious."

Nell only laughed though.

"Never mind!" they heard her say. "It's a silly old dress. I never liked it. Who cares!"

Wonderingly, Emily and Ursula exchanged glances.

"She is very strange sometimes, isn't she?" said Ursula.

Emily shrugged her shoulders. "Come back to my room," she said. "I want to get a clean handkerchief."

The light was out in Emily's room, but before she had time to put her hand to the switch a voice came out of the dark.

"Hello, Emily. Hello, Ursula."

"Why, Dolly!"

As the light flashed on and lit up the room, they all — not just Dolly — blinked their eyes. Emily's brain must have blinked too because of the way she blurted out the first thing that came into her head.

"We thought you were down in the woods, Dolly," she cried, and even before Ursula kicked her in the shins she blushed furiously, all over.

"Down in the woods? Whatever made you think that?" Dolly too blushed all over.

She was sitting in the middle of Emily's bed in her stocking feet. Her slippers were on the floor, one lying on its side near the door, and the other slap up against the wainscot. "I hope you don't mind my being on your bed, Emily," she said, quick upon her disclaimer about the woods. "I turned back the coverlet," she said earnestly.

"Of course I don't mind." Emily's heart was rent with remorse. "You didn't need to bother about the bedspread."

"Oh, I always turn it back at home when I sit on my bed," Dolly said. "Mother says it's the little things that are important in life."

At the mention of Dolly's mother, Emily and Ursula looked at each other.

"Why aren't you dancing?" Emily asked, quite crisply considering how her heart burned with chagrin at their unjust suspicions.

There was one second's silence.

"I got a nosebleed," Dolly said then. "See!" She pulled out a little lacy square of cambric and showed the dots of blood on it. "I thought I'd better come up here and lie down for a minute."

"Oh, Dolly!" Emily's heart nearly broke into pieces. "I'm so sorry. Why didn't you tell us? Or ring for the maid? Was it bad? Did you get blood on your dress? Oh, I'm so sorry. What can I get for you? Would you like a drink of water?"

So great was Emily's contrition that it was almost implicit that she was atoning for something. "I'll tell you what — " she said. "I'll get something cold and put it down your back. That's what Father always does when I get a nosebleed. I'll get the key of the garden gate. It's always icy cold."

"But it's stopped bleeding now. It's all right again," Dolly said.

"Oh, good." Emily earnestly examined the patient. "It looks all right," she said, anxious to be reassuring. "You don't look as if it bled at all!"

But here Ursula gave her another and more violent kick on the shin.

"Let's go down and tell Nell we found her," Ursula said in an urgent whisper. "Do you feel like coming down now, Dolly?" she asked coldly.

"I think I'll stay here for another little while," said Dolly weakly. "Perhaps if the car calls for me early, I might just slip away and not spoil the fun. You wouldn't mind, would you, Emily? It was a lovely party. I hate leaving, but it might be sensible. And anyway, Mother likes me to be home early."

Impulsively Emily put her arms around Dolly and kissed her.

"Poor Dolly," she said; again she tried to undo in one burst of feeling all the unkind things she had thought and said about her in the past hour. "Are you sure you're all right? Are you sure you wouldn't like us to stay with you? We wouldn't mind a bit. We were just saying we didn't feel a bit like dancing. And it's frightfully hot downstairs." It was hot upstairs too though. Emily felt hot anyway. "Would you like me to open the window, Dolly? Even a little bit? Or I could leave the door open. You'd hear the music better?"

But the last question was the only one to which Dolly made answer.

"I'd like the door shut," she said, "if you don't mind."

"Very well," Emily said. "We'll come up again to see how you are." Tenderly she closed the door after herself and Ursula. "I feel so mean," she said. "We were horrid about her. It's awful to think the poor thing was up here all the time, lying down with her nose bleeding."

But Ursula looked at Emily with pity and contempt.

"Her nose wasn't bleeding. The blood came from her wrist. Why didn't you look, when I gave you that kick. Her wrist was all scratched. I saw it although she tried to hide it under her dress. And didn't you see the end of the dress?"

"It was tucked under her!"

"Well, I saw it before she got time to hide it. It was all torn and muddy. But come on! We must tell Nell!"

As Emily hesitated, Ursula stamped her foot. "What are you staring for? Didn't we suspect the worst! Wait till Nell hears!"

Nell, however, was nowhere to be seen. But they found Harry.

"Where is Nell?" Ursula asked him urgently. She wasn't the least bit shy all of a sudden.

"Why do you want her?" Harry asked. "Come and dance with me." He put his arm around her. "What is the mystery?" he asked as he whirled her away. "I know there is one! You girls are up to something. I can tell. You must let me in on it. I thought you had something up your sleeves — to let off fireworks or something, but Nell said it was something much more serious."

"Did she say anything else?" Ursula asked cautiously.

"No," said Harry, but he was not very concerned. "Isn't it a pity we didn't think of fireworks in time."

"We have some at home," said Ursula unexpectedly.

"You have? Honestly?" Harry could hardly believe it. "You don't live far away either, do you?" he cried. "How about me getting the car and driving us over to get them. We could let them off on the terrace and give everyone a surprise — or better still, down by the river! We wouldn't tell anyone till they were in full spate. I can just imagine them running out astonished. Wouldn't it be fun?" He was very excited, but Ursula had doubts.

"Just you and me!" Harry pressed.

"All right," Ursula said, capitulating all at once. "They're great ones. Ferris lights and all. We tried them the other night."

"Oh great!" Harry was quite excited. "Let's hurry."

Nell was nowhere to be seen. As they went out the hall door they caught sight of Emily.

"Quick, before she sees us!" Harry said.

Too late.

"Where are you going, you two?" Emily cried. "Ursula! Harry! Wait for me." And she was starting to run after them when her mother rose like a pillar of cloud, right in her way.

"Where have you been, you tiresome child? I'm most annoyed with you. I don't know what kind of a girl you are — straying off and no one knowing where to look for you. I should imagine you'd remain at hand to attend to our guests. It's very extraordinary of you to wander away and ignore them. Have you no interest in the party? Are you not concerned for the enjoyment of others? And what about your own little friends? They don't know many people here. You should be on the spot to introduce them and make sure they have a good time."

Her mother's gaze was vigilantly scanning the dance floor, but as she looked back at Emily her vague dissatisfaction gave way to very positive annoyance. "Why are your slippers wet? Don't tell me your dress is wet too — there at the end — what on earth have you been up to, Emily? Are you out of your mind, dabbling with water on the night of a party! You look so tossed and untidy. Really I don't see that these parties are worth all the trouble I take with them if you children just wander off where you please and leave your guests to fend for themselves." Lost for words, she paused. "All I can say is that I'm very displeased with you, Emily!"

When her mother walked angrily away, Emily stood by the newel post, right in the middle of the hall, where everyone could see her, and yet to save her life she could not keep back the tears that gushed into her eyes.

Not a single tear had time to fall, however, because at that minute a voice spoke to her from one side. And although it was a particularly clear strong voice, and came from a young man standing at least two feet away from her, Emily got the impression that he was whispering into her ear, secretively and sweetly.

"Aren't you the younger sister?" the voice asked, and turning around Emily saw a young man rather like her brother Harry, only taller and fairer, and far better looking really. He had blue eyes. "I am Stephen Martin," this idol said. "I am a friend of your brother. May I have the next dance?"

As they whirled around Emily saw Nell standing beside the piano talking to Harry's tutor, and Harry's tutor was behaving exactly as he did when he was talking to Ena. He kept running his hand through his hair and every other minute he took out a white silk handkerchief and wiped his mouth. How on earth could Nell be so interested in what he was saying? And Ursula? Where was she going with Harry, of all people? Above the sound of the music she could hear the sound of a car outside on the gravel sweep at the front of the house. They weren't going off in the car! Hardly! Perhaps it was the car calling for Dolly? The music was threaded with her questions, but as it got faster the questions got mixed. Her head began to spin, and the other dancers and the colored dresses of the girls ran together till they seemed to circle around her head like a bright lasso.

"Happy?" Stephen asked.

Emily smiled up into his face, but it was a mistake to smile because she couldn't stop.

"Everything is whirling around and around," she said.

"That's the way things ought to be!" he said.

He smiled. She smiled. And the music went faster and faster. Emily got panic-stricken. What would she do if she couldn't stop smiling — ever?

A HAPPY DEATH

"ARE YOU UP THERE, Mother?" The child's thin voice shrilled up the dark stairs, as she stood at the bottom and looked upward, her small, white face tilted back on her thin neck.

"What do you want?"

The mother came to the banister rail on the landing overhead, and leaned across it. It was the custom of the household to eliminate footsteps whenever possible by carrying on conversations from room to room, and even, as in this case, from one landing to another, but the lodger in the lower-front room, who was understood to be connected with the stage, had a cold in the head and had not gone out to the theater that day, and it was in deference to the unusual presence by daytime of a stranger in the house that the woman came out to lean over the banister.

"What are you shouting for?" she demanded. "What do you want?"

At the response, however unsatisfactory, from the woman above, the child straightened her neck with relief, but a minute later some urgency in what she had to say to her mother made her strain her face upward again.

"Are you coming down, Mother?" she said, in a whimpering voice that seemed to expect a short answer.

"What do you want me for, might I ask?" the mother demanded, uncompromisingly. "Hurry up! I can't stand here all day with my two hands idle down by my sides."

The child was reluctant to give the reason for her request. She thought desperately for a minute, trying to find something to say that would bring the woman downstairs. She had apparently no faith in the efficacy of the truth, but as the woman on the upper landing shrugged her shoulders and made a move to go back into the room she had been dusting, the child was forced, against her judgment, to make what use she could of the truth, weak as it was.

"He's bad, Mother," she said. "He's coughing and moaning."

There was no need to mention a name. There was only one man in the family, and the lodgers were all women. A pronoun identified him at any time. He was rarely called Father by any of the children, which was hardly surprising since he had less authority in the house than any of them. As for their mother, it was years since she had called him by his Christian name, and there would appear to be something unseemly now in her doing so. Indeed, it was such a far cry from the time she had called him Robert that it hardly seemed possible to the children that Robert and he could ever be the same person. Not that they had ever heard much about Robert, either, but judging from the few fragments of the past they had pieced together from occasional words their mother had let fall, it seemed to them that Robert must have been the kind of young man with whom they themselves would have been proud to have been seen out walking. He seemed to be the romantic kind of young man who could never grow old. He certainly could never have become the hollow-faced nonentity that stole apologetically in and out of the house, and ate his meals in the darkest corner of the kitchen between the sink and the yard door. Why! Robert was their ideal young man. And to Mary, the oldest girl, who had a crippled back, due to a spinal injury in her childhood, Robert was the dominant figure in the long romances she wove as she sat sewing all day. Mary was apprenticed to a dressmaker, being unfit for anything more strenuous. To the youngest child, Nonny, who was now calling up the stairs to her mother, it was doubtful if the name Robert meant anything at all, for Ella had long given up even the most casual remarks about the past by the time Nonny was born.

Nonny was now eleven years old. And, this morning, with her small face, startlingly white in the dark hallway, she looked less than eleven as she stared anxiously up the stairs, at a loss to know what to do. At last she stood up uncertainly and went up a few steps.

She could hear her mother in the room above. She could hear the sound of the sweeping brush knocking against the wainscoting and against the legs of the bed.

"Please come down, Ma," she pleaded. "He's sick. He's bad. He's sitting in the kitchen moaning."

The woman came out to the landing again, but her intention was only to pacify the child.

"Did you ever see him any other way?" she asked.

The child, whose eyes had lit with a flicker of hope, said nothing at this, but after staring helplessly up the stairs, her teeth bit slowly into her lower lip, and, sitting down abruptly on the stairs, she broke into silent, helpless tears.

The woman looked down at her impatiently and frowned. She resented this implication of sympathy with the man in the kitchen. She resented any sympathy with him, from any of the children. She always fought her corner with them viciously.

"It's easy for him to sit around and complain. Look at me! My back is broken with trying to keep this ramshackle house in some kind of order. I declare to heaven I seldom or never see the daylight; stuck indoors from one end of the day to the other, with a sweeping brush in one hand and a mop in the other. Did I ever think I'd live to see the day that I'd be sunk to this level? I that was never called on to soil my hands in my mother's house, and had nothing to do when I wanted a new hat or a pair of gloves but walk out to the shop and put my hand in the till!"

It was an old song. The children knew it by heart. They had heard it so often they never doubted the truth of it, and before they were of an age to form a judgment the poison of it had entered their hearts. But they got sick of it sometimes. All the same, they despised their father when he took Ella's part.

"That's what spoiled your mother," he said. "She had too much money, and not enough to do with it. She had nothing to do but walk out into the shop and put her hand in the till and take out all the money she wanted."

Indeed, the girls were never quite clear what the trouble was between their parents. Their mother's complaints, and their father's justification of her, were expressed in such similar words they missed the distinguishing emotion that underlay the words.

On this day, as Nonny sat on the stairs, the tears streaming down her face and her satchel strapped across her thin shoulders, the mother was more than usually irritated. She came out again to the head of the stairs.

"Why aren't you gone to school?" she demanded. "Do you know the time? Get up out of that and get out of my sight."

As she spoke, however, a door opened in the lower hall, and the lodger in the front room came out. She did not at once see the child crouched on the steps of the stairs, but she stared down the dark passage to the kitchen from which at that moment there came a low moan. The woman on the upper landing drew back hurriedly to avoid being seen. The child knew without looking up that her mother was standing back out of sight, but that she was listening intently to all that went on below, her features hard and unrelenting, her hands tightened irritably around the sweeping brush, and her bitter expression heightened by the uncompromising way in which her hair was tied up in an old duster. Out between the banister rails the child could see the other woman, the lower-front lodger. She peered down out at her. And a look of cunning came into her face. Her foxy little eyes took in the painted cheeks and dyed hair and the big breasts heaving inside a tight red silk blouse, as the muscles of a fine mare ripple under the silk skin. She saw the gaudy turquoise jewelry that dangled from the woman's ears and crusted her fingers and throat. And she sensed their purpose unerringly; they were designed to give pleasure. She longed to have this warm, big-breasted woman go in to her father.

She stirred on the stairs, but the woman did not notice her. She moved her foot. The woman looked as if she was about to go back into her room and shut the door. The child coughed, and then, overcome by consciousness of her secret motives she was seized by a fit of timorous shivering and could not raise her head to see if she had been noticed. But the lodger had heard her. Putting up her hand hastily to the palpitating red silk blouse she gave a startled exclamation.

"Nonny! How you startled me, child. Why are you sitting there in the dark? Why aren't you at school?" Then, looking at her more intently with the forced stare of the shortsighted, she spoke more sharply. "Was it you I heard moaning?"

"No." Nonny, conscious of the unseen listener, was afraid to say more.

"Who was it so?" the woman asked. Then getting no answer she looked down the dark passage again. "Was it your father?" she asked.

The child nodded dumbly, hoping the woman overhead could not see her. But the lodger's next question betrayed her.

"What's the matter with him? Is there anyone with him? Is he sick?" Lifting her head she listened for a minute. "There he is again!" she said. "Is there no one to do anything for him?" She started as if she would make her way down to the kitchen, and although the child longed to let her go, fear of the woman overhead was uppermost in her, and she knew she must not let the lodger into the kitchen. She thought hard, and then as the woman took another step forward, inspired with a sudden duplicity, the child spoke again shrilly.

"It's all right," she said, shrill and loud. "My mother is coming down to him."

"Oh!" said the lodger, and she looked irritably at the child. "Why didn't you say that sooner?" She felt the wastage of her sympathy. She felt thwarted in her desire to be of use. But the child did not heed her. She sat on the stairs, hard and tight, waiting to hear her mother descend. She had triumphed over her. She had forced her to come down against her will. Already, she could tell from the sounds above that her mother was gathering her cleaning utensils together to bring them down with her. "I may as well go back to my room," the lodger said, ungraciously. She patted her hair absently. "Let me know if I can do anything."

The child sat up. She must detain the woman, or her plan would fail.

"He's calling you, Mother," she called again urgently.

The lodger turned back.

"You've better ears than I have," she said, and she listened again.

But the small delay had fulfilled its purpose.

"I'm coming," the mother said sourly, and she began to come down the stairs.

The lodger stepped forward eagerly. She'd wanted to get a look into that kitchen. None of the lodgers had ever put foot in it, and a great deal of curiosity about it was shown from time to time in the gossip between the different roomers.

"Can I be of any assistance?" she cried.

Ella's face was expressionless, but she was torn between resentment at the other woman's interference, and a consciousness of the necessity to be civil.

"No, thank you," she said. "He's all right."

"But I heard him moaning," said the woman.

Ella stepped over the child huddled on the bottom step.

"He thinks he's worse than he is," she said, and then, as if to dismiss the stranger, she turned back to the child. "What are you doing there?" she said in a harsh loud voice. "You'll be late for school!"

She caught the child by the strap of the satchel and lifted her to her feet and pushed her forward. In the narrow hall the woman from the lower-front room felt that she was blocking the child's way. She saw no course but to go back to her own room. The child, however, suddenly realizing the inadvisability of being left alone with her mother, held the flapping satchel to her side and darted up the hallway past the lodger. She had got what she wanted. She had brought her mother downstairs. There was a defiance in the way she shut the hall door after her with a loud clap.

The lodger turned in to the open doorway of the lower-front room.

"You know where I'm to be found if you want me," she called back over her shoulder.

"I won't want any one," said Ella, tartly. "He's not as bad as he'd have people think!"

Beyond an occasional mention like this, she made a point of never talking about her husband to the lodgers; never telling them her affairs. She walked down the hallway, and as she did, the man in the kitchen was seized by another violent fit of coughing, which, however, he seemed to be trying to suppress as he heard the footsteps in the passage.

Ella, however, after a secretive look about her to see that the child had really gone to school, and that the front-room lodger had closed her door tightly, walked quickly past the closed door of the kitchen and went and stood at the back door. She had her own plans. She knew her own business, she told herself savagely, and she looked around the yard to find something to occupy her. She was determined not to go into the kitchen. She thought with irritation of the work she had been doing when Nonny interrupted her. If Nonny had not been such a busybody she would have had the top of the house cleaned by this time. Could she go up again, she wondered, now that Nonny was gone? She was inclined to turn and go up again when she remembered the woman in the front room. Ella jerked her body irritably. There was another busybody! There was another person poking her nose into what didn't concern her! Why couldn't they leave her alone? If she went back upstairs, and he continued to cough and moan, that woman would be out in the passage again wanting to know what was wrong. Ella turned back to the yard door. She might as well put out of her head all idea of going back upstairs. She looked around her to find some way to use up the nervous energy that was consuming her. Suddenly, as she stood at the back door, she started into activity. She'd clean out the yard. A vision rose up before her of the yard as she had kept it in the first year of her marriage. Robert used to say that he didn't miss a garden she kept the yard so nice. She used to whitewash the walls every spring, and she had butter boxes painted white and filled with red geraniums. But it wasn't long before she got sense. It wasn't long before she came to the end of such foolishness. Still there was no need to have a place like a pigsty. She looked around at the walls on which there was no longer a vestige of lime. They were covered with a powdery green lichen. The same unhealthy green growth covered the sunken flagstones, making them slippery and malodorous. And everywhere the refuse of years was strewn: rusted canisters, empty boxes, old bottles, and articles of broken crockery.

She could get rid of some of the rubbish anyway. That was one thing she could do. She rolled up her sleeves. She could clean out the drain; it was choked up, and lately the water never went down completely so that there was always a stagnant pool lying over the grating like a disk of discolored glass. She caught up a piece of rusty wire and began to tackle the drain. She began to work with a furious energy and as she did so, it seemed to her that in a little while the yard would be again white and sweet-smelling as it was years ago, and that nothing would be lacking but the white-painted boxes and the red geraniums. And they could be easily got. Robert would get them.

At the thought of him, however, her depression returned, and hearing him cough again at that moment, she frowned. Then she remembered her secret plans, and obstinately shutting her ears, she began to probe the drain with the rusty wire. As long as the lodgers would leave her alone! She dreaded to hear the creature in the front room coming out again to the hall to listen. She dreaded to have her come along again with her interfering offers of help. Why couldn't she see that her help wasn't wanted? Had she ever been asked to help? Had she ever been given any encouragement?

Ella pulled up the wire and with it there came up a clot of green slime that gave out a foul stench.

She never encouraged the lodgers. She never told them her troubles. She never told anyone her troubles, but her pride in her own reticence was spoiled for her by a guilty feeling that if she had concealed her resentment from strangers she had vented it all the more fiercely on the poor wretch himself, and although she defended her conduct on the grounds of loyalty, in the depths of her mind she was uneasy. And it did not make things any better to think that he took all her gibes in silence. As a matter of fact, that was what made her most bitter; his silence.

"I suppose he keeps his complaints for the ears of his friends down at the library," she said to the children time and again. "I suppose he makes himself out to be a great martyr when he's talking to them."

The children said nothing on those occasions. It was true their father must have a great many friends among the subscribers to the library where he worked, because he was always bringing home presents he got from them, sweets and cake, and pots of honey or jam.

"He makes out he's to be pitied, I suppose," Ella would say, as she took up the things he had brought, having waited until he had gone to bed before she as much as looked at them, in case it might give him any satisfaction to see her do so. And then she would let the children eat as much as they wanted without stopping them, as if she hoped they would sicken themselves and that there would be a scene over them next day. As a matter of fact, whether it was a coincidence or not, it seemed as if he never brought home anything without there being dissension over it.

"I wish people would keep their rubbish to themselves," she'd say triumphantly, when one of the children would get sick, or when the floor would be messed with crumbs, or when a wasp would come into the kitchen to annoy them, drawn by a sticky jam jar.

On those occasions he used to rouse himself to defend the donors.

"They sent them out of kindness!" he'd say.

"Kindness?" Ella would curl her lip contemptuously. "Pity would be more like it! I suppose you tell them how badly treated you are."

He would make no answer to this and so she had to fall back on another familiar gibe.

"I'm glad to see you're ashamed," she would say.

But in her heart she knew that she was making false accusations against him, and that if he talked about her to strangers it would only be to tell them about the old days, about how pretty she used to be when she was a girl, and about how they had eloped together in spite of her parents, and in spite of their having no money, in spite of how young they were — she was only nineteen that summer, and he was only twenty.

Still the thought of his loyalty to their outworn romance did not soften her, and she told herself that it was easy for him to talk about those days, down at the library, where there was no one to see how the romance had turned out, where there was no one to see the drudge he had made her, and the way she had gone to pieces. She'd like to tell people about the old days too, but she had to hold her tongue, for who'd believe now that she was ever young, or that she ever had soft hands and fine skin. Sometimes she'd like to tell those painted old actresses that rented her rooms that she'd had more beaus than any girl in the town where they'd lived while her hair was still down her back. But they wouldn't believe her.

That made her hold her tongue. They'd only ask themselves why she married a broken-down wreck like the man in the kitchen if she had such a great choice. They wouldn't know how good-looking he was when he was young, any more than she could have known then how much he'd change.

That was what galled her most. It wasn't the fact that she was worn out and had lost her looks, she could have put up with that, but it hurt her sense of pride that he should have lost his own good looks, and grown into such a poor shriveled wretch of a man. Who'd ever have thought it? And yet, she supposed, there were some girls who would have looked ahead, who would have foreseen how things would turn out. Why! her own mother had been able to see clearly what would happen. That was why her mother had been so dead set against the marriage. Her mother had seen what she was too blind to see, that the very things that attracted her to him were the things that would have made another girl cautious. She loved his white skin that was as fine as a girl's. How did she know it would get sickly and yellow? She loved the way the blue veins showed in his white hands. How was she to know that was a sign of delicacy? And one summer, when he was swimming in the river outside the town, she had come upon the riverbank suddenly and seen his white body, hairless and smooth, flashing through the heavy river water. How was she to know that hair on a man's body was a sign of strength, and that only a foolish, ignorant girl would disgust to it? She knew nothing, it seemed, in those days. And she was so obstinate. She wouldn't look at any other fellow after she met Robert. They all looked so coarse. There was her third cousin, Mat, and her mother thought he would be a good match for her, but she couldn't bear the thought of him after Robert. She hated his thick coarse skin and his black hair that always smelled of stale pomades.

"He's dirty!" she said to her mother. "He has warts all over his hands."

"Warts aren't the worst things in the world," her mother said. "Warts are a sign of strength. And anyway you could get them off with caustic."

The thought of treating Mat's warts made her sick in the pit of her stomach. The thought of touching his thick oily skin at all made her shudder. But her mother was right. There were worse things than warts. And as for strength! She met Mat a few years ago, and he was as strong as ever, although he was four years older than she. He was like a bull. Such health! Such a red face! Such good humor! He had grown into a fine man. And wasn't it right for a man to be strong? Wasn't it natural for men to have coarse skin and strong hair. They had to be rough to work the way they did. Anyone but she would have known that Robert wasn't made for hard work. Fine skin and soft hair were only for women. Warts indeed! How particular she had been. Why! the welts on her own hands sometimes now after scrubbing down the whole house, were as bad as warts any day. But there again she didn't mind that. All she minded was for the way he had broken down himself. It was for that she blamed him. She had been so proud of him. She would have worn herself to the bone working for him if he had kept his looks and stayed the way he was back home when she used to steal out of the house and meet him in the Long Meadow back of the churchyard. He always looked so much cleaner than other men. He wore white shirts and white collars, and they were always dazzlingly white. And his clothes were always brushed and pressed, with creases in them as sharp as the blades of a knife. And his shoes were always shining. You could see yourself in his shoes. She'd gladly have worn herself out if he had kept up his appearance. She'd have broken her back polishing his shoes. She'd have worn her fingers to the bone to keep him in white collars and shirts. But you can't keep the color in shirts forever, and a shirt never looks the same after it's patched. And shoes won't give the same shine when the leather is cracked. As for brushing his clothes! It came to a point where she used to hide the clothes brush.

"They're worn enough," she'd say to him, "without you brushing the threads asunder!"

Long ago in the evenings in the Long Meadow, when they were making their plans for running away, they used to count on the fact that they had plenty of clothes anyway.

"They won't wear out for a good while," Robert used to say. "We have enough clothes to keep us going for a long time."

But it was surprising how quickly the clothes wore out. Before they were a year married every suit he had was threadbare. But he wore most of them out sitting about on the benches of the registry offices looking for work. And when he got an odd job now and again, it seemed as if you could see the clothes wearing away with the strain. The elbows would get rubbed, the fabric thin, and the back of the trousers would begin to shine, and in the winter the coat would get dragged out of shape with the way he had to pull up the collar against the cold. Clothes didn't last long when you put them to the test. She could see now how unreasonable she used to be about the rough clothes Mat used to wear.

"I can't wear clothes as fancy as certain gentlemen in this town who sit about reading poetry all day," Mat said once, giving a dig at Robert.

"Robert isn't reading poetry," said her mother. "He's studying." Her mother was set against Robert, but when she was talking to Mat she never let on to be against him. It was part of her mother's plan to make all Ella's suitors appear to be worth nothing in their own eyes, but worth a great deal in the eyes of each other. But Ella couldn't let that remark pass. She was determined to contradict it, partly because she wouldn't give in to her mother, and partly because she wanted to annoy Mat.

"It is poetry!" she said. "He reads nothing but poetry!"

She was proud then of the fact that Robert read poetry. That was another thing she could laugh at now. She used to like to see him with a book of poetry in his pocket, or rather she used to like the rest of the people in the town to see him. She didn't like him to read it to her though, and he was always wanting to read it aloud to her. She only wanted to talk, or to tease him. Once in a while she liked to look into the books, and see how strange they were, for the more incomprehensible the poems were to her the prouder she felt of him and the more confidently she could boast of him to others.

"What good is poetry to anyone, I'd like to know?" her mother said, and to this she always made the one reply.

"Don't show your ignorance, Mother," she used to say.

And then too, although she was often impatient with him for reading when they were out in the meadow, she knew that after he had read a few poems in the book he was always more loving to her, and she felt too that it was because he read poetry that he could say such flattering things about her hair and her eyes and her lips. Other men were so tongue-tied. You'd catch them looking at you. That was the only way you'd know what they thought of you. And even then it was your bosom or your legs they'd look at, but Robert was always praising little out-of-the-way things about her, like her ears or her fingernails. He loved her ears. He'd talk about her ears sometimes for ten minutes. And he said her fingernails were like shells. What other man would ever say a thing like that? Shells! It was the poetry put such things into his head. It was the poetry made him different from other men. She had known that then, but to her cost she had known it better later on. More than his compliments came out of the poetry books; all his nonsense came out of them as well. She wasn't long about telling him so, either. And in the end he admitted she was right. The day she gathered up all the old books and threw them into the fire he said nothing for a minute, and then he said she had done right.

"You're right, Ella," he said. "They were my undoing. A man can't expect to walk with his face turned up to the sky without losing his foothold on the ground. You must keep your eyes on the ground."

"Oh that's more of your talk!" she said, but she was glad she had forced him to give in to her.

He gave in to her in most things, and if he protested at all it was only a feeble protest.

"You used to like to have me read to you, Ella," he said one day.

"I never liked it!" she said, in a fit of temper. "I only let on to like it!"

But she regretted saying that when she saw the look on his face. She wasn't long in learning that he could take any stings she gave him about the poverty and degradation into which they had fallen, but he could not bear her to say anything that spoiled the past. She took back her words that day.

"I didn't mean what I said," she muttered grudgingly, but she was swallowing her words so that she couldn't be sure if he heard her or not. "I've more to do now than listening to poetry, with those children to get ready for school."

That was the first quarrel they had.

"What can I do?" he said. "What do you want me to do? I'm doing my best." He had got a job as an assistant in a lending library at this time, but the salary was small. "I give you every penny I earn!"

That was true. But it wasn't enough.

"I don't know why it isn't!" he said. "There are bigger families than this living on less!"

"And how are they living!" she flashed out at him, and she drew his attention to his clothes. "I want you to look respectable," she said, "like you used to look at home. If you'd only do as I say."

"What do you want?" he asked again.

"Why do you keep asking that!" she said. "You know what I want! I want to let the front room, and add a bit of money to the house."

But it was two years before he gave in to let her take lodgers; not that he could be said to give in, even then, but she took things into her own hands and let the room.

"It's for you I'm doing it," she said. "The first money we can spare I'm going to buy you a new suit, the one on your back is falling to pieces. It's no wonder you got a hint about them cutting down the staff at the library! They saw the state of your clothes. They wouldn't want to have a shabby person giving out the books. It wouldn't look well. People are particular about things like that!"

"That's not why they gave me the hint," he said. "What's the use of them having signs up all over the place asking for silence, if I keep coughing all the time? I got a bad fit of coughing this morning."

"Oh, don't start complaining. If you had a decent overcoat, you'd get rid of your cough." She thought for a minute. "While we're letting one room we might as well let two. The children could all sleep together, and we could let the middle room as well. Then I could buy you a new overcoat. That would get rid of the cough, you'd find. Never fear! It's not the cough that they don't like; it's your shabby appearance."

They didn't get the overcoat. The day the rent was paid on the rooms, two of the children got the measles and from that day on through the whole winter there wasn't a single week without some new expense.

"Now what would we do without the rent?" she asked, at the end of every week when she laid the household bills beside his salary, and went over to a tin box on the dresser and triumphantly took out her own money.

Although the money all went to meet the bills, still she didn't forget about the clothes for him. She was bent on getting them. But she never seemed able to scrape up enough money.

"What's the use," she said one day, "of having a parlor and a dining room? We never go into the parlor." Her eyes were deep with calculation. "The parlor would make a grand bedroom, only some people don't like sleeping downstairs."

He didn't see what she was aiming at, and he joined in the conversation on its face value.

"Delicate people wouldn't mind," he said. "Some people are not allowed to climb a stairs."

"The very thing!" she said. "I'll put an advertisement in the paper, saying there's a room suitable for an invalid." She made it seem as if it was his idea, and he wasn't able to protest. As it turned out they got a better rent for the parlor than for any of the bedrooms.

"Who'd ever have thought it!" she said, as she took down the tin box and counted the money in it. "I'll get you a new suit," she said, "as well as the overcoat. The mistake most people make is not getting enough clothes at the one time. If you have enough clothes you can be easy on them, and wear them turn about." She had been very excited and animated, but he was hardly listening.

"I don't think the new clothes will make any difference," he said morosely.

"Oh, you make me sick," she said impatiently.

Nevertheless, when she brought home the new suit, her heart missed its first beat. He didn't look like he used to look back home before they were married. There was some change. She couldn't say just what it was, but there was a change. What harm! she said to herself — it'll take time to bring him back to what he was. I'll get him some new shirts and new collars. She looked at his feet — I'll get him new shoes. She looked at his hair — I'll get him some brilliantine for his hair. Then her eyes brightened — I'll get him a gold tiepin! she said. The thought of the gold tiepin caused her mind to spin round in furious excitement. She was determined to make him again what he was when they were courting. "We could let the other room. We could eat in the kitchen. It would save my feet, too. I'm worn out carrying heavy trays backward and forward."

She bought Robert the new collars and the new shoes. She bought the brilliantine and she bought the gold tiepin, and the morning he was going out in the new clothes she was unusually excited.

"There's a lovely color in your cheeks, Ellie," he said.

She ran over to the mirror and laughed happily at her reflection, but when she turned round she noticed how pale he was himself. Her heart misgave her again, but she pushed him toward the door with affected good humor.

"You'll see! There'll be no more hints about cutting down the staff. I'll make you look the way you looked when you were hired. I don't blame them for getting uneasy. You were looking terribly shabby lately."

She watched him out of sight, and that day she felt that perhaps the bad times they had gone through were over, and that things would take up again, and be like she thought they would be before she was married.

But the minute he walked in the door that evening she knew something was wrong. When you went downhill it wasn't as easy as all that to get up again.

"Well?" she said, and her face darkened, and the light that had shone in her eyes since morning died out.

He stood in the doorway and looked at her in a strange way.

"I knew it wasn't the clothes," he said.

"What do you mean?" she cried. Why couldn't he speak out plainly!

"It was the coughing," he said, and then, as if to convince her, he was shaken with a hard dry cough. "They said they were sorry, but they couldn't have me disturbing people trying to read."

She stared at him, and he stared back at her helplessly. Then, before she said anything, he recovered himself and put up a hand to his necktie.

"Where did you buy the tiepin?" he asked. "Would they take it back and refund the money?"

At this some of her old fire came back.

"Leave that pin where it is!" she cried, and she slapped his hand down from his neck just as she'd slap one of the children's hands. He stared at her. All at once he felt like one of the children. He felt that her authority over him was going to grow into something enormous and unnatural that would shame his manhood. He was confused and weary, but yet he felt that he must defend himself against this wrongful authority of a woman over a man. And although he couldn't collect himself for a minute or two he knew that he had a weapon against her. What was it? He tried to concentrate, and then suddenly he remembered.

"You needn't worry about the money," he said. "I'll still be bringing in my share."

He spoke defiantly but she didn't seem to heed his words. It wasn't the money she had minded. She had forgotten about the money. It was the humiliation of their not wanting him anymore at the library. She had been so proud of him when he first got the job there. She used to pass by at night when the windows were lighted, just to see him, sitting at his desk in his white collar giving out the books and stamping the date on the flyleaves. And although she had had to give that up when she had the lodgers on her hands, it was only that morning she had been thinking that she'd try and walk down before closing time and see him in his new suit. She had been thinking of it all day. She'd like to have caught a glimpse of the tiepin. She'd like to see if it attracted any attention.

And now they didn't want him there anymore!

She couldn't believe it. A nervousness overtook her suddenly. Was there anything wrong with the clothes? Were the sleeves too short? Why were his wrists sticking out like that? — and how thin they were!

There was nothing wrong with the clothes, however, and she was forced to take heed of the way his frame had shrunk. He had changed. Yes, he had changed, and it wasn't the money she was thinking of at all but of this change, when he spoke. Yet she looked up at him.

"If you're not wanted at the library, where will you get the money?" she asked, dully, because she wasn't interested in this aspect of the thing, but as she looked at him she felt frightened, because she saw that he himself was frightened of telling her where he was going to get it. "Where will you get it?" she asked again, more urgently.

"At the library," he said.

"I thought you said . . . ?" She stared at him stupidly.

He swallowed hard and moved back from her.

"They said they didn't like letting me go — "

"Well?"

" — they said they didn't like letting me go, but that there were people complaining about my coughing."

"Well?"

" — so they said that I'd have to leave the reading room."

"Well?"

He simply couldn't go on. He began to cough again.

"They said they could give me another job — if I had no objections to it," he said at last, " — a job where I wouldn't disturb people."

"In the office?" she asked quietly enough.

"No."

"Well, where?" There was fear in her eyes and before that look of fear his voice failed and he was hardly audible.

"The man that looks after the books in the basement — the stockman, we call him — is leaving at the end of the week," he said. "They thought maybe . . . in these hard times . . . temporarily you know . . . till something better turns up . . . that some money would be better than none."

He allowed the words to fall from his lips, nervously, because her silence upset him. Why was she so silent? He had expected abuse.

But she was stunned; stupefied. The man that handled the books! A porter! a kind of janitor, you might say! Suddenly she burst out crying, and through her fit of tears her anger could only break out erratically.

"A porter! How dare they make such an offer! How dare they! How dare they!" She sat down weakly on the edge of a chair. Robert stayed on his feet, looking down at her. He was somewhat confused. It appeared that she was not annoyed with him; that all her anger was directed against the people at the library. But one thing was clear. He was not going to suffer a storm of abuse any-way, and with this thought he felt relieved, and as the phlegm that he had been trying to keep back rose again in his throat he was about to give himself the further physical relief of coughing when he was suddenly seized with a feeling of fear. She wasn't going to let him take the new job. That was her plan. He summoned all his strength once more. He'd have to take it. He'd have to keep his independence. He'd have to pull his weight in the house. And so before he was overcome by another fit of coughing, he managed to summon breath enough for one remark. "I'm going to take the job," he said chokingly. And then the coughing started and he had to sit down.

That day had been the beginning of all their misery. That was when the real trouble had started between them. It was not until that day that the irreparable bitterness had come into every word they said to each other.

He persisted in taking the job. The new clothes were laid aside, and the tiepin was stuck on the wallpaper over the mirror. He wore his old clothes frankly after that. Ella gave up trying to darn them or patch them. She no longer even brushed them or made any ef-fort to keep them clean. He wore the new shoes, though, because after a bit his feet came out through the old ones. But the rest of the clothes were put away in a cupboard.

"They would only attract attention," she said. "They would only draw people's attention to the fact that you were lowering yourself below your station!"

Her bitterness knew no bounds. Every hour that he was in the house she upbraided him, and where before she had regarded the money from the lodgers as an addition to their joint money, now she regarded herself as the sole support of the family, and sneered at the small sum that he laid on the table every Saturday.

"Is this for your keep?" she used to ask, and throw it contemptu-ously to one side. And at other times, when they were eating their meals, she would laugh bitterly as she filled his plate.

"You get good value for your money," she said. Sometimes she called him The Boarder. "There's more profit on lodgers than boarders," she'd say.

Things went from bad to worse. He got more and more shabby-looking, and as well as that he seemed to shrink and grow smaller and meaner-looking every day. The more sickly and ill he became, the more bitter she grew toward him.

One day, when he left his few shillings down on the table, she snarled at him.

"Why don't you keep it!" she said, throwing back the money to him. "Keep it and buy lozenges with it; not that you'll get much for that!"

He seldom protested against this treatment, and when the children appeared occasionally to take his side he always discouraged them. "Your mother is tired, girls," he used to say. "Don't let her think you are going against her. She has a lot to put up with, and she wasn't used to hardship."

When he said that Ella was not used to hardship, Robert's eyes would sometimes seem to dim with recollection, and sitting there in the squalid kitchen he would stare out the window where a few bits of green fern in a pot on the sagging windowsill had power to draw his heart back into the past. He would sit there, thinking especially of the Long Meadow back of the churchyard in the old town where he and Ella were born. And when he came back up out of the depths of these memories, he was brighter and more cheerful looking, and the girls felt reassured enough to resume their plans for their own enjoyment. They felt they could forget him with impunity, and they crushed against each other, and jostled each other for preference of place in front of the dirty mirror, mottled with splashes, that hung over the sink, as they powdered their faces and combed their hair before going out for the evening.

"None of you have hair like your mother," he said, sometimes on those occasions, and he would start to describe how Ella's hair had been, how bright, how glossy, and how it curled around her forehead if the weather was damp. But they didn't want to hear.

"There's not one of you like her," he said sadly, and Dolly, the second youngest tittered.

"It's a good thing we're not," she whispered under her breath, because they couldn't see back into the past when Ella was young and decked out for love. But Mary shuddered. She was, in fact, somewhat like her mother, and she trembled in her secret soul at the thought that if her mother was once beautiful and yet got like she was, then she, Mary, might someday get like her mother.

"Let's hurry!" she'd say, anxious to be out in the impersonal streets. Being the most sensitive of them all to her father's suffering, she was nevertheless least able to bear the sight of it, just as, most sensitive to the strain between her parents, she was least able to stand it, and rushed out of the house as often as she could.

"Goodbye, Father, goodbye!" They would soon be gone, leaving him in the dark kitchen, knowing that Ella would not stop working and scrubbing until he was out of it too. She would not please him by stopping. She would not give him the satisfaction of seeing her sit down for a few minutes to rest. He began to go to bed earlier and earlier, until soon it was only a question of taking his meal and standing up from it to go to bed. When he was out of the way, he thought, she might sit down and eat, or rest herself by the fire.

One Saturday the strain was too much for Mary. After her mother had made some contemptuous remark about the weekly money that he left obstinately down on the table every Saturday, she burst out before him.

"Why are you always picking at him, Mother? What do you want him to do? Kill himself? He can't earn any more than he does. He shouldn't be working at all! He's not fit for it."

The mother stared at her.

"Keep out of what doesn't concern you," she said angrily. But after a minute she softened. "I'm not making him work. I'm against it. I was always against it from the start. Isn't that the cause of all our misery?" She was speaking to Mary, but out of the corner of her eye she tried to see the effect of her words on the man. "I want him to stay at home. I want him to give up that humiliating job. What he earns isn't as much as what I get for one room!"

Mary was surprised. She looked at her father.

"Why don't you do what Mother says?" she asked.

But Robert shook his head. "You don't understand," he said.

"There you are!" Ella went out of the room impatiently.

But if Mary didn't understand, Ella herself understood less. The only difference between herself and Mary was that Mary honestly tried to understand, but she had shut her mind against him long ago and never tried to see his point of view. She saw her own only, all the time, day after day, and when he got fits of coughing, or an attack of the cramping pains across his chest that he got lately, her own viewpoint narrowed down the more.

"I don't know what notions you have in the back of your head," she said to him, "but let me tell you this! You're keeping me back. People won't take rooms everywhere and anywhere, and when they hear my husband is a janitor they think the place isn't class enough for them. And when they see you going in and out, in your dirty old clothes, coughing and spitting, that turns them more against the place; whereas if you were to give up that job and stay at home and wear your good suits and put on clean collars it would make the place look respectable. You could help me out too. There's many a thing you could do. You could order the provisions. It would look well to see you going into the shops. And you could be seen about the place. That counts for a lot. It gives a place a respectable appearance to see a well-dressed man taking his ease in the middle of the day. It would let people see we weren't lost for their last penny. It would let them see we were independent, and that if the price didn't suit them they could go elsewhere. As it is they think because my husband is a janitor I ought to be glad to take whatever they like to offer me!" A frown settled on her face as she thought of past scenes of haggling over the price of the rent, but it lifted suddenly as she let her mind fly forward to a vision of things as they would be if she had her way. "I'd like to see you with a clean collar on you every day," she said, "and your good suit, and your tiepin, sitting on the bench outside the front of the house. That would give a good appearance to the place."

She paused to picture him sitting on the bench, and then as if the picture was not complete she bit her lip and seemed to be thinking. After a minute she looked up eagerly. "You could have a carnation in your buttonhole."

She was so carried away with her idea that from that day forward she never stopped appealing to him. But gradually the appeals grew sour, and took the form of complaints. He, however, remained steadfast in his resistance to her. He resisted her all the time. And the weaker his power to express it, the stronger his resistance seemed to grow, until sometimes it shone at the back of his eyes in a wild light. He was steadfast in his determination to keep his job. She was steadfast in her determination to make him give it up. But although they were equal in obstinacy and will power, she had an advantage over him because of his own decreasing strength. He'd never endure the hardship. His cough was worse week after week. And so, as she went about the kitchen, she used to watch him out of the corner of her eye. He thought he was going to best her, but she knew that she'd win in the end. And when the children worried about his cough, and came to her, and tried to make her get a doctor for him, she smiled in a curious way and gave them evasive answers. For it seemed now that the cough was her friend. It would accomplish what she had failed to do; it would force him to give up.

And when that day came she'd have him where she wanted him. She'd get down his good suits. She'd shake them out and press them, and she'd put a great gloss on his collars, and she'd get him two new pairs of shoes at least, as well as a couple of pairs of socks. She'd get black lisle socks with colored clocks embroidered on the ankles. As for his cough! That didn't worry her. She'd cure that in a few weeks. When he had nothing to do but sit out in the sun and take his ease the cough would go. There would soon be a great change in him. He would soon get back his looks.

Ella straightened her back. The yard didn't look much better, but she had made some improvement in it.

Just then there was another fit of coughing in the kitchen, and after it she heard a distinct moan. Several times she had fancied she heard moaning, but she'd been able to persuade herself that she was mistaken because she had been making a good deal of noise herself in the yard. But now as she stood idle to rest her aching back she heard it clearly. If only the lodger didn't hear it! If she heard it she would be likely to come out again. They were so curious and interfering. And if that inquisitive creature came out now, it would spoil everything. Doggedly Ella stood and listened to the sounds inside the small window that opened on the yard from the kitchen. She felt that as long as there was no interference with her plans she would soon come to the end of her struggle with him. She was near the end of it now, she felt, and with this thought she permitted herself to move nearer to the kitchen window and listen more intently. But when she listened deliberately there was no sound. Then, when she was moving away, the man in the kitchen was seized with a most violent attack of coughing that was only interrupted by moans and gasps that seemed to be as involuntary as the coughing. The woman leaned forward. He was bad. He was worse than ever he was. A sudden wild elation took possession of her. At this rate he wouldn't be able to go to work today. This was the beginning of the end. What time was it? She strained her head backward to try to see the time by the church clock that could be seen in the distance between the city roofs. Ten o'clock. Could it be that late? Why, he should have been gone long ago! She listened. Her elation grew. Morning after morning he had been getting later and later, but he had never been as late as this! How she had hoped time and again they would discharge him altogether. Seemingly, however, they were prepared to stand anything from him. They pitied him, she supposed, and her resentment burned more bitterily at the thought that he should make himself the object of pity, of charity. Then, as the clock began to strike, she listened intently to the chimes pealing out loudly overhead. He must not be going out at all today. Exultantly she wiped her hands on the sides of her dirty dress. Her day had come. He was defeated at last. Now she had him where she wanted him. She would not be humiliated any longer by having people know that her husband was a janitor. He would be a gentleman again. That was why she had married him; he had been such a gentleman.

Ella sat down on an upturned box in the yard. She felt weak all of a sudden, but it was a gratifying weakness; bearable, and endurable, after a long hard fight in which victory, although certain, had been a long time deferred. After a few minutes the tiredness from the heavy work in the yard began to stream away from her, and with it there seemed to stream away the unhappiness that had lain on her now for so many years. Suddenly she felt that all was going to be well. She looked around at the squalid yard, and up at the loose bricks of the house, that needed to be pointed, and then she looked at the windows of her house, where, in their early years of occupation, neat curtains of white frilled muslin had made all the windows alike, but where now the different occupants of the different rooms had hung their own different curtains. A tenement! That's what it was. But all that would be changed. She would get a better-class lodger. She might try giving board as well as lodgings. There was more money to be made that way, and it was more respectable. Things would be easier now that she would have Robert at home with her. Before he put on his good clothes at the beginning of the day he could do odd jobs for her about the house. They would coin money. And there wouldn't be as many expenses as there were long ago. The girls were all through school except Nonny. Mary's apprenticeship to the dressmaker would be at an end in two months' time and she could ask for a salary any day after that, or set up on her own. She was as good as any dressmaker already. And Dolly was no worry. Dolly's salary at the factory was more than Robert ever earned, even in the good days when he was in the reading room. Then, too, Dolly was as good as married. And Nonny? Ella's worn face brightened even more. She had not done too well for the girls. But there was still time to do something for Nonny. It would be nice to send her to classes and get her made into a typist. Typists didn't get tired and drawn-looking. And she could keep her hair nice, and her hands would be soft and not pricked all over with needles like Mary's, or dyed with chemicals like Dolly's.

Ella looked down at her own hands. If Robert was at home all the time she'd have more heart to keep herself clean. She pulled a hairpin out of her untidy knot of hair, and began to pick the hard black dirt from under her nails. She put up her hand to her hair again. It wouldn't be so coarse if it was washed once in a while. She felt her neck with her fingers. It was dry and rough. But was that any wonder? She only washed her neck when she was going out in the street. You got into dirty habits when you were all alone all day in a dirty, dark house. It would be different if Robert was with her all day. She'd get through her work early, and they might go out for a walk. They used to go out every Sunday when they were first married. She could remember well how proud she was of him. The brightness in her face was a hard defiant brightness. She'd be proud of him again. The suits she'd bought him a few years ago were still as good as new. And they were a better quality than could be got nowadays. As for his appearance, he'd get back his looks in no time after a few days' rest. That was all he needed; rest. He would look older, of course, but he would be distinguished looking, and that was what counted with people.

She began to visualize how he would look, clean and rested, and dressed in his good suits, but the only Robert she could see was the Robert of long ago, the Robert who used to sit on the wall outside his father's house reading poetry and looking down the street to see if she was coming. Once or twice she made a deliberate effort to take his age into consideration, but the Robert she called up before her eyes was a Robert decorated rather than blemished by the marks of age.

She drew a deep breath. Things had been bad, but they were going to come right in the end. Now that the struggle was over she was prepared to acknowledge that she had been bitter, but not without cause. An intolerable burden had lain on her for so many long dark years. And although behind her was the dark, decaying house, with its damp and slimy yard, its ramshackle windows through which there came so often the stench of conflicting smells that hung about the house all day long from the various and inferior foods the lodgers cooked in their rooms at night, nevertheless it seemed to her that these things were nothing, mere details, or external manifestations of a nameless, obscure trouble that had lain over her ever since she was married. A nameless obscure obstacle had been set in her way and prevented her from fulfilling the bright dreams that had glanced back and forth in her pathway so convincingly and alluringly when she was a girl, contemptuously swinging her foot under the table while her mother abused Robert and said he was good for nothing. Perhaps it had been some fear that her mother was right, and that she was wrong, that had lain on her all those years. And Robert himself seemed to have taken her mother's side. He seemed readiest of all to agree that he was worthless and that she had thrown herself away on him. Why had he not helped her to keep up a show? He had given in so early to other people's opinion of him. He had not put up any fight. He hadn't ever cared if he put her in the wrong with her own people. But oh, now wasn't she glad she had not given in to him! She had held out all the time. She had fought. And now she had won. In her limited experience and knowledge she knew little of the abstract differences of the sexes, but from some dim memory of a national-school primer she had an idea that women were the upholders of spiritual values and she felt that in all the weary years she had been championing a cause. People might have blamed her for her methods, but they didn't understand: she had had her plans. She had known what she was about. And now her reward had come. Even Robert would have to see that she had been acting for the best. She had been making a way for them both out of the dark forest in which they had been imprisoned, and together now they would flash out into the open glade. That it would be like the green glades of their early youth she did not for a moment doubt.

She stood up. As her tiredness and misery had given way to excitement and exultation, so this exultation had in turn given way to a feeling of infinite peace. She moved toward the back door that led into the house.

But as she entered the mean hallway, her nostrils were assailed by imprisoned odors of the stale past, and she heard his feet scrape on the broken cement floor of the kitchen. And immediately her spirits were dampened. She felt tongue-tied. The habits of years were not to be broken so easily. What would she say to him? For she would now have to deal with the real Robert; the bodily Robert, and whereas it had seemed in her mind, as long ago it had seemed in her heart, that they were one person, indissoluble in intimacy, who could say or do whatever they liked to each other, she had no sooner heard him cough and scrape his foot on the floor than she was aware again that two people never are one, and that they were, as they always were, and always would be, two separate beings, ever at variance in their innermost core, ever liable to react upon each other with unpredictable results. She was uneasy. She had lost her surety before she had crossed the threshold.

And when she heard him call her name in a strange voice, as if trying to penetrate some incredible distance between them, while she was actually within a few yards of him, with her hand on the kitchen door, all her old irritation came back.

"I'm here," she said. "There's no need to shout."

"Didn't you hear me moaning?" he asked feebly and without accusation. Her antagonism gathered.

"Are you ever doing anything else?" she asked. Her flock of hopeful thoughts had taken flight again.

Robert was dressed for work, and the coarse ugly clothes put a barrier between them instantly. But he, who for many, many years had been so sensitive to the strain between them, seemed suddenly unaware of it now. He put out his hand, and it seemed as if he was unconscious of all the other barriers that the years had erected between them. Before she had time to draw it away, he had taken her hand in his.

At the feel of his hard, coarsened hand when it caught hers, Ella drew back roughly and attempted to release her own hand. But Robert only held it tighter and in his eyes there was a strange expression, and he looked at her in a curious way, almost, she thought, as if it were twenty years back and that she was standing in front of him in the Long Meadow. He seemed to ignore or not any longer to see her worn face. And when she tried again to pull her hand away, he seemed not to understand the rough gesture, or to think of it as the capricious withdrawal of bashfulness.

"Don't draw away from me, Ella," he said. "I have something to say to you. I was calling you all morning. I wanted you."

She was disconcerted. The man in front of her had the shrunken appearance of the man she had lived with in misery for the last twenty years, but his voice and his manner were those of the young man who used to read poetry to her long ago. As a few minutes earlier in the yard, once again she got the astonishing sensation that she had made her way out of the depth of a forest in which she had strayed for a long time. Over her head the trees were laced together less tightly. Through chinks between the leaves the light was breaking in ever brighter shafts. But whereas in the yard she had thought she would have to explain all this to Robert, it appeared now that he too had broken his way through to the light. Snatching back her hand, she put it to her head. It was too sudden. It had all come about too unexpectedly. They had flashed out into the glade too fast. She was dazzled. And so she tried to draw back and take refuge in the habits of the past.

"I heard you!" she said. "And so, I suppose, did that creature in the front room! What did she think, I wonder? It's a wonder any of them stay in the place at all. And as for coming in to you — you know as well as I do that I can't be running in and out every minute for nothing. I have things to do! I wasn't out in the yard for my own pleasure, I assure you!" The flood of words, once released, poured out in a bitter stream. Then as she saw him staring at her, she faltered. "Anyway," she said, defensively, "I didn't know whether you were calling or coughing!"

Still he stared at her, but his eyes were gentler.

"Would it have been such trouble to come to the door and find out?" he asked. And she was put into confusion both by his glance, and by the fact that he had never before in all the years made any protest against her, even a gentle protest like this one.

"Every step counts," she said doggedly.

She persisted in hanging back in the sheltering darkness of former habits. But when she looked at him she realized that he had already traveled far faster than she. His eyes shone. And in spite of the way the fits of coughing had stooped his shoulders of late, his head was high.

"Every minute counts, too," he said. And this time when he put out his hand and took hers, she let it remain with him, and further than that, looking at him, and feeling her hand in his, she ventured a fearful step forward with him into the brightness.

"Are you not going to work?"

He looked at her steadily.

"You've always looked forward to the day I'd have to stay at home, haven't you?"

So he *was* going to stay at home! Without further hesitation she rushed into the light.

"You're not going?" she cried. "You've got sense at last!" She looked back for an instant with a vain regret. "If only you'd given it up long ago, as I asked you," she said, but her joy was too headlong to be impeded. Her heart exulted even as she spoke. "You were killing yourself down there! And for what? As I often told you, I get more for one room than you earn in a week." She paused. "At least I would if I had the right kind of people in the house as I could if the rooms had a bit of decent paper on the walls and a few sticks of furniture in them." She sprang to her feet. "I'll go up and look at the front room this minute and see the condition of the walls. Even a dab of distemper would work wonders with it. And we could give the woodwork a coat of white paint. Better-class people like white paint. They see the worth of keeping it clean. I'd never have put on that ugly mahogany paint if it wasn't for the poor type of people I had to take. I knew they weren't likely to go to the trouble of keeping white paint clean." She was silent for a minute, and her mind was busy making calculations. "New curtains wouldn't cost much," she said. "And we could get a few pieces of furniture out of the money in the tin box." She ran over to the dresser and took it down, but instead of opening it herself, as she always did, she thrust it into his hands. "How much is in it?" she cried, taking him into partnership. "Count it." Her own mind had leapt away and was making other plans. "If we got thirty shillings for the front room," she said, "I'd give notice to quit to the women in the middle room and we'd do it up too." She looked at him as she spoke, but unseeingly. "We might be able to do it ourselves, indeed, and then it would only cost us the price of the paint. I often thought that if I had help I'd never need to get a paperhanger; I could do it as good myself, so now, with you at home to help me, I might manage to do it." She had been talking in a headlong fashion, but suddenly she felt weak from the fever of her excitement. She went over and sat down on a chair at the other side of the table, opposite him, and as she did her eyes rested on him with more attention as he sat with the tin box in his hands.

"You didn't open the box?" she exclaimed suddenly in surprise, but rushing ahead she interpreted his motives for herself without waiting for a reply. "I know it's hard to think of spending the money, but we can look on it as an investment." She sighed happily. "That box won't hold all the money I'll make now that you're going to be a help instead of a hindrance."

But when Robert made no reply at all, not even to her last remark, which she felt to be very gracious and generous, she looked sharply at him. To her astonishment there were large tears glistening in his eyes, and a heavy tear was making its way slowly down his coarse cheek, running irregularly between the stubbles of his unshaven face.

"What's the matter with you?" she cried, starting up anxiously.

"I don't feel well, Ella," Robert said weakly.

"Oh, is that all?" She leaned back with relief. "I wouldn't mind that. A few days at home will set you up again as good as ever."

But the tears continued to roll down his face.

"I'm afraid I'll be more of a hindrance than ever now!" he said, and then when he conquered a fit of coughing he looked across at her. "How could I be any help papering the rooms?" he asked passionately. "How could I help you at anything? I'm fit for nothing now."

Ella pressed her lips together. So this was the way he was going to act. She stood up and glared across at him, about to give him a cutting answer, but what she saw in his face silenced her. He did look bad. There was no mistake about it. For a moment her resentment against him returned. To think that he might die now just at the moment of her triumph! But a minute later her heart began to ache and she recollected that when this stubborn creature died, there died also the young man with the fair hair who used to sit on the wall reading poetry, and furthermore there died also the fine man in the new suit, with a gold tiepin in his cravat and a carnation in his buttonhole, that she counted on having the lodgers see sitting on a bench outside the house. She ran over to him.

"Don't talk nonsense, Robert. You had yourself worn out, but now things will be different." As she spoke she patted him on the shoulder and tried to brighten him up too. "Why don't you change your clothes and sit in the sun? I'll make a cup of hot soup for you." She darted over to the cupboard to get a saucepan.

Robert did not stir.

"Do as I say," she said. "This kitchen is no place to sit."

For the first time in years she seemed to see its filth and squalor, and leaving down the saucepan she ran about straightening the chairs, gathering up the rags and rubbish that littered them, and finally, snatching up the sweeping brush, she began to sweep an accumulation of dirt and crumbs into the corner under the sink. This furious activity absorbed her entirely for a few minutes. Then she turned around.

"You couldn't find a healthier spot in the world than that bench outside the house. Why don't you go out and sit there? Why don't you go out there now?"

"Ella, please! Let me sit where I am for a while," said the man wearily.

She laid down the sweeping brush, only half convinced that he was unwilling to comply. Then she gave in to him.

"Well, you can sit out there tomorrow. And it will give me time to have your suit aired and pressed. But you'd better not sit here in the dirty kitchen. I'll help you into your room." She went to catch him by the arm. But he shrank from being touched.

"I'd like to stay where I am for a while," he said pathetically, and then got such an attack of coughing there was nothing for her to do but go back to what she had been doing until he got over it. The coughing sounded bad. It distressed her to hear it. He seemed worse all right. And when he stopped coughing he tried to speak but she couldn't hear what he was saying. She went over to him and bent down her ear to him.

"I like to be here where I can watch you, Ella," he said.

She laughed uneasily.

"Oh go on out of that!" she said roughly, but it was a roughness he knew of old, a roughness of embarrassment, a righteous unwillingness to give in to the pleasurable vanity roused by his words. "I'll have a drop of soup for you in a few minutes. Wait till you see! You'll be a new man after it."

It took a long time to make the soup, because in her excitement she tried to do several things at the one time, only thinking to run over and stir the soup when it boiled over and there was a smell of burning. She dragged the ragged net curtains from the window and threw them into a basin of water. She snatched down the mirror that was over the sink and tried to wipe off the flyblows that covered it like a pock. But when the soup was ready at last he could only swallow a few mouthfuls.

"What harm!" she cried. "It will be all the thicker for leaving it on the fire. You can have it later on."

Later on, however, he was less inclined for the soup than before, and although she patiently held the spoon to his mouth and coaxed him to take a spoonful, he swallowed only a few drops. The rest ran down on his chin and slobbered his clothes.

At last he protested against the effort of trying to swallow it.

She looked at the clock.

"But you must eat something. You've been sitting there all day without a morsel inside your lips!" A frown of worry came on her forehead. "What will I do with you?" she asked, but more to herself than to him, for although he kept his eyes fixed on her, watching all her movements, she was beginning to have a curious feeling of being alone. There was certainly no use in expecting any cooperation from him. She wished the girls were home. The day had flown and yet it would be a long time still till they got back from work. Nonny would soon be back from school, but what use was Nonny? She'd be peevish and tired and crying for her dinner.

There was a sound in the passage. That was probably Nonny now and there was nothing ready for her to eat. Even the soup was boiled away. Well, Nonny would have to wait. Ella went out and banged the kitchen door shut.

It was not Nonny, however. It was just a door that had slammed in a draft. The child did not come in until some time later.

The instant Nonny did come home, and stepped into the hall, however, the child was aware at once that some change had come over the house, although she could not tell what it was. The dark hallway was the same, and the same damp smell came out from the walls. There was the same cold, empty sound as she ran down the bare cement passage. Yet something in the atmosphere had lightened and brightened. She pushed open the door of the kitchen, but as she did so her mother shot out a hand and pushed her back into the passageway.

"Go easy!" the mother cried crossly. "Your father is asleep. What's the meaning of making such a noise? Can't you walk gently? Have you no respect for people's nerves!"

The child stopped in astonishment. This was something new!

Her mother had never before greeted her in this manner. Then recalling that her mother had said something about her father, she looked scared.

"Where is he?"

"He's in the kitchen," the mother said. "You can go in to him if you go quietly."

Fearfully and on tiptoe, not knowing what to expect, Nonny went in, but her father was still sitting where he sat that morning, only now his feet were lifted onto a stool and there was a blanket thrown over them. There was also a pillow behind his back.

The child looked timidly at him, but when she saw that he was not going to speak to her she stared at him curiously. Ella had to push her out of her way at last, and after that the child stole about the kitchen getting herself some bread and butter. When she had cut and buttered two or three uncouth and crooked slices of bread, she crept out again on tiptoe to eat them in the yard. She had not been sent out to the yard, but all the time she had been in the kitchen she had felt nervous and uncomfortable and she had knocked into the chairs, and clattered the cups on the dresser, and once she had stumbled. Each time she made a noise she felt her mother turn and glare at her, although she did not dare look up at her. It would have choked her to eat in the kitchen. It was better out in the yard. She sat down on an upturned box and began to chew the bread and ponder on the change that had come over her mother. It used to be her father that was ordered about and glared at, and it used to be herself that was petted. She sat chewing the bread without relish. And she wished her older sisters were home.

The first thing the older girls noticed when they came into the house was the smell of soap and disinfectant, and they saw at once that the passage had been swept. Then, before they went into the kitchen they saw Nonny sitting disconsolately on a box in the yard. They went to the door of the yard to talk to her and tease her, but when they saw the way the yard had been cleaned up and tidied, they forgot Nonny. What was the meaning of this? They exchanged glances, arching their eyebrows. Then they smelled the soup. This was most unusual. And all these unusual things prepared them in some way for a change, so that unlike Nonny, when the older girls went into the kitchen they went quietly, and were hardly surprised at all to see their father wrapped up in a blanket in the corner. As if they were in a strange house, the two girls politely refrained from looking around at the freshly scrubbed dresser and the clean curtains, but they were aware of every change, and under their feet they missed the grit and dirt that was always on the floor, and, when they went to sit down, they were astonished to find the chairs were free of their usual clutter. There was no sign of their supper, however, and their mother, who was always in a fuss at this time of day, belatedly getting something hot for them after their day's work, turned around to them with an anxious face and ignored all mention of food.

"How do you think he is looking?" she asked them earnestly, and although they had not been told their father was any worse than usual, they felt instantly that he must be bad, from their mother's solicitude for him. It shocked them too to hear her speaking of him to his face as if he neither heeded nor heard.

"He didn't go to work today," Ella said. Then she questioned them anxiously once more. "How do you think he looks?"

Mary drew back, uneasy at talking about him in his presence.

"Don't mind him! He won't hear you," Ella said. "He's sleepy. He's been like that all afternoon."

Dolly was less sensitive. She stared into the corner where her father sat.

"He looks bad," she said bluntly.

Ella said, scathingly, "He's very bad!"

Dolly was tired and hungry and her mother exasperated her.

"He's no worse than he has been for months past," she said viciously.

For a moment Ella pondered over Dolly's words and her face clouded with worry as she looked distractedly at Robert, then as she became conscious of the mood in which her daughter had spoken, her face darkened still more.

"If that's the case," she said, "you might have spoken sooner! You might have drawn my attention to him."

The rebuke was hurled at Dolly, but the bitter glance that went with it included Mary in its wide reckless orbit. The two girls looked at each other again. Like Nonny they had never before been in disfavor with their mother, but unlike Nonny, they sensed that after twenty years the habits and instincts of acerbity were unlikely to be stifled at will, and that at best they could be but diverted from one person to another. They felt that it was they, now, and not their father, who stood in the path of their mother's wrath.

Ella herself, however, was unconscious of all except the needs of the invalid. After her bout with Dolly she looked at Robert critically, but after a few minutes she was able to disregard her daughter's words again and blind herself to his poor appearance.

"He'll be all right in a day or two," she said defiantly, and she went over to him and repeated the same words, but in an utterly different tone of voice; half coaxing, half bullying. "You'll be all right in a couple of days, Robert," she said, and she tucked the blanket tighter around him and gave the pillow behind him a jerk.

Robert said nothing. His eyes were shut. It gave Ella a shiver to have him sit so patient and quiet. She caught up the blanket and gave it another and unnecessary shake, and she gave the pillow another and more violent jerk.

All of a sudden, looking at his sunken cheeks, she felt that no assurance from the children would be of any use to her. He must assure her himself. For the third time she repeated the words but this time they were in the form of a question.

"You'll be all right in a couple of days, won't you?" she asked, and although she stood over him with her arms on her hips in a truculent attitude that seemed to defy him to give her any answer but the one she wanted, into her voice there had crept a whining tone that was new to her.

Robert opened his lusterless eyes and looked up. And for a moment there was a sign of struggle in his face as he tried to summon up enough duplicity to give a cheerful answer, but he was already too far gone in weakness to do any more than tell the truth. The truth was the easiest. He had no energy for subterfuge.

"I don't know," he said. "I feel bad."

"Oh, nonsense," Ella said impatiently, but she wasn't convinced by her own exclamation. He did look bad. She could see that now. What would she do? She looked around her helplessly for a moment, but the only words that came to her were the old, ready words that she had used a hundred times. "You'll be as well as ever you were in a few weeks. And you'll have the best of times. You can lie in bed till the day is well aired, and when you get up you can put on your best clothes, and go out and sit on the bench in front of the house, and be called in to your meals, with plenty of time to eat them slowly and chew your food. Oh you'll be all right. Wait till you see. That bench gets all the sun. I don't know how it is, but the sun shines on it from one end of the day to the other. I often wonder that the lodgers don't make more use of it. But, as a matter of fact" — and here she brightened considerably — "as a matter of fact, I'm just as well pleased they never got into the habit of sitting on it, because of course you won't want to make free with them when you're sitting out there yourself." The bright picture she drew of him, sitting proud and aloof on the bench in front of the house made her forget the dismal picture he presented huddled in the chair. "You'll be all right in a couple of days," she said. "After all you have something to look forward to now. It would be a different matter if you were going back to that old library! Yes! You have something to look forward to now, Robert!"

But the truth had stolen into the diminished citadel of Robert's soul and, taking advantage of the weakness of his body, it was in possession now for the rest of his earthly sojourn.

"It's not much to look forward to, Ella," he said, and he looked up at her. "I thought I'd come to a better end! I thought we'd make more of our lives than this!" And in spite of the leaden weights that hung on his arms, he struggled to put out a hand from under the covering and make a gesture to include the house.

"What do you mean?" She was frightened.

"It's not much to live for — is it?" Robert said. "The thought of spending the end of your days sitting in front of a lodging house. Do you remember what we planned? Do you remember how we wanted to be together always, just you and I, without anyone else? Do you remember the way we used to be so mad when your young sister Daisy hung on to us, and wanted to come for a walk with us, and we couldn't get rid of her? And now," his voice weakened, and he had to stop to draw a long breath, "look at the way things have turned out!" He made a disparaging gesture. "Look what happened!"

"What happened?" she asked in a whisper. She truly did not know.

He seemed to be getting weaker every minute. With a great effort he concentrated his forces for an answer, but he could only manage to give utterance to it in fragments.

"Strangers," he said, and drew a long breath. "Strangers everywhere." He began to cough. She wanted to hear what he had to say, but it was so painful to watch him she was ready to forgo her curiosity. But when, rather than see him laboring to talk, she tried to interrupt him, he put up his hand to make her listen to him. "We wanted to be together, Ella. We wanted to be alone. That's why we left home. And here we are finishing our days in a houseful of strangers. Strangers; strangers; strangers. Strangers in every room. I'm so ashamed! To think we should come to this!"

His voice was stronger toward the end of what he was saying, but suddenly he stopped speaking and sat silent again, and this time it seemed that it was words that had failed him, and not his voice.

In the silence the two girls who, after the first few minutes of curiosity, had begun, like Nonny, to look around and prepare some sort of food for themselves, began now to whisper to each other. Dolly took up her father's words.

"I told you," she said, turning to Mary. "I often said it was degrading to keep lodgers. I am always afraid they'll find out at the factory that we keep a lodging house. They'd look down on me so much!"

From the corner her father had caught the sound of her voice, but it seemed he could not see well because he suddenly broke out again in a passionate complaint, and his anger gave a spasm of strength to his voice.

"Listen," he cried. "I hear people talking over there at the sink. Who are they? Why must there be strangers everywhere? Why must they be in here?"

The girls were startled.

"He's delirious," Dolly said under her breath. "He doesn't know who we are!" And she turned around as if she would go over to him, but Mary suddenly caught her by the sleeve and held her back.

"He knows who we are all right," she said. "He just doesn't want us here." But she herself made no move to go out because to stay where she was seemed less conspicuous, and Dolly, who hardly comprehended her, just stood where she was also, staring at the sick man — a pot of tea in one hand and a cup in the other. But now Nonny who under cover of the older girls had stolen back into the kitchen, and had been listening to the last few words that had passed between her sisters, caught at their skirts in fright, unable to understand what was wrong. She had known all day that something was wrong and had hoped to find out when the other girls came home, but although she had hung on every word that was uttered the meaning of the words was incomprehensible to her.

"Who doesn't want us?" she asked, dragging urgently at Mary's skirt and then at Dolly's. Getting no satisfaction from them she was just beginning to cry when suddenly their mother created a diversion. For Ella had suddenly flung herself on her knees in front of the sick man.

"Why didn't you ever tell me you felt like that?" she cried, in bitter reproach. "I thought you wanted us to make money. You used to say we'd make our fortune in the city. I only tried to help." She put her hand to her forehead distractedly. She was bewildered. They had wanted to make money, hadn't they? That was why they had come to the city, wasn't it? She tried to recall the long talks they used to have in the days before they ran away from home. But it was all so long ago. She couldn't remember. Yet surely they had been determined to make money. Wasn't that what all normal people wanted — to make money, and rise in the world?

But Robert was muttering something different.

"The two of us. Just the two of us; that's what we wanted," he murmured. "To go away together, and not have your mother all the time nagging at us!" His face brightened as he spoke, and it was almost as if it was of the future he spoke and not of the past that had never fruited. "The two of us. Just the two of us." He began to smile. But suddenly his glance grew dark again and he tried to see across the room into the corner where the girls were whispering together. "And now," he cried in a loud bitter voice, "now I'm going to die in a house full of strangers."

The girls looked at each other. Dolly plucked her mother by the sleeve.

"Tell him it's only us."

But her mother swung around.

"Don't bother me, I'll tell him nothing. What are you doing in here anyway? Get out of the room. Can't you see you're irritating him?"

In their surprise the girls made no protest, but moved to the door, and as they went they heard their mother speaking to their father again, but her words were hardly coherent.

"It's not too late. We can go away now, Robert. We'll get a cottage. We'll go away, and get a little cottage, and be together, Robert! Robert!" She raised her voice as if she would force him to hear her. "Do you hear me? We'll get out of this place. We'll get a cottage, away out in the country, just the two of us; like you wanted." She sprang up and rushed across the kitchen. "There was a cottage advertised in yesterday's paper," she said, and the girls could hear her searching for the paper. Then they heard her run back to their father. "I can't find the paper now," she cried, "but it's somewhere about the place; I'll look it up. That cottage might be the very thing for us. Three rooms, it said, three rooms, and a garden at the back. Think of it, Robert! You'd like that, wouldn't you?" She was suddenly secure again, a person who could not be bested. For a moment it had looked as if something had gone wrong. But everything would be all right after all.

Outside in the passage Dolly and Mary listened.

"Did you hear that?" Dolly said. "The two of them! And what about us?" Angry spots of red burned in her cheeks.

But Mary looked pale. "I think Father is delirious," she said. "I think he's forgotten about us." Her eyes opened wide. "I think he doesn't remember we were ever born!"

"But what about Mother?" Dolly demanded. "*She* knows we were born! *She's* not delirious. What does she mean, talking about a cottage in the country with three rooms?"

All of a sudden Nonny began to whimper.

"Now see what you've done," said Mary to Dolly. "Hush, Nonny. It's nothing to worry about. Mother and Father are only planning a holiday."

But it was their mother alone who was making plans. She dashed out into the hall just then.

"Where is yesterday's paper?" she cried. She was angry and querulous, as if one of them had deliberately withheld it from her. She went over to the miscellaneous pile of things that she herself had gathered together in armfuls earlier and flung out into the hallway, but she was too distracted to know what she was doing. Mary went over to help her and soon found the paper. When she handed it to her mother Ella snatched it up and eagerly searched out a small paragraph in the advertisement columns. Then she ran back to the kitchen with it.

"Look at that," she cried, and pressed it into Robert's hands, but she was too impatient to wait for the tired eyes to focus on it and she caught it up again. "I'll read it for you," she cried. "Listen! Three rooms! And a garden! Think of that, Robert. Just what we want. Just suitable for two people. Just what you wanted. Just the two of us."

In the hallway Dolly put an arm around Nonny. She felt suddenly sad, but it was not sadness for herself, it was for Mary and Nonny. After all, she would be getting married soon. She looked down at Nonny. She might be able to have Nonny to live with her. Then what would become of Mary? But Mary was smiling.

Yes, Mary was smiling, although it was a weak, sad smile. And it faded when they heard their father trying to say something. Their mother evidently could not hear what it was either because she came to the door and called them.

"What is he trying to say?" she asked, and she beckoned them to come back into the room.

The girls listened. Their father spoke again. Dolly couldn't catch what he said at all, but Mary bent close to him.

"It's too late now." That was what Robert said.

Mary raised her sad eyes. "He said it's too late now, Mother."

"Too late? What does he mean?" Ella stared at Mary. She wanted to contradict him, but she had no longer the strength to argue. "Tell him he'll be all right in a couple of days," she said to Mary. "Tell him the country air will cure him. Tell him about this — " and she pointed to the paper in her hand. "Tell him about the cottage that's advertised here."

But when Mary bent down again to her father he put out his

hand, and with a violence unexpected from one in his weak condition he gave her a push and knocked her back against the table.

"Strangers," he said bitterly. "Strangers everywhere."

Mary turned to her mother.

"I think he's raving, Mother," she said, but even as she spoke she was struck by the expression in her father's eyes as compared with that in her mother's face. Her mother was the one who looked distracted, whereas her father, in spite of his rambling talk, was looking at her with a fierce and, it seemed, a conscious antagonism. But such a groundless antagonism was in itself unnatural. "You ought to get the doctor for him, Mother," she said.

Ella however was not listening.

"It's *her* mind that's wandering," Dolly said impatiently. "Just listen to her!"

For Ella was sitting down with the paper in her hands, staring at the advertisement for the cottage.

"I'm sure there wouldn't be many people would want that cottage," she said. "I'm sure they couldn't ask a high rent for it in the heart of the country. I'm sure we could get it."

"What will we do?" Mary asked despairingly of Dolly.

The man in the corner was muttering louder and louder, and shouting out against the strangers that he seemed now to imagine all around him. He even made efforts to struggle to his feet in order to get at them and put them out of the house.

"We'll have to do something," said Mary, wringing her hands, and she caught her mother by the arm. "Mother! Mother! Listen to me! We ought to get the doctor for him."

Ella shook off Mary's hand.

"Get me a scissors," she said. "I'll cut this piece out of the paper so that it won't get lost. Someone might tear up the paper on me."

But Dolly went over and took the paper out of her mother's hands.

"We can talk about the cottage later on," she said, "but we must get the doctor for him now."

It was Nonny who brought things to a head. She was sorely perplexed; the strain had told on her. Sisters were only sisters, but what she wanted was a father or a mother. And now there was this strange talk about her parents going away. Where were they going?

And what was to become of her? She looked from one of her parents to the other. Which of them would tell her? The distraught condition of her mother and the bright alive look in her father's eyes determined her to turn to him, and running over she buried her golden head in the blanket about his knees. Instantly there was tension in the room. Mary started as if to pull her back, but she was too late. She could only stand by and stare.

It seemed for a minute that Robert knew the child, so concentratedly did he stare at her, but after a moment they saw it was the concentration of unutterable anger. Gathering up unbelievable strength, he put out his thin bony hands and gave Nonny a violent push backward.

"Who is this child?" he cried. "Take her away. Am I never to have any peace?" And then raising his voice he began to shout. "Strangers!" he cried. "Strangers! Strangers!"

There was dead silence after that, and then Nonny began to scream. Opening her mouth to show her small stunted teeth, she screamed and screamed. Ella came to her senses.

"Come here, Nonny," she cried, and she caught the child to her breast. "He doesn't know you, darling," she said appeasingly, and tears began to flow down her own face.

"We'll have to take matters into our own hands," said Dolly. "I'll go for the doctor. What doctor will I get?"

But there was no need to take things into their own hands. Nonny's tears had roused Ella. She had begun to capitulate to the force of events. She got to her feet. She was more urgent now than any of them.

"We should have got the doctor hours ago," she said, and now she was blaming everyone. "I'll go for the doctor myself," she said. "He wouldn't come quick enough if one of you went. But I'll make him come." And snatching her coat she ran toward the door. "I won't get the dispensary doctor. I'll get a private doctor." At the door she halted. "Which is the best doctor to get?" she cried, and then she ran back into the room and threw herself down on her knees again. "I'll get the best doctor in the city for you, Robert," she said, shaking him to make him hear. "He'll have you as good as new inside an hour!"

Mary was strained to breaking point.

"Get some doctor anyway, quick, Mother, for God's sake," she said, "or it will be too late."

When the doctor came he said that Robert would have to be taken to hospital. The girls dreaded the effect this would have on their mother, yet Ella took it fairly well and began at once to busy herself with preparations for his removal.

"Get the best ambulance you can, Doctor," she said, and she kept impressing this injunction on him all the way down the hall as he took his leave.

And when the ambulance came it was she who saw to everything, and made the ambulance men promise not to jolt the stretcher, and even went out into the street with them and sent away the crowd of children that had collected to gape at the spectacle. She would have ridden to the hospital in the ambulance with him but the regulations forbid such a thing.

"No one is allowed to ride in the ambulance, ma'am," the stretcher bearers said as they prepared to take their departure.

She had to give in to them of course, but she ran to the front and spoke to the driver.

"Drive carefully," she cried to him, and then, just as they moved away she remembered something else and she ran along the path beside the moving vehicle. "Take care you don't let him be put in a public ward!" she cried. "I want him put in a private room."

As the attendants did not appear to hear her she turned frantically to her daughters. "Hurry, girls!" she cried. "Go after them. You can go quicker than me. Go down to the hospital, and be sure he's put into a private ward. And tell the nurses he's to get every attention. Tell them that. Let them know we can pay for it all. Let them know he has people that care about him. That counts for a lot with those nurses." They were standing out in the street, and the girls were ready to go, but she called them back. "Wait a minute. You'll need money. I want to give the porter at the desk a tip. It will let him see that Robert is a person of some importance. He'll be able to let us in and out, you know, on the sly, outside the regular visiting hours." She rummaged in the pocket of her skirt and pulled out several notes and some small coins. "Have you enough, do you think?" she cried, as she pressed the money into their hands. They took the money and turned away, but as they went they heard her calling after them urging them to hurry. Yet they had not reached the end of the street when they heard her running after them. "Come back a minute," she cried, and she was panting from lack of breath. "I forgot to tell you — find out if there's anything he wants, and if there is, get it for him. Insist on seeing him. You'll be allowed up to him if you're persistent enough."

"Aren't you going to come to the hospital yourself, Mother?" Mary asked.

"I am, of course," said Ella, "but I want to go down to the shops and get him a few things. I'll bring them with me. His nightshirt is a show. I want to get him a new one. I wouldn't want him to be ashamed in front of the nurses. And I'll get him some oranges. Oranges are a great thing to have beside your bed when you're sick."

Robert, however, was a bit far gone for oranges. And as Dolly remarked to Mary it didn't make much difference to him whether he was in a private ward or not, although their mother, when she arrived, was insistent that he be changed. For Robert had been put into a temporary ward, until a bed would be vacated in one of the wards proper, and although it was a long airy passage with only another occupant in a bed at the far end, Ella kept after the authorities all that evening and all the next day to get him moved into a proper ward on the first floor.

The girls were embarrassed at the fuss their mother made.

"They'll move him when they get a chance, Mother," said Mary, "and this place is nice and bright." She was thinking of the damp room at the back of the kitchen where he had slept for the last twenty years.

Dolly protested also, and she tried to kill two birds with the one stone, and make her mother see how bad their father was.

"I don't see what it matters where he is at the moment, Mother," she said. "I don't think he knows where he is at all. He doesn't take any notice of anything."

"It does matter," Ella insisted. "We must let the nurses see that we are particular about him." She looked down at the lifeless figure stretched on the hospital bed. "He's quiet because he's resting. That's what he needs; rest. Don't disturb him." She looked around. "I hope there won't be noise here," she said, and the girls were embarrassed again because of there being only one other patient in the ward. This patient was a brawny young man, whose leg was tied up in some kind of splint, and whose main object was to get the nurses to sit on the side of his bed and talk to him. He looked good-natured and considerate and they hoped he would not think their mother's remarks were a reflection on him. They whispered together and then Mary drew her mother's attention to him, but Ella when she turned to look at him saw only the table beside his bed, for on it there was a plate with a large bunch of purple grapes. "Grapes!" said Ella. "I should have got Robert some grapes. I heard one time that a person can swallow the pulp of a grape when nothing else will stay in the stomach." She opened her bag and pulled out a half crown. "There's a shop around the corner. I saw it when I was coming in here — and they had lovely fruit in the window. Run out and see if you can get some grapes." She looked back at the other bed and her eye fell on a pile of papers and magazines. "Get him some papers too. He used to like reading the paper."

Mary hesitated. She did not take the coin.

"I have the money you gave me yesterday," she said evasively.

But Dolly spoke out.

"What's the use of spending money foolishly?" she said. "He's too far gone to eat anything. And it's only nonsense to think of him reading, when he doesn't even know where he is!"

"Mind your own business," her mother said sharply. "You ought to be ashamed of yourself, talking of saving money at a time like this. Wouldn't I get him anything in the whole world that he wanted?" She raised her voice and bent over the man in the bed. "Wouldn't I?" she cried. "Wouldn't I, Robert?"

Robert was moved next day to a ward on the second landing. Ella was more or less satisfied.

"It shows they think something of him," she said, and she looked around her with satisfaction. "You can see that this is a good ward by the class of patients in it."

There were five other beds in the ward. One was unoccupied. In one there was a young man who was still under the influence of an anesthetic. In another there was a small boy with a bad leg. The third bed was occupied by an old man who was allowed to get up and move about the ward in his dressing gown. And one bed they could not see because there was a screen around it.

Ella looked at the other patients and noted the crowded condition of the small enamel tables beside their beds, and everything she saw with these other patients she wanted to get for Robert.

"I must get him some apples," she cried, as she saw the old man painstakingly peeling a large red apple while he sat on his bed with his legs dangling. And when she saw some story books on the young boy's table she went home and rooted out two or three mildewed volumes of poetry in old-fashioned bindings with gilt edges that had somehow been saved from destruction, and she brought them up to the hospital. "When he starts to come round to his senses," she said, "he'll be glad to see them."

Dolly nudged Mary. "It's a good job there's a screen around the bed at the end so she can't see what's behind it, because if she brings any more stuff in here it will have to be put under the bed." She laughed.

But Mary could not laugh. She looked down the ward uneasily. "I wonder what's the matter with that patient? He must be dying."

The bed at the end of the ward had a screen around it all the time, and nothing could be seen of the patient, although at visiting hours a thin nervous woman in black came up the ward and noiselessly passing behind it took up a position of vigilance at the bedside of the patient. Through the joints of the screen the thin black figure of the woman could be seen sitting silent and tight-lipped, her fingers ceaselessly moving as she passed the beads of a worn rosary through them with the dextrous movements of a card player slickly dealing out cards. The woman never seemed to bring anything to the patient behind the screen.

"He's too ill to appreciate anything, I suppose," Mary said.

"She has more sense than Mother," Dolly said. "I suppose she's his wife."

The woman was at that moment passing down the ward, unsmiling and walking noiselessly with her eyes to the ground. The two girls looked after her curiously, but they were recalled to their surroundings by Ella.

"Calf's-foot jelly!" she said in a loud voice, speaking out of a deep reverie. "There's nothing like it for a sick person. I'll get him a jar of calf's-foot jelly."

"For goodness' sake, Mother, don't bring anything else for a while," said Mary. "Wait till he's able to enjoy things."

Dolly nudged her.

"Don't be giving her false hope," she said. "He'll never enjoy anything again." And she looked at the man in the bed, the counterpane motionless under his inert body, and she looked at the littered table beside the bed. "Those grapes will get rotten," she said. "He'll never eat them!"

As a matter of fact, after a day or two the grapes began to lose their bloom, and the girls themselves ate one or two of the oranges. The magazines began to get crumpled and used-looking and marked with wet rings from the glasses and medicine bottles that the nurses left down on them. As for the poetry books, the nurses put them into the locker under the table because they were only cluttering up the small space of the cubicle.

But still Ella brought in paper bags of fruit and biscuits and sweets. And all the time Robert remained unconscious of her ministrations, or at least as indifferent to them as he had been to her promises of the bench outside the house and the carnation for his lapel. He just lay on his back looking up at the ceiling, and Ella's consolation in the fact that he sometimes nodded his head when she bent down and spoke to him was spoiled somewhat by the fact that he also did it once or twice when no one was speaking to him at all. He divided his time between long periods of complete unconsciousness and shorter periods when he seemed to recover consciousness only to carry on long incoherent conversations with himself in an undertone.

When he was three days in the hospital there was hardly room to sit beside him in the cubicle with all the things Ella had brought with her to try and attract his attention.

"Look, Robert," she'd cry, bending over the bed and holding out something for him to see. But Robert gave no sign that he saw anything.

Finally the nurses got impatient with Ella, and spoke irritably to the girls.

"I wish that woman would stop bringing in this rubbish," one of them said one day when she found it difficult to make a place for the thermometer on the top of the crowded table. She turned to Mary. "Can't you make your mother see that he is too far gone to take any notice of these things? What kind of a woman is she? Why can't she behave like other visitors? Look around! No one in the ward is treated the way she treats this man. No wonder he doesn't come back to his senses. She has him bothered. She shouldn't be let in here at all!"

Mary was embarrassed. She resented the harshness of the nurse. But Dolly could understand the nurse's irritation and she defended her. "It's true for her," she said. "I wonder why Mother's behaving like this? I suppose it's remorse for the way she treated him in the past!"

But Mary looked away and the sad look came into her pale thin face and her eyes shone with tears.

"It's not as simple as that," she said. "Mother doesn't feel any remorse. If she did she would be more upset. It would probably break her heart. I don't think she realizes how unkind she has always been to him. I don't think she is aware of the way their lives were wasted away in bitterness. I think it just seems like a bad spell they got into, and that it will pass away and they will come out again into happy times like they used to have long ago. She doesn't blame herself at all. She thinks they were *both* the victims of misfortune."

Dolly looked at her sister. She didn't fully understand what Mary was saying. She was thinking how different they were. She is more like Father, she thought. I'm more like Mother. And she felt irritated with Mary's subtlety and gentleness.

"I think it's us who were the victims of misfortune," she said.

"We've heard nothing but quarreling and fighting since the day we were born." Suddenly she wanted to hurt Mary. "Thank goodness I'm going to be married soon and get away from it all." Then as she looked back at the unconscious man in the bed a disturbing thought came into her mind. "If he dies now I suppose I'll have to put back my wedding plans for another six months."

Mary's face quivered and she looked anxiously at her father. "Mind would he hear you, Dolly!"

"Don't be silly," said Dolly. "You're as bad as Mother with her grapes and her nonsense. Can't anyone with an eye in their head see that he's unconscious?" But she looked at him guiltily, regretting her words. Then she went over and bent down. "Father!" she said, and her voice was firm and authoritative, unlike her mother's cringing appeals to him. "Father! Can you hear me?" There was no recognition whatever on the white face. Dolly straightened up. "It's my belief that he won't come back to his senses at all."

Mary nodded her head in agreement. "Poor Mother," she said. "I wish for her sake that he would come around just long enough to notice all she tried to do for him. If she could have the satisfaction of his seeing all the things she brought him." She brightened. "It would be nice for him too. I'd love him to know how she tried to make up to him for the past. He would think it was like the old days." She caught Dolly's arm eagerly. "Do you remember he used sometimes to talk about the time when they were young, and how yellow her hair used to be, when she went walking in some meadow with him. I often think of that. I think that if he could only see all she's doing for him now it would be just like as if the sun had burst out again after a long time, and it wouldn't matter how dark it had been, or how long the darkness had lasted. Nothing would matter if that sun shone again, bright, bright, bright, even for a few minutes." She moved nearer to the bed and gazed down at her father with a passionate look in her eyes. "If only he'd open his eyes. If only he'd speak. How happy they both would be!"

But Dolly shrugged her shoulders. She was still irritated by the thought that she might have to postpone her own plans.

"I don't think they deserve to be happy!" she said bitterly.

"Don't say that," Mary said sharply.

"I will!" said Dolly. "I'm sick of it all." But as her father murmured and seemed to be in pain, she was filled with remorse. "Do you think he's suffering?" said Dolly. "Poor Father! I suppose he deserves it."

"Deserves what?"

"Oh, what you were saying about the sunshine, and all that. I wish for his sake he could see the way she is trying to make up to him. If he did, I suppose he'd die happy." But her softness only lasted a moment. "I can't say our mother deserves much though!" she said. "It would serve her right if he died without getting back his senses." She looked angrily at the plate of grapes. Several of the grapes were beginning to rot, and around them a fly buzzed. "I'm going to throw them out!" she said, and breaking off some of the rotted grapes she caught them up in the palm of her hand with an expression of disgust and looked around for somewhere to throw them. At the far end of the ward there was an open window, and walking across to it she threw them out into the street. "I don't care!" she said, in answer to the unspoken criticism of her sister's face. "I was sick of the sight of them."

When Ella arrived the first thing her eye fell on was the plate of grapes from which the large bunch had been cut. Her face, that was furrowed by fatigue, straightened out, and a light came into her eyes.

"He ate the grapes?" she cried, in delight.

The girls said nothing although Mary's lips moved and if Dolly hadn't been listening she might have told a lie, and said he had eaten them. But she felt her sister's eyes upon her, defying her to give in to such weakness.

Ella read their faces. Her eyes grew dull again. She took out a soiled handkerchief and began to wipe her neck. There was sweat on it from the strain of climbing the stairs in a hurry.

"Don't cry now, Mother," Dolly said crossly, and Ella looked meekly at her and put away the handkerchief. Her old obstinacy was breaking down. She was getting uncertain about everything. She would have liked to talk about her disappointment over the grapes, but she was afraid of Dolly. But just then the Sister-in-Charge came into the ward. She was a small red-faced nun, with a

kind face, secure and complacent in her own beliefs. Ella turned
to her eagerly.

"I thought he ate the grapes," she said, and she sat down despon-
dently on the bed, another paper bag of fruit unopened in her hands.

But the Sister had heard the complaints of the nurses. She dis-
regarded Ella and spoke in an undertone to the girls.

"I think it would be better if she could be made to understand
that he's too far gone for these things. It's only waste of money."
She looked at their poor clothes, and Mary blushed. She knew what
the nun was thinking.

"We don't mind the money!" she said defensively.

Ella raised her head. She overheard the last sentence.

"That's right," she said, looking at Mary. "Spare no expense!"
She even appealed to the Sister. "Is there nothing I can get for
him?" She turned and threw herself across the coverlet of the bed.
"My poor darling," she cried. "Robert! Robert! Is there nothing I
can do for you? Why don't you know me? It's Ellie. It's your own
Ellie! Ellie — who'd do anything in the world for you!" But the
impassive face had no reply, and she turned back to the others. "If
only there was something I could get for him; something to ease
him!"

The girls said nothing. They looked at the nun. The nun looked
back at them as if she would like to have conferred with them alone,
but since this was impracticable just then, she nodded her head to
signify that she could not neglect the opportunity afforded by Ella's
own words. She put her arm around Ella.

"You want to do something for your husband, do you, you poor
woman? Well, there is only one thing you can do for him. You can
pray that God will give him the grace of a happy death."

Ella drew back from the nun's embrace.

"He's not going to die!" she said fiercely.

But the nun had entered into a familiar domain. She ignored the
nervous murmuring of the girls, and even a slight stir in the man in
the bed.

"We must all die, sooner or later," she said. "It doesn't much matter when we go. But what does matter is the manner in which we
die! Will we get the grace to die a happy death, or will we not?
And if we are unable, like this poor man, to pray for that grace our-

selves, what more can those do who love us than pray that God will give us the grace we are unable to ask for with our own dying lips?" The words fell easily from the untroubled lips of the nun, like a lesson long learned, and it echoed in the ears of those around with the familiar notes they had heard a hundred times in sermons and mission lectures. Then the nun's voice grew warmer, and more personal. She took Ella's hand and pressed it.

"Pray for him, my child. Pray that God will give him that inestimable thing that surpasses all else in the world — the grace to die a happy death. You can give him no greater thing."

Ella pulled away her hands but this time it was to wipe her face. Her tears had begun again. The nun looked around her quickly, and taking up a bunch of the decaying grapes she held it in front of Ella.

"Think of all the Masses that could have been said for the benefit of his soul with money that was spent on this perishable matter!"

There was a pause. Had the nun succeeded? The girls held their breath. In the next bed the old man who had been putting on his socks sat listening, with one sock on and one sock off. The nun herself could be seen silently moving her lips in prayer while under the fold of her habit her fingers ran over the wooden beads of her rosary.

Suddenly Ella stood up.

"How long is it since he was at the Sacraments?" she asked the girls.

They all exchanged glances. She had not only comprehended the nun's words, but with her impetuous nature she had already outstripped her in thought.

"Do you think is there any danger he would die without recovering consciousness?" she asked, but she didn't wait for an answer. "We should have sent for the priest for him," she said. "We should have done it long ago. Why didn't someone mention the matter to me?" But when the girls made a stir as if they would do something about it, she pushed them aside. "I'll attend to this. Some priests are more sympathetic than others. I don't want him to be upset. Some priests have very poor manners! I'll get a Franciscan; that's what I'll do. The Franciscans are all lovely men." Her enthusiasm swelled into a great flood.

Like the bench in front of the house, like the cottage with the three rooms, like the grapes, the oranges, the books of poetry with the gold edges, now it was eternal salvation she wanted for him. She was ready to dart away at once to get it. But she stopped, frightened, and caught at the nun by the arm.

"What will I do if he doesn't recover consciousness? He won't be able to make his confession! He won't be able to talk!" She was startled. She was terror-stricken.

"The priest has already paid him a routine visit," the Sister said more gently. "And of course we'll let him know the minute there is a change. He has been anointed and been given conditional absolution."

But this wasn't good enough for Ella. For days it had been impossible to convince her that he was dying, but in her determination to procure him all the rites of the Church she was instantly reconciled. These rites might be the last thing that she could procure for him.

"Conditional absolution isn't enough," she cried. "He'll have to come around to his senses." Suddenly she threw herself down on the bed again. "Robert! Robert!" Then she looked around her wildly. "He'll have to come around. Couldn't the doctor give him something to bring him around, just for a few minutes; just for long enough to make an act of contrition?" Then she remembered something else. She straightened up. "There should be a blessed crucifix placed in front of him so that his eyes would fall on it if he opened them. Just to look at the crucifix could save your soul, even if you weren't able to speak. Did you know that? I always heard that said. Where will we get one?" She began to fumble in her pocket for money to send the girls out to buy one. The nun put out a hand to calm her, and detaching the long brass crucifix that dangled from her belt she proffered it. But Ella pushed it aside. "It should be made of wood," she said authoritatively, and drawing still further upon some obscure fund of theological superstition she cried out again. "A habit!" she cried. "He should have a habit ready. If he only got one arm out in the sleeve of it he'd be saved. The left arm; nearest the heart." Hastily drawing out a greasy purse she gave it to Mary. "Get a habit," she ordered, "and a crucifix. I'll stay here and try and bring him around." A fever of energy had made her cheeks glow, and from the depths of some repository of knowledge and superstition, long undisturbed, she brought up a score of suggestions. "If we held a lighted candle in front of his eyes, he might open them!" she cried. "If we wet his lips he might speak! Do you think it would be any use to wipe over his face with a cloth wrung out in cold water?" She was determined to bring him around, if only, as she said, over and over again, if only for one moment.

From that hour there was continual excitement. Ella was in and out of the hospital as often as she could gain admittance, and in the intervals she did not rest but sped all over the city, going from church to church lighting blessed candles and arranging to have Masses said for her special intention. The special intention was always the same. The prayers were all offered for Robert's return to consciousness. And when she was in the ward there was such confusion that they put a screen around Robert's bed, while the mother of the small boy in the opposite bed made so many complaints about the noise they had to move the boy to another ward.

"What will we do with her at all?" said the nun who had first put the idea of a happy death into her head. For Ella was inconsolable. "After all," the nun said at last, "you haven't such great cause to worry. Your husband led a good life. He was a good man. And he has already been given conditional absolution. God is merciful, you know. But what would you do if you were that poor creature?" She nodded down toward the end of the ward where, behind the screen, the woman in black was just discernible sitting alert and vigilant beside her husband's bed. "That poor woman down there has cause to worry. Her husband is unconscious too like yours, but how different his life has been!"

Ella was barely listening, but the girls looked curiously at the screen.

"An atheist!" the nun said in an undertone, and she made the sign of the cross over her breast as inconspicuously as possible, because the woman in black had raised her head and seemed to be looking in their direction. "She can't hear us," the nun said reassuringly as Mary's face reddened. "And even if she did, she wouldn't mind. She's a saint if ever there was one. She doesn't mind who knows her story. She is aware that it could be a lesson to others. That's what she said to me. And so it will. There he is now, after his life of sin and blasphemy, stretched speechless without the power to utter one syllable in supplication for God's pardon!" The nun shook her head sadly. "That poor woman's life has been a trial to her from the day she married him, but she never lost her faith in God's goodness. She offered up all her sufferings to the Almighty. And she never ceased praying for her husband's return to the Faith. Even now, she has not lost hope, and every hour that she spends by his bedside is occupied in silent prayer for him."

The girls felt uncomfortable at this point, fancying that there was an implied criticism of their mother in the nun's words.

"Is he unconscious too?" asked Dolly.

The nun shook her head sorrowfully. "Alas, not all the time. How much better if he were!"

Dolly did not understand.

"Whenever he comes to his senses," the nun said, "it is only to utter curses and blasphemies. Fortunately the periods of consciousness are getting fewer. When he was first brought in here it was terrifying to listen to him. The night nurse would not stay on duty alone. She said it was as if there was an Evil Presence in the ward!" The nun shuddered. Then she looked at Ella. "It should console your mother, to hear about that man. What would she do if she was the wife of that man?"

But Ella was not to be so consoled by anything. She had set her heart on one thing, and she was determined that Robert would come to his senses.

"If we brought Nonny up to him!" she exclaimed when the girls were trying to make her listen to what the nun had told them about the other man. "He might hear Nonny. He might heed her where he wouldn't heed anyone else. A child's voice is very penetrating."

But when they brought Nonny she was so timid she could hardly be persuaded to open her mouth. And when they urged her forward to the bedside, she hung back and clutched at Mary's skirt.

"Call him, Nonny!" Ella ordered. "Call him. He'll know your voice. He'll hear you! He'll come back to his senses when you call him. Go on. Call him." Nonny opened her mouth, but she could hardly be heard by those standing beside her. The mother gave her a jerk. "Who could hear that?" she exclaimed irritably. "Where is your voice? Call him again. What are you afraid of anyway? Raise your voice. Go on! Call him. Call him again." But the child was nervous and overconscious, and would only utter a few weak cries. Finally Ella sent her home in disgust. "No matter! When the priest comes he'll bring him back," she said. "The priests have wonderful power in their tongues. Wait till the priest comes."

The Franciscan Father, when he came, however, occupied himself more with Ella than with Robert.

"You must not give way to despair," he said. "You must trust in God. God's ways are strange. God's ways are not our ways." Then he became more practical. "There doesn't seem to be any immediate danger, or I would anoint him, but I'll look in later in the night to see how he is getting along. At the least sign of danger I can assure you I will exercise my powers." He patted Ella's shoulder reassuringly.

"You're not going, Father!" cried Ella. She was afraid to let him away. "He might take worse suddenly."

But the priest had other duties, as he explained rapidly to the girls in a low voice.

"I have other sick calls to make," he said. "I must try to be where I am needed. I do not think I am needed here — not just yet."

Afterward they all recalled his last words.

"God's ways are wonderful indeed," the nun said.

For just as the priest was leaving Robert's bedside, there was a sudden sound of a chair being pushed back and a woman's voice rose in a sharp exclamation. A minute later the screen by Robert's bed was pushed aside and the woman in black rushed into the cubicle.

For a moment the others hardly recognized her. The face that had for so long outstared the enemy wore a defeated look that was at odds with the words she uttered.

"My prayers have been heard," she said. She looked as if she might at any minute start to laugh foolishly. Ella and the girls could not immediately comprehend what had happened. But the nun understood at once.

"God be praised," she said, and forgetting Robert, forgetting Ella, forgetting even the Franciscan Father, she pushed aside the screen, and followed by the excited nurse, she hastened to the end of the ward. The Franciscan then, although he had no previous history of the case, seemed to divine what had occurred. "Thank God I was here," he said. "His ways are indeed wonderful!" And like the others, forgetting Robert, forgetting even to push aside a chair over which he nearly fell, he too hurried down the ward to the bedside of the penitent, from whom there had come a despairing cry.

"A priest! For God's sake, get me a priest!" the man cried. "Don't let me die in my sins."

It was a miracle. Word of it flew all over the hospital. Nurses and Sisters whom Ella and her daughters had never seen came running to proclaim it. There was untold activity. Screens were hurriedly pushed back to permit the passage of those carrying candles, holy water — a crucifix.

As for the man himself, who had lain prone so long, he had started up from the pillow, and in spite of the hands that tried to hold him down he was almost standing in the bed, his eyes burning as in fever, and the sweat beading his face.

"Mercy!" he cried in a voice for all to hear, and terrifyingly lucid. "Oh God, have mercy on me, miserable sinner that I am," he cried. But when way was made at the bedside for the Franciscan he did not recognize his garb and tried to push him away. "Mercy! Mercy! Mercy!" he screamed. It was as if he already gazed upon the Face of the Godhead, but being perhaps blinded by the lightning flash of his conversion, he could not distinguish upon that Dazzling Countenance the attributes of mercy from the attributes of wrath. "I am lost!" he cried. "Lost!" And even when he was at last made to understand that the priest was there, it was some time before he could be convinced that it was not too late for him to seek salvation. Babbling bits of half-forgotten prayers, he clutched convulsively at the priest's hands and covered them with kisses.

In the other beds in the ward the patients were all sitting up in excitement, except for Robert, who lay silent and still behind his screen, which was slightly awry after the abrupt departure of the Sister and the nurse. And then, suddenly, the Sister, who had gone hurriedly out of the ward a few moments previously, came back carrying in her hand two tall black candlesticks in which burned long wax candles, the flames of which, as she moved, flowed backward so swiftly that the eye could hardly see the tenuous thread that connected wick with flame. When the Sister was halfway down the floor of the ward she stopped, and beckoning one of the nurses she nodded her head in the direction of Robert's bed.

"Take that screen," she said. "We can get another one later for that patient."

Before Ella could protest, the screen had been whisked away and a moment later, although Ella still stared in the direction of the penitent's bed, she could see nothing but the shadows of those behind the screen, chief amongst which was the shadow of the priest with a raised crucifix in his hands. Then the Sister appeared again around the corner of the screen. She came toward Ella who was standing alone by Robert's bedside. "My daughters had to go," Ella said. "The little one was frightened and they had to take her home. It's too bad. I thought Nonny's voice might reach him. She has a very penetrating voice." But the nun wasn't listening to Ella. Her thoughts were still occupied with the man at the other end of the ward.

"A miracle!" she exclaimed. "That's what it is; a miracle. God works in a mysterious way. How I hope that I may be shown the same mercy when my turn comes. Think of it! A man who lived a life of sin; an enemy of the Church; a blasphemer. Ah yes; it is true indeed; God loves the sinner." The nun folded her arms in the form of a cross. Then suddenly she uncrossed them again and looked around her. The light in the ward was fading rapidly now. She became aware of the irregularity of Ella's presence.

"I'm afraid it's time for you to go," she said, but she spoke kindly, and as Ella looked back in anguish at Robert she nodded her head in understanding.

"Don't lose hope," she said. "God's ways are wonderful. I'm sure your husband will regain consciousness. You'll see. God will not fail to give him a happy death." She nodded back over her shoulder at the patient at the far end of the ward. "You ought to be greatly encouraged," she said, "by this marvelous example."

As Ella went toward the door, she caught a last glimpse of the other patient. The excitement had abated, and except for the Franciscan, who stood at the end of the bed, his hands joined in prayer, and the candles that fluttered and strained upward, the scene was almost the same. The woman in black still sat with stiffly folded hands at the bedside, and the man, exhausted now, lay on his back staring up at the ceiling.

"And no wonder he was exhausted!" Ella said later that night, when she was telling the girls. "I never heard such shrieks. They were hardly human." She sighed. "When that shrieking didn't rouse your father, nothing will rouse him. Oh, what will I do? What will I do?" And frantically she looked at the clock to see if there was yet time to arrange for another Mass for him. "If he'd only come to himself for five minutes. Five minutes would be enough."

"Even if he doesn't, Mother," said Mary, "you have no need to worry. Poor Father. He'll go straight to heaven. What did he ever do that was wrong? He never hurt anyone in all his life."

Under her breath, Dolly was muttering.

"The only one he ever hurt was himself. He put his purgatory over him here in this world."

Ella wasn't satisfied.

"How do we know what sins he might have on his soul?" she cried, and she threw up her hands and began to wail. "I'll never rest an hour if he dies without recognizing the priest. What does anything matter as long as a person gets a happy death? Isn't it the only thing that counts in this world?"

And it seemed to her that morning would never come when she would renew her vigil at his bedside, where by now instead of bags of oranges and apples there was an accumulation of crucifixes and blessed candles, holy water and medals, all of which by turns she pressed against his lips and his forehead and his hands in the hope that they would bring him back from the bottomless silence into which he had sunk.

The next day when it came at last, and they went back to the hospital, passed in much the same manner as the day before it. Robert's condition was unchanged. But there was no sign of the man who had occupied the bed at the end of the ward. The nurse said he had died shortly after Ella had left the hospital the previous night.

"It was an edifying sight," the nurse said. "To see a man who wouldn't let the Name of God be mentioned in his presence, die clutching the priest's hand and crying like a child. An exemplary death! Is there any end to God's mercy? To think that a man like that should be given the grace to die such a death!" Then the nurse remembered Robert's state and she reddened. "Please God your husband will get the same grace," she said. Ella and she glanced at the bed on which they were all accustomed now to see Robert's motionless face. When she glanced at him now, the nurse gave a startled cry and bent closer. Then she caught Ella's arm. "His eyes are open!" she cried, and she rushed over to the bed, but Ella, who reached the bedside almost as quickly, pushed her aside with a violent arm.

"The crucifix! Let him see the crucifix!" she cried, and snatching it up she held it in front of him, almost pushing it into his face. "Robert! Robert! Look at the cross. Can you see it?" She stared into the open eyes, but there did not seem to be any answering response in them. "Can you see me at all?" she cried. And then, more anxiously still she shook his arm. "Can you hear me?" she asked. "Can you hear me? I want you to repeat an act of contrition. Can you hear? Keep your eyes on the crucifix." And while she held it in front of him, she looked around at the girls. "The priest!" she gasped. "What are you thinking about? Get the priest at once!" Then, turning back to the man on the bed, she entreated him to try and hear her. "Repeat after me, Robert," she said, and she began to enunciate the act of contrition. " 'O my God,' " she said, and waited for him to repeat the words. "Robert! Can you hear me? 'O my God.' Say that after me. 'O my God, I am heartily sorry for ever having offended Thee.' Robert! Robert! Repeat it after me. Can you hear me?" And the last words were almost a wail because, although the light of recognition had flickered for a moment in his eyes, it had gone out again. She leaned closer. "Robert! Don't you know me? It's Ellie; your own Ellie!" But in spite of her appeal it seemed as if there would be no change in the face on the pillow. Then suddenly a faint light flashed in the dark eyes of the dying man, and the lips moved as if they would say something. Ella put her face down to the pillow. Yes, he was saying something. But what it was she could not hear. She bent so close she could feel his breath on her face, and then, faint as the breath itself, she caught the word that with great difficulty was formed on the parched lips.

"Ellie!"

That was the word.

Ella straightened her aching back with a sob of relief, and as the nurse came hurrying into the ward, followed by the Sister, she turned around to them, her worn face bathed in happiness.

"He has come to his senses. He spoke to me," she cried. Tireless, she bent down over the bed once more.

"Robert darling, you know me? You can hear me? It's your own Ellie. And she wants you to do something for her. She wants you to make an act of contrition. Repeat the words after me — 'O my God —'"

The girls, who had arrived, crept closer, and the nurse, without saying anything, sat down on the chair beside the bed and took the thin wrist in her hand to feel its pulse. Then she looked at Robert's face.

"He's trying to say something," she said, for although no sound came from the lips, it seemed that the man was making some effort to speak by the way the muscles of his worn face had begun to work. They listened.

Then, scarcely audible, a few words struggled from his lips.

"Ellie, my own Ellie!" he said.

Ellie's face showed some relief, but there was still a certain anxiety in her eyes.

"Yes, yes, your own Ellie," she said impatiently. "But now, Robert, I want you to repeat something after me."

"Just a minute," the nurse said. Taking a spoon and a bottle she went over to the patient and forced something between his lips. "Now!" she said, nodding encouragingly to Ella.

Ella bent down again.

"'O my God!'" she said. "Repeat that after me, Robert. 'O

my God, I am heartily sorry for ever having offended Thee.'
Repeat that. 'O my God . . .' "

But it seemed as if Robert had slipped back into his world of
darkness. His eyes closed, and an imperturbable look had settled
once more on his ashen face.

"Robert! Robert!" Ella's voice implored him to hear her. "Don't
slip back on me, Robert," she cried. "You know me, don't you?
It's Ellie, Ellie!" she cried.

The dying man opened his eyes again and again he spoke.

Although showing signs of exhaustion, Ella wasted no time.

"Repeat this after me, Robert," she cried. " 'O my God, I de-
test all my sins,' " she said, and then, confused, she began to forget
the wording of the prayer. " 'I am heartily sorry,' " she said.
" 'Never more to offend Thee.' " But now she was not looking at
the silent lips, she was turning in despair to the Sister and the nurses.
"What is keeping the priest?" she cried. "Why doesn't he come?
This may be our only chance. He may slip back altogether after
this!" She was distracted. She was on the point of collapse.

But just then the priest appeared at the door. Under a white cloth
he had the Sacrament for the dying.

"God is good," he said, by way of salutation to those around
the bed, who all fell to their knees before the Presence he brought
with him. The priest moved over to the bed, but first he stopped to
whisper to the Sister. "If he wants to make his confession," he
said, "I'd like you all to draw back from the bedside. Just a few
paces is all that will be necessary."

Those around the bed immediately withdrew.

"The goodness of God! Two such miracles in the one day."
The nun took Ella's hand in hers. "God has heard your prayers!"
she said. "You have a lot to be thankful for. I must admit there
were times when I thought your husband would never regain consciousness."

Then the priest, who had bent over the man in the bed, straightened up and looked back over his shoulder. He appeared to be in
some difficulty. The nun stood up and went over to him.

"Do you want something, Father," she asked, and she prepared
to hand him first the crucifix and then the holy water.

But the priest wanted Ella.

"I think he wants to say something to you," he said. "He keeps calling your name. It might be better if you remained within his range of vision."

"Ellie!" said the man in the bed, and he stared up into her eyes, and now to her joy his eyes seemed once again to be clear and lucid and to shine with all the brightness of consciousness. "Ellie. My own darling girl." Like the man who had died at the other end of the ward, he struggled to raise himself on the pillows.

"He's near the end," the nurse said to Mary, and she hastened to support him, but Robert pushed her aside. The nurse motioned to Ella then, and Ella put her arms around him and held him up. He turned his head and looked at her, and it seemed that he saw nothing else.

"Just the two of us!" he said, and he put up his hand and stroked her hair with a perfectly normal gesture. The onlookers exchanged glances of satisfaction, but a minute afterward they were in doubt again, because although now he spoke clearly, the words he uttered were inexplicable to them. "Your lovely golden hair," he said. Taken aback, they all looked at Ella's gray hair on which his hand rested.

Ella continued to support him, but she turned frantically to the priest.

"What will I do?" she said. "Will I repeat the prayers?" The priest nodded his head. " 'O my God,' " said Ella. "Can you hear that, Robert? 'I am heartily sorry.' Can you hear that?" And this time Robert seemed to hear.

"Sorry?" he repeated, questioningly. Then he closed his eyes for a moment again, but when he opened them they were filled with a rapturous light, astonishing to behold in a face etched with the lines of an almost lifelong sadness and weariness.

"Yes, yes," said Ella eagerly, repeating the line that seemed to have caught his attention, while the priest nodded his acquiescence. " 'I am heartily sorry,' " she said, speaking slowly and distinctly.

Robert put out his hands and eagerly caught at her hands.

"Sorry?" he said again weakly, then his voice grew suddenly strong and vibrant. "There's nothing to be sorry about, my darling," he said. "We were unfortunate, that was all. It wasn't your fault.

I wasn't much good. That was the trouble. I should never have taken you away from your comfortable home. I'm the one who should be sorry, not you." He had raised himself higher in the bed, and some of the lines of hardship had gone from his face, and an assuredness that was like the assuredness of youth came back into his voice. "But I'm not sorry," he said. "You were all I wanted in the whole world. When I had you I had everything. Even when you spoke harshly to me, I knew it was because you were tired. I knew that I had failed you, and I always forgave you." He pressed her hand tighter. "Don't talk about being sorry," he said again, urgently searching her face for the effect of his words. "There's nothing to be sorry about. You always made me happy, just by being near me. Just to look at you made my heart brighter. Always. Always. It was always like that." He sighed then with a long peaceful sigh, and seeing that he had relaxed, the nurse motioned Ella to lower him again onto the pillow. Back on the pillow he closed his eyes, then, but he closed them deliberately and not from fatigue, for a smile played over his face, and showed that he was yielding to some happy thought. "The meadow," he said then, in a soft voice little more than a sighing breath. "Do you remember the meadow? How happy we were walking along the headland holding each other's hands. You could never understand why we had to keep to the headland. You used to want to walk in the high grass. 'I'd love to wade through it like water.' You said that one day. Do you remember? You wanted to wade through and pick the clover that sweetened the air with its warm scent, and when I told you it would spoil the harvest, you wanted to trample it all down. You were so willful! So willful, my darling. That was what I loved best in you; your willfulness." Suddenly his voice grew stronger and there was a harsh note in it. "Your mother knew you were willful. That was why she was afraid to speak out against me. That was why she did no more than throw out hints about my health. My health was all right then. It would have been all right if she had let us alone, and let us stay where we were happy. We could have got a little cottage outside the town, with a small piece of land. That was what I always wanted." Suddenly he struggled to sit up in bed again. "I don't like that woman," he said.

Ella, who had been listening with suppressed sobs of remorse and joy, suddenly stopped sobbing. Her mother had been dead for years.

"I don't like her," said the man at the top of his voice. "I won't be humiliated by her. I'll take you away. I will!" His voice was fierce. "Will you come with me, Ellie?" he cried. "I'll make you happy. Trust me! Trust me, Ellie." The fierceness that flared up so suddenly as suddenly died out. "Trust me, Ellie," he said then in a soft sweet voice, the voice of a young lover. "I'll make you happy. I promise. I know I can do it. We'll go away from here where we'll be alone; just the two of us. Just the two of us. You and I."

Since the first mention of her mother, Ella had been sitting with a dazed look on her face, unable to comprehend what had happened. She turned around now with a vacant look at the priest. The priest moved over to the bedside.

"Perhaps after all it might be well for you to stand aside where he wouldn't see you," he said, "and then I might be able to regain his attention." But when the priest came within his range of vision Robert's face changed, and his eyes took on again the wild unnatural glitter.

"There's someone coming!" he shouted, warningly. "I think it's your sister Daisy. She'll want to come with us! And we don't want her, do we? It's so much nicer alone, just the two of us. Let's hide, Ellie. Let's hide, sweetheart. Let's get behind that tree over there!" Dragging his hand free from Ella he began to point wildly.

The priest shook his head, and moved back to the footrail of the bed where he began to confer earnestly with the nurse and the Sister. Ella sat still, stunned into silence. Dolly coughed nervously. She felt embarrassed at the incongruous intimacy of her father's outburst, even in delirium. She turned to Mary in her discomfort. But Mary was smiling strangely, and staring at her father with a secretive smile that was like a smile of complicity. Dolly was aware again, as she had been a few days earlier, of a great difference between herself and her sister. Mary was like their father. She herself was more like her mother. She looked at her sister's face, and then at the face of her father, but as she looked at him Robert began to move his lips again.

"Just the two of us!" he said, the look of rapturous happiness returning to his face.

And something about that rapturous look caused the nurse to start suddenly to her feet and make a sign to the priest. After one startled glance at Robert, without waiting to stir from where he stood, he raised his hand in the blessing of conditional absolution. At the same time the nurse put her arm quickly around Ella's shoulders to lead her away.

Ella pushed the nurse's arm away, and, not comprehending what was happening, she looked in bewilderment at Robert. But the serene smile that had taken the place of the rapture of a moment before deceived her, and she did not recognize in it the serenity of death, until her daughters, both together, put their arms about her and began to reassure her.

"Never mind, Mother. Never mind! He led a good life. He never did anyone any harm."

Then Ella understood. Throwing up her arms she began to scream.

Still screaming and sobbing, she was led out of the ward, and it was utterly incomprehensible to her that God had not heard her prayers, and had not vouchsafed to her husband the grace of a happy death.

THE SAND CASTLE

JOHN was the oldest. He had straight black hair and a pale face. Emily came next. She had bright hair. Every summer they got gold freckles, but in the winter they went away. Alexander was the youngest. His freckles never went away, but Alexander did not mind. He did not mind about being fat, either, as long as he was getting big, one way or another.

One summer they went to stay in Howth, a small seaside resort. It had a silver bay and a bright green boat-slip, a silver strand and a cold white harbor. There were things to do, every hour of the day, and the nights fell even faster there than they fell at home. When the tide was out, you could dig for cockles and go down so deep with the spade that you came to jet-black clay underneath the silver sand. You could skim stones on the shallow waters. When the sea was full and high, you could fish from the pier with a string and a pin. You could vault over the old pier stakes that stuck up in the sand like stunted trees. You could sit on the slimy boat-slip and talk to the fishermen as they mended their nets. You could pile up big stones and try to knock them down again with smaller stones. You could walk out to the end of the cold white harbor wall and look down over the sides at the great green tongues of the sea that licked up the walls. You could do This. You could do That.

Emily and John quarreled all day long because they could not decide between This and That. Even Alexander was independent in his ideas, for a four-and-a-half-year-old.

"What will we play today?" he asked, on their second day there, as they sat at their lunch in the window alcove of the hotel.

"You can do what you like," said Emily. "You won't play with us!"

"Why?" said Alexander. "Why won't I play with you?"

"You're too small," Emily said.

Alexander could not accept this familiar insult. He stared at his plate. The tears splashed onto the surface of the shining porcelain.

"Alexander is not as small as you think," said Nurse. "He walked to the end of the pier yesterday afternoon, all by himself." She looked anxiously at Alexander, whose tears that were now falling on his plate, with the loud, steady fall of the first raindrops that herald a thunderous downpour. "Tell them about your walk, Alexander!"

Alexander looked up, with such a jerk that two tears sped into the air on either side of him. He entered at once upon the narrative with a vigorous faith in the fact that it would vindicate him from future charges of being too small to play with the others.

"I walked to the end of the pier," he said, "all by myself. Nurse sat on a lobster pot. I walked to the very end, and when I got there I sat down on a seat." As he spoke he was impressed by the exactitude of his memory, but when his narrative was over he became aware of a certain paucity of detail. Moreover, when he looked at his audience, he realized that he had held their attention to no purpose, for the story was ended and his audience clearly expected more.

"Well?" said Emily.

"What happened then?" said John.

Alexander was humiliated. Desperately he tried to remember further incidents about the walk, but, although he could call up a picture of the pier, it was a cold, straight pier, without turns or steps, and all he could see on it was himself, walking along toward the seat at the far end, and a solitary, dull sea bird. Alexander was forced to fasten upon the sea bird. "While I was sitting on the seat," he said, taking up the narrative after the most fragmentary and imperceptible pause, "a big bird came along and sat beside me."

"Did you catch him?" John asked with a spurt of interest.

Fearing that he might be expected to produce evidence if he answered in the affirmative, Alexander shook his head.

"Before I had time to catch him," he said, earnestly staring at his listeners, "he ran away."

"You mean he flew away." Emily was beginning to look incredulous.

"No, he ran away," Alexander said, having learned that it is best to stick to one's first story even if it is a poor one. Emily looked at John.

John fixed Alexander with a fierce and unblinking stare. "How many legs had he?"

"He had four legs, of course," Alexander said, indignantly, but immediately he began to doubt his statement, and when at that moment a sea gull flew past the window, with no legs visible at all, his doubts became more serious.

"A sea gull with four legs!" said John, and he began to laugh.

"I knew he was lying all the time," said Emily.

Nurse looked up. "Emily! That is not a nice way to speak about your little brother."

"Make him tell the truth then!" said Emily, turning to Nurse.

"Tell the truth, Alexander," Nurse said, frowning.

Alexander began again, but this time his voice was humble and his story was interrupted by apologetic sniffling. "It's true that I walked to the end of the pier," he said, "but it's not true about the bird. There was a bird, but he just stood on the ground."

"Did you sit on the seat?" John asked.

"I did."

"Did the bird come near the seat?"

Alexander did not reply for a minute, and then he straightened up. "No," he said, "but he looked at me." And proudly, putting his own head to one side and shutting an eye, he showed how the bird looked when it looked at him. "I am going to walk down the pier again today," he said, after he had opened his eye and straightened his neck again.

"You are not," said Emily.

"I am," said Alexander.

"You will do as we say," said Emily.

The tears came into Alexander's eyes again. Nurse frowned and bit her lip. Nurse was pale, and there was a dark stain under the lashes of her young blue eyes. "Why are you children so difficult?" she said. "Why aren't you like other children? Why are you always quarreling?" She paused, and then she brightened. "Why don't you build a nice big sand castle?"

"A sand castle!" John was almost speechless with indignation.

"The sand is dirty," said Emily. "I heard a lady say that she saw fleas in it, hopping up and down!"

"Emily!" Nurse looked around hastily to see if there was anyone within earshot. "There are some things that are not mentioned at table."

There was silence then for a few minutes, and Nurse looked out between the stiff lace curtains at the far blue sea, and the gray beach lit along its length with bright cockle streams catching the silver sunlight. When she spoke again it was softly, as if to herself. "Very few people can build a good sand castle. It takes skillful planning. It takes a strong steady hand."

Alexander looked rapidly from Emily to John and from John to Emily, no doubt regretting that he could not look in two directions at one time. Emily and John were looking at Nurse. But Nurse still looked at the sea.

"I could build the best castle that was ever built," John said.

Nurse continued to look at the sea. She said nothing, but she allowed a faint and supercilious smile to fashion itself at the corners of her mouth.

John addressed the smiling mouth. "I'll show you!" he said, angrily, and he beckoned to Emily. "Are you coming?" he said to her, and he strode out of the room. Emily strode after him.

Alexander had some difficulty descending from his chair, and so he could not stride out after them with the arrogance he would have liked to show, because they were already going through the swinging glass doors of the vestibule, and he had to run or he would have been left behind altogether.

Outside the hotel, the air was bright and challenging. The wind shook the red geraniums that stood in glaringly white urns on the terrace and threatened to dash their petals all over the green grass.

Alexander caught up with Emily. He drew a deep breath and pulled her by the skirt. "Wait for me," he said, mysteriously, and disappeared around the corner in the direction of the hotel. When he came back he carried a rusty, corrugated bucket. He had seen it sometime previously but had been unable to devise a use for it.

"Where did you get that?" Emily asked, enviously, stretching out her hand for it.

"Finders, keepers!" Alexander said, retreating a pace or two, putting the bucket behind his back.

"Oh, keep it!" Emily said, tossing her hair angrily. She ran after John. Alexander ran after her.

They caught up with John in the long dune grasses that separated the hotel lawn from the flat sand on the lower shore.

"Here is a good place to build the castle," Alexander said, setting down his bucket. The soft white sands lifted into streamers on the air. John looked at Alexander with contempt.

"Is that all you know about building?" he said, as he strode ahead, his feet sending up branching sprays from the sand, as a clipper sends up sea spray.

"What is the matter with this place?" Alexander asked Emily, in a whisper.

"You have to have wet sand to make the walls firm," Emily said.

"I could get water from the sea to wet the sand." Alexander held up the bucket, and looked out through the handle at the tempting blue waters with which he would fill it.

"The sea is too far away from here," Emily said.

Alexander put the bucket on his head, tilted it forward, and put the handle under his chin as a chin strap.

"If we were playing soldiers," he said, with infinite regret, "I could be the General."

"You know John is always the General," Emily said, scathingly.

Down on the hard, damp, corrugated ripples of the lower shore, John had taken off his coat. Emily sat down with her legs spread out. Alexander sat on his upturned bucket. For a time John dug in the sand silently, mounting it high. Then he looked up and glanced around at the shell-strewn shore.

"Get me an oyster shell, Emily," he ordered.

Emily poked Alexander in the ribs.

"Get him an oyster shell," she said, pointing to the cockle beds that were rippling with shallow water, blown by the wind. Alexander sped for the shallows. The other two watched him as he went, and listened with satisfaction to the flat flapping sound that his feet made as he ran through the waters of the cockle stream and reached the far side where shells littered the sand. In a few minutes they saw him bend and pick up something, and then they saw him turn and run back across the flat and empty beach, starting a flurry among the feeding gulls and splashing water up each side of himself.

"Is this right?" he shouted, holding up a great shell.

John put out his hand and took the shell without speaking.

"Do you want anything else?" said Alexander, panting.

John did not hear him.

Alexander turned to Emily. "Will I get another shell for him?" he asked, politely.

But Emily was sitting with her legs spread out wide, and she was absorbed in the task of taking a lollipop out of her pocket. She had run into difficulty because the lollipop had melted and become somewhat stuck to the inside of her pocket. She did not answer. Alexander, however, had forgotten his question in the intensity of watching for the lollipop to emerge. His eyes opened wider and wider. As the lollipop came unstuck at last, he clapped his hands.

"Can I have a lick?"

Emily took a long steady lick of the lollipop and said nothing.

"Just one lick?" said Alexander.

"Go away," Emily said, taking two short licks and one long, defiant one.

"Please!" Alexander said humbly.

"Don't bother me!" said Emily. "Go away!" and she took up a fistful of sand and threw it at the pleading Alexander. Alexander pursed his lips. He made a dive upon the sand to gather a fistful of retaliation, when a more effective method of achieving his object occurred to him. He glanced up at the dunes to see that the setting was right, and seeing, as he had hoped, that Nurse was sitting there, within earshot under her striped sunshade, he threw back his head, and putting his hands to his face, gave a long, thin, penetrating wail of anguish.

"There's sand in my eye!" he wailed. "Oh, oh! there's sand in my eye. I'm blinded." And he began to stagger, very blindly, up the beach.

"Come back, Alexander," Emily said urgently, and she pulled John by the sleeve. "What will I do?" she said. "He'll tell Nurse that I threw it at him."

"You did!" John said, without looking up.

"We'll be kept in after tea!" Emily warned.

John looked up. "Give him the lollipop," he directed. "That's what he wants."

Alexander had paused momentarily in his blind stagger forward, and his wailing had grown less loud because it interfered somewhat with his hearing. When Emily made no move to give him the lollipop, however, he set off once more and threw back his head with a view to louder wailing.

"Alexander." Emily stood up. "Alexander," she called, running after him. "Will you stop crying if I give you my lollipop?"

Alexander turned around slowly, and came back with his tear-wet hand outstretched. He took the lollipop and sat down on the sand. Emily sat with her back to him. John resumed his work.

"I am going to dig the moat now," John said after a while, and he began to dig around the castle with both hands, throwing up the sand on all sides.

Wildly the sand rose in the air. Lightly it floated downward again. It lay like a fine mist of rain on Emily's bright hair. And it drifted all over Alexander, but he sat in beatific unconcern of it, although the fastly falling grains settled upon the sticky lollipop and impeded the progress of his bright, industrious tongue, that licked and licked and licked.

"This will be the best castle that was ever built," John declared, and he wiped his hand across his mouth, leaving a whisker of sand upon his chin.

"Oh, look," Alexander said. "John has a beard. John has a beard."

And throwing away the lollipop stick, clean as if it had been licked
by the briny tongues of the sea, he lifted a fistful of sand and began
to decorate his own sticky chin with blond whiskers.

"Stop that," said John, "we have no time to waste." He picked
up Alexander's bucket where it lay on its side forgotten, and put it
into Alexander's hand. "Get me water for the moat," he said.

"The bucket is leaking," Emily said, disparagingly.

"He can run quick, so the water won't have time to leak out,"
said John.

Alexander ran off like mad toward the thin sea waves, with his
battered bucket swinging in his hand. Every time he let it down
to chase a sea gull, or to poke his finger into a pool, John called
out to him, and the sea birds rose in a flurry, and he picked up the
battered bucket again and ran toward the waves with fresh vigor.

In a short while he was racing back, with all the fury of a full-
blown wave racing for the shore.

"Is it spilling? Is it spilling?" he shouted, as he ran, not daring to
take time to look behind him.

"Hurry! Hurry!" John and Emily shouted together, and they
stood up and cheered him, as he dashed through the last cockle stream
an inch ahead of the racing drops of water that seemed to be chas-
ing him like a swarm of silver bees.

John rushed forward and caught the bucket from him and dashed
the remaining water into the moat. Triumphantly the three of them
flung themselves face-down on the sand and leaned over the edge of
the moat to gaze with pride and admiration. But in a few minutes
the water had stolen out of sight between the grains of sand, and
soon there were defiant gleams of granite as the sand dried out again
to a pale silver color. Then there was nothing left of the perilous
water but a few iridescent bubbles.

"The water is gone!" Alexander said, and the statement of this
truth seemed to be more bitter than the truth itself, for the tears
welled into his eyes.

"What will we do?" said John, looking at Emily.

"We'll think of something," said Emily, and she got down on her
knees and inspected the bottom of the moat. "Perhaps, if we put
stones along the bottom it might keep the water from leaking away."

Alexander got up and moved a bit away. He sat down on his hunkers and began to root in his pockets. After a minute he produced a ball of silver paper, and began to tear off pieces of the thin tinfoil and lay them along the bottom of the moat.

"Look at the water!" he said, pulling Emily by the sleeve.

"It's just like water," said John, and he got down on his knees. "Give me some, Alexander," he said. "It's just as good as water. You'd think it was water," and he began to line the moat upon the opposite side from Alexander until the whole circle of the dike around the castle shone with fake silver water.

So, gradually, although at first he wanted to work at the castle alone, John allowed the others to offer suggestions and give him help. When the artist first begins to shape his creation he is filled with a pride in himself and cannot bear to think that any hand but his could shape the perfection of the dream behind his brain, but as the dream emerges into a tangible form his selfish pride in his own power fades before a pure, unselfish pride in the thing he has created. Then he is willing and anxious to accept help from others, and is even ready, if necessary, to make the tragic abnegation of abandoning his task to other hands if those hands seem better fitted than his own to consummate the task.

Emily pinned back her hair. Alexander took off his shoes. Sitting with their legs spread out, all three of them worked without talking. They patted and dug, they mounded the sand, they smoothed it, and they piled it high. And soon a noble castle, with a noble crenelated tower, rose out of the sand and stood between them and the sun. It rose so high, so proud, so tall, that it cast a deep blue shadow on the pale sand.

"What kind of doors will we have?" said John. "We could have real wood for doors."

"We could have real glass in the windows," said Emily.

"I'll get the wood," said Alexander. "I'll get the glass." And he ran up to a bank of seaweed, higher up on the shore, where broken china, bits of glass, splinters of driftwood, tin, pearl buttons, shells, and empty bottles were tangled in the mesh of seaweed. He ran back with his arms filled and let fall a glittering cascade of treassures.

John began to pick out suitable pieces of glass, but all at once Emily clapped her hands. "I have an idea," she said. "We could have real doors and windows; that you could see through!" And picking up a shell she began to dig a hole in the side of the sturdy wall.

"Be careful," warned John. But the idea gripped him, and picking up another shell he began to tunnel into the castle upon the opposite side from Emily. "Be careful," he called out, from time to time. "We are nearly meeting!" And indeed, even as he spoke he felt something alive stirring within the castle, and a minute later he felt Emily's hot fingers underneath his own.

"Hurrah!" said John, and throwing himself on his face he peered into the tunnel. "Can you see me?" he yelled in delight as he caught sight of Emily's blue eyes at the other end.

"Can you see me?" screamed Emily.

Alexander jumped up and down. "Can I have a look? Can I have a look?" he yelled, but without much hope of being heard. All the same he continued to jump up and down.

When at last the furious ecstasy of creation had wasted his strength John sat back and drew a deep breath of renewal.

"What do you think of it, Alexander?" he asked patronizingly.

But Alexander was speechless. He jumped up and down more furiously, and all he could say, as he stared at the castle, was "Gosh." "Gosh," cried Alexander. "Gosh! Gosh! Gosh!"

But as Alexander said "Gosh," a faint voice in his ears whispered it back again, slyly. "Gosh."

Alexander stopped jumping up and down. Emily and John stared at him suspiciously.

"Gosh," said Alexander, once more, bravely, but while he spoke he put out a hand, edging near to Emily, and caught at her skirt. "Gosh," said the small white voice behind him, "Gosh, gosh, gosh."

They all swung around, with their lips apart, their hands groping out for each other. There, at their feet, were the thin white lips of the cold sea waves, saying over and over again, without even waiting, now, for Alexander, "Gosh — " and then, "Gosh." "Gosh — " and then, "Gosh — "

John looked at Alexander; Alexander's ears were sticking out with excitement. His chin was pulled in tight. He was staring at the waves, mesmerized with their words. The castle was forgotten behind him. But when John looked at Emily her lips were pressed tightly together. John pressed his own lips together. Stronger than the bitter odor of the sour seawater that stole into his nostrils was the first bitter foretaste of human impotence. "What will we do?" he cried. "Our castle will be destroyed!" But as he spoke a combative spirit woke within him. "We will fight back the sea!" he cried. "We will rout the enemy. Arm yourselves, my men! Arm yourselves." And taking up stones he led his men. "I am the king of the castle!" he cried.

Missile after missile was hurled into the water, breaking the faces of the pale waves but unable to silence their chuckles of triumph or stem their relentless advance. The green regiment outnumbered even the stones on the shore, and soon the defenders had to lay down arms as the castle keep began to collapse with a slow sliding of grain after grain.

Big tears ran down Alexander's red cheeks. But Emily's eyes were dry, and they seemed to have taken on the agate color of the sea.

"There is one thing we can do!" she said, and she bit her lip and looked at the castle. She turned around and looked at the boys. "I am queen of the castle!" she said, then in a loud voice, and raising her arms like a bird lifting his wings for flight, she leapt into the air, and landed with both feet upon the crenelated tower. The castle crumbled around her feet.

Her feet sank into streaming sand. She raised them heavily, one after another, and rivers of sand ran lightly over the white knobs of her ankles. Her dress belled out like a tulip. Her bright hair blazed. "Now you can't have our castle!" she cried to the greedy reaching waves.

Uncomprehendingly, John and Alexander looked on for a moment. Then they, too, ran forward and, jumping into the air, landed upon the castle with a shout, and began to leap up and down. "Gosh!" said Alexander. "Gosh! Isn't this great? Isn't this the best game ever?"

They jumped and jumped, all three of them, while the waters stole around their feet, with swirling foam, and writhing seaweed, and millions of grains of sand restlessly traveling.

And soon they forgot the reason why they were jumping and they began to see who could jump the highest, and who could make the biggest splashes in the rising water. And as they rose up and down, in their hearts also there rose and broke, and rose again, and broke, the silent waves of a wild intuition that was carrying them forward, nearer and nearer to the shores of adult knowledge — those bright shores of silt.

THE SMALL BEQUEST

IT WAS GENERALLY UNDERSTOOD that when Miss Tate died she would leave a small bequest to her companion, Miss Blodgett. There had never been any direct statement of the old lady's intention in the matter, but it was felt by all their friends to be an understood thing. Meanwhile, of course, Miss Blodgett was getting an excellent salary, most of which she should have been able to put aside, for not only was her keep provided but, as well as sharing the necessaries of life with Miss Tate, she had full enjoyment of all the luxuries that the Tate family were continually bestowing upon the old lady: the sweets, the fruits, the books, the papers. For Miss Tate, at eighty, was able only to appreciate the kind thought of the giver; the bodily appreciation of the gifts fell entirely to Miss Blodgett. As she herself often remarked, Miss Blodgett was just like one of the family. And indeed it was as such she was always treated.

The Tates felt themselves greatly in Miss Blodgett's debt for her tireless devotion to Miss Adeline Tate. It was now twenty-seven years since Miss Blodgett had moved into the elegant house in Clyde Road, with her big wicker suitcase and her tin trunk. They didn't know what Miss Adeline Tate would have done without her. Lord Robert, Miss Tate's oldest nephew, expressed the feelings of the whole family one evening after a visit to Clyde Road.

"What a good job it is," said Lord Robert, "that Miss Blodgett is only sixty. She's fairly sure of outlasting Aunt Adeline."

There had been a large family gathering in Clyde Road that afternoon, and some of the family were dining that night with Lord

THE SMALL BEQUEST　　　　　215

Robert. They all agreed with their host except Honor Tate, his
first cousin, who, being a lady barrister, felt compelled to point
out that then, instead of Miss Tate, they would have Miss Blodgett
on their hands.

"Oh, not at all!" said Lord Robert impatiently. "Aunt Adeline
will see that Miss Blodgett is well taken care of after her death."

"How?" asked Lucy Tate, Lord Robert's youngest daughter.

"Don't be silly, Lucy dear," said her father. "You know it is
understood that Aunt Adeline will make a substantial mention of
Miss Blodgett in her will."

"Oh, of course," Lucy was abashed. She blushed. "I forgot!
The bequest!" She recalled at once that she had often heard her
aunts and uncles mention Miss Blodgett's small bequest. "Dear Aunt
Adeline!" she murmured.

Miss Tate of course was not Lucy's aunt at all. Miss Tate was her
grand-aunt, but like all the younger members of the family she had
grown into the habit of calling the old lady by the name she'd heard
on the lips of her elders. Miss Tate was Aunt Adeline to all of them.
They never called her anything else.

It was quite disconcerting at times to hear some of the extremely
young members of the family calling the old lady by such a familiar
name. But it was even more disconcerting to hear Miss Blodgett
calling all the family by their familiar names, although perhaps it
was natural enough for her to do so, considering that she had known
them all since they were in their cradles, and had dandled most of
them on her knee with as much affection, and a great deal more
energy, than Miss Tate had ever done. Sometimes, indeed, it seemed
as if Emma Blodgett had never noticed that they had grown up,
and in some cases, even grown old. Lord Robert was always Robbie
to Miss Blodgett. The caustic Honor was still Honey. And I never
heard her call Lady Elizabeth Tate-Conyers anything else but
Bessie.

The Tates were an old family that went back for nine recorded
generations of plain but prosperous people, who had, however,
linked themselves all along the way with the best stock in the
country. The root was a plain and sturdy natural growth, but suc-
cessful grafting had resulted in the frequent breaking out of blos-

som. The family had rarely failed in any decade to show a famous belle, a great soldier, or a poet. When Miss Tate's nephews, nieces, grand-nephews, grand-nieces, and great-grand-nephews came to pay their respects to her on a Sunday afternoon, the drawing room in Clyde Road was filled with a gallant company, of which the old lady might well be proud.

And Miss Tate was extremely proud of them all. So, too, was Miss Blodgett. Although, here again, when one heard Miss Blodgett familiarly chaffing with judges and peers, and scolding a bishop for having snuff on his cuff, it was a little surprising to recollect that she had originally joined the Tate household in a humble capacity.

The only trace that still remained to indicate Miss Blodgett's original position in the family was that Miss Blodgett herself was never called by her Christian name. Miss Tate was the only one who called her Emma. The others delicately shrank from doing so in case it might seem to be taking advantage of her dependence. They felt it better to emphasize the difference between her and Hetty. Hetty was Miss Tate's old maid-servant who had been with the family for fifty years. Hetty was a treasure too, but of course she was only a servant.

The first day I moved into the house next door to Miss Tate, I found two visiting cards lying in the empty letterbox. On one neat glossy card was engraved the name of Miss Adeline Tate. On the other card, which was equally neat, equally white, if perhaps a little thinner, a little less glossy, was printed the name of Emma Blodgett in pen and ink.

That afternoon I saw Miss Tate in her garden. It was some few days before I saw Miss Blodgett.

As a matter of fact, I was at first under the mistaken impression that I had seen both Miss Tate and Miss Blodgett, for there were two old ladies in the garden, and the two were dressed remarkably alike. They both wore long blue silk gowns, with tightly clipped bodices and the hems were weighted with rows and rows of heavy braid. Both ladies wore wide and delightfully dilapidated blue straw hats, wreathed — overpowered you might say — with large floppy silk flowers shaded from deep rose to pale pink, which the bees, that clouded around them like halos, must have mistaken for real blooms. It is true that one of the old ladies was extremely elegant,

and that the other was distinctly shabby, her gown having indeed
innumerable patches and darns, but nevertheless I think my mistake
was pardonable. I ought perhaps to have guessed that the old heiress
would give away her worn gowns to her servant, but how on earth
could I have known that Miss Tate's fanatical affection for animals,
birds, insects, and even slugs, was so great that on no account would
she allow old Hetty to come out into the garden in her cap and
apron in case their white glare might startle her beloved pets, the pet
dogs, the tabby cats, and the countless tame pigeons who wandered
about the garden with as much composure as the ladies. Within
doors, with the blue gown hidden under an old-fashioned capacious
apron I would never have mistaken poor old Hetty for Miss Blodgett. Indeed, no two people could have been more dissimilar, although as a matter of fact Hetty and Miss Tate were not too unalike
at all. Both were small and frail, but at the same time agile and keen.
And in Hetty's face, as well as in Miss Tate's, the flesh had thinned
away with the years, and the bone was seen to be fine and well-
chiseled. Miss Tate's face had, of course, the more delicate outline.

It was a pity that Miss Tate had never married. It was a pity she
should have thought fit to discontinue the work of nine generations,
for there could be no doubt, I think, that this charming old figurine
was the result of careful selection and breeding. Yet, it was surprising to see how a generation or two of poverty and privation
could accelerate the pace of bone refinement, too, because there was
undoubtedly something fine and compelling in old Hetty's clear and
angular face. All the same, it was stupid of me to have mistaken
Hetty for Miss Blodgett. And when I saw Miss Blodgett go down
the steps into the garden a few days later, it was immediately clear
that Hetty was the servant.

"Hetty," Miss Blodgett called out, "I forgot my sunshade. Run
into the house and get it for me."

And when Hetty, who had been putting some seedlings into the
ground for Miss Tate, stood up to do the errand, she lowered her
eyes deferentially while Miss Blodgett sailed past.

There could be no mistake this time. This could be no other than
Miss Blodgett. When she got to the end of the garden I was amused
to see her wag her finger at Miss Tate.

"Not so much bending!" she cried. "Not so much bending!"

Then drawing up a garden seat, she called Hetty, who had returned with the sunshade, and sent her into the potting shed for an iron footrest. "The grass is so damp in the garden," she said, as she settled herself plumply down to watch Miss Tate and Hetty continue their work with the seedlings.

Emma Blodgett was a big woman. She had a soft, warm, friendly face; a very nice person, one would say unhesitatingly, but rather dull, perhaps even stupid. She was only about sixty; much younger than Miss Tate, much younger even than Hetty, but less active. Her round plump face was perpetually flushed. She had a mass of gray hair, strong, straight, and unruly. Her figure was stout too, and she had a surprisingly matronly bosom for a spinster of her years.

Miss Blodgett also wore blue. As a matter of fact, she, too, was dressed somewhat similarly to Miss Tate, and yet there was some very great difference which even I, from my study window, could see but could not at once define. First I thought it was a matter of length, for although, like Miss Tate, Miss Blodgett wore her skirts longer than was fashionable, they were not as long as Miss Tate's. Whatever impulse made her disregard fashion had not been as strong as the old lady's, and was probably only imitation of her, for where Miss Tate's long blue hemline hung down to hide her ankles, Miss Blodgett's stopped short a cowardly inch or two farther up from the ground, and revealed a pair of fat ankles with a tendency to swell, and possibly some other weakness as well, because Miss Blodgett wore thick blue woolen stockings even at the hottest time of the year. It was impossible to tell what kind of stockings Miss Tate wore; no one ever saw Miss Tate's little ankles. But to go back to Miss Blodgett's dress again. As I said, I thought at first it differed only in length from Miss Tate's blue gown. Then I thought I detected a slight difference in the shade, and later still I thought it was a matter of age. But I soon dismissed these solutions because Hetty's gown, although tattered and shabby, was in other respects exactly like Miss Tate's new gown. It was not until the first day I went to take tea with the ladies that I discovered the difference between the three blue gowns. It was simply this: that Miss Blodgett's gown did not rustle! You know what that meant. It was blue. It was silky. It was cut to much the same pattern as the gown Miss

Tate wore. But it didn't rustle. In other words, it was not quite the same quality. It was not real silk, not the genuine thing. And of course Miss Blodgett did not realize this at all.

"Look at Miss Tate," she said to me one day after we had become familiar over many cups of tea in their house and in mine. "Look at Miss Tate! She pays twice what I pay for the material in her gowns, and mine is just exactly the same. No one could tell the difference. But the shopkeepers impose on Miss Tate. They know she has plenty of money. They don't impose on me! I'm well able for them!" And having triumphantly said this, Miss Blodgett begged me to have more cake, and as she went over to the table, I heard the slight creak of artificial silk. Whereas a moment later, Miss Tate delicately rustled across the room. And indeed, as my ear caught that rustle, which was as faint as a sigh, at the same time, in the far corner of the room where Hetty was pouring out tea, I caught the sound of another rustle fainter still. If the rustle in Miss Tate's gown was like a sigh, the rustle that came from under Hetty's voluminous white apron was the echo of a sigh.

I became very friendly with the ladies in the house next door, but long before I met them I had become extraordinarily familiar with the sight of Hetty and Miss Tate in the garden.

The gardens of the houses in Clyde Road were large and secluded for city gardens. They were separated from each other by high walls of beautifully cut granite, on which stonecrop and red valerian flowered freely. But from the upper windows of the houses the gardens were not so secluded, and from my study at the back of the house in the second story I could see into every nook and cranny of my neighbors' gardens. The best comment I can make upon Miss Tate's garden is that from the first day I looked down into it I never bothered to look into any other garden. The others, like my own, were plain city gardens, with a plot of grass at the top and a few apple trees at the end. But Miss Tate's garden — well, I was hardly a day in Clyde Road when I realized I would have to change my study to the front of the house if I was ever to do any work. It was the most distracting garden I had ever seen.

In the first place, it was almost entirely given over to the old lady's pets, and everywhere on the small plot of lawn near the house, upon the grass and upon the green metal seats, and even raised on specially constructed standards, there were bowls of water of all shapes and sizes, wide and narrow, deep and shallow, to facilitate the different needs of bird and beast and butterfly. And although to either side of the grass plot there were small flower-beds, in them there bloomed only a few of those fragrant old flowers that were fashionable when Miss Tate was a girl: musk roses, heliotrope, lavender, and clove carnations, and a few other flowers of unpretentious aspect, whose names I did not know, but which I afterwards found out were grown specially for the bees and the butterflies. There were no vegetables, unless you count a giant clump of catmint in the corner under my window which was grown specially for the tabby cats.

This grass plot with its border of flowers was, however, only one small fraction of the garden. The rest was planted with small flowering trees in which the birds and bees kept up a continual orchestration, the bees and pigeons supplying the bass, the blackbirds and thrushes breaking in with high trebles. These flowering trees, although fully matured, were of such a nature that, although as old as Miss Tate, they were, like her, frail and delicate even in their age. And in comparison with the plain old trees in the public park beyond the lane at the back of our gardens, they looked like mere branches stuck into the ground and tied all over with paper flowers, some pink, some yellow, some blue.

Viewed from my study window, indeed, the whole of Miss Tate's garden looked as unreal but as entrancing as the miniature Japanese gardens that children used to construct long ago in shallow saucers, which, when made, tantalized them with a longing to be small enough to wander in them.

Watching Miss Tate and Hetty down in their dreamy unreal garden, under the small flowering trees, I was often tantalized myself with a desire to close up my books and join them under those bloom-laden branches that seemed to be continually shedding either petals or fragrance, or fragments of birdsong.

It was at night, however, that Miss Tate's garden was most tantalizingly beautiful. Then, the moon shone down in misty brightness over it, leaving the dark depths undisturbed and mysterious as the

cold sea, but washing the tops of the small trees with light, and striking gleams from the glossy leaves as gleams are struck from the
pointed wave. And in the middle of this misty moonlit sea the small
white-painted glasshouse with its pointed roof seemed to float
through the night like a silver bark of romance.

If ever a house was a harbor of happiness, it ought surely to have
been the house looking over that blossom-tossed garden. Yet, the
first day I ever set foot in it, I felt there was something wrong.
There was some uneasiness in the air. There was some slight strain
between Miss Tate and Miss Blodgett. But what it could be was
impossible to imagine, for seldom had two people more to give each
other. On the one hand Miss Tate gave Miss Blodgett not only a
home but a beautiful one, not only a salary but a bountiful one.
And last, although not least, there was this understanding about the
small bequest. Miss Blodgett, on the other hand, was a perfect companion for Miss Tate. She not only ran the house, and supervised
Hetty, but she had, it appeared, no friends or relatives at all of her
own, and so even such time as she was supposed to have free for her
own purposes was lavished also on Miss Tate, and occupied in doing
errands and messages for her in town. In short, Miss Tate gave Miss
Blodgett a share in everything she possessed and made no distinction
whatsoever between them, and Miss Blodgett, although she could
only give Miss Tate her time and her interest and her care, gave
them without stint and kept back not one morsel for herself.

Yet I felt there was something uneasy in their relationship. I felt
it instinctively on the first day I took tea with the ladies, although
I could not name it nor trace it to any cause. And when I became a
habitual visitor in the house next door, never a visit passed, however
happily and pleasantly, without my getting at some time or another
this feeling that all was not well. At some time or another I would
see a little arrow in Miss Tate's blue eyes, and something sharp
would shoot across the room. At first I merely felt a vibration in the
air. But one day I actually saw it flash out; a little arrow of dissatisfaction. I saw it flash out, yes, but I was no wiser afterwards. I still
could see no cause for Miss Tate's sharpness. And when, afterwards, I pieced together the conversation of that visit, a more in-
nocuous conversation could not be imagined. There wasn't a single

remark that could have rasped anyone's nerves as far as I could see. And Miss Blodgett, who was helping Miss Tate to pick up a dropped stitch, had contributed to it only by smiles and nods or at most, I am almost sure, a single remark. Yet it was at Miss Blodgett that the arrow had been aimed.

There was only one child to tea that day: Honor's eldest girl, Martha, one of the quietest of the family, a bit dull you might even say. Whenever Martha was there the conversation was always somewhat slow. The two ladies knitted, and the talk never ventured far beyond worsted and yarn. It is hard to recall an insipid conversation. But I took pains to recall every word in order to see why that little arrow had been sped from the bow.

Tea was over and Hetty was clearing the cups away.

"That's pretty wool, Aunt Adeline," Martha said, looking at the candy pink wool that Miss Tate was knitting.

"You saw it the last time you were here," said Miss Tate.

"Did I? Are you sure, Aunt Adeline? I thought you were knitting something with blue wool the last time."

"It's two years since I knitted anything blue," Miss Tate said. "The last thing I knitted in blue wool was a scarf for your brother Edward."

"Oh, but this was only the other day, Aunt Adeline," said poor Martha, "and it wasn't a scarf for Edward, it was a shawl for Miriam's child."

Miss Tate looked up. So did Miss Blodgett.

"This is the same shawl," the two ladies said, speaking at the same time, and then Miss Tate said that she had been working at it for at least six weeks. "I'll never make a shawl again," she said; "it's so tiresome."

Poor Martha put out her hand and drew over a corner of the pink knitted shawl.

"Such an intricate pattern!" she said to cover her embarrassment. "You have wonderful patience, Aunt Adeline."

At this point — I remember it all exactly — Miss Tate dropped the stitch, and while she and Miss Blodgett were trying to take it up she did not catch Martha's last remark.

"What did you say, Martha dear?" she asked, when the stitch was safe back on the needle again.

"I said you have wonderful patience, Aunt Adeline," poor Martha repeated.

But Aunt Adeline did not hear it the second time either. Now Aunt Adeline was not deaf, but she was decidedly nervous in case she might get deaf, and so, if for any reason she failed to catch something that was said, whether due to a noise in the room or an indistinctness on the part of the person who spoke, or, as in this case, because she just wasn't listening, she always got flurried. The result was that the remark had to be repeated several times after that before she caught it. I often noticed that on such occasions Miss Blodgett was invaluable. She either repeated what had been said calmly and clearly, or better still, she diverted Miss Tate's attention so that she forgot she had missed something. But on this particular occasion when Miss Blodgett came to the rescue, I, in my ignorance, thought it was her interference that annoyed Miss Tate, for it was right after Miss Blodgett spoke that I saw the arrow.

"Martha said you have wonderful patience, Aunt Adeline," Miss Blodgett said kindly. And she was just putting out her hand to re-arrange a cushion that had slipped out of place on Miss Tate's chair when Miss Tate let loose the arrow.

"All old people are patient!" she snapped. "But the Tates were never patient before ninety."

Poor Martha blushed. But it was not at Martha the arrow was aimed. It was at Miss Blodgett. I saw it. I saw it go forth, aimed straight for Miss Blodgett's heart. But somehow it missed. Miss Blodgett sat knitting as placidly as ever, smiling, and nodding her head in rhythm with the clicking needles. Perhaps the arrow had hit and splintered against the large cameo brooch that rose and fell on her big bosom. I don't know. Martha, however, was upset. She had not been quick enough to see the arrow, but she was not dull enough to be unaware that something was amiss. She thought, poor girl, that she was at fault, that she had said something to offend. Her eyes filled with tears.

The minute Miss Tate saw those tears, she understood at once what had happened. I thought I saw her give an angry look at Miss Blodgett's cameo brooch. Then she turned around with a gracious smile to Martha.

"Come, we will go into the garden, Martha my dear," she said.

"Give me your arm. I must get a rose for my favorite grand-niece." The old lady was her gracious, sweet self again. Over me, too, she shed her graciousness. "Will you come with us," she asked, turning toward me, "and I'll get one for you too." But at the door she paused. "Martha, like all the Tates, loves flowers," she said. Turning around again sharply she nodded at Miss Blodgett who had gone over to the window and was sitting with her back to it. "Miss Blodgett wouldn't know a rose from a cauliflower," she said. And in an instant another little arrow went through the air.

But Miss Blodgett smiled. Miss Blodgett had not felt any prick this time, either. Before she turned around to answer I saw that her dress was fastened up the back with a row of little pearl buttons. I was not near enough to see if one of them was scratched or broken, but I think it could hardly have been otherwise.

Miss Blodgett noticed nothing.

"Oh I don't mind gardens," she said complacently, "but there are so many unpleasant things in a garden, bees and wasps, and ants and slugs. I'm quite satisfied to sit here at the window and get the sun through the glass." Smiling benignly, she went on with her knitting.

Miss Tate took Martha's arm, then mine, and we went out gossiping lightly. As if to make up to her, she was making an unusual fuss over the girl all the time, picking her the best and most beautiful roses, and several times asking me if I saw any likeness between them.

She insisted on giving me a bouquet too, and as she pressed the bunch of red roses into my hand I felt that this charming old lady may have known that I saw that arrow speeding through the air, and wanted to divert my mind from what I had seen. In fact, when I was leaving, she kept me standing at the small green gate at the end of the garden telling me how good Miss Blodgett was to her, and how much she was indebted to her dear companion.

"She has a kind heart. Not like the Tates. The Tates all have a bitter streak in them." She smiled at me then, and she smiled at Martha. But unfortunately Martha protested.

"Oh, Aunt Adeline! you're very naughty! Such a thing to say about us!" the poor girl said. She was destined to be the cause of more trouble, for just then Miss Blodgett came to the steps leading down to the garden and overhearing Martha's remark, she smiled at her with her wide benevolent smile.

"Did I hear you say Aunt Adeline was naughty, Martha?" she asked, and then before she said another word, there in the brilliant sunny air, with the birds singing and the bees humming as they went from flower to flower, Miss Tate let fly a third and dreadfully sharp arrow.

What was the meaning of it at all? I hugged my roses tightly, said goodbye, and went into my own garden greatly perplexed.

After that I saw the arrow several times, but only when I was near at hand.

At other times I would sit in my window and look down at Miss Tate and Hetty in the garden and think how gentle and sweet Miss Tate looked. And even when Miss Blodgett came out, and the two of them took tea together under the trees, they presented a charming picture of peace, tranquility, and sweetness. They would sip tea, the two of them, and Miss Tate would perhaps call Hetty and pour a cup of tea for her, and insist on the old servant drinking it there and then, standing beside them at the tea table with perhaps one of the lap dogs she had been combing caught up under her arm, or a bundle of weeds that she was going to burn at the bottom of the plot. On those occasions I saw no arrows.

Yet as surely as I went to tea with the ladies, at some point in the afternoon an arrow would pierce the air, and make straight for Miss Blodgett's heart.

I pondered a great deal over the whole thing. At first I thought there was some deep and serious reason for Miss Tate's antagonism to Emma Blodgett. Then a small incident occurred to make me veer around to quite the opposite opinion, and decide it was something very trivial that was getting on the old lady's nerves. Another case of the Princess and the Pea.

Then one afternoon when I had not called on the ladies for some days, I went to their garden gate and pushed it open to pay them a short visit. They were going to take tea in the garden, and Hetty had just laid the tray on the wicker garden table. When I walked across the grass the old ladies were pulling up their chairs to the

table, and Miss Blodgett had just relieved Miss Tate of a large catalogue at which they had both been looking. She threw it down on
the grass underneath the table.

"Hetty, another cup," Miss Blodgett called out, and Miss Tate put
one of the tabby cats down from its chair and invited me to take its
place. Then as Hetty brought out a cup and turned to go back into
the house, Miss Tate called her back.

"Hetty," she said, "will you please put on your hat and coat and
go down to the hospital to ask how Mr. Robbie's baby is getting on
today."

"Is the baby sick?" I cried. "In hospital, did you say?"

Lord Robert's son and namesake, young Robbie, had recently
married, and there had been great excitement at the birth of his first
son, Lord Robert's grandson, and another great-grand-nephew for
Miss Adeline Tate. I was sorry to hear the infant was not doing well.

"The doctor says it won't live," Miss Tate said, when I begged her
to tell me what was the matter with him. "There's something wrong
with its spine. It was weakly from the start."

Miss Blodgett sighed sadly.

"Oh, dear," I said. I felt uncomfortable, and rose from my chair.
"Perhaps if I hadn't come you would be going to the hospital,"
I said. "Please don't let me intrude. I only called for a minute.
I'll call again another day."

But the ladies excelled each other in assuring me that I must on
no account leave. Miss Blodgett rose to press me down into my
chair again, while Miss Tate insisted over and over again that a few
minutes before I appeared they were planning to send Hetty out
with a note asking me to call.

"Because we just got a present of some rose geranium jelly that
we want you to sample with us," Miss Tate said. "Sit down! Sit
down!" And Miss Blodgett poured out three cups of tea and took
the cover from the geranium jelly that its fragrance might tempt me
to stay.

I stayed. But I was uneasy waiting for Hetty to come back. She
was a long time away. In fact, she did not come back until I was
just leaving. I was letting myself out by the front door when I met
her in the hall.

I looked inquiringly at her. "Is he better?" I asked eagerly.

Hetty was calm. "No," she said, "he's dead. But it was a good job I went up there." Then with a remarkable compromise between deference and impatience, she prepared to pass me. "I must tell Miss Tate," she said.

I was confused. I tried to detain her. Surely she was not going to rush into the garden and blurt out the news like that? So bluntly?

"Hetty, wait," I cried. "Are you going to tell them at once?"

Hetty looked surprised. "What else would I do?"

"Don't you think you should wait a little while, and break it more gently to them?" I stumbled with my words. Had Hetty no sense? Couldn't she see what I meant? "If you said he was worse at first, and then later on suggested he wasn't expected to live, then perhaps they might be prepared for the shock and you could tell them the truth?"

But Hetty stared at me.

"What about the wreath?" she asked.

"The wreath?" I repeated.

Hetty looked at me impatiently. "Miss Tate will want to order it at once. She'll want time to decide what flowers to have put in it. She'd be most annoyed if she wasn't told in good time." Then, taking into consideration that I was, after all, a comparative stranger, the old servant paused to give me an explanation. "Miss Tate always sends a magnificent wreath to all funerals within the family," she said.

And with this Hetty hurried away. I stood uncertainly looking after her. I saw her run down the steps into the garden. I saw her go across the grass and I saw the ladies look up expectantly. I saw Hetty say something to them and I waited, holding my breath. In spite of what Hetty had said, I felt I might be needed. And I was on the point of going back to the garden, when I saw the two ladies rise excitedly to their feet. And in the soft, summer air Miss Tate's voice carried in to me distinctly.

"The wreath! Quick! Where is the catalogue?" she cried. And hastily pushing aside the tea table Miss Blodgett picked up the catalogue from the grass; the catalogue that they had been scanning when I went in. It was a florists' catalogue, and even from a distance I could see the illustrations of wreaths and artificial bouquets, flowering crosses, and glass-domed immortelles. "Give it to me," said Miss Tate, putting on her glasses and stretching out her hand.

"Wait a minute," said Miss Blodgett, withholding it. "We marked a pretty one, don't you remember?"

I didn't wait to hear any more. I could see why it had not occurred to Hetty to break the news gently. The ladies had long since passed into that time of life when they were no longer capable of feeling the great emotions. Like children, their joys and sorrows were as real as other people's, but arose from smaller things.

I stood looking at them in their sunny garden for a few minutes longer, and as I did it occurred to me that whatever discord was between them, it must have sprung from something trivial. I decided to put them out of my mind, and not to let the matter bother me further.

This, however, it was impossible to do for long. I never went into the house next door without feeling the familiar quiver in the air. The room might be filled with nieces and nephews. The talk might be gay and general and happy. But at some time or another, I would see the little arrow in Miss Tate's eye. And at the most unexpected moment she would let it fly. Perhaps one of the young people would say something to her across the room, and Miss Tate, talking to another member of the family, would not hear.

"Aunt Adeline!" the young thing would call out again; and then Miss Blodgett would step in.

"Aunt Adeline! Aunt Adeline! Lucy is calling you."

Miss Tate would look up. She never failed to hear Miss Blodgett. And inexplicably then, she would let fly the dart.

"I hear! I hear!" Miss Tate would say. "It's nothing important, I suppose!" and she would glance very fiercely at Miss Blodgett. But to the young thing who had called her she would cross the room courteously and, sitting down beside her, she would listen to all she had to say.

This, as a matter of fact, was a common scene. But one day when the drawing room was crowded with a great many Tates, and their husbands and wives, their children and their betrotheds, there was a slight difference in the atmosphere. This time Lucy called out to her grand-aunt and Miss Blodgett drew Miss Tate's attention to her. But Miss Tate, who had been sitting beside me, stood up, and so fierce a light was shining in her eyes I positively trembled. I felt she was going to let loose a whole quiverful of arrows.

"Aunt Adeline! Lucy is calling you." That was all Miss Blodgett had said; but Miss Tate turned to Lucy, and spoke quite crossly.

"I can't come now," she said, and she nodded to indicate me, as I sat behind her on the sofa. "I just promised our neighbor here that I would show her the family photographs."

I felt more uneasy than ever. This was the first I had heard of the promise. I saw, too, that Lucy was crestfallen at the snub. But Miss Tate was inexorable. She moved over to the mantelpiece on which there were set out anything from twenty to thirty photographs in silver and filigree frames, showing a bewildering array of ladies and young girls, babies and young men, men with great impressive beards and men so beardless they were like girls. There were small girls in frilly dresses and little boys in sailor suits. There were brides without number, in silks and lace. There were at least six men in uniform. There was Lord Robert in his wig, Lucy in a ball dress, Honor in her college gown — but it would have been simpler to say who was absent than who was present in that crowded gallery on the mantelpiece. Miss Tate beckoned me to follow her and took up the frame nearest to hand.

"This was my mother," she said, pushing the silver frame into my hand. But I had hardly time to glance at it when it was snatched away and another was pushed into my hand. "That was my grand-uncle," she said. "He would be the children's great-great-grand-uncle." Then she snatched back the great-grand-uncle. "This is a nephew," she said. "He was killed playing polo." One after another, she rammed the silver frames into my hands, and snatched them away again almost as quickly, so that I had hardly time to do more than glimpse the broadest details of them. At first I strove to keep pace with her; tried to exclaim that the old ladies were charming, the young officers handsome, and the soldiers fearless and brave. But as frame after frame was rammed into my hands and snatched away again, I became aware that behind this plan of showing me the photographs there was some hidden motive.

At last she came to the end of them.

"Well?" she said in a loud voice, and I saw her look around the room. She wanted everyone to hear. "Well?" she said. "What do you think of that for a family?"

"They all have remarkably fine faces," I said, awkwardly. It was true. But I felt embarrassed saying it out loud.

"But didn't you notice anything?" Miss Tate asked. I knew then that it was not my comment she wanted but an opportunity to make one of her own. "Didn't you notice how strong the likeness is all down the line?" She turned back and took down the great-grand-uncle again. "The Tates all had aquiline noses. The dead Tates had them. The living Tates have them." I looked around nervously, and true enough, although I had not noticed it before, there was a large number of noses in the room, and they were all aquiline. But just then Miss Tate snatched up another frame. "Look at great-uncle Samuel's nose!" She snatched up another. And another. "Look at this nose. Look at that nose!" Then, putting down the last frame so carelessly that the young man in uniform who was looking out from it over his aquiline nose fell flat on his face on the marble slab, Miss Tate held up her little head. "Look at my nose!" she said triumphantly. Then in still a louder, clearer voice, that had by now caught the attention of the whole room, she repeated her first statement. "Yes, the Tates all have aquiline noses. And the men are all tall, and the women are all small. And" — here Miss Tate drew a deep breath — "we were always noted for our ankles." She turned swiftly to Lucy. "Look at Lucy," she said. "Pull up your skirt, Lucy, and show your ankles." She turned to Martha. "Look at Martha!" she said. "Martha, my dear, why do you wear such dark stockings? It's a shame. Dark stockings are all right for women with ugly legs." And then, to my astonishment, Miss Tate's little hand swooped down and lifted the hem of her own blue gown. "In my day," she said, "we might as well have had no legs at all, but I have the Tate ankles, too. Noses and ankles: that's how you can always tell the Tates!"

And then, deliberately, Miss Tate turned and looked at Miss Blodgett, and distinctly, as on the other occasions, I saw it flash out, the glance of hatred. And where did it fly? It flew straight for Miss Blodgett where nearby she sat smiling complacently upon all the company. And it was aimed, of all places, at a point just below the hemline of the gown of imitation silk where Emma's fat ankles were comfortably crossed one over the other in their thick-ribbed, woolen stockings.

All at once I understood.

And I think that Lucy, who was a sensitive girl, must have understood too, for she gave an embarrassed laugh.

"You're as vain as a young girl, Aunt Adeline," she said.

But Miss Blodgett did not betray the slightest upset. As a matter of fact, she laughed heartily.

"That's good! Did you hear what Lucy said?" she cried, poking Miss Tate with the end of her knitting needle. "You're as vain as a girl, Aunt Adeline."

Aunt Adeline!

There they were, the simple words that had occurred in all the simple sentences I had analyzed so unsuccessfully in my effort to find out what was poisoning Miss Tate against Miss Blodgett.

Aunt Adeline. Aunt Adeline. I recalled at once that these words had occurred on every occasion just before the venomed arrow was let fly. Everything that Miss Tate possessed in the world was at the disposal of Miss Blodgett, except one thing — the family blood. Miss Blodgett had no drop of it and without it, and without the Tate nose and the Tate ankles, she was guilty of a grievous lapse every time she called Miss Tate by the familiar name reserved for the use of the Lucys and the Robbies.

I felt a pang of apprehension. I recalled the gossip I had heard about the small bequest. What if Miss Blodgett should jeopardize her chance of it? What if she should forfeit it?

I positively trembled. Why, Miss Blodgett, according to herself, was so much a part of the Tate family that most of her salary, lavish as it was, went in buying wool for the bonnets and shawls she was continually knitting for the Tate progeny and in small but frequent purchases of confetti and ribbons and good luck tokens for the numerous Tate brides. Why! I thought in panic, what a lot of money she must have spent if it was on nothing more than wreaths for the Tate corpses. Miss Blodgett could hardly have saved a penny. She would be absolutely dependent on that small bequest.

Really, I felt so bad I took my leave shortly afterwards. And all that week the affair preyed on my mind. I began to dread going into that house. For every time that Miss Blodgett addressed Miss Tate as Aunt Adeline, I felt my heart freeze. Every time she said it I felt the small bequest was more and more in jeopardy.

And so, when at the end of the summer I was about to leave for West Ireland as was my custom, I felt a certain relief as I said goodbye to the ladies. They came to the door to wave me out of sight. They seemed sorry to part with me. And Miss Blodgett had tears in her eyes. As I went down the steps from the hall door she linked her arm in Miss Tate's arm and called out after me.

"Aunt Adeline will miss you. Won't you, Aunt Adeline?"

Those were her last words to me before I set out. I didn't dare turn around. I simply could not bear to see the look in Miss Tate's eyes.

The following spring when I came back, the house next door was boarded up for sale. A few forlorn pigeons hovered uncertainly on the eave shoot. A stray cat or two slunk in and out between the railings. These of course were not the regular pets that belonged to the house, but it was clear they had had claims on its hospitality and could not realize their claims had ceased.

Miss Tate was dead.

There was no sign whatever of Miss Blodgett.

However, about a week after my return, as I was walking into town, I took a shortcut through one of those dreary intermediary streets that lie between the business section and the residential areas like Clyde Road, but which have not yet degenerated into slums. Here fine old houses that had once been fashionable residences stood forlorn, bereft of their elegant curtains, their gay window boxes, and elaborate brass knockers now painted to save labor. The particular street through which I passed had been saved from complete degeneration by reason of the fact that several of the houses had been turned into offices and service flats, and the few that had remained in private hands had been retained by their owners at the cost of turning them into respectable boardinghouses.

And coming down the steps of one of the most precarious and ramshackle of these boardinghouses, who should I see but Emma Blodgett.

Dear Miss Blodgett! How glad I was to see her! I waved to her, and hurried across the street with hands outstretched. But even before I reached the other side I saw with a sinking of the heart that, although only a few short months had passed since I had last seen her, Miss Blodgett was decidedly shabbier in her appearance. Her clothes were as clean and neat as ever; but she no longer had that sheltered look that all Miss Tate's household had had last summer, from Miss Tate herself down even to the sleek cats and the fat pigeons. Indeed, Miss Blodgett, at that moment, reminded me of the poor perplexed pigeons that I had seen clinging to the eaves in the empty house in Clyde Road.

Of course I did not pretend to notice any change, but I felt dreadfully upset about the poor thing, and feared that my worst forebodings about the bequest had been true. And yet somehow it did not seem like Miss Tate, dead or alive, to break her promise. I found it hard to see how she could have omitted Miss Blodgett's name from her testament when it was, as it were, an understood thing that it would be included.

"Dear Miss Blodgett!" I cried, and I sympathized with her on the loss of Miss Tate. And yet I felt a necessity to be guarded in my condolences. "So poor Miss Tate has left her garden," I said, and I watched Miss Blodgett carefully as I said it.

But Emma Blodgett's eyes filled with tears.

"Yes," she said. "Poor Aunt Adeline!" And then she took out a small handkerchief, that was not, alas, as spotlessly laundered as it might have been last year, but which, from the border of real lace that ran delicately around its hem, I took to be one of the many small treasures Miss Blodgett had amassed in her years at Clyde Road. "Yes," she said, and she blew her nose. There was no mistaking her sorrow.

I felt very much better. I felt I had been unjust to the memory of Miss Tate. Miss Blodgett's shabby appearance was due no doubt to the fact that she now had to be more prudent. She was living her own life now, and not the life of an heiress. And wasn't she justified in her prudence? Wasn't thrift a virtue when you were poor? And when you had no home, but had to pay for every morsel you ate, and for the roof over your head, could you afford to be prodigal with your money?

All those years when there had been constant talk about the bequest that Miss Tate was expected to leave her companion, had it always been particularly stated that it would be a small bequest? Why — another aspect of the situation struck me. Goodness knows how small it might have been. It might have been a mere nothing; a paltry sum. Then a worse thought struck me. Perhaps it had not been money at all. How often old ladies and gentlemen of eighty or ninety have set such a value on small personal possessions that they have carelessly disposed of their impersonal millions on the advice of lawyer or vicar, to lavish all their attention on the disposal of some worthless trinket — a lock of hair, or an old watch — because, in these last sad hours of abnegation, they had set more value on it than upon all their money. Perhaps into this worthless object they feel they have distilled the essence of a life, and they are loath to leave it behind them. Unfortunately it is of no more value than a stone, and like a stone alas, negotiable into nothing.

I looked hurriedly at Miss Blodgett, who was now weeping copiously, as between sobs she described Miss Tate's last hours to me.

"I was with her to the last breath," she sobbed. "I held her hand all the time. She clutched my fingers till the very end."

Here poor Miss Blodgett put out her hand and clasped mine in illustration of that last touching scene, but she was recalled swiftly from the bedside of her dead friend as her eye, and mine, caught sight of a large hole in the finger of her cotton glove. She hurriedly withdrew her hand.

"Oh, dear," she cried, "I must have caught my glove in something. It seems to be torn."

But the tear was not a new one. It had a frayed edge that told its own story. And irresistibly my eye traveled to Miss Blodgett's other hand. In the other glove too there was a hole: a slightly larger hole, and through it showed another finger, a finger which, alas, was not as immaculate as one would have expected. The fingernail was indeed decidedly grimy, and clearly showed that Miss Blodgett's landlady allowed her paying guest the privilege of doing out her own room, and blacking her own fire grate.

I looked away hurriedly. But you know how it is? The eye is a most unruly member. Do what I might, it would rove back irresistibly to the hole in Miss Blodgett's glove. And where my eye went, irresistibly it seemed Miss Blodgett's blue eye followed.

At last a point was reached at which I must either go away or one of us must make some telling remark. We had to lay the ghost of that torn glove that hovered between us interrupting our conversation, making us awkward and ill at ease.

It was Miss Blodgett who laid it. "Poor Miss Tate," she said suddenly, and she held out her hand and frankly displayed not only the torn tips of the gloves but the fact that the palm of one glove was worn so thin that her pink flesh showed through it. "Poor Miss Tate. How distressed she would be if she saw me looking shabby!"

I didn't quite know what to say, but remembering that Emma Blodgett was probably friendless, with no one, perhaps, in the whole wide world to take an interest in her, I felt that I could venture a step further without danger of being thought vulgarly curious.

"I hope her death has not caused too great a change in your circumstances," I said, and then feeling that I had not handled the situation very well, I ran on impulsively. "I mean, I always understood that Miss Tate intended to arrange matters so that you should never want for anything after her death." I hurried my words. "You know! The small bequest!"

I spoke hurriedly with my eyes on the ground. I was afraid to look up. But Miss Blodgett had dissolved into tears again, and lo! they were tears of love.

"Poor Aunt Adeline!" she said. "A small bequest? That was so like her, to underestimate every impulse of her dear, kind heart." She looked at me a little sternly. "You wouldn't call a thousand pounds a small bequest, would you?"

I was astonished; astonished. I had never thought about how much Miss Tate was likely to leave her companion, but I must admit I had hardly expected it to be more than a few hundred.

"Oh, Miss Blodgett," I said, putting out my hand again and taking hers, "I congratulate you!" But what, I wondered, was the mystery of the torn gloves?

Miss Blodgett withdrew her hand quickly.

"Congratulate me?" she asked. "Sympathize with me, you mean. There's nothing to congratulate me about. You see, I didn't get the money. And what is more, it looks as if I'm never going to get it."

"What?" I was bewildered. Surely the noble and wealthy Tates were not going to contest this reasonable, if generous bequest?

Considering how much they must have shared among themselves, the size of the bequest — even if its size had surprised them — should have added to the family's pride in its own magnanimity. "Surely they're not going to contest the will?" I cried.

"Oh, dear no." Miss Blodgett was shocked at the thought. "They feel worse than I do. In fact, Lord Robert is doing all in his power for me. He insisted on my getting the best solicitor I could get, and Miss Lucy Tate couldn't be surpassed for her kindness. They are all so kind to me, and so upset on my account. The Tates are like that, you know! The kindest people in the world. They think of me as one of themselves." She sighed. "And poor Aunt Adeline! She was the kindest of them all. I can only hope she is not looking down now and seeing all the trouble she caused, without realizing it, out of the goodness of her heart. For you see," and Miss Blodgett looked up at me earnestly, "it was because she was trying to be *too* kind to me that I lost the legacy."

I didn't pretend to understand. Miss Blodgett hastened to explain.

"Well, you know the way she always considered me one of the family. You know how she liked me to call her Aunt Adeline, just as if I was related to her in blood? You know all that, don't you? You could see it for yourself?" Miss Blodgett looked at me earnestly with her big obtuse face and her big stupid eyes filled with love and affection. I felt a great uneasiness gather again in my heart. I didn't answer, but there was no need, for Miss Blodgett rushed on. "Well!" she said. "Poor Miss Tate, when she drew up her will, put in a few words as a last message to me, I suppose. She wanted to let everyone see my place in her affections. She wanted to let me see how close she considered me to her. And so," here poor Miss Blodgett forgot for a moment about Miss Tate as she was recalled to the dreadful weeks that had passed, spent mostly in a solicitor's office, being questioned and browbeaten, and for a moment she broke down and her poor lower lip fell open, and a tear, that was not for Miss Adeline Tate, but for poor Emma Blodgett, stole down her cheek. "And so, in the will, Miss Tate designated me as her fond niece Emma. '*And to my fond niece, Emma,*' she said, '*I hereby leave and bequeath the sum of one thousand pounds.*'" Miss

Blodgett spluttered. "A . . . a . . . a thousand pounds! And to think that I'll never touch a penny of it." She suddenly tucked her handkerchief into her sleeve again, and looked up at a clock on a church tower that showed between the high offices. The little gold wrist watch she used to wear was no longer on her arm. "I am on my way down to the solicitor now," she said. "I have to go down every other day. They're doing their best for me. Lord Robert is most upset. And Miss Lucy too. Indeed, they all are extremely kind. But as for myself, I haven't much hope. You see, it would have been all right if poor Miss Tate had not tried to show me that last mark of affection. It would have been all right if she had left the money to Miss Emma Blodgett. That was what the solicitor said. 'You are Emma Blodgett,' he said. 'Of that there is no doubt. But who is this *fond niece Emma?*' There is no such person. There are fifty-four nieces, counting grand-nieces and two great-grand-nieces; but none of them is called Emma!" Miss Blodgett sighed. "It was perfectly clear, of course, to everyone that it was me that was meant. But" — Miss Blodgett's lips trembled again — "but what good is that to me?" She put out her hand. "I must be going," she said. "Those solicitors are very exact. They don't like to be kept waiting, although they think nothing of keeping others waiting. I'm often kept up to an hour there, and at the end I sometimes have to go away without seeing him. If an urgent call comes for him on the telephone, he has to attend to it. But his typist is very nice. She always gets me a chair." For an instant Emma brightened as she held my hand. "Do you know what I discovered the other day? The typist is a niece of Hetty's. You remember Hetty? Hetty was always very careful with her money, you know, and she educated all her brother's children. They all have good jobs. This girl in the solicitor's office is a very well-educated girl. She's very civil. And she's always very sorry for me if I have to go away without seeing the solicitor. 'Don't worry, Emma,' she says. 'Everything will be all right!' She's a very exceptional girl. Her name is Miss Hynes. Hetty's name was Hynes, you know."

I had almost forgotten to ask about Hetty.

"And how is Hetty?" I asked.

"Oh, Hetty is all right," said Miss Blodgett. "She's gone to live with her brother. They're glad to have her, of course; she has a nice nest egg saved. And then, of course, Miss Tate left her a nice little sum too."

"And Hetty got it all right?"

Miss Blodgett's big, stupid, blue eyes turned on me in swift surprise.

"Why, of course! Why wouldn't she get it? It was left to Hester Hynes. That was Hetty's right name. Hetty was nothing to Miss Tate! Miss Tate had no special feelings for Hetty. She just mentioned her name as a matter of course." Miss Blodgett had risen again for a moment to the height of the old days. Her bosom swelled. Her eye gleamed. "Hetty was only a servant! She was nothing to Aunt Adeline! Well, I must be going. Sometimes, you know, I get tired of going up to the solicitor's, but I say to myself that Aunt Adeline will never rest in her grave until I have made the last possible effort to rectify her mistake." She put out her hand. "Thank you for your sympathy. I'll let you know how things turn out. Goodbye, my dear."

She turned away then, but I saw that the tears had gathered again in her eyes. I heard her mutter something to herself as I stood looking after the blue imitation silk dress, and the ample ankles in the blue woolen socks. I couldn't be sure, but I think what I heard was an exclamation.

"Poor Aunt Adeline! Poor Aunt Adeline!"

A VISIT TO THE CEMETERY

"What a pity she had to be buried here!" said Alice, for the hundredth time since their mother died, as she took the key from her younger sister Liddy and struggled with the iron gate of the Old Cemetery.

The New Plot was about a mile outside the town, on a nice dry hill that commanded a fine view of the countryside. And it was just a nice walk out to it, not too far, but above all not too near.

"I can't think why on earth they ever put a cemetery here in the middle of the town," cried Alice, as the key turned at last in the corroded lock, but the heavy old gate refused to budge.

"Oh, Alice!" Liddy had to laugh at her older sister's ignorance, because of course the cemetery was far older than the town. It was the site of an ancient friary of which only one stump now remained, sticking up like an old tooth rotted down to its obstinate root, but which must once, upon the open fields, have floated free as an island.

Alice, however, was not concerned with antiquity.

"Come on," she cried. She had got the gate to open. The next minute they were inside, finding their way through the neglected grass and high rank nettles, following the faint track of the funeral still visible after four months. There was no real path anywhere now, and funerals had to make their way on foot, in and out, worm-like, between tottering tombstones. No hearse had entered the place in living memory; coffins had to be shouldered to their last resting place.

"Mind your clothes!" cried Alice sharply. She still had memories of the humiliation she suffered at the funeral, when the mourners came out into the street with burrs stuck all over their good black clothes.

"I'm all right," said Liddy. She was holding up her skirt. All the same they both had to stop more than once where their dresses caught in the briers.

But at last they came to their mother's grave and knelt down quickly, crossing themselves before their knees touched the clay. And, as they brought their hands together again in front of them, they closed their eyes tightly.

For the next second or so their lips moved with the quick pecking movements of a bird, as they got through what might almost have been a prearranged ration of prayer, so neatly did they come to an end together. Yet they did not immediately make the sign of the cross, neither wanting to be the first to move. But someone had to be the first, and so at last Liddy glanced across at Alice and raised her eyebrows questioningly.

At once, just as if she had been audibly addressed, Alice answered.

"I am. Are you?" she said, and she blessed herself and got to her feet. Liddy also scrambled to her feet.

"That grass was damp," she said crossly, and she began to rub her knees.

"It's always damp in this old place," Alice said very crossly. "I always say I'll bring something with me to kneel on — even an old newspaper — but I forget every time." She, too, rubbed her knees, but it was her black dress that concerned her most, and lifting up the hem, she submitted her skirt to a close scrutiny. "I'll never forget those burrs."

"Nor I," said Liddy, but she didn't bother to look at her dress, because after all they had to make their way back to the gate again. Wasn't it a wonder no one took any care of the place? Even to scythe the weeds would help. But then of course hardly anyone ever came here, except themselves. What a lonely place it was. And although where she stood she could hear the people talking in the street outside, and only a little farther away the thudding of a ball in the ball-alley, it seemed that she was cut off from them so that they would not hear her, not even if she were to scream at the top of her voice. But that was absurd. Why should she scream? It was broad daylight and there was Alice a few feet away calling out to her impatiently.

"Are you coming?" Alice cried.

But Liddy still loitered, and as if she had never before been in it, she looked around the old cemetery. As far as they could be made out in the rank growth in which they were submerged, there wasn't a tombstone or a headstone that wasn't slanted or tottering. It was almost as if the earth had quaked and the quiet dead — momentarily dislodged — had settled down again in postures, unquiet and disorderly. And ah — just behind their mother's headstone there was an unsightly grave where a rabbit — no, it must have been a badger — had burrowed, and from it — yes — though Liddy quickly averted her eyes — yes, from it a large bleached bone stuck upward. Almost falling forward into the high grass she ran after Alice, and caught her by the sleeve.

"Poor Mother!" she cried. "I can't help thinking how much nicer and cleaner it would have been for her in the new cemetery!"

"Isn't that what I'm always saying!" Alice looked at her. Liddy was slow sometimes. "Are you coming or are you not?" Pulling her sleeve free, she went on a few steps.

"Alice?"

Alice didn't want to turn around, but there was something in Liddy's voice that compelled her to turn. Liddy was standing just where she had left her, looking back at their mother's grave.

"What?"

Alice knew her voice was grumpy, but she really wanted to get out of the gate. How she hated it! And Liddy looked as if she were prepared to stay there forever.

"Do you ever think about it at all, Alice?"

What Liddy meant Alice both knew and did not know, so she hedged. "I don't know what you're talking about," she said.

Liddy turned around slowly and in her eyes there was an expression that could not be misread.

"It's so awful, isn't it?" She shuddered.

Almost as quickly as Liddy herself had averted her eyes from the grave, Alice averted hers from her sister.

"Oh, Liddy! If I'd thought you were going to take on like this I'd never have come with you." She paused, casting around in her mind for something to say that might get them over the silence that fell. "After all we must all die — we know that," she said lamely.

But Liddy was incorrigible. "That's what I mean," she said quietly.

Alice was at a loss. "Well, after all we can console ourselves that it's only the body that is buried, the soul . . ."

Not exactly rudely, however, and not exactly impatiently, Liddy shrugged her shoulders.

"I sometimes think that's the worst of it," she said, in a voice so low Alice had to bend to hear. "I can never believe that I won't go on feeling: feeling the cold and the damp — you know, even after — "

"Liddy! Liddy!" Alice stumbled toward her across the tufted grass. If Liddy had said a single other word she would have clapped her hands over her sister's mouth.

But Liddy didn't finish it. She had begun to sob softly.

"And to think," she said after a minute, "that in a few years, perhaps sooner, poor Father — " she sobbed, "just think of it — poor Father will be put down here too."

This was dreadful. Alice felt helpless. She always knew Liddy took things differently from her, but she never knew her to carry on like this. She couldn't think what to do, and when at that moment near her foot she saw a bone she gave it a kick. Hateful place: it was all bones. That one might have been brought in by some mongrel, but it could just as easily be a human bone. The place was disgusting. It was enough to give anyone the creeps. Oh, if only Mother had been buried in the new cemetery where everything was so neat and orderly, Liddy would not have got into this state! The gravedigger up there always boasted that he'd give five pounds to anyone who found a bone after him!

"Well, thanks be to goodness we won't be buried here, anyway!" she said impulsively.

"We won't?" Liddy looked up in such surprise a tear that was slowly rolling down her cheeks was jerked into the air.

"Of course not," Alice cried. "Not unless we are old maids!" But that seemed so untoward a thing that she made a playful face.

Then, seeing that Liddy had smiled, if wanly, she put on an arch expression. "We'll be buried with our husbands."

"Oh, Alice!" Liddy knew that Alice used to talk about boys with her friends, but she had never said anything like this to her before and she felt herself blushing. She was furious with herself about it until she saw that Alice was blushing a little too.

"It's true!" said Alice defensively. "The first death in the family means that you have to buy a plot. Surely you know that! That's why Mother was buried here, because of that baby she had before any of us, the one that died. Father bought a plot here then, and even though it was years ago, and there is a new cemetery now, poor Mother had to be buried here. And so will Father himself. But there aren't any more plots to be got here now, thanks be to God, so our husbands will have to provide them — in the new cemetery — thanks be to God again!"

Their husbands: it was an intoxicating thought. Liddy looked up at the sky. It was turning out to be a beautiful evening, although you wouldn't notice it so much in the old graveyard, where the ivy made everything so dark, and the shadow of stones overlapping made a sort of double gloom.

Although there was hardly room for two to walk together, she recklessly linked her arm in her sister's and began to draw her toward the gate. A great feeling of sisterly affection had come over her, and it seemed to her that it wasn't just a matter of chance that they had picked this evening to come out together. It was as if something for a long time suppressed had at last begun to force upward toward the light.

"Just think, Alice — about that baby, I mean. Mother was younger than us — than you, anyway — when that baby was born, and we — " she hesitated.

"I know," said Alice glumly. "I was thinking that myself a few minutes ago. But times were different then; girls were encouraged to have boys then. Not like now."

"You mean Father would — "

"He'd be just wild. You know that as well as me. And he will probably be ten times stricter now because he used to rely on Mother to look after us."

"Poor Mother! She wasn't strict at all."

"I expect that was because she was so ill for the past few years. You remember everyone said it was a happy release for her."

"I suppose it was too," Liddy said.

But they had reached the gate at last, and she sighed. Their adventure for the day was over. It was a pity they had started out so early in a way; if they had started half an hour later they would be coming in the gate now instead of going out. And she was right about the evening; there was a remarkable change in the air. It was like an evening in spring. Just as they stepped out into the street a breeze that came up out of nowhere, oh, so fresh and sweet, blew their skirts around their legs like an umbrella around its stem. It would be such a nice evening to go for a walk outside the town; to hold up their faces, to look, to smell, and above all to talk; to talk.

"Oh, isn't it too bad, Alice," she cried, as if it was the first time anyone had expressed the idea —

" — that she wasn't buried in the new cemetery?"

Liddy nodded. "It must be lovely up there on an evening like this: we could walk around and read the names on the stones — they're all names we know, not like in this old place. I don't suppose — " she hesitated — "I wonder if we might — "

"You mean — walk out that way?" said Alice, taking up her meaning immediately, but she looked frightened. "We didn't tell them at home that we were going for a walk."

"We said we were going to the cemetery, didn't we?" cried Liddy. "We didn't say which one!" She gave Alice's arm a pull. "Oh, come on, I've something to tell you, anyway. I've kept it a secret, but I think I could tell you now."

For an instant Alice was almost livid with jealousy. Could it be that Liddy had a boy? Liddy who was two years younger than her. And she hadn't had a single flutter. Unless you could count what happened after the choir the other evening. She wondered what Liddy would think about that? She might tell her as they went along.

"Come on so," she cried. "We'll chance it."

They almost forgot to lock the gate.

"What about this?" Liddy held up the key which she managed to get out of the lock.

They were supposed to hand it back where they got it, at the parochial house.

"Oh, we'll leave it back on the way home," said Alice. She was impatient to start.

But before they set out, one after the other, the sisters gave the gate a push to see that it was locked, and to make doubly sure Liddy put her shoulder to it.

"It's locked all right," she said. "Come on."

A TRAGEDY

ON THEIR WAY to meet Sis they went through Trim to get the evening papers, otherwise they would have had to depend on the radio. There would probably be pictures in the paper. After all, they would only lose two or three minutes!

But the papers gave little more than they had already heard on the wireless. And the pictures didn't show much at all, just the side of the snow-clad mountain and the big crater where the plane had nosed down into the black earth. Bits of wreckage blackened the whiteness in the immediate vicinity of the accident. And a large black "X" marked the spot at the extreme front edge of the picture where a portion of the undercarriage had been found, three hundred yards from the spot where the crash occurred.

"A terrible tragedy," Tom said. He folded up the paper and beckoned to Mary.

She would have been inclined to stay and listen to the comments of the other people in the shop. As soon as another customer came up to the counter and opened his paper, there was a fresh outburst of discussion.

"A fault in the engine — what else could it be!"

"I don't agree; those planes are too well tested for that."

At first even Tom had been inclined to delay.

"You must allow for the possibility of human fallibility," he said, and he might have enlarged on the point if at this stage the news agent hadn't joined the conversation.

"I believe — " he said, and he lowered his voice.

That was enough for Tom; the lowering of the voice. He knew at once the way the level of the discussion would drop.

It was then that he beckoned to Mary.

But even before they had got out of earshot they could hear someone saying something about the arm of a doll sticking up in the snow.

Mary hung back for a moment straining to catch more, but she saw Tom shudder and hurried out after him.

"There's no purpose to be served by that kind of talk," he said. He jerked his head in the direction of the shop. "Sensation mongers," he muttered.

The doll's arm, he meant, Mary supposed. And, as always, she felt rebuked by his power to discriminate. He was just as interested as anyone in the tragedy but he kept his interest free from base curiosity and sensation-seeking. Left to herself she would have wallowed in the gruesome details. With remorse she recalled how her fingers had fumbled unfolding the paper. What had she hoped to find? But having been brought to book she began at once to behave better. In the shop she had put out her hand for the paper, but when she got into the car she threw it on the back seat.

"I suppose by rights one shouldn't read about it at all," she said.

Tom started up the engine.

"Oh, I wouldn't go so far as to say that," said Tom. "And a lot depends on the newspaper. On the whole, Irish newspapers are well intentioned. They don't distort the facts, anyway; they don't dwell unnecessarily on morbid details." For a few minutes he drove along in silence out of the town, into the dark country. "Where did he read that?" he asked then, suddenly, specifying neither subject nor object.

The doll's arm again, Mary thought. How well I know him.

"It's always the same in this country," he said, as if he himself were a foreigner, or at least an extensive traveler. "It's impossible to keep a conversation on the right level. There is no such thing as general conversation. Someone always butts in and drags it down to particulars. How I'd love a few words with the people at the airport, the officials, I mean, of course. I'd like to hear what they have to say tonight. I was reading a very interesting report on aeronautics the other day in an American pictorial — by an expert, of course. And it is his opinion — ”

Unfortunately it was at this point that Mary, thinking of Sis, leaned forward to see the time by the light on the dashboard.

“Oh, we’ll be very late,” she burst out impulsively, without thinking.

It was so rude! He always hated to be interrupted. Desperately she tried to link her exclamation with the topic they were discussing. “We oughtn’t to have stopped for the old paper at all,” she cried. “It’d be a different matter if the inquiry was on. There’ll be an inquiry, won’t there? That will interest you, I know, won’t it, Tom?”

But Tom had slowed down to look ostentatiously at his own watch.

“Four minutes,” he said succinctly. “We lost exactly four minutes as I estimate it.” And she could see that his face had a sneering expression for all the world as if he knew Sis would be difficult over the little delay.

She knew immediately then that they were going to have a row. She might have known, of course, that even at this remove (for they still had a long way to go) Sis would be the cause of an argument, discord, unhappiness. Poor Sis! Just because she had been away from them for a few months, Mary had begun to forget the drag it was on them to have her living with them, and had even begun to look forward to seeing her again, and some of her sister’s good points had floated to the surface of her mind. Sis used to be so lighthearted when they were girls, before her awful marriage, and the frightfulness with which it came to an end. She was such a good companion when they shared a flat, taking everything as it came, and making little of all their difficulties. And earlier still, when they were at school, she was a positive scream. She used to call the nuns by their nicknames right under their noses. All the same she was the one you’d run to with your troubles. She was so human. But it was no wonder she’d changed. Yet, even as Mary was saying this to herself, she felt guilty. In her heart she knew it was not Sis who had changed, but herself, who under Tom’s influence had come to see her sister in a new light.

One thing Tom had shown her was that facetiousness was the mark of a mediocre intellect. And as for the word "human," she forgot herself when she used it. It was one of poor Sis's words, one of the words she was always using, and which made Tom say she was a loose thinker. He was right about that, of course, but she wasn't going to let him be unfair. And it was grossly unfair to suggest that Sis would be ratty with them if they were three or four minutes late.

"The bus may have been ahead of time: she may have been waiting for ages!" she cried, to justify Sis, in anticipation, for the mood he implied they would find her in when they got to Ballivor.

Tom took her up sharply.

"Would that be our fault?" he demanded.

With a great effort she said nothing. Perhaps it might still be possible not to quarrel. She reminded herself that he had had a long day at the office, and that it was asking a lot of him to get into the car again with no supper — only a cup of tea which he had had to swallow down in a hurry — and rush off to this godforsaken place.

"It's a pity we arranged to meet her at Ballivor," she said, thinking of him, and of the nuisance the driving must be to him.

She wasn't expecting his reaction.

"Well, that's a good one! I like that!" he cried, grinding down the brake and bringing them to a stop with a sickening jerk. "Did you say 'we' arranged it? As far as I can recall it was your dear sister who arranged it, and by the way I'd very much like to know what motive she had? The obvious thing to do was to go on to Dublin. We could have arranged to meet her in some hotel, where she would have been comfortable and warm, and we wouldn't have to break our necks like this!" They were belting along again.

"Poor Sis was probably looking into the money!" she said defensively. "The fare to Ballivor is almost a third less than it would cost to go on the whole way to Dublin."

"And just how much do you think it's costing us to come over here to Ballivor, in petrol and oil, to say nothing of the wear and tear on the car along these cursed cross-country roads? I must say it's a good idea to save money at our expense, when to put it mildly

I don't know that we're under any great compliment to your sister."

"On the contrary? Is that what you mean?" She could have bitten off her tongue for saying anything about money. "As a matter of fact poor Sis probably only wanted to make the bus trip as short as possible. She hates going anywhere by bus; she gets deadly sick. It probably seemed a good idea to get out at the nearest point to us as long as the bus was going through this part of the country. You must admit it would be a bit stupid to practically pass here and go on another thirty miles and then have to turn around and come back all the way again."

"My dear Mary, there are so many inaccuracies in what you just said I cannot put them *all* right for you, but I must point out to you — and I wish you'd point it out to your sister for future reference — that Ballivor is thirty-three miles and a quarter from our hall door. It's only twenty-nine miles to Dublin, apart altogether from the fact that one can always find business to do in the city, whereas no one in his sane senses would want to spend three minutes in this little pothole."

For they were getting into Ballivor.

"Now, where did she say she'd meet us? There's only one shop in the place as far as I remember, and it's probably closed at this hour."

Up to this, bad and all as it had been, there was a connubial privacy about their quarrel, but in a minute now they would be exposed to Sis.

Mary lowered the car window that was misted with the night air. She was filled with such forebodings of an unpleasant scene that she expected to see the one and only shop shuttered and dark, and Sis, numb and pinched, sitting on her suitcase outside it in the street.

As a matter of fact there was more than one shop in the village, and they were all brightly and cheerily lighted. It wasn't long since the bus had gone through, either, because in the shop outside of which they drew up — it seemed the largest — people were standing around with the evening papers held out in front of them.

And Sis was one of them. Standing familiarly among the Ballivorites, she was holding up her paper in front of her, as good as any of them, and lowering it every other minute to exchange com-

ments on what it contained. In spite of Tom, Mary glowed for a
moment with the old warmth and admiration for her. She made
herself at home wherever she went. Then Sis looked up and saw
the car.

Immediately, impetuously, she threw the paper down on a heap
of biscuit tins and ran out to them.

"Oh, there you are, you clever things — I thought you'd mistaken
the day. Not that I'd care. This is the dearest little village; I'd
stay here for ever. And the people in the shop are the sweetest people you could imagine. Just fancy, they let me have an evening
paper although, strictly speaking, they're only for customers, who
have one ordered; there's only a *very* limited number. But then, I
suppose they could see I was particularly interested. Wasn't it
dreadful, the crash, I mean? I know everybody is interested in it,
but can you imagine, Molly's mother-in-law — by the way Molly
sent her love to you both and all that — well, her mother-in-law
was almost in it — the plane, I mean, the one that crashed. Can
you imagine it! She telephoned Molly just after the crash because
she was sure Molly would think she was in it. She was supposed
to be in it but she was at the airport early and she got a chance of another flight and took it. Wasn't that luck? As a matter of fact
Molly didn't know when she was traveling — you know Molly —
she thought she was coming by boat in fact. A bit casual, don't you
agree? But then Molly is casual. She's a dear, I know that, but I
must say I was getting a bit sick of her. You know how it is when
you're at very close quarters with someone, without any bond, any
real bond? Oh, but I'm keeping you. Just hang on a second more,
will you, while I get my case. No, Tom! Please! It's as light as a
feather."

As quick as she had darted out she darted back again, her long
legs glinting with the flashy sheen of her stockings, and her chest
flopping like an adolescent's.

She was looking awfully well after the holiday with her old
friend Molly, whatever she herself might think. For a girl so
recently widowed, she was certainly looking extraordinarily well.

Ah, here she was now with the case, or rather with the cases, for
there was a hatbox and a shoe-box as well, and several packages. But
everyone in the shop seemed anxious to assist her.

"Oh, thank you so much, Mr. — er, I didn't catch the name," said Sis, taking the hatbox from a young country boy, but turning at the same time toward the shopkeeper himself who had her shoe-box. "So kind of you. It will be Ballivor for me every time!" she called back gaily, as they drove away.

Impossible not to be a bit proud of her. Clearly Tom's opinion of her was not shared by everyone, or else they didn't object to her being a nitwit — she was such a charmer as well.

"Are you all right, Sis?" she asked. "Perhaps I ought to have let you sit in the front. Are you cold? Would you like to change places with me?"

Fortunately Sis preferred to stay where she was, because after Mary had made the suggestion, Tom gave her a dig in the ribs.

"Oh, I'm as snug as a bug in a rug," said Sis. "And how are you two? Tell me your news? I suppose like everyone else you're all agog over the crash. Wasn't it too ghastly for words? I believe the papers were censored. They were half an hour late anyway, and someone said they were off the press and all when the Government stepped in and made them make a lot of cuts — in the interest of commerce. The Government have a big share in the airline, you know. I'd just love to see that first run-off. I suppose there are people who will get hold of a sheet of it. I believe there were pictures too that had to be scrapped. Not that I'd care to see them. Even the one I saw gave me the creeps, it did really! I kept peering and peering and my flesh was creeping. I don't know what I expected to see, but my hair was standing on end. But I mustn't do all the talking. What about you two? What's your news?"

"We're nearly home, Sis," Tom said, and Mary could see it took a lot of self-control for him to speak so quietly. "Suppose we keep what we have to say to each other until we've had something to eat and are sitting at the fire. We've had a long day; all of us."

It was so plain to Mary that he was ticking off Sis that she tried to catch her eye. She wanted to make a sign to her to indicate that he didn't like talking when he was driving at night, or something like that.

But there was no need. Sis was madly rummaging among her cases.

"Did you take the evening paper from me? Did I hand it to you?

I hadn't read a quarter of it. And you might like a look at it? I hope I didn't leave it behind. Oh, good: I knew I couldn't be that stupid," she said, coming upon the paper Tom had bought in Trim.

She took out a flashlight and by its feeble beam she began to read the print.

That was the way she used to read illicit magazines in the dormitories at school, Mary thought. She was always full of dash; no one could put her down. But all the same Mary wished that they had made some other arrangement about her getting back, it seemed such a long time since they had had anything to eat. Her own feet were frozen and the fire would probably be out when they got home.

The fire wasn't quite out; but the heart had burned out of it and the logs had fallen to one side, charred and blackened. As Tom poked dry kindling between the hot embers, Sis surveyed the charred logs.

"It must have been simply ghastly," she said irrelevantly. "I don't know how that rescue party could endure all they must have had to endure."

Mary looked nervously at Tom. Such a wrong note.

"Please, Sis!" she cried. "Please. I thought we weren't going to talk about it till after we'd had something to eat."

But two, three times, during the meal Sis broke the rules.

"I must say," she said, on the third occasion, "I think it's frightfully heartless of you both not to want to talk about it. I bet there isn't a tea table in the whole of Ireland this minute where they aren't talking about it, ten to the dozen."

Bitterly, Tom glanced at the clock. It was ten o'clock.

"There aren't many people having their tea at this hour," he said.

"Oh, you always have a clever answer!" Sis said, and she giggled. "But seriously, I think you're frightfully unnatural not to want to talk about it. I had such a lot to tell you that wasn't in the papers: oh, not creepy things!" she said, as she saw Mary give a frightened glance at Tom. "Ah, I fetched you that time," she cried, as Tom looked up with curiosity.

"Had Molly some information?" he asked. He knew that Molly's husband had some connection with the airlines, something indirect like having a contract for supplying them with oil, or something. But there was always the chance that he might have some information that wasn't submitted to the press. "A fault in the engine is everybody's guess," he said. "But for my own part I shouldn't be at all surprised if it shouldn't be put down, plainly and simply, to human fallibility."

Mary was so glad he was going to have an audience after all for his theories of human fallibility.

"Oh, I haven't the foggiest idea what caused it, if that's what you mean," Sis said. "Neither has Molly, but you remember there was a dentist among the victims? Well, his wife was a great friend of Molly's, and she rang up Molly just before I left and she told her something awfully sad: it's not generally known, she's hoping it will be kept out of the papers, but she's going to have another baby! Isn't that frightfully sad?"

The fire had blazed up and in the kitchen the kettle for their hot water bottles had begun to hop on the range. But Tom's humor had not improved. He made absolutely no comment on the information Sis had volunteered, but turned to Mary.

"I'm not staying up for the late news, Mary," he said curtly, and without further explanation. "I'm going to bed." But when she followed him out to the foot of the stairs, he didn't trouble to lower his voice. "It would have been doing me a favor if you could have made that sister of yours talk about something else for a change besides the one topic. I knew she was a fool, but I didn't realize she was such a complete one."

"Oh, Tom, please! You don't want her to hear you. I'm sorry: I wish you hadn't had that trip to Ballivor, but please don't go to bed without your hot water bottle. I'll hand it up to you."

"There's one thing you can do: leave me alone! Will you do that?"

He went up the stairs, into the dark, without even putting on the light on the upper landing.

"So you heard him?" said Mary, when she went back to the sitting room and saw Sis sitting dejected, looking into the fire.

"As a matter of fact I heard nothing," Sis said. "But I can guess a lot, you know. It was quite plain to me all the time that there was something wrong with him. I just ignored it at first, but naturally, I thought that like everyone else in the country he was upset over the disaster. If I had only known! Oh, he's the hardhearted man. Not that I care a snap of my fingers for him. It's not him that's depressing me. It's you, Mary. It's you. Oh, to think he has you so much under his thumb that you've made yourself into a little model of him. Yes, that's what you are! Why, there was a time not so long ago and you couldn't have heard enough of what I had to say when I'd come back after a holiday with Molly, or with anyone! And a tragedy like this would have turned you inside out: you'd have talked of nothing else all night. You'd have stayed up till three in the morning if you got someone to stay with you. Oh, I couldn't have believed you'd change so much if I hadn't seen it with my own two eyes. That story I was telling you about Molly's friend, the one that's going to have the baby, that story would have melted a heart of stone, but what effect did it have on you? Well, I'll tell you — I was watching you both, though you mightn't have thought it while I was telling it. I could see *at once* the superior attitude of your husband. I expected a lecture on dragging things down to particulars, or to a personal level, and all that tripe I've heard so often from him, but instead of that he decided to be rude to me: to walk out of the room — where is he, by the way, gone to bed? — but as I say, I don't care about him: he's no more than a stranger to me. But you! Oh, it made me sick to see the way you were hardly looking at me, but all the time looking at him out of the corner of your eye to see what way you ought to take it: what way he'd like you to take it. Do you know what I thought? I thought you were like a little dog, sitting up on its tail end, waiting for someone to throw a stick for you to catch. Which way will he throw it? you wondered. This way? That way? Whichever way it goes, I'll go after it. Good lord, how you make me sick! You've lost every scrap of personality you ever had. You've just become a second skin for that inflated windbag. You — "

But of course, she couldn't be let go any further. Right across the face, with the flat of her hand, Mary slapped her.

Or had she? Was it possible, she thought, the next minute, that she had hit Sis: she, the younger of the two, the one who until she met Tom was always the disciple, the one who was always in tow?

But Sis took it almost as if she had been expecting it.

"So we've come to this, have we?" she said. "Well, it's been brewing for a long time. Before I went away it was threatening. I know now how you feel about having me here in spite of your talk about this being my home. A nice home. But it's the only place I have to lay my head for all that, and you know it! So whether you like it or not I'm here to stay!"

She gave a laugh and stood up.

"I won't wait for my hot water bottle either, thank you very much. And you needn't bring it up to me."

So she *had* heard Tom? It made it a little bit better to think there was an immediate cause for their misery, thought Mary, but she ran out to the foot of the stairs, as she did after Tom.

"Oh, Sis, how can you be so mean to me? You know I haven't changed, not toward you anyway, but even if I had, surely you ought to be able to understand that things happen to people when they" — she was going to say "when they marry," but evidently it wasn't generally applicable, and so she changed it — "when they're as happy as Tom and I. And you see Tom is very logical, and philosophical" — what else was he? — "and he discriminates very much. Living with him one is bound to be influenced a little bit and one tries to be less impulsive — to think before one speaks and use a little judgment — "

"Oh, skip it, will you? I'm going to bed," said Sis. "Something may turn up yet. I may win the sweep, or meet some other mutt. I may not be stuck with you all my life." But she paused. "All my life!" she repeated. "And I'm only twenty-nine!" She put her hand on the newel post. "I wonder if any of those people in the plane had got their lives into a mess like me?"

"Oh, Sis!" Sis hadn't exactly said it, but she had as good as said that she envied them. "Oh, please, Sis. Try to understand," she implored, following her up the stairs a step or two.

She wasn't expecting Sis to turn around and question her so plainly.

"Understand what?" said Sis.

"That I can't change," she said. "Not twice. Not back again. For good or bad, I've made myself over into Tom's ways now. You'll have to be patient with me, that's all."

It seemed as if Sis was softening. Mary went up another step. "Perhaps if you had tried to — " she began.

But her sister's face froze.

"We'll leave my marriage out of this conversation, if you don't mind," she said, and her face hardened again as she turned and ran up the stairs. And she didn't turn on the landing light either.

Mary sat down on the stairs.

Oh, it was so unfair. That last rebuff was the limit. She had opened her door, taken her into her home, but Sis on the other hand, was not going to open any doors. Failure though it had been, finished and done with, Sis had managed to keep her own marriage in some way sacred and private.

For a long time Mary sat there on the stairs. Perhaps she thought that one or other of them would come down again. But no; she could hear Sis stomping about in her bare feet, making more noise that way than when she was teetering about in her high-heeled shoes.

And Tom? He had probably read for a while after he went to bed, and when she went up she would find him lying with his mouth open, the light shining full on his face, and a nimbus of moths circling his head.

Oh, it was all very well for those two; they were strangers to each other. What did they care if they had an odd bicker now and then? But between them, she was being torn to pieces. My heart is broken, she told herself, over and over again, sitting on the stairs, even though she knew it was the kind of loose talk that Tom deplored. And when finally she went upstairs to Tom and put out the bedroom light (on account of the moths) her nerves were so strained it was like a pain to her when, through the thin walls, she heard the bedsprings creaking under Sis. And when she was ready to get into bed herself she stood for a long time in her bare feet on the cold linoleum, because it was absolutely unbearable to think that Sis in her turn would hear their bed creaking. At last, cold as a stone, she lowered herself cautiously into the bed beside her husband, and when, disturbed in his rest, Tom gave a great clumsy heave, and the bed groaned, she began to tremble with the violence of her feelings. We have no privacy, she whispered, not even in our bedroom; in our bed.

Suddenly she sat up straight and clenched her hands. A new idea had struck her, and it seemed that the circumspection and delicacy that was imposed upon them by the presence of another person in the house was in some way responsible for her not having yet conceived a child. Tom might say that was nonsense, but she knew that, right or wrong, this new idea was pervasive, and would make her relations with Sis more sour and bitter still.

After a long time lying in the dark, Mary looked at her watch. It was only a little after eleven. By rights, they should still be downstairs, she and Tom, sitting over the last of the fire, drinking cocoa.

Without the cocoa she'd never get to sleep. Her feet were like ice. Would she get up again and go downstairs and make some, she wondered? But instead, she decided that she would try once more to go to sleep. She would think of something other than Sis and the problems she created. But when she forced her mind to let go its hold upon those problems, it fastened instantly on the broken plane, half buried in the ground on Snowdon. The bodies that had been recovered were to be removed for burial, but owing to weather conditions and the treacherous nature of the snowy slopes at that point, all further search for bodies had been abandoned. A burial service would be read in the air from another plane, flying at low altitude over the spot.

She could see that plane, flying so low that its shadow, like the shadow of a bird, flew with it across the white wastes.

Was it possible that Sis really envied those who had won eternal peace in that way — in that place? A deeper, and more terrible desolation took hold of her.

"Tom!" she whispered. She gave him a poke. "Tom, I'm worried about Sis."

Tom only grunted something in his sleep.

"Please wake up! Please listen, Tom," she said. "I'm awfully upset about her. She must be terribly unhappy. I didn't realize it, but do you know what she said tonight?"

"Oh, shut up," said Tom.

"No, you must listen. She said she wished she was dead. Do you hear me?"

"I hear you," he said then, and he opened his eyes and looked at her. "Did she say that?" he said. "Well, I'll tell you what you'll do: ask her to tell it to the dead on Snowdon, and see what they'll say to her."

She thought he was half asleep and didn't rightly know what he was saying. But when she thought for a minute over his words she knew he wasn't asleep, and he wasn't joking.

Not one of them — those undiscovered dead in their far-flung graves, not one of them, she knew, but would fling back, if he could, that mantle of snow and come back to it all: the misunderstandings, the worry, the tension, the cross purposes.

With a heave that shook the whole bed she flung her arm across Tom.

Her husband was right, as usual. Words were cheap, and Sis was a fool. That was all that was really the matter. And for the moment, anyway, their rooms were separate worlds that whirled away from each other through vast infinities of space.

THE LONG HOLIDAYS

"You may as well call me Dolly," said Dolly, whenever she was being introduced. "Everybody does. It's silly really, now that I'm a grown-up woman; but what can I do?"

And she laughed: a little dolly laugh.

But for the most part, people were relieved to have her mention her size. It put them at liberty to utter all the exclamations that rose to their lips the moment they set eyes upon the tiny little figure, with its tiny feet and hands, and tiny, tiny waist.

"I have a friend who can span it with one hand," Dolly said, and presumably the friend was a gentleman.

Dolly had lots of gentlemen friends. Just to look at her made gentlemen feel big and strong. But she had the same effect upon ladies; she made them feel big and strong too; and so she had not many lady friends. This didn't matter because Dolly didn't care much for ladies, anyway. They always seemed to be jealous of her, although most of them had so much more of everything than she did: more hip, more middle, more bust. Dolly was frightened of them really. She made it a point never to be alone with them, but sometimes she got caught by them, in the ladies' cloakroom, for instance, and it terrified her the way they seemed to pen her up in a corner and pluck at her.

"How do you ever get things to fit you?" they cried. "Fancy having to have everything altered!" The married ones were the worst. One of them leaned over her and whispered into her ear, one day, "I suppose it's *deliberately* you never got married?"

The implications of this were so enormous, and undiscoverable to her, that she was frightened to death for weeks. Because, of course, it was not deliberate at all.

So when the Major came along, Dolly had no hesitation; on any account whatever. With the Major at her back, even metaphorically, she wasn't half as frightened as she used to be of other women; and she didn't mind at all when they exclaimed at the size of her waist.

"You should see me beside my fiancé," she'd say. "I'm like a real doll beside him," and opening the beak of her little handbag she would take out a snapshot.

There she was, on the left of the picture, as small as ever, in a long white dress and a big white hat, with a parasol on one arm, and the Major on the other, although considering the size of Dolly, and the size of the Major, who was six feet one in his socks, it might have been more exact to say it was a picture of the Major with Dolly on his arm. One usually associates the lesser as belonging to the greater. But there are exceptions, of course, as one can see by looking at the *Tatler*, which often shows a photograph of a little man in white ducks and topi holding up by his side some mighty monster of land or sea. The Major was definitely Dolly's trophy.

Even in our hour of glory, however, we have our detractors. And some people wondered if Dolly would have captured the Major so readily if he hadn't been a widower with a small son on his hands. But Dolly seemed to take Vinnie in her stride.

"He's only a baby," she said, "hardly eleven! I'm longing to give him the comfort of family life. I haven't met him yet; he's away at boarding school — but I'm looking forward wildly to when he comes home. I bet I'll turn out to be a born stepmother!"

She turned to the Major. "Has he a tuck-box, darling?"

And when she heard the boy didn't, one of the first things she did after they were married was to buy a big box, and off she went to the station with it strapped to the back of the little red car the Major had bought for her. And as for letters; there was hardly a day she didn't drive to the post office to send off a postcard or a bundle of comics.

"You won't feel right till he's home for the holidays, ma'am," the postmistress said.

But two days before the holidays Vinnie got the mumps!

Dolly was so disappointed. The Major had to keep reminding her that the next term was a short one. But when that term came to an end, there was another disappointment. It appeared that his housemaster had planned to take a party of boys to Switzerland, and it seemed wrong to deprive Vinnie of going. They hated to disappoint the young teacher too; he was so madly keen on the idea. He hadn't been abroad before, and this was such a great chance for him, because one of the big travel agencies was sponsoring the trip, as an advertisement, and was issuing free travel vouchers to any teacher who succeeded in rounding up a party of twenty boys. The young man might never get another chance, because the whole thing was an experiment, and might easily be a dismal failure. Boys were so troublesome, always getting into mischief, and liable to every kind of accident, to say nothing of the danger of taking children abroad in any case. Anything might happen to them! And of course if anything happened to one of them, that would be the end of the idea as far as the travel agency was concerned.

"As for Vinnie," the Major said, "the ups and downs will be good for him. We simply cannot refuse him. We must be firm, though, when it comes to the summer holidays, because he'll probably be asked to stay with people. When I was a little chap the parents of other chaps were always inviting me to stay. My mother used to be furious; she said she hardly ever saw me."

"Surely you're thinking of some other holidays," said Dolly. "Not the *long* holidays. Who could possibly want another person's child around the place for three months — and in the dead of summer? I'm sure we can count on having him here. In fact, I'm going to begin making preparations right away."

The Major couldn't but be proud of the way Dolly threw herself into the preparations. Every day she seemed to have a new idea for making the boy's holidays enjoyable. "Will we get his room repapered?" she'd cry, one day. And the next day she'd want to know if he had a bicycle.

"We'll have to get him one then," she'd cry, when she found he hadn't. "And what about a fishing rod? And roller skates? Or is he too small for them?"

"Too big, I think, my dear," the Major said. But Dolly felt one was never too old to have fun. "What else can we get him?" she cried. Every day there was a fresh excitement; it was a regular plan of campaign. One day, about a fortnight before Vinnie's arrival, the Major's eye fell on the little silver calendar on Dolly's desk. He was deeply touched. For the date on which Vinnie was expected home had been singled out by Dolly from all the other dates in the month, and ringed around with red ink, till it stood out like a military target. And the days that lay between her and her objective, like cities in the path of an advancing army, had been heavily crossed out; devastated; sacked.

Looking at that calendar, the Major was ashamed of how little he personally had done to prepare for his son.

But what was there left to do? Dolly seemed to have bought the boy everything under the sun.

Suddenly the Major got a brain wave. Boxing gloves!

The boxing gloves had to be ordered, and they didn't arrive until the very day that Vinnie was coming home. By this time Dolly was suffering from nervous exhaustion, and when she saw them on the hall table she shuddered.

"Ugh! Aren't they ugly!"

She couldn't get them out of her mind all day. Like big bloated human hands, of abnormal size, they floated before her as she rushed around putting last minute touches to things. In the end, a morbid fascination made her pick them up and examine them. She put them down hastily.

"I never really saw a pair before," she said. "Not so close to me." She shuddered again.

"I had no idea they'd upset you like this," said the Major. "I wish I hadn't got them!"

But Dolly told him not to be silly.

"Oh! the boy has to have them," she said; and then she paused. "It would be different if it were a little girl."

And indeed, a few minutes later when they were upstairs taking a last look around Vinnie's room to see that nothing was missing, she sighed.

"It would have been much easier to get the room for a little girl,"

she said, "and it would have been so much more fun. I'm sure that
if I had had a child of my own it would have been a little girl —
because I'm so small," she added quickly, when the Major turned
a hurt eye upon her. "Let me see," she said dreamily. "I'd have
the walls pink instead of that bright blue — it's too bright I think,
don't you? I'd have little white ruffles — "

But the Major had to cut her short. It was time to go to the station to meet Vinnie.

The minute Vinnie jumped out of the train, Dolly got a
start. He was so big. He rushed up to them like a young bull.

I'll scream if he puts his arms around me like he put them round
his father, she thought.

But it was worse when the Major intervened.

"Shake hands nicely with your mother!" he said.

"Oh, don't you think he ought to call me Dolly?" Dolly cried.
People might think he was her real son, and her mind revolted
against such an error, as against some abnormality of nature. Wasn't
there a mathematical law of some kind that said the part could
not be greater than the whole — oh, it wouldn't be seemly at all to
have people think she was his mother, this great lump of a boy. Already she thought she had seen a woman on the platform sniggering.

"Let's hurry home," she said, anxious to be out of the station
anyway.

The drive home was far from pleasant though. Vinnie was sitting on the back seat but he kept leaning forward and breathing
down her neck all the way.

And such facetiousness.

"Thanks for the lift!" he said, as he bounded ahead of them out
of the car and up the steps to the house.

"We'll have to draw his attention to the foot-scraper," said the
Major placatingly, when they saw the marks he had made on the
parquet floor.

"I think it would be better to draw the attention of the cobbler
to his boots," Dolly said, because the floor was scratched as well.
"Oh, never mind," she said resignedly, "we may make it less noticeable with sandpaper. Oh, dear! What was that?"

There was *such* a crash.

But it was only Vinnie's door banging, as he went out to the toilet. After he had gone into the toilet a second time, and come out again, and gone back to his own room, Dolly began to realize she might as well get used to doors banging.

"Better call him down for his sandwiches, dear," she said to the Major, because, it being mid-afternoon, she had had some sandwiches cut for him and covered with a napkin so that she wouldn't have to set the table again before suppertime. But what a quantity he ate of the sandwiches! To begin with, he took two at a time, and then he seemed to let half of the filling fall all over the carpet. It would have been far better to have set the table.

Well, I'll know next time, she told herself resignedly.

But long before suppertime came around she began to think that no woman's memory could possibly store as many precautionary plans for the future as were necessitated by Vinnie's behavior. And of course one would always have to deal with unlooked-for accidents that couldn't possibly be foreseen.

She had to admit that the boy was willing enough to please her. He even suggested taking off his hobnailed boots every time he came in through the hall door.

It was on one of these occasions, when he was crossing the hall in his bare feet, that Dolly noticed the peculiar marks his stockinged feet had made; sticky, like paw marks.

"Are your feet wet, Vinnie?" she called after him.

"How could they be wet?" Vinnie looked at her with surprise. It was a hot summer day. Then he looked at the marks on the floor. "Maybe it's sweat!" he said.

Dolly turned aside hastily. It was too near suppertime to let one's mind dwell on such a thought.

But just as they were sitting down to supper, with the soup in front of them, the Major gave a sniff.

The evening was very hot, and the odor of food hung heavy in the air, the odor of food and — yes — of something else.

"Peculiar smell, isn't there?" the Major said.

Dolly glanced at the window.

"Something outside, I dare say. Something dead in the wood perhaps? Shall we shut the window?"

But when the window was shut the smell was worse.

Vinnie tried to be helpful by sniffing harder than anyone.

"That's enough," the Major said at last.

They ate in silence for a few minutes after that, and then suddenly Vinnie put down his soupspoon.

"Perhaps it's my feet that smell," he said, helpfully.

"Is that meant to be a joke, young man?" the Major asked icily.

It was not a joke.

"Don't they have any regard for personal hygiene in those schools?" Dolly said faintly, addressing herself to the Major.

But fair was fair; Vinnie didn't want his school maligned. He hurried to correct a false impression.

"It's not my feet, it's my socks," he said — and he turned to Dolly aggrievedly. "I told you in a letter that we have to pay out of our pocket money for getting our socks washed. They don't go on the bill like shirts and things; a woman in the village does them whenever we want. Some fellows don't get theirs done at all, she charges too much — threepence a sock. It's a bit thick, isn't it?"

Dolly turned to the Major.

"Please, dear!" she said, "do something!"

And Vinnie was sent off at once to change.

"Take a pair of mine if necessary," the Major shouted.

Vinnie wasn't long changing.

"This calls for a fresh start I think, don't you?" he said as he sat down, and he took a second helping of soup; a much larger helping than the first.

"You're spilling it," Dolly said, as he carried his plate from the sideboard to the table.

"Only a small drop," said Vinnie.

The meal continued.

It was in the middle of the custard and apple that Dolly saw the warts.

"How did you get those disgusting things on your hands, Vinnie?" she cried, and taking out her handkerchief she held it to her mouth with the most powerful implications of the way her stomach felt. "On his hands," she said impatiently, pointing them out to the Major. "Around his thumb. You must be blind if you can't see them. And there are more on his wrist, under the strap of his watch. I never saw anything so unsightly in my life. Really! It does seem odd that something wasn't done about them if the school is as good as it's said to be."

The Major examined the warts.

"I must say they are not a pretty sight," he said, "but I don't know that it's fair to blame the school. At a certain age boys are inclined to get warts, I believe — and some people say they are contagious too, which makes it more difficult to control them. Indeed, I seem to remember having heard it is very hard to get rid of them; there isn't any really good cure."

"Nonsense," Dolly said. "That's all superstition and ignorance. I'll bring him down to the dispensary first thing in the morning and get them taken off with caustic."

Vinnie was the only one still eating while this conversation was going on, but he was evidently following closely what was being said. Ramming a last piece of cake into his mouth, warts or no warts, he wiped his mouth clean with the back of his hand.

"Will they charge you for taking them off?" he asked, with great interest.

"Only a few shillings each time," Dolly said. "You'll have to go down there two or three times. I don't think the caustic removes them at once; it withers them away gradually. But anyway the cost is unimportant."

It was not unimportant to Vinnie.

"Oh, shucks!" he said. "I wouldn't waste good money like that if I were you! I'll get them off when I go back to school. Can't think why I didn't have them off before the holidays! I can get them off for nothing! There's a chap in the lower form that takes them off for everybody — and he gets them off right away — first go — you don't have to go back to him — and all you have to pay him is do his sums for him every night for a week. A week a wart — that's his charge."

Then and there he began to calculate how many weeks' sums he'd have to do for his warts.

"Seven weeks!" he said, partly in awe, partly in dismay.

In spite of herself, Dolly was interested.

"How does he do it?" she asked, as she took up her fork again.

Vinnie looked surprised that she should have to be told.

"Bites them off — how else did you think?" he asked, and then he looked at the Major. "What's the matter with her?" he demanded.

For Dolly had rushed from the room.

She didn't come down anymore that evening, but next morning, when the Major was passing her desk, he noticed that the little army of black numbers on her calendar was once more on the march. Away at the bottom of the calendar, the date of Vinnie's departure was singled out as the new objective. And in the vast desert of days that had yet to be traversed before that objective was reached, only one had been passed. For unlike the short, quick campaign that had just been concluded, this new campaign would be a long-drawn-out affair, lasting the whole summer. And the forecast gave it for hot.

MY VOCATION

I'M NOT MARRIED yet, but I'm still in hopes. One thing is certain though: I was never cut out to be a nun in the first place. Anyway, I was only thirteen when I got the Call, and I think if we had been living out here in Crumlin at the time, in the new houses the Government gave us, I'd never have got it at all, because we hardly ever see nuns out here. And somehow, a person wouldn't take so much notice of them out here anyway. It's so airy you know, and they blow along in their big white bonnets and a person wouldn't take any more notice of them than the sea gulls that blow in from the sea. And then, too, you'd never get near enough to them out here to get the smell of them.

It was the smell of them I used to love in the Dorset Street days, when they'd stop us in the street to talk to us, when we'd be playing hopscotch on the path. I used to push up as close to them as I could and take great big sniffs of them. But that was nothing to when they came up to the room to see Mother. You'd get it terribly strong then.

"What smell are you talking about?" my father asked one day when I was going on about them after they went. "That's no way to talk about people in Religious Orders. There's no smell at all off the like of them."

That was right, of course, and I saw where I was wrong. It was the no-smell that I used to get, but there were so many smells fighting for place in Dorset Street, fried onions, and garbage, and the smell of old rags, that a person with no smell at all stood out a mile

from everybody else. Anyone with an eye in his head could see
that I didn't mean any disrespect. It vexed me shockingly to have
my father think such a thing. I told him so, too, straight out.

"And if you want to know," I finished up, "I'm going to be a
nun myself when I get big."

My father only roared laughing.

"Do you hear that?" he said, turning to Mother. "Isn't that a good
one? She'll be joining the same order as you, I'm thinking." And he
roared out laughing again: a very common laugh, I thought, even
though he was my father.

And he was nothing to my brother Paudeen.

"We'll be all right if it isn't the Order of Mary Magdalen that one
joins," he said.

What do you make of that for commonness? Is it any wonder I
wanted to get away from the lot of them?

He was always at me, that fellow, saying I was cheapening myself, and telling Ma on me if he saw me as much as lift my eye to a
fellow passing in the street.

"She's mad for boys, that one," he used to say. And it wasn't true
at all. It wasn't my fault if the boys were after me, was it? And
even if I felt a bit sparky now and then, wasn't that the kind that always became nuns? I never saw a plain-looking nun yet, did you?
Not in those days, I mean. The ones that used to come visiting us
in Dorset Street were all gorgeous looking, with pale faces and not
a rotten tooth in their heads. They were twice as good-looking as
the Tiller Girls in the Gaiety. And on Holy Thursday, when we'd
be doing the Seven Churches, and we'd cross over the Liffey to the
south side to make up our number, I used to go into the Convent of
the Reparation just to look at the nuns. You'd see them inside in a
kind of golden cage, back of the altar, in their white habits with
blue sashes and big silver beads dangling down by their side. They
were like angels; honest to God. You'd be sure of it if you didn't
happen to hear them give an odd cough now and again, or a sneeze.

It was in there with them I'd like to be, but Sis — she's my girl
friend — she told me they were all ladies, titled ladies too, some of
them, and I'd have to be a lay sister. I wasn't having any of that,
thank you. I could have gone away to domestic service any day if

that was all the ambition I had. It would have broken my mother's heart to see me scrubbing floors and the like. She never sank that low, although there were fourteen in her family, and only eleven of us. She never sank lower than a wards maid in the Mater Hospital, and they're sort of nurses, if you like. And when she met my father she was after getting an offer of a great job as a barmaid in Geary's of Parnell Street. She'd never have held with me being a lay sister.

"I don't hold with there being any such thing as lay sisters at all," she said. "They're not allowed a hot water bottle in their beds, I believe, and they have to sit at the back of the chapel with no red plush on their kneeler. If you ask me, it's a queer thing to see the Church making distinctions." She had a great regard for the Orders that had no lay sisters at all, like the Little Sisters of the Poor, and the Visiting Sisters. "Oh, they're the grand women!" she said.

You'd think then, wouldn't you, that she'd be glad when I decided to join them. But she was as much against me as any of them.

"Is it you?" she cried. "You'd want to get the impudent look taken off your face if that's the case!" she said, tightly.

I suppose it was the opposition that nearly drove me mad. It made me dead set on going ahead with the thing. You see, they never went against me in any of the things I was going to be before that. The time I said I was going to be a Tiller Girl in the Gaiety, you should have seen the way they went on — all of them. They were dead keen on the idea.

"Are you tall enough though — that's the thing?" said Paudeen.

And the tears came into my mother's eyes.

"That's what I always wanted to be when I was a girl," she said, and she dried her eyes and turned to my father. "Do you think there is anyone you could ask to use his influence?" she said. Because she was always sure and certain that influence was the only thing that would get you any job. But it wasn't influence in the Tiller Girls: it was legs. I knew that. And my legs were never my strong point, so I gave up that idea.

Then there was the time I thought I'd like to be a waitress, even though I wasn't a blonde.

But you should see the way they went on then too.

"A bottle of peroxide would soon settle the hair question," my mother said.

They were always doubtful if I'd get any of these jobs. But they didn't raise any obstacles, and they didn't laugh at me like they did in this case.

"And what will I do for money," said my father, "when they come looking for your dowry? If you haven't an education you have to have money going into those convents."

I turned a deaf ear to him.

"The Lord will provide. If it's His will for me to be a nun He'll find a way out of all difficulties," I said in a voice as near as I could make it to the ladylike voices of the Visiting Sisters.

But I hadn't much hope of getting into the Visiting Sisters. To begin with, they always seemed to take it for granted I'd get married.

"I hope you're a good girl," they used to say to me, and you'd know what they meant by the way they said it. "Boys may like a fast girl when it comes to having a good time, but it's the modest girl they pick when it comes to choosing a wife." They were always harping on the one string. They'd never get over it if I told them what I had in mind. I'd never have the face to tell them!

And then one day what did I see but an advertisement in the paper.

WANTED, POSTULANTS, it said, in big letters, and, underneath in small letters, was the address of the Reverend Mother you were to apply to, and in smaller letters still, at the very bottom, were the words that made me sit up and take notice. NO DOWRY.

"That's me," said I, and there and then I up and wrote off to them, without as much as saying a word to anyone, only Sis.

Poor Sis, you should have seen how bad she took it.

"I can't believe it," she said, over and over again, and she threw her arms around me and burst out crying. She was always a good sort, Sis. After that, every time she looked at me she burst out crying. And I must say that was more like the way I expected people to take it. But as a matter of fact Sis started the ball rolling, and it wasn't long after that everyone began to feel bad, because, you see, the next thing that happened was a telegram arrived from the Reverend Mother in answer to my letter.

"It can't be for you," my mother said, as she ripped it open. "Who'd be sending you a telegram?"

And I didn't know who could have sent it either until I read the signature. It was Sister Mary Alacoque.

That was the name of the nun in the paper.

"It's for me all right. I wrote to her," I said, and I felt a bit awkward.

My mother grabbed back the telegram.

"Glory be to God," she said, but I don't think she meant it as a prayer. "Do you see what it says? 'Calling to see you this afternoon, Deo Gratias?' What on earth is the meaning of all this?"

"Well!" I said defiantly. "When I told you I was going to be a nun you wouldn't believe me. Maybe you'll believe it when I'm out among the savages!" Because it was a missionary order: that's why they didn't care about the dowry. People are always leaving money in their wills to the Foreign Missions, and you don't need to be too highly educated to teach savages.

"Glory be to God," said my mother again. Then she turned on me. "Get up out of that and we'll try and put some sort of front on things before they get here. There'll be two of them, I'll swear. Nuns never go out alone. Hurry up, will you?" Never in your life did you see anyone carry on like my mother did that day. For the few hours that remained of the morning she must have worked like a lunatic, running mad around the room, shoving things under the bed, and ramming home the drawers of the chest, and sweeping things off the seats of the chairs. "They'll want to see a chair they can sit on. And I suppose we'll have to offer them a bite to eat."

"Oh, a cup of tea will do," said my father.

But my mother had very grand ideas at times.

"Oh, no, I always heard you should give monks or nuns a good meal," she said. "They can eat things out in the world that they can't eat in the convent. As long as you don't ask them! Don't say will you or won't you! Just set it in front of them — that's what I always heard."

I will say this for my mother, she had a sense of occasion, because we never heard any of this lore when the Visiting Sisters called, or even the Begging Sisters, although you'd think they could do with a square meal by the look of them.

There was never before seen such a fuss as was made on this occasion.

"Run out to Mrs. Mullins in the front room and ask her for the lend of her brass fender," she cried, giving me a push out the door. "And see if poor Mr. Duffy is home from work — he'll be good enough to let us have a chair, I'm sure, the poor soul — the one with the plush seat," she cried, coming out to the landing after me, and calling across the well of the stairs. As I disappeared into Mrs. Mullins's I could see her standing in the doorway as if she was trying to make up her mind about something. And sure enough, when I came out lugging the fender with me, she ran across and took it from me. "Run down to the return room, like a good child," she said, "and ask old Mrs. Dooley for her tablecloth — the one with the lace edging she got from America." And as I showed some reluctance, she caught my arm. "You might give her a wee hint of what's going on. Won't everyone know it as soon as the nuns arrive, and it'll give her the satisfaction of having the news ahead of everyone else."

But it would be hard to say who had the news first. I was only at the foot of the steps leading to the return room when I could hear doors opening in every direction on our own landing, and you'd swear they were playing a new kind of Postman's Knock, in which each one carried a piece of furniture round with him, by the way out friends and neighbors were rushing back and forth across the landing; old Ma Dunne with her cuckoo clock, and young Mrs. McBride, that shouldn't be carrying heavy things at all, with our old wicker chair that she was going to exchange for the time with a new one of her own. And I believe she wanted to get her piano rolled in to us too, only there wasn't time!

That was the great thing about Dorset Street: you could meet any and all occasions, you had so many friends at your back. And you could get anything you wanted, all in a few minutes, without anyone outside the landing being any the wiser. My mother often said it was like one big happy family, that landing — including the return room, of course.

The only thing was everyone wanted to have a look at the room.

"We'll never get shut of them before the nuns arrive," I thought.

"Isn't this the great news entirely?" old Mrs. Dooley said, making her way up the stairs as soon as I told her. And she rushed up to my mother and kissed her. "Not but that you deserve it," she said. "I never knew a priest or a nun yet that hadn't a good mother behind them!" And bumping into Mrs. McBride who was coming out, she drew her into the conversation. "Isn't that so, Mrs. McBride?" she cried. "I suppose you heard the news?"

"I did indeed," said Mrs. McBride. "Not that I was surprised," she added, but I think she only wanted to let on she was greater with us than she was, because as Sis could tell you, there was nothing of the Holy Molly about me — far from it.

What old Mr. Duffy said was more like what I'd expect.

"Well, doesn't that beat all!" he cried, hearing the news as he came up the last step of the stairs. "Ah, well, I always heard it's the biggest divils that make the best saints, and now I can believe it!" He was a terribly nice old man.

"And is it the Foreign Missions?" he asked, calling me to one side, "because if that's the case I want you to know you can send me raffle tickets for every draw you hold, and I'll sell the lot for you and get the stubs back in good time, with the money along with it in postal orders. And what's more — " he was going on, when Mrs. Mullins let out a scream.

"You didn't tell me it was the Missions," she cried. "Oh, God help you, you poor child!" She threw up her hands. "How will any of us be saved at all at all with the like of you going to the ends of the earth where you'll never see a living soul only blacks till the day you die! Oh, glory be to God. To think we never knew who we had in our midst!"

In some ways it was what I expected, but in another way I'd have liked if they didn't all look at me in such a pitying way.

And old Mrs. Dooley put the lid on it.

"A saint — that's what you are, child," she cried, and she caught my hand and pulled me down close to her — she was a low butt of a little woman. "They tell me it's out to the poor lepers you're going?"

That was the first I heard about lepers, I can tell you. And I partly guessed the poor old thing had picked it up wrong, but all the same I put a knot in my handkerchief to remind me to ask where I was going.

And I may as well admit straight out, that I wasn't having anything to do with any lepers. I hadn't thought of backing out of the thing entirely at that time, but I was backing out of it if it was to be lepers!

The thought of lepers gave me the creeps, I suppose. Did you ever get the feeling when a thing was mentioned that you *had* it? Well, that was the way I felt. I kept going over to the basin behind the screen (Mrs. McBride's) and washing my hands every minute, and as for spitting out, my throat was raw by the time I heard the cab at the door.

"Here they come," cried my father, raising his hand like the starter at the dog track.

"Out of this, all of you," Mrs. Mullins cried, rushing out and giving an example to everyone.

"Holy God!" said my mother, but I don't think that was meant to be a prayer either.

But she had nothing to be uneasy about: the room was gorgeous. That was another thing: I thought the nuns would be delighted with the room. We never did it up any way special for the Visiting Sisters, but they were always saying how nice we kept it. Maybe that was only to encourage my mother, but all the same it was very nice of them. But when the two Recruiting Officers arrived — it was my father called them that after they went — they didn't seem to notice the room at all in spite of what we'd done to it.

And do you know what I heard one of them say to the other?

"It seems clean, anyway," she said. Now I didn't like that "seems." And what did she mean by the "anyway" I'd like to know? It sort of put me off from the start — would you believe that? That, and the look of them. They weren't a bit like the Visiting Sisters — or even the Begging Sisters, who all had lovely figures — like statues. One of them was thin all right, but I didn't like the look of her all the same. She didn't look thin in an ordinary way; she looked worn away, if you know what I mean? And the other one was so fat I was afraid if she fell on the stairs she'd start to roll like a ball. She was the boss; the fat one. And do you know one of the first things she asked me? You'd never guess. I don't even like to mention it. She caught hold of my hair. "I hope you keep it nice and clean," she said.

What do you think of that? I was glad my mother didn't hear her. My mother forgets herself entirely if she's mad about anything. She didn't hear it, though. But I began to think to myself that they must have met some very low-class girls if they had to ask *that* question. And wasn't that what you'd think?

Then the worn-looking one said a queer thing, not to me, but to the other nun. "She seems strong, anyway," she said. And there again I don't think she meant my health. I couldn't help putting her remark alongside the way she was so worn-looking, and I began to think I'd got myself into a nice pickle.

But I was prepared to go through with it all the same. That's me: I have great determination although you mightn't believe it. Sis often says I'd have been well able for the savages if I'd gone on with the thing.

But I didn't.

I missed it by a hair's breadth, though. I won't tell you all they asked me, but at the end of it anyway they gave me the name of the Convent where I was to go for Probation, and they told me the day to go, and they gave me a list of the clothes I was to get.

"Will you be able to pay for them?" they asked, turning to my father. They hadn't taken much notice of him up to that.

I couldn't help admiring the way he answered.

"Well, I managed to pay for plenty of style for her up to now," he said, "and seeing that this mourning outfit is to be the last I'll be asked to pay for, I think I'll manage it all right. Why?"

I admired that "why?"

"Oh, we have to be ready for all eventualities," said the fat one.

Sis and I nearly died laughing afterward thinking of those words. But I hardly noticed them at the time, because I was on my way out the door to order a cab. They had asked me to get one and they had given me so many instructions I was nearly daft. They didn't want a flighty horse. They didn't want a cab that was too high up off the ground. And above all I was to pick a cabby that looked respectable.

Now at that time, although there were still cabs to be hired, you didn't have an almighty great choice, and I knew I'd have my work cut out for me to meet all their requirements.

But I seemed to be dead in luck in more ways than one, because when I went to the cabstand there, among the shiny black cabs, with big black horses that rolled their eyes at me, was one old cab and it was all battered and green-moldy. The cabby too looked about as moldy as the cab. As for the horse — well, wouldn't anyone think that he'd be moldy too? But as a matter of fact the horse wasn't moldy in any way. Indeed, it was due to the way that horse bucketed about that the cab was so racked-looking. It was newer than the others I believe. As for the cabby, I believe it was the horse had him so bad-looking. That horse had the heart scalded in him.

But it was only afterward I heard all this. I thought at the time I'd done great work, and I went up and got the nuns, and put them into it and off they went, with the thin one waving to me.

It was while I was still waving, I saw the horse starting his capers.

My first thought was to run, but I was still afraid I'd have had to face them again, so I didn't do that. Instead, I ran after the cab and shouted to the driver to stop.

Perhaps that was what did the damage. Maybe I drove the horse clean mad altogether, because the next thing he reared up and let fly with his hind legs. There was a dreadful crash and a sound of splintering, and the next thing I knew the bottom of the cab came down on the road with a clatter. I suppose it had got such abuse from that animal from time to time it was on the point of giving way all the time.

It was a miracle the nuns weren't let down on the road. It was a miracle for me too in another way because if they had been, I'd have had to go and pick them up and I'd surely have been drawn deeper into the whole thing.

But that wasn't what happened. Off went the horse, as mad as ever, down the street, rearing and leaping, but the nuns must have got a bit of a warning and held on to the sides, because the next thing I saw, along with the set of four feet under the horse, was four more feet showing out under the body of the cab, running for dear life.

Honest to God, I started to laugh. Wasn't that awful? They could have been killed, and I knew it, although as a matter of fact someone caught hold of the old cab before it got to Parnell Street and they were taken out of it and put into another cab. But once I started to laugh I couldn't stop, and in a way — if you can understand such a thing — I laughed away my vocation. Wasn't that awful?

Not but that I have a great regard for nuns even to this day, although, mind you, I sometimes think the nuns that are going nowadays are not the same as the nuns that were going in our Dorset Street days. I saw a terribly plain looking one the other day in Cabra Avenue. But all the same, they're grand women! I'm going to make a point of sending all my kids to school with the nuns anyway — when I have kids. But of course it takes a fellow with a bit of money to educate his kids nowadays. A girl has to have an eye to the future, as I always tell Sis — she's my girl friend, you remember.

Well, we're going out to Dollymount this afternoon, Sis and me, and you'd never know who we'd pick up. So long for the present!

FRAIL VESSEL

WHO WOULD HAVE THOUGHT, as they stood by their mother's open grave, that they would both be married within the year? Why Liddy was only sixteen then! Wasn't it for Liddy's sake that she and Daniel had gone on with the arrangements for their own marriage? Wasn't it partly to give her little sister a home; a real family life again that they were getting married so soon? Everyone in town appreciated the fact that she wasn't in a position to postpone her marriage. And anyway, taking into consideration the precarious state of the business and the fact that it would have collapsed years ago only for Daniel's good management, everyone sympathized with the necessity for an immediate formal settlement. In their case, there was certainly no disrespect intended toward the dead.

But Liddy! Bedelia was shocked to find that Liddy had no regard at all: for the living or the dead.

Naturally she was opposed to the marriage. She made every effort to persuade Liddy to wait awhile. But she soon saw her efforts were useless. Whatever came over Liddy, she could get no good of her at all. She was like a person that was light in the head.

As for Alphonsus Carmody, Bedelia could make nothing out of him from the start. To begin with she never could stand solicitors. You could never feel at ease with them. They were always too clever for you, no matter what you did. And then, she never could think of Alphonsus Carmody as anything but a stranger. And what else was he?

He had been only a few months in the town; a total stranger,

with no connections — and no office you might say, except the use
of a room at the Central Hotel. He was a kind of laughingstock
right from the start, sitting inside the hotel window and not a soul
ever darkening the door. He made no effort to get to know people either. Their Liddy was the only one he ever saluted!

Daniel used to laugh at the child.

"He must expect to get a lot of business out of you, Liddy," he
said.

That was the whole trouble: they treated the thing as a joke, both
she and Daniel. And indeed, Liddy herself took it as a joke, in the
start.

No one in his senses could have believed that it could turn into
anything serious. No one could have foreseen that a young
girl would lose her head to an old fellow like Carmody.

Not that Alphonsus was so old; it was more that he was odd than
anything else. But he was certainly a bit old for a man said to
have just qualified.

"Just qualified!" Bedelia cried. "But he's gray!"

Daniel, however, was able to explain. He said probably Carmody
had been a law clerk.

"They have a hard time. So he mightn't be as old as he looked."

As a matter of fact Daniel was right. Alphonsus was a lot
younger than he looked, but all the same it never occurred to Bedelia that there could be anything romantic about him. And the
day that Liddy's face got so red when they were passing the Central Hotel, she simply could not account for it.

They had been out for a walk together, she and Liddy, and they
were coming home. They were talking about her own wedding,
as a matter of fact, when she noticed that Liddy wasn't paying attention. And when she looked at her she saw that she was blushing.

Whatever for? That was her first thought, and she looked
around the street. It could only be some boy, she supposed, and
she couldn't help feeling annoyed because Liddy seemed too much
of a child for that kind of thing. But although she scanned the street
up and down there wasn't a soul in sight except Alphonsus Carmody standing at the hotel door. It simply did not occur to her to
attribute those blushes to him; she contented herself by thinking

that they were due to embarrassment at the way the child was teased about him.

How differently she would have acted if there had been a boy in the street that day, a young man, that is to say. If there had been anyone presentable at all in sight it would have been a warning to her. And although she was nearly distracted, with plans for her own wedding, she would have kept a better eye on Liddy.

As things were, however, she did not give the incident another thought.

She did notice, however, that Mr. Carmody had taken to standing a lot at the door of the hotel, because whenever she paused to look out the window she saw him there.

One day when Daniel was dressing the window in the gable end, and she was looking out over his shoulder into the street, she commented on it.

"He's coming out of his shell," she said to Daniel.

"You'd feel sorry for him," Daniel said. "He can't be doing much of a practice."

Bedelia herself felt a bit sorry for him, but as Liddy came into the shop just then she thought she'd make her laugh.

"We're looking out at your friend Mr. Carmody," she said. "He's always standing in the doorway of the hotel. Maybe he's got a job as hotel porter."

"That must be it," said Liddy. And she laughed.

Yes, Liddy laughed at him too that day. That deceived them.

If she had shown the slightest annoyance or taken Carmody's part in any way they might have been suspicious. But she deceived them completely. Either that, or she really and truly did regard the whole thing as a joke at that time. She certainly didn't take his first proposal seriously. And no wonder!

As it happened, Bedelia herself was at the window, that day, and she saw him lean out as Liddy was passing and catch her by the plait.

She little knew what he had said to her!

"Well, Liddy?" she said, when the girl came running into the shop. "I saw you!" She was partly disapproving; partly amused.

"But you didn't hear what he said to me!" cried Liddy. "He

told me to go home and ask you when you'd let me marry him!"

"Well, the cheek of him!" Bedelia cried. "I didn't think he had it in him to make a joke." Because, of course, she took it as a joke.

But when it became a regular thing for the fellow to pull Liddy's plait every time she went up or down the street, Bedelia felt obliged to speak to her.

Liddy didn't take it well though. Bedelia noticed that at once, and for the first time she felt uneasy.

"After all, Liddy, you must remember that I stand in your mother's place and I am responsible for you. I think this thing is going beyond a joke."

But her words were truer than she knew: it was already beyond a joke.

So when Liddy paid no heed to her at all, but continued to hang about the hotel door laughing and talking to the fellow, Bedelia decided to have it out with her. The next time they were together upstairs, in the big parlor over the shop, Bedelia jerked her head in the direction of the Central Hotel.

"If this nonsense doesn't stop, Liddy, I'll have to speak to Mr. Carmody."

That was all she said, and indeed she hadn't any intention of carrying out such a threat. But to her surprise Liddy said nothing. Something odd about the girl's silence made her look sharply at her.

Liddy's face was covered with blushes.

"I think he wants to speak to you too, Bedelia," she said. Bedelia saw that her hands were trembling.

"To speak to me?" She was astonished.

Liddy's head was bent, but with a great effort she forced herself to look her in the face.

"I think he's coming to see you —" she said " — today!"

Today?

But Liddy could control herself no longer.

"Oh, Bedelia!" she cried. And Bedelia honestly could not tell whether she was crying or laughing. "Oh, Bedelia — you know the way he was always going on — about asking you if you'd let him marry me — you remember we thought he was joking — didn't we? Well — he wasn't!"

Bedelia could only gasp. And then, before she had time to get over the shock there was a loud rap on the hall door.

Never in her life was she thrown into such flurry. She stared at Liddy.

Liddy's blushes had died away.

"I expect that's him now," she said, coolly, calmly, as if it were the most natural thing in the world.

In the few minutes before Bedelia went down to the little front parlor to see her prospective brother-in-law, she tried to gather her thoughts together.

She was bewildered. What was she to say to this — stranger?

Her first impulse was to run down the backstairs and call Daniel in from the shop. But it didn't seem fair to drag Daniel into it. Anyway, she doubted if he would be much use in this kind of situation. Daniel's talent was for figures; for keeping books and attending to the financial side of things. Of course, there was a financial side to this situation too. How was this fellow going to support a wife? Where was he going to bring his wife to live? These and several other questions ran through her head as she stood where Liddy had left her, but it was only her mind that was working; her practical common-sense mind. What she felt about the matter she did not know; as to feeling, she was absolutely numb.

Then her eyes fell on the plain serge suit which was intended for her own wedding. It had just that day come from the dressmaker, and she was suddenly shot through and through with irritation. Why did this business about Liddy have to blow up almost on the eve of her own wedding?

Goodness knows, she hadn't expected much fuss to be made about her own marriage, what with not being out of mourning, and Daniel having always lived in the house anyway; but it did seem a bit unfair to have this excitement blow up around Liddy.

Two rare, very rare, and angry tears squeezed out of Bedelia's pale eyes, and fell down her plain round cheeks. Because, of course, mourning or no mourning, a young girl like Liddy wasn't likely to get married in serge!

Bedelia felt that a mean trick had been played on her. After all I've done for that girl! she thought. After being a mother to her! But this last thought made her feel more bitter than ever because it seemed to her that this was the measure of the difference between them as brides. Already she could imagine the fuss there would be over Liddy — the exclamations and the sighs of pity and admiration. Such a lovely bride!

Whereas when she — oh, but it was so unfair because never at any time did she regard her own marriage as anything but a practical expedient. It was only that she hadn't counted on being up against a comparison. It was the comparison she minded.

But here Bedelia called herself to order. Of course a lot depended upon when the other two intended to bring their affairs to a head. After all Alphonsus Carmody couldn't have much money. Perhaps he only wanted her sanction to his suit? It might be years before he could get married.

Yes, of course. Of course. That was it. She was letting her imagination run away with her. It would probably be years before poor Carmody would take the final step. Running across the landing to her bedroom, and dipping the corner of her towel into the ewer of water on her washstand, Bedelia rubbed her face and darted a look into the mirror. Smart and all as Liddy was, she might be old enough by the time her beau was in a position to lead her up to the altar! Bedelia ran down the stairs.

But at the bottom of the stairs another aspect of the situation struck her.

It was all very well for Daniel and herself to be making a home for Liddy when they regarded her as a child — but how would things be after this? Indeed if this had never occurred it might have been more awkward than they realized to have another person in the house with them right from the start — and another woman at that.

For the first time in her life, Bedelia felt bashful at the thought of the night when Daniel would move out of the little return-room on the back landing, where he had slept since he was a young apprentice, and, with his old alarm clock under his arm, take up his position in her room. It was only then — only at the last minute, with her hand on the knob of the parlor door, that it came over her that things might not be so bad after all. In any case what could she do about it? If they were bent on getting married, who could stop them?

It was all settled. It had taken less than five minutes, and yet everything was arranged. Daniel had been sent for and although he was as much taken by surprise as anyone, he was soon brought a-round more or less to Alphonsus Carmody's viewpoint. That was what came of being a solicitor, Bedelia supposed. They were so able. But I'll never like him, she thought. He could build a nest in my ear.

And that was tantamount to what her new brother-in-law proposed to do.

It seemed that Liddy had told him about the little house at the end of the street that the sisters owned; it was unoccupied, tumbling down in fact, but it had never seemed worthwhile repairing, for the small rent they would get for it.

It would be just the thing for himself and Liddy, Alphonsus said. With a bit of paint, and something done about the bad spot on the roof, it would serve until they had time to find something better, something more suitable.

"And it's so pretty," Liddy cried. "I always thought it was a dear little house! I used to peep in through the shutters and wish I could go and live in it" — she turned and smiled at Alphonsus — "all by myself."

But Bedelia had had enough without that. Such soppiness — and in front of Daniel. Well, Liddy might play the lovebird, but there no getting away from the fact that the romantic Mr. Carmody was almost gray — whereas Daniel had a head of hair like an infant. She turned around to Alphonsus on an impulse.

"It's a wonder you never married before now, Mr. Carmody," she said, and she looked archly at him to conceal the malice in her voice.

But perhaps he saw through her, because he put out his hand and drew Liddy nearer.

"I suppose I was waiting for Liddy, here," he said, and it was impossible to know whether he was serious or whether he was joking.

And it crossed Bedelia's mind that that was the way in which he had wormed himself into Liddy's affections: by mixing up sentiment and mockery. It was a kind of cheating, she thought. Nowadays people didn't go on with nonsense like that about waiting for the right person to come along. There was nothing like that between herself and Daniel! Daniel certainly didn't go down on his knees to her! She would have thought he was daft if he did. But all the same, as she looked at Alphonsus, she felt that he was the kind of a man who might easily fall down on his knees in front of a girl as a kind of a joke — and she'd know he was joking or partly joking — but all the same it would bring a kind of sweetness into her life.

But Bedelia had to call herself to order again, because Alphonsus was reaching for his hat and they had to see him to the door.

Bedelia was the first to speak, after the door was closed and they were back in the downstairs parlor. "Well, everyone to his own taste," she said, "but I must say I don't know how on earth you can bear that sloppy manner. You know what I mean," Bedelia added impatiently. She tried to think of something sloppy he had said, but it was like trying to remember a smell — she could only remember that it was sloppy. But at last she laid hold on one phrase he had used. "You know — all that rubbish he went on with — about you being the only one in the world for him — and that he was waiting all those years for you. How can you stand that kind of talk? It's so meaningless."

Liddy had caught up the tablecloth and was just about to spread it on the table, but instead she lifted it up to her face, as if it were a veil behind which she smiled, a dreamy, secretive little smile.

"Oh, Bedelia, *I* knew what he meant," she said, and then, over the edge of the cloth, her eyes seemed to implore something from Bedelia — but Bedelia turned aside. Really this sentimentality was more than she could bear. Her eyes narrowed.

"Liddy," she said sharply, "I hope" — she paused — "you know how I have always felt toward you, like a mother — well anyway, like a guardian," she corrected, "but perhaps lately with my own plans taking up so much of my time I may not have given you

as much supervision as I used — as much as you should perhaps
have had — I can only hope that you haven't abused your freedom
in any way?"

But Liddy had spread the cloth on the table and was bending
across it smoothing out the folds. Had she been listening at all? Bedelia gave a clap with her hands.

"What I mean is that I hope you haven't made yourself cheap in
any way? Men don't usually speak so sentimentally, unless — well,
unless a girl has let them become — well — familiar!"

After she'd said the word she was a little daunted herself by its
force, but to her surprise at first, and then to her unspeakable irritation, Liddy didn't realize its implications at all.

"Oh, but that's just it, Bedelia! I wanted to tell you! We've become *so* familiar really. Isn't it odd and to think that we've only
known each other for a few weeks, and that this is the first time
we've ever been together inside in a house." She gave a little high-
pitched laugh. And — yes — Bedelia could hardly bear it, she
hugged herself. "But I feel as if we've known each other for
years and years." A rapt look came into the girl's face. "Bedelia!
you don't mind my saying it, do you, because you want me to be
happy, don't you? But I feel more familiar with him than with you!
I do, really! I know it sounds queer, but it's true — " She paused as
if she was trying to think of some way to make herself clearer.
Then her face lit up. She didn't see the danger signals in Bedelia's
face. "Do you know what I was thinking last night?" She paused
— to take courage? — and then she rushed on. "In bed," she said
softly. "I was thinking about when I was small and used to sleep
with you in your big brass bed. Oh, I used to love it, you know
that! I used to be lonely when I got a room of my own: I was never
able to go to sleep for ages, and I couldn't warm up for hours! But
all the same, even when I loved sleeping with you — you don't
mind my telling you this, do you? I used to hate if your — I used
to hate if my — I mean I couldn't bear it if our feet touched!"

But here, her faint heart failed her again, and she had to rush over
to Bedelia.

"You don't mind my telling you, do you?"

Bedelia drew back. She did mind. She didn't want to hear it. It sounded a lot of rubbish to her. Still, in spite of everything, she was curious.

"I must say I don't see the point!" she said coldly.

Liddy brightened.

"Oh, I'm coming to the point. It's that although I never saw Alphonsus without his shoes and stockings on, of course, it came into my mind — last night in bed — that I wouldn't mind a bit if our feet touched — his and mine, you know — after we were married I mean!" It was said. She had said it. For a moment her face was radiant. Then she looked at Bedelia. "Oh, Bedelia! What's the matter?" She ran over to her. She couldn't understand the look on her sister's face. "You're not hurt, are you?"

"Hurt?" Bedelia put out her two hands. "Keep back from me," she shouted. "Hurt indeed. Revolted would be more like it! Such talk from a young girl. Do you want to know what I think? Well, I think you're disgusting!"

The sisters had both been married six months when Liddy came back to the old house one afternoon and, passing through the shop with only a word for Daniel, went straight upstairs to Bedelia's room over the shop.

"I want to ask you something, Bedelia," she said, straight-away, without preamble. "Will you let us off our share of the rent of the little house — it's such a small sum to you and — well, it's not so small to us — and I know you were only charging us something as a formality — to make us feel independent and all that — but the fact of the matter is — " Nervously she had run on without stopping ever since she came into the room, but as Bedelia, who was sitting at the window, stood up, she broke off — Bedelia was looking so queerly at her.

"Why, Liddy," she said, "I must say this is very surprising. Not that the rent means anything to Daniel and me — you're quite right about that — as a matter of fact Daniel was saying only the other day that no rent could compensate us for the loss of store-space — though mind you, Liddy, I would never have mentioned that if you hadn't brought up the matter yourself — but as I was saying, it isn't a question of money — you know that — you know the standard of living in this house, and you know your little contribution wouldn't go far to maintain it! And it hasn't changed, I can tell you that, although I must say Daniel is very particular about my keeping accounts — "

But marriage had quickened Liddy's perceptions.

"You're not going to let us off?" she whispered, not caring that she was interrupting.

Was she going to run from the room? Bedelia put out her hand. "Wait a minute, Liddy," she cried. "Don't be so hasty. I didn't refuse you, did I?" she asked when she saw with relief that Liddy had come back into the room. "I was taken by surprise, that's all. It's such a wretched little house — I thought perhaps that you were going to tell me that you'd found something better — you know it was never supposed to be anything but a stopgap. I thought you'd be out of it long ago, but of course, if Alphonsus hasn't been able to better his position — if indeed, as it seems, he's come down a peg instead — well then I think the least he could do would be to come and see me himself and not leave you to do his begging for him."

"Begging! Oh!"

For a minute Liddy's stricken face swam in front of Bedelia, but the next minute she could hardly believe that it was her own little sister who suddenly drew herself up, her eyes blazing.

"I'm glad he didn't come to you, Bedelia," she said. "I wouldn't like anyone, much less Alphonsus, to be hurt like you've hurt me. But before I go, I want you to know one thing — Alphonsus didn't send me. He didn't even know I was coming. And he had no idea I was going to ask you for anything." She softened for a minute. "I was going to pretend you suggested it yourself," she said, almost in a whisper. Then she drew herself up again. "I'm sorry I bothered you, Bedelia. Goodbye." At the door she paused. "Please don't say anything about this to anyone, Bedelia. After all, we *are* sisters." She half turned away again and then she turned back. "And just in case you might change your mind, I want you to know I couldn't accept now."

It was that last cut that hit Bedelia hardest, because she had changed her mind and she was already planning how she'd scribble a note when Liddy was gone and send it up the street after her; to overtake her before she got inside the door of the wretched little house.

As if she read her mind, Liddy looked at her sadly.

"You see, Bedelia, I couldn't ever pretend now that you had done it of your own accord. It would be telling him a real lie now, not just managing things a little bit, making things easy — like I meant it to be!"

She was gone.

"Liddy!"

Bedelia made her way clumsily to the door to call after her, but she could hear the light feet on the stairs. The next minute she heard the front door clapped shut. There was no question of going after her now. Bedelia was heavy with child.

It was two months later. Bedelia was once again sitting in the big parlor upstairs, and she was thinking of Liddy. Except when she caught glimpses of her in the street, she had not seen her since she ran down the stairs and out of the house, her pathetic request ungranted.

Oh, how could she have refused that miserably small favor? How could she have refused her anything: Liddy, her little sister? Only, of course, it wasn't really Liddy she wanted to refuse that day, it was Carmody. It was him she had wanted to humiliate, it was Carmody. Oh, how she had grown to hate that fellow. How had she ever consented to his taking Liddy away from her, because, after the tepid experience of marriage with Daniel, Bedelia had begun to feel that no matter what, no one can ever be as near to you as your own flesh and blood. And although poor Liddy didn't seem to have discovered that fact yet, it only made Bedelia feel more drawn to her, and recalled all her old feelings of motherliness for the child! For to Bedelia as she herself grew heavier in pregnancy, Liddy, when she glimpsed her in the streets, seemed as childish as ever — thinner, if possible, than before she was married. Oh, what had possessed her that she didn't make more effort to keep her at home?

This was the question that Bedelia asked herself over and over again, and not only did she completely forget the last minute impulse of selfishness that had activated her decision, but she was be-

ginning to think she had erred by being too selfless. And they were
both the losers. Liddy's loss was only too obvious, but it was very
hard for Bedelia to sit and think of all the help the girl could have
been to her in these last few months. To think of the way she could
have run up and down stairs, and stretched for things, and stooped
for things. It would have been so different from asking the maids.
The maids were so curious. It nearly drove her into a rage when she
caught them covertly glancing at her swollen abdomen.

Vain regrets weren't much use, however, and the most she could
hope for was that something or other would break Liddy's resolve,
and that she would sometime start running in and out again like she
did when she was first married, although it used to irritate her the
way Liddy kept looking at a clock. Still, she'd love the briefest visit
now. But the last words Liddy had flung at her as she ran out the
door were to the effect that she'd never set foot in the place again.

It was just as she was thinking of Liddy's last words that Bedelia
heard the footsteps on the stairs, the unmistakable light little steps
of her sister.

There was something wrong though. Bedelia's hand went to her
heart. Always, she was susceptible to wild premonitions of trouble when she heard those flying feet, coming along a passage or as
now, upon the stairs. But as she strained to get to her feet, she suddenly sank back again into the chair. For just as the protective waters within her lapped around her embryonic son, securing him from
hurt, so too a protective instinct warned her against giving way to
shock or distress.

Whatever was wrong, it was not her concern; unless indirectly.
She must not let herself become upset. She sat still.

"Oh, Bedelia!"

It was an exclamation, not a greeting; it was a sigh, a gasp. And
when Liddy came into the room, closing the door, she sank back
against it exhausted. But the next minute she drew herself together,
and even gave a little self-critical smile.

"I never thought I'd set foot in your house again, Bedelia," she
said, and to Bedelia there was something preposterously confident
and independent in the words, but the next minute Liddy's voice
broke, and a more familiar dependent note came into it.

"But I had to come, Bedelia," she cried. "I had no one else to turn to — no one."

Oh, what satisfaction those words gave Bedelia.

"Well, what's the matter?" she said briskly. "Don't stand there — come over here and sit down."

Obediently Liddy moved forward into the room and sat down on the edge of a chair, but almost at once she stood up again.

"It's Alphonsus," she said. "We're in such trouble, Bedelia."

Bedelia tried to look more surprised than she felt.

"It was all my fault, really," Liddy cried. "Only for the way he's always trying to make things easier for me it would never have happened."

Bedelia always hated vagueness.

"What wouldn't have happened?" she asked, sharply.

But it was clear Liddy didn't know how to begin her story.

"Well, you see," she said falteringly, "when we got married Alphonsus wanted to do everything he could to increase his income and so he took on an insurance agency — temporarily, of course, although lots of solicitors do it. He thought he might work it up a bit and that it would bring in a little regular money until his practice grew — you needn't look so contemptuous, Bedelia," she interrupted suddenly, "the commission wasn't very much, but Alphonsus's idea was to get as many policies as we could and last month" — here a weak note of pride came into her voice — "last month he collected eleven premiums totaling forty-seven pounds."

Weak and watery as was that little note of pride, it angered Bedelia.

"I presume the forty-seven pounds was the amount of the premiums, not the commission," she said.

"Oh, the premiums of course," said Liddy, somewhat flatter, "the commission was only — " But here she paused, and almost as if some inspired voice had given her the cue she needed, just at the moment when it had seemed utterly impossible to go on with the story, she threw out her hands and rushed on eagerly. "That was the beginning of it all. The insurance company gives a percentage on each premium but the agent is supposed to make out the amounts himself, subtract his commission, and forward the balance to the head office. It's not fair you know, really — they have such a staff up there and everything, while poor Alphonsus has no one to do anything for him — not yet, I mean." At this point she hesitated. "And so he got things a bit mixed up — only in arrears really, but — " Here, however, her voice failed utterly. But Bedelia had heard enough.

"Do you mean to tell me he laid hands on it all — the policy money as well as the commission?" she cried, and in spite of nature's elaborate provisions against such contingency, Bedelia's heart began to palpitate, and a pulse began to beat in her temple. She wasn't so indirectly affected at all. She had thought it might be some trouble that would affect Carmody only — or at worst the pair of them. But if the fellow had converted this money to his own use — newspaper phrases flashed to her mind — well then he might easily bring disgrace on them all.

"Well, answer me! Did he?" she cried.

Although she herself was in a fury, she didn't like the way Liddy's face was quivering. "I'll have to know sooner or later," she said, more kindly, "you may as well tell me."

But Liddy was crying.

"It's the way you put it," she stammered. "As if he was a thief — "

Bedelia bit back the retort she would have liked to make, and instead she shrugged her shoulders.

"Well," she said then, "what do you want me to do?"

As if she had been running blindly down a wrong pathway and suddenly through the blinding branches had seen another way, the right way, Liddy ran back to Bedelia.

"Oh, Bedelia, all we need is to get an advance of the money — it isn't as if we had to ask you for it outright — it's not even a loan really, because the minute the premiums become due again we'll hand the commission straight over to you — of course it will take a little while, I expect, for it to accrue into the full amount, but you can see, can't you, that it's hardly a loan at all — just an advance."

"Advance — accrue! You've got very glib with financial phrases, I see."

Liddy smiled, or tried to smile. She had foreknown that it would be part of her purgatory to humor Bedelia.

"I've become quite a bookkeeper," she said, but as Bedelia said nothing, she looked at her sharply, and then drew back. "I should have known! You're not going to give it to us!" she said. "I can see by your eyes you're not," and she began to back away from those cold eyes, as from something destructive.

But she didn't go farther than the door, against which she shrank back exhausted. For where could she go?

Bedelia, however, had risen to her feet. Although she didn't believe Liddy had strength or spirit left to do what she did last time, flounce away in a temper, she just wasn't going to take any chances this time, and going over to a chest of drawers she took out a black tin box. Liddy knew that box. There was no need to say anything. Bedelia put it down on the table and let back the lid.

"How much did you say?" she said.

But Liddy was crying; silly hysterical tears.

"Forty-seven — oh, but that includes the commission and we don't have to make that up — Oh, Bedelia, I knew you wouldn't fail me — I was only afraid on account of that other time I came about the rent — and that's another thing — I wanted to tell you — you were right about that too — I told Alphonsus and he said you were right, that I shouldn't have asked you, not without telling him, anyway. Oh, you're so good — so kind — "

But Bedelia plunged her hand into the box.

"I'd like to get this settled," she said. "I want to lock away the box again. How much did you say?"

"Oh, dear — how much?"

Liddy tried to wipe away the silly tears, tried to think, to calculate. On her fingers she counted up a few figures and then she threw up her hands.

"I'll have to ask Alphonsus," she said. "You see, there's no immediate hurry: the inspector won't be here until the afternoon, I'll have plenty of time to get Alphonsus to tot up the exact amount." She paused. "I'll get him to write it down so I won't forget it," she said. She wanted Bedelia to see that she was going to be efficient about the whole thing right from the start.

"Liddy, I want to talk to you. Sit down."

Bedelia's voice was so odd that Liddy's eyes flew to the table, as if in doubt of all that had gone before, but no: the box was still there, with the bundle of notes in it held with tape. And to corroborate her previous words, Bedelia was stripping off note after note and counting them, forty, forty-five, fifty. But still, there was that strange, cold note in her voice. "Sit down," she said again.

Liddy sat down.

"I want to ask you something, Liddy. If I didn't give you this money, what were you going to do?"

For a minute there was silence, then Liddy spoke so low Bedelia had to bend her head to hear.

"Alphonsus would have to go away." Liddy said in a little dead voice, "until he gathered up the money somewhere," she added with a little more, but not much more, life. Then she looked up straight into Bedelia's eyes. "He would have to go on the four o'clock train this afternoon."

"And leave you to face the music?"

Liddy's face flushed all over. But it was the flush of courage, not shame.

"They couldn't do anything to me," she said, and then she sprang to her feet. "Why are you torturing me like this? Are you going to give it to me or not? Because I don't care! Do you hear that! I don't mind the disgrace. It couldn't be much worse than this. And in any case you'll come in for your share too. Do you think people won't know you refused us!"

"Hush, hush. Stop shouting! Who said I refused you? I didn't refuse you anything. I'm giving it to you." Feverishly and without finishing the counting, anything at all to stop her — Bedelia began to stuff the notes into her hands. "It's only that I want to do my best for you, Liddy. Surely you must know that," she cried, and as she felt the other soften again she led her over to the chair once more. "Liddy," she said softly, tenderly. "Liddy, I want you to ask yourself something. Do you believe in your heart of hearts that Alphonsus will never do this again?"

What is weakness? What is strength? Liddy had stood up to every taunt and vilification, but she wasn't proof against this tenderness.

"Oh, Bedelia," she whispered, and she began to cry again.

So many tears; she had shed so many and so many kinds, silly tears, tears of temper and tears of bewilderment, but these were tears of defeat. "I don't know," she said.

"Well, look here!" Bedelia took her hands. "This is the way I see it — I'm going to give you this money, but it's not enough to do just that, I want to do more for you. I want to help your poor husband if I can — help him to help himself, I mean."

Liddy didn't follow.

"Now, listen carefully to me," Bedelia ordered. "When I first agreed to help you, you spoke of conferring with Alphonsus. Well, that, I am afraid, I can't allow. This is going to be a matter between you and me" — she paused — "between you and me and the insurance company. I mean Alphonsus is not to know anything at all about it. In fact — he won't know because he will be gone on the four o'clock train. Do you follow?"

No, no! Liddy didn't follow, it would seem from the way she pressed her hands over her face. But when she took them down again it was clear she partly understood.

"But why?" she cried.

"It will test him out, Liddy. Can't you see that?" Bedelia said. "The other way would be making things too easy for him: it would be doing him harm; moral harm. But this way you save his name — you hand the money over to the company, with some excuse — you might even consider having the agency transferred to your name — but that's another matter — the important thing is you must let Alphonsus think that it has to be paid back — let him think that he has to send back the money, bit by bit, if necessary, until the whole debt is cleared. And in that way — "

But as at that moment the clock struck three, the sisters both started.

"Is this the only condition on which you'll give the money, Bedelia?" Liddy said quietly.

Bedelia's eyes ran over every cranny of her sister's face. For a minute she was afraid of what she was doing: afraid of the strain she was putting on the woman in front of her, so thin, so white; so beaten-looking.

But when she had got rid of Carmody, for a while anyway — and had taken the girl back into her own care again, she could make amends to her — make more than amends — for what she was doing now. Why, if there were nothing more gained than the opportunity — even for a few months — of feeding her properly and seeing that she had warmer clothes — there would be something to be said for her action. The girl could come home again, for the present. And with that thought Bedelia was so pleased that all vestige of doubt vanished from her mind, and she sank back into her chair.

And when, at that minute a button popped off her dress and rolled under the table, she caught herself up in the act of stooping for it. Liddy could do that.

It was two hours later when Liddy came back. The train had gone. Bedelia heard it give a short whistle as it went under the railway bridge at the end of the town, and then a long clear blast as it cut its way into the wide open country beyond the town. And then, only a few minutes afterward, there was a noise outside the parlor door, a sound of something heavy bumping, now against the stair treads, now against the banister.

"In the name of God, what is that noise?" Bedelia cried. She thought it was one of the servants.

It was Liddy, and dragging after her, as she came in the door, was their father's big portmanteau that she had taken to carry her things when she went away to be married.

"What on earth have you got in the portmanteau?" Bedelia cried. She hadn't thought Liddy would have taken her up so quickly about coming back. "You're welcome, of course," she said quickly, when Liddy, taken aback, began to explain. "I hope there's a bed ready for you, that's all," she said. "You know I can't do much these days. I'm doing more than I ought already." But as she saw Liddy's face fall, she tried to be warmer. "It's all right, you know," she said, "it's all right. I meant you to come, only I thought you'd have arrangements to make. I thought it would take you a few days to settle your things, although I dare say you wouldn't have much to attend to in that little poke-hole of a place — "

"Oh, I have lots to do," Liddy said proudly. "I've nothing done at all yet. I'll have to go back during the daytime, but — " she paused, and involuntarily her glance traveled toward the high window in the gable where the clouds could be seen foregathering in heavy masses on the western horizon.

Bedelia understood the glance all right, but some unanalyzed association of ideas irritated her.

"I thought it was only spinsters that were afraid at night!" she said, but immediately, prompted by a movement in her body, she knew she must not make remarks like that. They could upset herself as much as Liddy. If she was to get anything out of the situation; if she was to get any return for taking Liddy back into the house, she'd have to learn not to give way to petty vexations. "Put down that heavy suitcase," she said abruptly.

Was the girl a fool that she was still holding it, her shoulder dragging down to one side. "Come over to the fire, can't you?" she said, "and sit down. You're tired, I expect. You're very white-looking. When did you eat anything? Are you hungry?"

She was trying to be considerate, but all her questions were irrelevant compared with the one question that she could not bring herself to ask. Ask it she must, however. "Well — how did he go off?"

For answer tears welled into Liddy's eyes.

"Oh, come now — it's not as bad as all that. You took the only course open to you, you must know that!" But as Liddy's tears still fell silently, Bedelia stood up and looked down at her. "Oh come, now," she said more kindly. "You'll be hearing from him in a few days; you may have a letter tomorrow if he gets to his destination in time to catch the post. By the way, I didn't ask where he went? Has he any people — any friends or relatives? We never heard of any, I know that," she added quickly, "but I suppose everyone in the world has somewhere to creep when they get into trouble." She stopped. "What's that?" she said.

For Liddy had spoken at last, but so softly, only a whisper, that again the other had to bend down close to hear.

"Like I crept back here," that was what Liddy had said.

Bedelia looked at her. Was she being clever; trying to get out of telling his whereabouts?

"You didn't say where he was going," she persisted doggedly. "Are you afraid to divulge his whereabouts in case something else comes to light about him? I'd hardly give him away — now!" It was cruel, but it wasn't cruel enough to make Liddy open her mouth. Bedelia stood over her. "Perhaps you don't know yourself," she said, moving still nearer. But she had to stand back suddenly as Liddy got to her feet unsteadily and swayed forward with her hand on her stomach.

"I think I'm going to be sick, Bedelia," she said, with a mawkish irrelevance.

It was such a shock. Bedelia gave a shout.

"Not on the carpet," she screamed, and frantically she pulled out a handkerchief from her sleeve. "Here, take this — try to swallow. Breathe — take a deep breath — it will pass off in a minute."

So it did; it was only a gust of nausea.

Liddy handed back the handkerchief and tried to smile bleakly through her tears.

"I'm all right now."

It was Bedelia who looked bad now. She sank down on a chair.

"I must say it's a queer way it took you!" she said crossly, and she placed her hand on her own stomach. "You gave me such a start."

Liddy saw the enormity of her offense.

"It must have been the portmanteau," she said apologetically, "the weight of it, I mean." Then gulping, she came to a quick decision. "I didn't tell you, Bedelia," she said, "but I'm not supposed to lift anything heavy just now — "

"Good God!"

Heavy and all as she was, awkward and clumsy, Bedelia was on her feet again in an instant.

"You don't mean — " Oh, but it was absolutely — oh, but absolutely unbelievable. It was the last straw. Why, she felt as if she had been tricked — as if between them they had made a fool of her, Liddy and Carmody, both of them. "Why didn't you tell me this before now?" she screamed, and as she screamed one question, others swarmed in her mind. What use would the creature be to her in this condition? This condition: it revolted her to think of them both — two of them! — in the same condition, in the one house — one as useless as the other as the days went on. And this brat? When he was born — what was going to become of him?

Would she and Daniel have to rear him too, as well as their own child? And for how long?

Before her mind's eye, she saw the face of Alphonsus Carmody but it was as inscrutable as ever.

She swung around. "Might I ask one thing," she cried. "Did he know about this when he embezzled the funds, or did it come as a glorious surprise to him afterward?"

Liddy hesitated before she answered, but her tears had dried, and she looked steadily into Bedelia's eyes.

"He didn't know," she said calmly. "And he doesn't know even now! I didn't tell him at all!"

"You didn't what?" Bedelia's voice had gone; she could say nothing now except in a shrill scream.

"I didn't tell him," Liddy repeated quietly. Her voice was growing in confidence. "I was going to tell him the very night — the night he had to tell me about the money and so I didn't tell him after all!"

"Why?"

"I wanted to keep it till — "

Anyone — anyone could see why she waited: in the hope that the clouds would be dispelled and that the sun would shine again, and her secret be given its golden due.

Yes, Bedelia too could see that was why she waited: could see but could not bear what she saw.

"You fool," she cried. "There may be a time for sentimentality of that kind, but this wasn't the time! You let him get away without knowing the full extent of his responsibilities. What in the name of God were you thinking about?"

Liddy's mind, however, was in no confusion.

"I knew what I was doing, Bedelia," she said. "I wouldn't have told him for anything. I wouldn't have made things harder for him. He mightn't have been able to make up his mind if he knew — or not so quickly, anyway."

Just as on the day she announced that Carmody wanted to marry her, there was a radiance and glory about her that Bedelia could not but perceive. Yet she could not see whence came this ambience, nor why it should be Liddy's due.

"I must say it's easy to be noble at the expense of others," she said. "Have you thought about us — about me and my husband? It was one thing to have you here — for a while — by yourself — till he sent for you — you might even have been some help in the house — Daniel would have been only too pleased. But how will he take it now — when I have to tell him we're saddled with rearing another man's brat! And for how long? That's the question."

It was the all important question.

Yet Liddy never seemed to have pondered it at all. Her body, beautiful, frail for all its fertility, was still a vessel for some secret happiness Bedelia had never known. Bedelia thrust her face, that was swollen with the strain she had undergone, into the face, now so serene, in front of her.

"Do you know what I think?" she cried. "I think you've seen the last of him — do you hear me — the last of him!"

But she couldn't make out whether Liddy had heard or not. Certainly her reply, when it came in a whisper, was absolutely inexplicable.

"Even so!" Liddy whispered. "Even so!"

BRIGID

THE RAIN came sifting through the air, and settled like a bloom on the fields. But under the trees it fell in single heavy drops; noisily, like cabbage water running through the holes of a colander.

The house was in the middle of the trees.

"Listen to that rain!" said the woman to her husband. "Will it never stop?"

"What harm is a sup of rain?" he said.

"That's you all over again," she said. "What harm is anything, as long as it doesn't affect yourself?"

"How do you mean, when it doesn't affect me? Look at my feet. They're sopping. And look at my hat. It's soused." He took the hat off, and shook the rain from it onto the spitting bars of the grate.

"Quit that," said the woman. "Can't you see you're raising ashes?"

"What harm is ashes?"

"I'll show you what harm," she said, taking down a plate of cabbage and potato from the shelf over the fire. "There's your dinner destroyed with them." The yellow cabbage was lightly sprayed with ash.

"Ashes is healthy, I often heard said. Put it here!" He sat down at the table, taking up his knife and fork, and indicating where the plate was to be put by tapping the table with the handle of the knife. "Is there no bit of meat?" he asked, prodding the potato critically.

"There's plenty in the town, I suppose."

"In the town? And why didn't somebody go to the town, might I ask?"

"Who was there to go? You know as well as I do there's no one here to be traipsing in and out every time there's something wanted from the town."

"I suppose one of our fine daughters would think it the end of the world if she was asked to go for a bit of a message? Let me tell you they'd get husbands for themselves quicker if they were seen doing a bit of work once in a while."

"Who said anything about getting husbands for them?" said the woman. "They're time enough getting married."

"Is that so? Mind you now, anyone would think that you were anxious to get them off your hands with the way every penny that comes into the house goes out again on bits of silks and ribbons for them."

"I'm not going to let them be without their bit of fun just because you have other uses for your money than spending it on your own children!"

"What other uses have I? Do I smoke? Do I drink? Do I play cards?"

"You know what I mean."

"I suppose I do." The man was silent. He left down his fork. "I suppose you're hinting at poor Brigid again?" he said. "But I told you forty times, if she was put into a home she'd be just as much of an expense to us as she is in the little house above there." He pointed out of the window with his fork.

"I see there's no use in talking about it," said the woman. All I can say is God help the girls, with you, their own father, putting a drag on them so that no man will have anything to do with them after hearing about Brigid."

"What do you mean by that? This is something new. I thought it was only the bit of bread and tea she got that you grudged the poor thing. This is something new. What is this?"

"You oughtn't to need to be told, a man like you that saw the world, a man that traveled like you did, a man that was in England and London."

"I don't know what you're talking about." He took up his hat and felt it to see if the side he had placed near the fire was dry. He turned the other side toward the fire. "What are you trying to say?" he said. "Speak plain!"

"Is any man going to marry a girl when he hears her aunt is a poor half-witted creature, soft in the head, and living in a poke of a hut, doing nothing all day but sitting looking into the fire?"

"What has that got to do with anybody but the poor creature herself? Isn't it her own trouble?"

"Men don't like marrying into a family that has the like of her in it."

"Is that so? I didn't notice that you were put off marrying me, and you knew all about poor Brigid. You used to bring her bunches of primroses. And one day I remember you pulling the flowers off your hat and giving them to her when she started crying over nothing. You used to say she was a harmless poor thing. You used to say you'd look after her."

"And didn't I? Nobody can say I didn't look after her. Didn't I do my best to have her taken into a home, where she'd get proper care? You can't deny that."

"I'm not denying it. You never gave me peace or ease since the day we were married. But I wouldn't give in. I wouldn't give in then, and I won't give in now, either. I won't let it be said that I had hand or part in letting my own sister be put away."

"But it's for her own good." This time the woman's voice was softer and she went over and turned the wet hat again on the fender. "It's nearly dry," she said, and she went back to the table and took up the plate from which he had eaten and began to wash it in a basin of water at the other end of the table. "It's for her own good. I'm surprised you can't see that; you, a sensible man, with two grown-up daughters. You'll be sorry one of these days when she's found dead in the chair — the Lord between us and all harm — or falls in the fire and gets scorched to death — God preserve us from the like! I was reading, only the other day, in a paper that came round something from the shop, that there was a case like that up in the Midlands."

"I don't want to hear about it," said the man, shuffling his feet. "The hat is dry, I think," he said, and he put it on his head and stood up.

"That's the way you always go on. You don't want to listen to anything unpleasant. You don't want to listen to anything that's right. You don't want to listen because you know what I'm saying is true and you know you have no answer to it."

"You make me tired," said the man; "it's always the one story in this house. Why don't you get something else to talk about for a change?"

The woman ran to the door and blocked his way.

"Is that your last word?" she said. "You won't give in?"

"I won't give in. Poor Brigid. Didn't my mother make me promise I'd never have hand or part in putting the poor creature away? 'Leave her alone,' my mother used to say, 'she's doing no harm to anyone.' "

"She's doing harm to our daughters," said the woman, "and you know that. Don't you?" She caught his coat and stared at him. "You know the way Matty Monaghan gave up Rosie after dancing with her all night at a dance in the Town Hall last year. Why did he do that, do you suppose? It's little you know about it at all! You don't see Mamie crying her eyes out some nights after coming in from a walk with the girls and hearing little bits of talk from this one and that one, and putting two and two together, and finding out for herself the talk that goes on among the men about girls and the kind of homes they come from!"

"There'd be a lot more talk if the poor creature was put away. Let me tell you that, if you don't know it for yourself! It's one thing to have a poor creature, doing no one any harm, living quiet, all by herself, up at the end of a boreen where seldom or never anyone gets a chance of seeing her. It's another thing altogether to have her taken away in a car and everyone running to the window to see the car pass and talking about her and telling stories from one to another till in no time at all they'd be letting on she was twice as bad as she is, and the stories about her would be getting so wild that none of us could go down the streets without being stared at as if we were all queer!"

"You won't give in?" his wife asked once more.

"I won't give in."

"Poor Mamie. Poor Rosie." The woman sighed. She put the plate up on the dresser.

Owen shuffled his feet. "If you didn't let it be seen so plain that

you wanted to get them off, they might have a better chance. I
don't know what they want getting married for, in any case.
They'd be better off to be interested in this place, and raise a few
hens, and make a bit of money for themselves, so they could be independent and take no notice of people and their gossip!"

"It's little you know about anything, that's all I have to say," said
the woman.

Owen moved to the door.

"Where are you going now?"

"There's no use in my telling you and drawing down another
stream of abuse on myself, when I mention the poor creature's
name."

The woman sighed and then stood up and walked over to the fire.

"If that's where you're going you might as well take over these
clean sheets." She took down a pair of sheets from where they
were airing on the shelf over the fire. "You can't say but I look after
her, no matter what," she said.

"If you remembered her the way I do," said the man, "when she
was only a little bit of a child, and I was growing up and going to
school, you'd know what it feels like to hear talk of putting her in a
home. She used to have lovely hair. It was like the flossy heads of
the dandelions when they are gone past their best. No one knew
she was going to be a bit soft until she was toddling around and beginning to talk, and even then it was thought she was only slow;
that she'd grow out of it."

"I know how you feel," said the woman. "I could cry sometimes
myself when I think about her. But she'd be so happy in a home!
We could visit her any time we wanted. We could hire a car and
drive over to see her, all of us, on a fine Sunday now and again. It
would be some place to go. And it would cost no more than it costs
to keep her here."

She didn't know whether he had heard the end of the sentence because he had gone out through the yard and was cutting across the
field, with his ash plant in his hand.

"He was cutting across the field with the ash plant in his hand,
when we were starting off on our walk," said Rosie, when she and

Mamie came in to their supper, and her mother asked her if she had
seen their father out in the yard.

"He was going up to your Aunt Brigid then," said their mother.
"Did you not see him after that?"

"That was three hours ago," said Mamie looking worried. "He
wouldn't be over there all this time. Would he? He must be doing
something for Aunt Brigid — chopping wood or mending something. He wouldn't be just sitting over there all this time."

"Ah, you wouldn't know what he'd be doing," the mother said,
and the girls looked at each other. They knew then there had been
words between their father and mother while they were out.

"Maybe one of you ought to run over and see what's keeping
him?" said their mother.

"Oh, leave him alone," said Mamie. "If he wants to stay over
there, let him! He'll have to be home soon anyway to put in the
calves. It's nearly dark."

But soon it was very dark, and the calves were still out. The
girls had gone out again to a dance, and it was beginning to rain
when Owen's wife put on her coat and went across the field herself,
and up the boreen to Brigid's.

How can she sit there in the dark? she thought, when she didn't
see a light in the window. But as she got nearer she saw there was
a faint glow from the fire on the hearth. She felt sure Owen wasn't
there. He wouldn't be there without lighting a lamp, or a bit of a
candle! There was no need to go in. She was going to turn back,
but it seemed an unnatural thing not to call to the door and see if
the poor creature was all right.

Brigid was the same as ever, sitting by the fire with a silly smile,
and not looking up till she was called three or four times.

"Brigid, did you see Owen?" his wife asked without much hope
of a reply.

Brigid looked up. "Owen is a queer man," she said. That was all
the answer she gave.

"So he was here! What time did he leave?"

Brigid grumbled something.

"What are you saying, Brigid?"

"He wouldn't go home," Brigid said. "I told him it was time to go home for his tea, but he wouldn't answer me. 'Go home,' I said, 'go home, Owen.' "

"When he did go? What time was it? Did you notice?"

Brigid could be difficult sometimes. Was she going to be difficult now?

"He wouldn't go home," Brigid said again.

Suddenly Owen's wife saw his ash plant lying on the table.

"Is he still here?" she said, sharply, and she glanced back at the door. "I didn't see him in the yard! I didn't hear him!"

"He wouldn't speak to me," Brigid said again stubbornly.

The other woman couldn't see her in the dark. The fire was flickering too irregularly to see by its light.

"But where is he? Is there anything the matter with him?" She ran to the door and called out into the dark. But there was no answer. She stood there trying to think. She heard Brigid talking to herself, but she didn't trouble to listen. She might as well go home, she thought. Wherever he was, he wasn't here. "If he comes back, Brigid, tell him I was here looking for him," she said. "I'll go home through the other field."

Brigid said something then, that made her turn sharply and look at her.

"What did you say?"

"Tell him yourself," said Brigid, and then she seemed to be talking to herself again. And she was leaning down in the dark before the fire.

"Why don't you talk?" she said. "Why don't you talk?"

Owen's wife began to pull out the old settle bed that was in front of the fire not knowing why she did it, but she could feel the blood pounding in her ears and behind her eyes.

"He fell down there and he wouldn't get up!" Brigid said. "I told him to get up. I told him that his head was getting scorched. But he wouldn't listen to me. He wouldn't get up. He wouldn't do anything."

Owen's wife closed her eyes. All of a sudden she was afraid to look. But when she looked, Owen's eyes stared up at her, wide open, from where he lay on his back on the hearth.

"Owen!" she screamed, and she tried to pull him up.

His shoulders were stiff and heavy. She caught his hands. They were cold. Was he dead? She felt his face. But his face was hot, so hot she couldn't put her hand on it. If he was dead he'd be cold. She wanted to scream and run out of the house, but first she tried to drag him as far as she could from the ashy hearth. Then suddenly feeling the living eyes of Brigid watching her, and seeing the dead eyes staring up from the blistered red face, she sprang up, knocking over a chair, and ran out of the house, and ran screaming down the boreen.

Her screams brought people running out to their doors, the light streaming out each side of them. She couldn't speak, but she pointed up the hill and ran on. She wanted to get to the pump.

It was dark at the pump, but she could hear people running the way she had pointed. Then when they had reached the cottage, there was no more running, but great talking and shouting. She sat down at the side of the pump, but there was a smell off her hands and desperately she bent forward and began to wash them under the pump, but when she saw there was hair stuck to her fingers she wanted to scream again, but there was a great pain gathering in her heart, not yet the pain of loss, but the pain of having failed; failed in some terrible way.

I failed him always, she thought, from the very start. I never loved him like he loved me; not even then, long ago, the time I took the flowers off my hat. It wasn't for Brigid, like he thought. I was only making myself out to be what he imagined I was. I didn't know enough about loving to change myself for him. I didn't even know enough about it to keep him loving me. He had to give it all to Brigid in the end.

He gave it all to Brigid; to a poor daft thing that didn't know enough to pull him back from the fire or call someone, when he fell down in a stroke. If it was anyone else was with him, he might have had a chance.

Oh, how had it happened? How could love be wasted, and go to loss like that?

It was like the way the tossy balls of cowslips they used to make as children were forgotten and left behind in the fields, till they were trodden into the muck by the cattle and the sheep.

Suddenly she thought of the heavy feet of the neighbors tramping the boards of the cottage up in the fields behind her, and rising up, she ran back up the boreen.

"Here's the poor woman now," someone said, as she thrust past the crowd around the door.

They began to make a way for her to where, on the settle bed, they had laid her husband. But instead she parted a way through the people and went toward the door of the room off the kitchen.

"It's Brigid I'm thinking about," she said. "Where is she?"

"Something will have to be done about her now all right," someone said.

"It will," she said, decisively, and her voice was as true as a bell. She had reached the door of the room.

"That's why I came back," she said, looking around her defiantly. "She'll need proper minding now. To think she hadn't the strength to run for help, or pull him back a bit from the fire." She opened a door.

Sitting on the side of the bed, all alone, she saw Brigid.

"Get your hat and coat, Brigid," she said. "You're coming home with me."

THE GREAT WAVE

THE BISHOP was sitting in the stern of the boat. He was in his robes, with his black overcoat thrown across his shoulders for warmth, and over his arm he carried his vestments, turned inside out to protect them from the salt spray. The reason he was already robed was because the distance across to the island was only a few miles, and the island priest was spared the embarrassment of a long delay in his small damp sacristy.

The islanders had a visit from their Bishop only every four years at most, when he crossed over, as now, for the Confirmation ceremony, and so to have His Grace arrive thus in his robes was only their due share: a proper prolongation of episcopal pomp. In his alb and amice he would easily be picked out by the small knot of islanders who would gather on the pier the moment the boat was sighted on the tops of the waves. Yes, it was right and proper for all that the Bishop be thus attired. His Grace approved. The Bishop had a reason of his own too, as it happened, but he was hardly aware of it anywhere except in his heart.

Now, as he sat in the boat, he wrapped his white skirts tighter around him, and looked to see that the cope and chasuble were well doubled over, so that the colored silks would not be exposed when the currach got away from the lee of the land and the waves broke on the sides. The cope above all must not be tarnished. That was why he stubbornly carried it across his arm: the beautiful cope that came all the way from Stansstad, in Switzerland, and was so overworked with gilt thread that it shone like cloth of gold.

The orphreys, depicting the birth and childhood of Christ, displayed the most elaborate work that His Grace had ever seen come from the Paramentenwerkstatte, and yet he was far from unfamiliar with the work of the Sisters there, in St. Klara. Ever since he attained the bishopric he had commissioned many beautiful vestments and altar cloths for use throughout the diocese. Once, at their instigation, he had broken a journey to Rome to visit them. And when he was there, he asked those brilliant women to explain to him the marvel, not of their skill, but of his discernment of it, telling them of his birth and early life as a simple boy, on this island toward which he was now faced.

"Mind out!" he said, sharply, as one of the men from the mainland who was pushing them out with the end of an oar, threw the oar into the boat, scattering the air with drops of water from its glossy blade. "Could nothing be done about this?" he asked, seeing water under the bottom boards of the boat. It was only a small sup, but it rippled up and down with a little tide of its own, in time with the tide outside that was already carrying them swiftly out into the bay.

"Tch, tch, tch," said the Bishop, for some of this water had saturated the hem of the alb, and he set about tucking it under him upon the seat. And then, to make doubly sure of it, he opened the knot of his cincture and retied it as tight about his middle as if it were long ago and he were tying up a sack of spuds at the neck. "Tch, tch," he repeated, but no one was unduly bothered — because of his soft and mild eyes. Didn't they know him? Didn't they know that in his complicated, episcopal life he had to contend with a lot? And it was known that he hated to give his old housekeeper cause for undue thumping with her flatiron. But there was a thing would need to be kept dry — the crosier!

"You'd want to keep that yoke there from getting wet though, Your Grace," said one of the men, indicating the crosier that had fallen on the boards. For all that they mightn't heed his little old-womanish ways, they had a proper sense of what was fitting for an episcopal appearance.

"I could hold the crosier perhaps," said Father Kane, the Bishop's secretary, who was farther up the boat. "I still think it would be more suitable for the children to be brought over to you on the mainland than for you to be traipsing over here like this, and in those foreign vestments at that!"

He is thinking of the price that was paid for them, thought the Bishop, and not of their beauty or their workmanship. And yet, he reflected, Father Kane was supposed to be a highly educated man, who would have gone on for a profession if he hadn't gone for the priesthood, and would not have had to depend on the seminary to put the only bit of gloss on him he'd ever get. Like me, he thought! And he looked down at his beautiful vestments again. A marvel, no less, he thought, savoring again the miracle of his power to appreciate such things.

"It isn't as if *they*'ll appreciate them over there," said Father Kane, with sudden venom, looking toward the island, a thin line of green on the horizon.

"Ah, you can never say that for certain," said the Bishop mildly, even indifferently. "Take me, how did I come to appreciate such things?"

But he saw the answer in the secretary's hard eyes. He thinks it was parish funds that paid for my knowledge, and diocesan funds for putting it into practice! And maybe he's right! The Bishop smiled to himself. Who knows anything at all about how we're shaped, or where we're led, or how in the end we are ever brought to our rightful haven?

"How long more till we get there?" he asked, because the island was no longer a vague green mass. Its familiar shapes were coming into focus; the great high promontory throwing its purple shade over the shallow fields by the shore, the sparse white cottages, the cheap cement pier, constantly in need of repairs. And, higher up, on a ledge of the promontory itself there was the plain cement church, its spire alone standing out against the sky, bleak as a crane's neck and head.

To think the full height of the promontory was four times the height of the steeple. The Bishop gave a great shudder. But one of the rowers was talking to him.

"Sure, Your Grace ought to know all about this bay. Ah, but I suppose you forget them days altogether now!"

"Not quite, not quite," said the Bishop, quickly. He slipped his hand inside his robes and rubbed his stomach that had begun already to roll after only a few minutes of the swell.

When he was a little lad, over there on the island, he used to think he'd run away, some day, and join the crew of one of the French fishing trawlers that were always moving backward and forward on the rim of the sky. He used to go to a quiet place in the shade of the Point, and settling into a crevice in the rocks, out of reach of the wind, he'd spend the day long staring at the horizon; now in the direction of Spain, now in the direction of the Norwegian fjords.

Yet, although he knew the trawlers went from one great port to another, and up even as far as Iceland, he did not really associate them with the sea. He never thought of them as at the mercy of it in the way the little currachs were that had made his mother a widow, and that were jottled by every wave. The trawlers used to seem out of reach of the waves, away out on the black rim of the horizon.

He had in those days a penny jotter in which he put down the day and hour a trawler passed, waiting precisely to mark it down until it passed level with the pier. He put down also other facts about it which he deduced from the small vague outline discernible at that distance. And now, sitting in the boat, he smiled to remember the sense of satisfaction and achievement he used to get from that old jotter, which his childish imagination allowed him to believe was a full and exhaustive report. He never thought of the long nights and the early dawns, the hours when he was in the schoolroom, or the many times he was kept in the cottage by his mother, who didn't hold with his hobby.

"Ah son, aren't you all I've got! Why wouldn't I fret about you?" she'd say to him, when he chafed under the yoke of her care.

That was the worst of being an only child, and the child of a sea widow into the bargain. God be good to her! He used to have to sneak off to his cranny in the rocks when he got her gone to the shop of a morning, or up to the chapel of an afternoon to say her beads. She was in sore dread of his even looking out to sea, it seemed! And as for going out in a currach! Hadn't she every cur-rach-crew on the island warned against taking him out?

"Your mammy would be against me, son," they'd say, when he'd plead with them, one after another, on the shore, and they getting ready to shove their boats down the shingle and float them out on the tide.

How will I ever get out to the trawlers if I'm not let out in the currachs? he used to think. That was when he was a little fellow, of course, because when he got a bit older he stopped pestering the men, and didn't go down near the shore at all when they were pulling out. They'd got sharp with him by then.

"We can't take any babbies out with us — a storm might come up. What would a babby like you do then?" And he couldn't blame them for their attitude, although by this time he knew they could often have found a use for him out in the boats when there was a heavy catch.

"You'll never make a man of him hiding him in your petticoats," they'd say to his mother, when they'd see him with her in the shop. And there was a special edge on the remark, because men were scarce, as could be seen anywhere on the island by the way the black frieze jackets of the men made only small patches in the big knots of women, with their flaming red petticoats.

His mother had a ready answer for them.

"And why are they scarce?" she'd cry.

"Ah, don't be bitter, Mary."

"Well, leave me alone then. Won't he be time enough taking his life in his hands when there's more to be got for a netful of ling than there is this year!"

The shop was always full of dried ling. When you thought to lean on the counter, it was on a long board of ling you leaned. When you went to sit down on a box or a barrel it was on top of a bit of dried ling you'd be sitting. And right by the door, a greyhound bitch might have dragged down a bit of ling from a hook on the wall and be chewing at it, not furtively, but to the unconcern of all, growling when it found it tough to chew, and attacking it with her back teeth and her head to one side, as she'd chew an old rind of hoof parings in the forge. The juice of it, and her own saliva mixed, would be trickling out of her mouth onto the floor.

"There'll be a good price for the first mackerel," said poor Maurya Keely, their near neighbor, whose husband was ailing, and

whose son Seoineen was away in a seminary on the mainland studying to be a priest. "The seed herring will be coming in any day
now.

"You'll have to let Jimeen out on that day if it looks to be a good
catch," she said, turning to his mother. "We're having our currach
tarred, so's to be all ready against the day."

Everyone had sympathy with Maurya, knowing her man was
nearly done, and that she was in great dread that he wouldn't be fit
to go out and get their share of the new season's catch, and she
counting on the money to pay for Seoineen's last year in the seminary. Seoineen wasn't only her pride, but the pride of the whole island as well, for, with the scarcity of menfolk, the island hadn't
given a priest to the diocese in a decade.

"And how is Seoineen? When is he coming home at all?" another
woman asked, as they all crowded around Maurya. "He'll soon be
facing into the straight," they said, meaning his ordination, and
thinking, as they used the expression, of the way, when Seoineen was
a young fellow, he used to be the wildest lad on the island, always
winning the ass-race on the shore, the first to be seen flashing into
sight around the Point, and he coming up the sands, keeping the
lead easily to finish at the pier head.

"He'll be home for a last leave before the end," said his mother,
and everyone understood the apprehension she tried to keep out
of her voice, that apprehension which steals into the heart of every
priest's mother thinking of the staying power a man needs to reach
that end. "I'm expecting him the week after next," she said. And
suddenly her joy in the thought of having him home again took
its place over everything else.

"Ah, let's hope the mackerel will be in before then!" said several
of the women at the one time, meaning there would be a jingle in
everyone's pocket then, for Seoineen would have to call at every single cottage on the island, and every single cottage would want to
have plenty of lemonade and shop biscuits, too, to put down before
him.

Jimeen listened to this talk with interest and pleased anticipation. Seoineen always took him around with him, and he got a share
in all that was set down for the seminarian.

But that very evening Seoineen stepped onto the pier. There was an epidemic in the college and the seminarists who were in their last year like him were let home a whole week before their time.

"Sure, it's not for what I get to eat that I come home, Mother!" he cried, when Maurya began bewailing having no feasting for him. "If there's anything astray with the life I've chosen it's not shortage of grub! And anyway, we won't have long to wait?" He went to the door and glanced up at the sky. "The seed will be swimming inward tomorrow on the first tide!"

"Oh God forbid!" said Maurya. "We don't want it that soon either, son, for our currach was only tarred this day!" and her face was torn with two worries now instead of one.

Jimeen had seen the twinkle in Seoineen's eye, and he thought he was only letting on to know about such things, for how would he have any such knowledge at all, and he away at schools and colleges the best part of his life.

The seed was in on the first tide, though, the very next day.

"Oh, they have curious ways of knowing things that you'd never expect them to know," Jimeen's mother said. It was taken all over the island to be a kind of prophecy.

"Ah, he was only letting-on, Mother," Jimeen said, but he got a knock of her elbow over the ear.

"It's time you had more respect for him, son," she said, as he ran out the door for the shore.

Already most of the island boats were pulling hard out into the bay. And the others were being pushed out as fast as they could be dragged down the shingle.

But the Keely boat was still upscutted in the dune grass under the promontory, and the tar wetly gleaming on it. The other women were clustered around Maurya, giving her consolation.

"Ah sure, maybe it's God's will," she said. "Wasn't himself doubled up with pain in the early hours, and it's in a heavy sleep he is this minute. I wouldn't wake him up whether or no — he didn't get much sleep last night. It was late when he got to his bed. Him and Seoineen stayed up talking by the fire. Seoineen was explaining to him all about the ordination, about the fasting they have to do beforehand, and the holy oils and the chrism and the laying-on of hands. It beat all to hear him! The creatureen, he didn't get much

sleep himself either, but he's young and able, thank God. But I'll
have to be going back now to call him for Mass."

"You'll find you won't need to call Seoineen," said one of the
women. "Hasn't him, and the like of him, got God's voice in their
hearts all day and they ever and always listening to it? He'll wake
of himself, you'll see. He'll need no calling!"

And sure enough, as they were speaking, who came running
down the shingle but Seoineen.

"My father's not gone out without me, is he?" he cried, not seeing their own boat, or any sign of it, on the shore. A cloud came
over his face that had been all smiles and laughter when he was running down to them. He began to scan the bay that by this time
was blackened with boats.

"He's not then," said Maurya. "He's above in his bed still, but
leave him be, Seoineen. Leave him be!" She nodded her head back
toward the shade of the promontory. "He tarred the boat yesterday, not knowing the seed 'ud be in so soon, and it would scald the
heart out of him to be here and not able to take it out. But as I was
saying to these good people, it's maybe God's will the way it's happened, because he's not fit to go out this day!"

"That's true for you, Mother," Seoineen said, quietly. "The
poor man is nearly beat, I'm fearing." But the next minute he threw
back his head and looked around the shore. "Maybe I'd get an oar
in one of the other boats. There's surely a scarcity of men these
days?"

"Is it you?" his mother cried. It mortally offended her notion of
the dignity due to him that he'd be seen with his coat off maybe —
in his shirt sleeves maybe — red in the face maybe along with that
and — God forbid — sweat maybe breaking out of him!

"To hear you, Mother, anyone would think I was a priest already. I wish you could get a look into the seminary and you'd see
there's a big difference made there between the two sides of the
fence!" It was clear from the light in his eyes as they swept the sea
at that moment that it would take more than a suit of black clothes
to stop him from having a bit of fun with an oar. He gave a sudden
big laugh, but it fell away when he saw that all the boats had pulled
out from the shore and he was alone with the women on the sand.

His face hardened.

"Tell me, Mother," he cried. "Is it the boat or my father that's the unfittest? For if it's only the boat then I'll make it fit! It would be going against God's plenitude to stay idle with the sea teeming like that. Look at it!" Even from where they stood when the waves wheeled inward they could see the silver herring seed glistening in the curving wheels of water, and when those slow wheels broke on the shore they left behind them a spate of seed sticking to everything, even to people's shoes. "And for that matter, wasn't Christ Himself a fisherman! Come, Mother — tell me the truth! Is the tar still wet or is it not?"

Maurya looked at him for a minute. She was no match for arguing with him in matters of theology, but she knew all about tarring a currach. "Wasn't it only done yesterday, son? How could it be dry today?"

"We'll soon know that," Seoineen said, and he ran over to the currach. Looking after him they all saw him lay the palm of his hand flat on the upturned bottom of the boat, and then they heard him give a shout of exultation.

"It's not dry surely?" someone exclaimed, and you could tell by the faces that all were remembering the way he prophesied about the catch. Had the tar dried at the touch of his hand maybe?

But Seoineen was dragging the currach down the shingle.

"Why wouldn't it be dry?" he cried. "Wasn't it a fine dry night? I remember going to the door after talking to my father into the small hours, and the sky was a mass of stars, and there was a fine, sharp wind blowing that you'd be in dread it would dry up the sea itself! Stand back there, Mother," he cried, for her face was beseeching something of him, and he didn't want to be looking at it. But without looking he knew what it was trying to say. "Isn't it toward my ordination the money is going? Isn't that argument enough for you?"

He had the boat nearly down to the water's edge. "No, keep back there, young Jimeen," he said. "I'm able to manage it on my own, but let you get the nets and put them in and then be ready to skip in before I push out, because I'll need someone to help haul in the nets."

"Is it Jimeen?" said one of the women, and she laughed, and then all the women laughed. "Sure, he's more precious again than you!" they said.

But they turned to his mother all the same.

"If you're ever going to let him go out at all, this is your one chance, surely? Isn't it like as if it was into the Hands of God Himself you were putting him, woman?"

"Will you let me, Ma?" It was the biggest moment in his life up to then. He couldn't look at her for fear of a refusal.

"Come on, Jimeen, didn't you hear her saying yes? What are you waiting for?" Seoineen gave him a push, and the next minute he was in the currach, and Seoineen had given it a great shove and he running out into the water in his fine shoes and all. He vaulted in across the keel. "I'm destroyed already at the very start!" he cried, laughing down at his feet and trouser legs, and that itself seemed part of the sport for him. "I'll take them off," he cried, kicking the shoes off him, and pulling off his socks, till he was in his bare white feet. "Give me the oars," he cried, but as he gripped them he laughed again, and loosed his fingers for a minute, as one after the other, he rubbed his hands on a bit of sacking on the seat beside him. For, like the marks left by the trawler men on the white bollard at the pier, the two bleached oars were marked with the track of his hands, palms and fingers, in pitch-black tar.

"The tar was wet!"

"And what of it?" cried Seoineen. "Isn't it easy to give it another lick of a brush?"

But he wasn't looking at Jimeen and he saying it. His eyes were leaping along the tops of the waves to see if he was pulling near the other currachs.

The other currachs were already far out in the bay. The sea was running strong. For all that, there was a strange still look about the water, unbroken by any spray. Jimeen sat quiet, exulting in his luck. The waves did not slap against the sides of the currach like he'd have thought they would do, and they didn't even break into spray where the oars split their surface. Instead, they seemed to go lolloping under the currach and lolloping up again on the far side, till it might have been on great glass rollers they were slipping along.

"God! Isn't it good to be out on the water!" cried Seoineen, and he stood up in the currach, nearly toppling them over in his exuberance, drawing in deep breaths, first with his nose, and then as if he were drinking it with his mouth. And his eyes at the same time were taking big draughts of the coastline that was getting farther and farther away. "Ah, this is the life: this is the real life," he cried again, but they had to look to the oars and look to the nets, then, for a while, and for a while they couldn't look up at sea or sky.

When Jimeen looked up at last, the shore was only a narrow line of green.

"There's a bit of a change, I think," Seoineen said, and it was true.

The waves were no longer round and soft, like the little cnoceens in the fields back of the shore, but they had small sharp points on them now, like the rocks around the Point, that would rip the bottom out of a boat with one tip, the way a tip of a knife would slit the belly of a fish. That was a venomous comparison, though, and for all their appearance, when they hit against the flank of the boat, it was only the waves themselves that broke and patterned the water with splotches of spray.

It was while he was looking down at these white splotches that Jimeen saw the fish.

"Oh look, Seoineen, look!" he cried. Never had he seen the like.

They were not swimming free, or separate, like you'd think they'd be, but a great mass of them together, till you'd think it was at the floor of the sea you were looking, only it nearer and shallower. There must have been a million fish; a million million, Jimeen reckoned wildly, and they pressed as close as the pebbles on the shore. And they might well have been motionless and only seeming to move, like on a windy day you'd think the grass on the top of the promontory was running free like the waves, with the way it rippled and ran along a little with each breeze.

"Holy God, such a sight!" cried Seoineen. "Look at them!"

But Jimeen was puzzled.

"How will we get them into the net?" he asked, because it didn't seem that there was any place for the net to slip down between them, but that it must lie on the top of that solid mass of fish, like on a floor.

"The nets — begod, I nearly forgot what we came out here for!"

Seoineen cried, and at the same time they became aware of the activity in the other boats, which had drawn near without their knowing. He yelled at Jimeen. "Catch hold of the nets there, you lazy good-for-nothing. What did I bring you with me for if it wasn't to put you to some use!" He himself caught at a length of the brown mesh, thrown in the bottom of the boat, and began to haul it up with one hand, and with the other to feed it out over the side.

Jimeen, too, began to pull and haul, so that for a few minutes there was only a sound of the net swishing over the wood, and every now and then a bit of a curse, under his breath, from Seoineen, as one of the cork floats caught in the thole pins.

At first it shocked Jimeen to hear Seoineen curse, but he reflected that Seoineen wasn't ordained yet, and that, even if he were, it must be a hard thing for a man to go against his nature.

"Come on, get it over the side, damn you," Seoineen cried again, as Jimeen had slowed up a bit owing to thinking about the cursing. "It isn't one netful but thirty could be filled this day! Sure you could fill the boat in fistfuls." Leaning down suddenly over the side, and delving his bare hand into the water, with a shout he brought up his hand with two fish, held one against the other in the same grip, so that they were as rigid as if they were dead. "They're overlaying each other a foot deep," he cried, and then he opened his fist and freed them. Immediately they writhed apart to either side of his hand in two bright arcs and then fell both of them, into the bottom of the boat. But next moment they writhed into the air again, and flashed over the side of the currach.

"Ah begorra, you'll get less elbow room there than here, my boys," Seoineen cried, and he roared laughing, as he and Jimeen leaned over the side, and saw that sure enough, the two mackerel were floundering for a place in the glut of fishes.

But a shout in one of the other currachs made them look up.

It was the same story all over the bay. The currachs were tossing tipsily in the water with the antics of the crews, that were standing up and shouting and feeding the nets ravenously over the sides. In some of the boats that had got away early, they were still more ravenously hauling them up, strained and swollen with the biggest catch they had ever held.

There was no time for Seoineen or Jimeen to look around either, for just then the keel of their own currach began to dip into the water.

"Look out! Pull up the net! Catch a better grip than that, damn you. Do you want to be dragged into the sea. Pull, damn you, pull!" cried Seoineen.

Now every other word that broke from Seoineen's throat was a curse, or what you'd call a curse if you heard them from another man, or in another place, but in this place, from this man, hearing them issue wild and free, Jimeen understood that they were a kind of psalm. They rang out over the sea in praise to God for all his plenitude.

"Up! Pull hard. Up, now, up!" he cried, and he was pulling at his end like a madman.

Jimeen pulled too, till he thought his heart would crack, and then suddenly the big white belly of the loaded net came in sight over the water.

Jimeen gave a groan, though, when he saw it.

"Is it dead they are?" There was anguish in his voice.

Up to this, the only live fish he had ever seen were the few fish tangled in the roomy nets, let down by the old men over the end of the pier, and *they* were always full of life, needling back and forth insanely in the spacious mesh till he used to swallow hard, and press his lips close together, fearing one of them would dart down his gullet, and he'd have it ever after needling this way and that inside him! But there was no stir at all in the great white mass that had been hauled up now in the nets.

"Is it dead they are?" he cried again.

"Aahh, why would they be dead? It's suffocating they are, even below in the water, with the welter of them is in it," Seoineen cried. He dragged the net over the side where it emptied and spilled itself into the bottom of the boat. They came alive then all right! Flipping and floundering, some of them flashed back into the sea. But it was only a few on the top that got away, the rest were kept down by the very weight and mass of them that was in it. And when, after a minute, Seoineen had freed the end of the net, he flailed them right and left till most of them fell back flat. Then, suddenly, he straightened up and swiped a hand across his face to clear it of the sweat that was pouring out of him.

"Ah sure, what harm if an odd one leaps for it," he cried. "We'll deaden them under another netful! Throw out your end, Jimeen," he cried.

As Jimeen rose up to his full height to throw the net wide out, there was a sudden terrible sound in the sky over him, and the next minute a bolt of thunder went volleying overhead, and with it, in the same instant it seemed, the sky was knifed from end to end with a lightning flash.

Were they blinded by the flash? Or had it suddenly gone as black as night over the whole sea?

"God's Cross!" Seoineen cried. "What is coming? Why didn't someone give us a shout? Where are the others? Can you see them? Hoy there! Marteen! Seumas? Can you hear — ?"

For they could see nothing. It was as if they were all alone in the whole world. Then, suddenly, they made out Marteen's currach near to them, so near that, but for Seoineen flinging himself forward and grabbing the oars, the two currachs would have knocked together. Yet no sooner had they been saved from knocking together than they seemed so far sundered again they could hardly hear each other when they called out.

"What's happening, in Christ's name?" Seoineen bawled, but he had to put up his hands to trumpet his voice, for the waves were now so steep and high that even one was enough to blot out the sight of Marteen. Angry white spume dashed in their faces.

"It's maybe the end of the world," said Jimeen, terror-stricken.

"Shut up and let me hear Marteen!" said Seoineen, for Marteen's voice was coming over the waves again.

"Let go the nets," Marteen called. "Let go the nets or they'll drag you out of the boat."

Under them then they could feel the big pull of the net that was filled up again in an instant with its dead weight of suffocating fish.

"Let it go, I tell you," bawled Marteen.

"Did you hear? He's telling us to let it go," piped Jimeen in terror, and he tried to free his own fingers of the brown mesh that had closed tight upon them with the increasing weight. "I can't let go," he cried, looking to Seoineen, but he shrank back from the strange wild look in Seoineen's eyes.

"Take care would you do anything of the kind!"

"It's cutting off my fingers!" Jimeen screamed.

Seoineen glared at him. "A pity about them!" he cried, but when he darted a look at them, and saw them swelling and reddening, he cursed. "Here. Wait till I take it from you," he cried, and he went to free his own right hand. But first he laced the laden fingers of his left hand into the mesh below his right hand, and even then, the blood spurted out in the air when he finally dragged them free of the mesh.

For a minute Seoineen shoved his bleeding fingers into his mouth and sucked them, then he reached out and caught the net below where Jimeen gripped it. As the weight slackened, the pain of the searing strings lessened, but next minute as the pull below got stronger, the pain tore into Jimeen's flesh again.

"Let go now, if you like, now I have a bit of a hold of it anyway, now I'm taking the weight of it off you," Seoineen said.

Jimeen tried to drag free.

"I can't," he screamed in terror. "The strings are eating into my bones!"

Seoineen altered his balance and took more weight off the net at that place. "Now!"

"I can't! I can't!" Jimeen screamed.

From far over the waves the voice of Marteen came to them again, faint, unreal, like the voices you'd hear in a shell if you held it to your ear.

"Cut free. Cut free," it cried, "or else you'll be destroyed altogether."

"Have they cut free themselves? That's what I'd like to know?" cried Seoineen.

"Oh, do as he says, Seoineen. Do as he says," screamed Jimeen.

And then, as he saw a bit of ragged net, and then another and another rush past like the briery patches of foam on the water that was now almost level with the lip of the boat, he knew all the boats had indeed done what Marteen said: cut free.

"For the love of God, Seoineen," he cried.

Seoineen hesitated for another instant. Then he made up his

mind and, reaching along the seat, without looking, he felt for the knife that was kept there for slashing dogfish.

"Here goes," he cried, and with one true cut of the knife he freed Jimeen's hands, the two together at the same time, but, letting the knife drop into the water, he reached out wildly to catch the ends of the net before they slid into it, or shed any of their precious freight.

Not a single silver fish was lost.

"What a fool I'd be," he gasped, "to let go. They think because of the collar I haven't a man's strength about me anymore. Then I'll show them. I'll not let go this net, not if it pull me down to hell." And he gave another wild laugh. "And you along with me!" he cried. Then, as if he had picked up a word from a voice in the wind, he roared it out. "Murder? Who said that? What if it is murder? Sure it's all one to God what a man's sin is, as long as it's sin at all. Isn't sin poison — any sin at all, even the smallest drop of it? Isn't it death to the soul that it touches at any time? Ah then! I'll not let go!" And even when, just then, the whole sea seemed littered with tattered threads of net, he still held tight to his hold. "Is that the way? They've all let go! Well then, I'll show them one man will not be so easy beat! Can you hear me?" he cried, because it was hard to hear him with the crazy noise of the wind and the waves.

"Oh, cut free, Seoineen," Jimeen implored, although he remembered the knife was now gone to the bottom of the sea, and already Seoineen's fingers were mangled in the strings of the net.

"Cut free, is it? Faith, I'll show them all," cried Seoineen. "We'll be the only boat'll bring back a catch this night, and the sea seething with fish." He gave a laugh. "Sure that was the only thing that was spoiling my pleasure in the plenty — thinking that when the boats got back the whole island would be fuller of fish than the sea itself, and it all of no more value than if it was washed of its own accord onto the dirty counters of the shop! Sure it wouldn't be worth a farthing a barrel! But it will be a different story now, I'm thinking. Oh, but I'll have the laugh on them with their hollow boats, and their nets cut to flitters! I'll show them a man is a man, no matter what vows he takes, or what way he's called to deny his manhood! I'll show them! Where are they, anyway? Can you — see them — at all?" he cried, but he had begun to gasp worse than the fishes in the bottom of the boat. "Can you — see them — at all? Damn you, don't sit there like that! Stand up — there — and tell me — can — you — see — them?"

It wasn't the others Jimeen saw though, when he raised his eyes from the torn hands in the meshes. All he saw was a great wall, a great green wall of water. No currachs anywhere. It was as if the whole sea had been stood up on its edge, like a plate on a dresser. And down that wall of water there slid a multitude of dead fish.

And then, down the same terrible wall, sliding like the dead fish, came an oar; a solitary oar. And a moment afterward, but inside the glass wall, imprisoned, like under a glass dome, he saw — oh God! — a face, looking out at him, staring out at him through a foot of clear green water. And he saw it was the face of Marteen. For a minute the eyes of the dead man stared into his eyes.

With a scream he threw himself against Seoineen, and clung to him tight as iron.

How many years ago was that? The Bishop opened his eyes. They were so near the shore he could pick out the people by name that stood on the pier head. His stomach had stopped rolling. It was mostly psychological, that feeling of nausea. But he knew it would come back in an instant if he looked leftward from the shore, leftward and upward, where, over the little cement pier and over the cranebill steeple of the church, the promontory that they called the Point rose up black with its own shadow.

For it was on that promontory — four times the height of the steeple — they had found themselves, he and Seoineen, in the white dawn of the day after the Great Wave, lying in a litter of dead fish, with the netful of fish like an anchor sunk into the green grass.

When he came to himself in that terrible dawn, and felt the slippy bellies of the fish all about him, he thought he was still in the boat, lying in the bottom among the mackerel, but when he opened his eyes and saw a darkness as of night, over his head, he thought it was still the darkness of the storm and he closed them again in terror.

Just before he closed them, though, he thought he saw a star, and he ventured to open them again, and then he saw that the dark sky over him was a sky of skin, stretched taut over timber laths, and the star was only a glint of light — and the blue light of day at that — coming through a split in the bottom of the currach. For the currach was on top of him! Not he in the bottom of it. Why then was he not falling down and down and down through the green waters? His hands rushed out to feel around him. But even then, the most miraculous thing he thought to grasp was a fistful of sand, the most miraculous thing he thought to have to believe was that they were cast up safe upon the shore.

Under his hands though, that groped through the fishes, he came, not on sand, but on grass, and not upon the coarse dune grass that grew back from the shore at the foot of the Point. It was soft, sweet little grass, that was like the grass he saw once when Seoineen and he had climbed up the face of the Point, and stood up there, in the sun, looking down at all below, the sea and the pier, and the shore and the fields, and the thatch of their own houses, and on a level with them, the gray spire of the chapel itself!

It was, when opening his eyes wide at last, he saw, out from him a bit, the black gray tip of that same chapel spire that he knew where he was.

Throwing the fish to left and right, he struggled to get to his feet.

It was a miracle! And it must have been granted because Seoineen was in the boat. He remembered how Seoineen prophesied the seed would be on the tide, and in his mind he pictured their currach being lifted up in the air and flown, like a bird, to this grassy point.

But where was Seoineen?

"Oh Seoineen, Seoineen!" he cried, when he saw him standing on the edge of the Point looking downward, like they had looked, that other day, on all below. "Oh Seoineen, was it a miracle?" he cried, and he didn't wait for an answer, but he began to shout and jump in the air.

"Quit, will you!" Seoineen said, and for a minute he thought it must be modesty on Seoineen's part, it being through him the miracle was granted, and then he thought it must be the pain in his hands that was at him, not letting him enjoy the miracle, because Seoineen had his two hands pressed under his armpits.

Then he remembered the face of Marteen he had seen under the wall of water, and his eyes flew out over the sea that was as flat and even now as the field of grass under their feet. Was Marteen's currach lost? And what of the others?

Craning over the edge of the promontory he tried to see what currachs were back in their places, under the little wall, that divided the sand from the dune, turned upside down and leaning a little to one side, so you could crawl under them if you were caught in a sudden shower.

There were no currachs under the wall: none at all.

There were no currachs on the sea.

Once, when he was still wearing a red petticoat like a girsha, there had been a terrible storm and half a score of currachs were lost. He remembered the night with all the women on the island down on the shore with storm lamps, swinging them and calling out over the noise of the waves. And the next day they were still there, only kneeling on the pier, praying and keening.

"Why aren't they praying and keening?" he cried then, for he knew at last the other currachs, all but theirs, were lost.

"God help them," said Seoineen, "at least they were spared that." And he pointed to where, stuck in the latticed shutters on the side of the steeple, there were bits of seaweed, and — yes — a bit of the brown mesh of a net. "God help you," he said then, "how can your child's mind take in what a grown man's mind can hardly hold — but you'll have to know sometime — we're all alone — the two of us — on the whole island. All that was spared by that wall of water — "

"All that was on the sea, you mean?" Jimeen cried.

"And on the land too," Seoineen said.

"Not my mother — ?" Jimeen whimpered.

"Yes, and my poor mother," said Seoineen. "My poor mother that tried to stop us from going out with the rest."

It was a grief too great to grasp, and, yet even in face of it, Jimeen's mind was enslaved by the thought of their miraculous escape.

"Was it a miracle, Seoineen?" he whispered. "Was it a miracle we were spared?"

But Seoineen closed his eyes, and pushed his crossed arms deeper under his armpits. The grimace of pain he made was — even without words — a rebuke to Jimeen's exaltation. Then he opened his eyes again.

"It was my greed that was the cause of all," he said, and there was such a terrible sorrow in his face that Jimeen, only then, began to cry. "It has cost me my two living hands," Seoineen said, and there was a terrible anguish in his voice.

"But it saved your life, Seoineen," he cried, wanting to comfort him.

Never did he forget the face Seoineen turned to him.

"For what?" he asked. "For what?"

And there was, in his voice, such despair that Jimeen knew it wasn't a question but an answer; so he said no more for a few minutes. Then he raised his voice again, timidly.

"You saved my life too, Seoineen."

Seoineen turned dully and looked at him.

"For what?"

But as he uttered them, those same words took on a change, and a change came over his face, too, and when he repeated them for the third time, the change was violent.

"For what?" he demanded. "For what?"

Just then, on the flat sea below, Jimeen saw the boats, coming across from the mainland, not currachs like they had on the island, but boats of wood made inland, in Athlone, and brought down on lorries.

"Look at the boats," he called out. Four, five, six, any amount of them; they came rowing for the island.

Less than an hour later Seoineen was on his way to the hospital on the mainland, where he was to spend long months before he saw the island again. Jimeen was taken across a few hours later, but when he went it was for good. He was going to an aunt, far in from the sea, of whom he had never heard tell till that day.

Nor was he to see Seoineen again, in all the years that followed.

On the three occasions that he went over to the island, as Bishop, he had not seen him either. He had made inquiries, but all he could ever get out of people was that Seoineen was a bit odd.

"And why wouldn't he be?" they added.

But although Seoineen never came down to the pier to greet the Bishop like the rest of the islanders, it was said he used to slip into the church after it had filled up and he'd think he was unnoticed. And afterward, although he never once would go down to the pier to see the boat off, he never went back into his little house until the boat was gone clear across to the other side of the bay. From some part of the island it was certain he'd be the last to take leave of the sight.

It had been the same on each visit the Bishop made, and it would be the same on this one.

When the Bishop would be leaving the island, there would be the same solicitous entreaties with him to put on his overcoat. Certainly he was always colder going back in the late day. But he'd never give in to do more than throw the coat over his shoulders, from which it would soon slip down onto the seat behind him

"You'd do right to put it on like they told you," said the secretary, buttoning up his own thick coat.

But there was no use trying to make the Bishop do a thing he was set against. He was a man had deep reasons for the least of his actions.

THE MOUSE

LEILA wasn't my real aunt at all, although I called her Aunt Leila in affection. She was only a dear friend of my mother. They were girls together, not, I gather, such *very* great friends at all in those days, but when my father died and my mother came back to her hometown, the friendship really developed. Aunt Leila being an old maid, you see, and Mother being a widow, they were in greater need of each other's company than when they were young, and separated by their hopes and dreams.

They saw a certain amount of each other, of course, even in those days, because they were the only three girls in their town who went by train each day to the convent school in Galway. They had a pass on the railway, the three of them: my mother, and Leila, and Mina.

Mina was never a friend of my mother. Indeed, they disliked each other. My mother said so straight out one day to Leila.

"I *never* liked her, Leila, as you know. I never could understand what you saw in her."

And Leila sighed.

"It just was to be, I suppose," she said, and her face was so sad that later, when she had gone, I asked my mother about it.

She hesitated for a minute.

"Well, there's no reason why you shouldn't know — what little there is to know. You see, Leila was going to be married one time, to a most suitable person too, and then — well — no one knew exactly what happened, but one night he eloped with Mina. Leila behaved wonderfully. Nobody ever heard her say a word against either of them. Not a word. Can you imagine that!" cried my mother. "Wouldn't you think she'd just have to unburden herself to someone? We may not have been bosom friends in those days, but she could have told *me*. Yet their names never passed her lips. It was very strange. The whole town was a hive of gossip. Everyone wanted to know what had happened, but all they could make out was that there was a bit of an estrangement between Arthur and Leila, and that he was seen talking to Mina a few times, but no more than that! Nothing to explain the next thing that happened, the two of them eloping — Mina and Arthur, I mean — and getting married in Dublin. Poor Leila; even now it seems hard to believe it happened."

"But, why didn't she marry someone else?" I cried. "She must have been very good-looking."

"She was!" cried my mother. "She was absolutely lovely; a most striking face, as you can still see, but unfortunately as she said to me recently, *she didn't know it*."

I didn't see how that counted for anything.

"Oh, it made all the difference in the world," cried my mother. "Why, even that awful Mina, who was hardly to be called pretty, even in the commonest way, was so well read about her own looks that I used to think she'd know how to show herself off to the best advantage if she were to be laid out dead! Oh that one! She was good-looking, I'll admit, but there was a lot of trickery to that one's looks. Whereas Leila had a kind of unregarding beauty that was there *all* the time, no matter whether it was being shown up or not. If she took any thought of it, she could have dazzled people. Not that I think she would have liked dazzling anyone. I think that, no matter what happened, it might have been a matter of luck for the right person to come along. She was a kind of person that you would have to put something into, before there'd be anything to get back from her, if that's not beyond you to understand? That was what Arthur did, you see.

"We all noticed the change in her when he began to walk out with her. We all saw suddenly that she had a beautiful face, and we hadn't realized it. But it wasn't everyone would have acted on her like Arthur, and that's why it was so terrible when that awful Mina got mixed up with them. Only for her, they'd be happily married today, like me — like I was, I mean."

"All the same, it's a wonder she didn't marry someone else," I said quickly, "if she was so good-looking."

"You poor child," said my mother, "you don't understand. She couldn't possibly have married anyone else. They were made for each other, she and Arthur; made for each other! It was like your father and me! You might as well think I'd have married someone else if *he* had jilted *me*."

I'm afraid I took this avowal lightly. I wouldn't say there was a lot to choose between Mother and Mina when it came to having boys, just that Mother was a nice girl, and Mina — well, of course, I didn't know her, but she didn't *seem* nice, that's all. Whereas Leila — ah, there was someone who might easily be the kind of person to give her heart once, and once only.

"You see, Arthur was a bit of a stick really," my mother went on. "At least, that's how he appeared to us at first. I don't think I told you that I used to know *him* too, long ago, when we were going in and out to school on the train every day. There were three of us girls — I told you that — but there were five boys as well, although they traveled in a separate compartment. They were always pulling our plaits and jeering at us, and showing off before us too, but they never mixed with us all the same. They wouldn't be caught dead in the same compartment as us. I remember once one of them was late — I do believe it was Arthur! — and he came running onto the platform as the guard was locking the doors, and what did the guard do but open the door of our carriage and shove him in on top of us. Oh, such laughing; we nearly died laughing, but when Arthur saw it was our compartment, he wrenched open the door again and jumped down on the line, although the train was moving fairly fast. He nearly broke his neck. And the stationmaster half killed him, and, needless to say, he missed school that day on top of everything else: but he'd suffer all that rather than have the indignity of traveling with us girls. He was always sort of shy. Not but that the others would have acted the same, and some of them were a long way from knowing the meaning of shyness. There was one big fellow — I forget his name, but if you knew what Mina told me" — but here Mother stopped — "looking back on it," she said, "I suppose Mina could have made up that story, or the half of it anyway. But I know there was something gentler about Arthur than there was about the others, although to tell you the truth, I don't remember much about him, and he was only a short time going in and out on the train. He wasn't living in the town, you see, only staying with people who lived in a big house on the outskirts. His own people were abroad, or something — I don't remember — but in any case he went back wherever he belonged after a bit — I forget where — somewhere in Enniskillen, I think — not that it matters. And he went clean out of my thoughts, and out of Leila's too, I'm sure, because it was only a coincidence that he came back to the town later. There must be dozens of branches of the Ulster Bank in the Twenty-six Counties! But there you are! It was to our town he was sent. Can you blame us for thinking it was Fate? And when we heard Leila's mother was going to take him as a paying guest, well, anyone could guess what would happen!

"To begin with, they were both Protestants, did I tell you that? And then they were both the moody type — quiet, and willing to say nothing if they weren't pressed. They were great readers, too — both of them. I like a good book myself, but if I take one up I can't put it down — it's the story I'm after, you see — but I often saw Leila take up a book — any book! — and start reading it — anywhere — in the middle or the end — anywhere, just for the sake of reading! And he was the same. And such books as he had in his room — Leila took me in one day — not a novel among them, would you believe it? And he was finished his studies at that time. It wasn't compulsory, I mean, if that's what you're thinking. Not that Leila thought it remarkable. It wasn't to show me the books she took me into the room, but for some other reason, which I forget as a matter of fact, but looking back now I think it might only have been for the pleasure of going into his room. Would you believe it? I think she'd be too shy to go into it alone, and he away on his holidays in Enniskillen! That was Leila!

"It wouldn't be Mina's way, I can tell you. And talking about books, do you know I only saw that one with a book in her hands on one occasion, and it turned out to be one that, when you opened the cover, wasn't a book at all but a cigarette box! You couldn't imagine two people more unlike than Mina and him. But Leila and he looked sort of alike. I noticed it right away, a few days after he came to the town, when I saw them in the street. Don't laugh. Why shouldn't people be a bit alike outside if they can be exactly alike inside like those two?

"Arthur was good-looking, too, you see, in an odd way. I would even go so far as to say that, like Leila, he was the kind, too, who was better looking than you'd think at first sight. I know if he had half the notions about himself that some men had, he'd have put more oil in his hair, for one thing, and not have it sticking up like a sweeping brush. Most people saw the shock of yellow hair on him before they saw what good features he had.

"I remember Mina laughing the first time *she* saw him.

"That was the funny part of it. Mina didn't think anything of him at first. We were all dying to see what the new bank clerk would be like, and of course Mina — trust her! — was the first to clap eyes on him. 'Tow-pate: that's his name, girls,' she said, when she came back from some trumped-up message at the bank. She didn't even recognize him, or know she'd ever seen him before in her life. And when she heard Leila's mother was having him in the house as a paying guest, she pitied Leila.

" 'Isn't it a shame,' she said to me, 'that when Leila's mother got it into her head to take a lodger, that she didn't get somebody eligible. Because you know, Leila will never marry anyone — she'll be an old maid for certain — unless somebody is thrown at her head — there'd be some hope for her in propinquity!'

"Oh, she was very well-up, Mina. But it wasn't propinquity that brought Arthur and Leila together, of course — because I suppose that implies only a sexual attraction, and really, I sometimes thought that was one thing they didn't have at all! It would have come, of course. Oh, it would have come for certain when they were married, which would have made everything perfect, but I don't think it was there at the time, unfortunately for Leila — "

And here my mother stopped.

"I wonder if I ought to be talking to you like this at all," she said, dubiously, "but then, you young people nowadays seem to know all that's to be known about everything without ever being told!" She sighed. "Anyway, that's all that's to the story, so there's no harm done."

"You mean you don't know what happened?"

I never felt more let down in my life.

"I told you she never mentioned his name," said my mother, with asperity.

"But perhaps Mina — ?"

"As if I'd demean myself by talking about it to *her*," said Mother. "And anyway, who'd believe *her* version?"

"Do you know something, Mother?" I cried suddenly. "You ought to ask Leila what happened — ask her *now!*"

"Are you out of your mind?" said my mother. "When I kept my mouth shut at the time, I'm hardly likely to bring it up now, when she's mostly forgotten it, I hope."

"She's not forgotten it," I said. "You'd know by a certain look in her face. Oh Mother, it was wonderful of you not to have said anything to her then — at the time, I mean — but somehow I think it's almost unkind never to refer to it *now*. You see *now*, it's all she has ever had, or ever will have; that romance, and even if it never came to anything in the eyes of other people, it must comfort her to feel her life wasn't always empty and cold! Oh, I *do* think you ought to bring it up some day. It would be like talking about the dead — you said it yourself about Father! — they are only really dead when they are no longer remembered by the living — and it may be the same with Leila. You might be able to put a little more reality into her memories."

"I never thought of that," said my mother. "And after all, there was a good deal of reality in it. Arthur *did* love her, I know that for certain. And he never loved Mina — I told you that, didn't I? — the marriage was an awful failure — I haven't heard anything about them for a long time. They left the town after a few years. I knew from the start it could never be the way it should be. So maybe, in a way, Leila ought to be made to feel she had more than Mina in the long run. Oh, the past is a queer place surely! I think sometimes, it's like what we're told to believe Heaven is like, with no marriage, and no giving in marriage; I mean the bodily memories die away, and you only remember the love after a while. If it weren't for that, the pain of love would be unbearable. Perhaps I hadn't so much more than Leila myself when all is said and done. It was only Mina who had less; less than either of us. You're right about talking to her: I will."

And I knew she would. So that evening, when I was out for a cycle run, and passed Mother and Leila pacing slowly along the country road, I didn't get off the bicycle, but just waved as if I was going somewhere, because I knew they were deep in it. Indeed, Mother gave me one of her flashing blue glances that conveyed all and more than she wished to convey.

It was a beautiful evening. I cycled for miles, but I wasn't really going anywhere in particular, and there was only the one road back, so I had to pass them again whether I liked it or not. They were still walking up and down when I passed the second time. I was a bit embarrassed, but I don't think Leila noticed me at all. Mother saw me all right; but the look she gave me wasn't at all the same as earlier in the evening. Even flying past on the bicycle, I could see she was impatient, not only with Leila, but with me. The evening was coming down, and it was chilly for all that it was spring. She was probably cold, I thought, walking up and down the road, and so slowly too.

When she did come home, about an hour later, her hands were icy. And she was inclined to be irritable with me.

"I hope you're satisfied," she said. "I'm two hours listening to her. And what about? I'll tell you! About nothing! All about nothing!" she cried, as she threw off her coat and began to fill the kettle for a cup of tea.

"Look — " Suddenly she put down the kettle, and left the tap running gaily. "Look! You wouldn't think Leila was a bit — a bit strange, dear, would you — from thinking about the past too much?"

"Hadn't you better tell me what happened first?"

"But that's what I'm trying to tell you: nothing happened; only she thinks the nothing was something! Oh dear, it was so hard to follow her, and she went on and on, once she started, and my shoe was hurting, and it was getting cold, and I don't see that it did any good, one way or another. Not that I'm sorry I spoke to her, because you were right, you know, about how precious the memories were to her, and I could see that my remembering them too made a difference to her. She said so. She said she sometimes found herself doubting that there had ever been anything between them. She began to wonder if she had only invented the things he said, just to fill up the terrible vacancy in her heart. Like as if she was getting queer, she meant, I suppose. I was so glad to be able to reassure her. Because, of course, everyone knew how he loved her. 'It was plain to be seen in his eyes when he looked at you, Leila,' I said. 'And he was so manly about it, walking along the roads with you, right from the start, where another fellow would be afraid of getting named along with you.' The tears came into her eyes when I said that.

" 'Oh, those evenings,' she cried, and she lifted her head — you know how lovely she can look even now — and it was like as if the same sweetness was in the air for her still. 'Oh, those evenings,' she cried. 'We were only getting to know each other then; only talking about books.' And she laughed.

" 'Just the same!' I said. 'It was manly of him to be so open about you; and later in the summer, when you *really* were caught up with each other, it impressed everyone the way you still walked out together in the daylight, and sat down on the banks by the side of the road for everyone to see you together, although you weren't engaged really, were you? I mean, you hadn't a ring from him. There was something so innocent about you both.'

" 'Too innocent maybe,' she said quietly, and then she started to talk in earnest.

" 'Mina passed that remark, you know,' she said, quickly. 'Only Mina had an ugly way of saying things, and yet, do you know, I often wondered afterwards if she was trying to warn me; warn me against herself even! There was one day she met us on the road.

" ' "Well, you two don't deserve to live in a place like this," she said, "with all the little lovers' lanes and shady paths there are! I know where I'd go if I was spooning." I remember she looked queerly at us: at me in particular. I think it was that day she first got interested in Arthur. After that we met her once or twice in about the same place, and she was always alone, and that wasn't like Mina. She'd stop when she came to where we'd be sitting, and she'd sit down on the bank on the other side of Arthur, and sometimes she stayed with us till it was nearly time to go home.

" ' "I mustn't spoil sport," she'd say then. I always thought that was a vulgar expression — a bit common — but I think there was more than commonness in it when Mina said it. I think she was sneering at me. But maybe I was wronging her.

" 'Another day she said it was well for us to be so innocent. "Have you nothing to hide at all?" she said.

" 'We hadn't. And even now, even the way things turned out, I'm still glad we were like that, and that Arthur felt like that about me, wanting it to be all in the sunlight, and out in the open. Yes! I'm glad, or I would be only for one thing. Only one thing. I used to think that if we were the kind that wanted to go down the lanes, and climb through the hedges to the quiet of the fields, Mina wouldn't have come on us, and hung around the way she did! I suppose if I got time I'd have shaken her off, but I got no time. It all happened so quickly. She only joined us a few times at first, and even when she did it two or three times running, it was all still less than a week — a Thursday first, and then the Friday, and then Saturday. It was the Saturday I felt really hurt, because we were out for the whole afternoon. I thought she'd see that that was different from our little walks in the evenings, when we went out as much for the air as for anything else.

" 'And as a matter of fact we weren't sitting on the side of the road that day either. Do you know the first field outside the ramparts, with the little stream running through it? There are stones from the rampart fallen into the water, and when it's sunny, the water sparkles and sings going over them. It still does. But it was heavenly that afternoon. The wall was all down in a couple of places, and what did we do but climb over it and sit down by the stream. I may have had it in the back of my mind that Mina wouldn't see us if she passed. Not that we weren't plain to be seen from the road, but I thought she wouldn't think of looking across the wall. But we weren't settled when I heard her voice.

" ' "Can I come in?" she cried, as if it was into a parlor. And the next minute she flounced down beside us.

" ' "I hope the ground isn't damp," she said. "My mother told me not to sit down without something under me. Give me that book, and I'll put it under me."

" 'Arthur laughed.

" ' "Oh no, you won't," he said, snatching it away. He had a great respect for books. "Anyway, the grass is dry. Look at us sitting on it. I must say I didn't think though that you were the kind of girl that would heed all her mother's warnings."

" ' "Oh, not all of them!" said Mina, and she laughed. And Arthur laughed again. "Anyway," said Mina, "she died when I was ten, so she didn't have time to warn me about everything."

" 'Arthur laughed again. I never heard him laughing just like he did that day. But I was glad. Although it was his seriousness that I liked, I'd have loved to see him laughing too, if he felt like it. Even then, sitting there with Mina and me, he soon got serious.

" ' "My mother died too when I was about ten."

" ' "Then you're in the same boat as me!" said Mina.

" 'But I don't think he heard her.

" ' "I only remember one thing about my mother," he said. "When she came to say good night to me, I used to hold up my face to be kissed, and then I used to hold out my wrist to her. *Do the mouse! Do the mouse!* I'd say, because sometimes — not always — she used to put her hand up my sleeve and run her fingers over the inner side of my wrist where the veins are — pretending her fingers were little mice-feet."

" 'Suddenly he pulled back the sleeve of his coat, and tugged at his cuff to show us his wrist.

" ' "I never forgot it," he said. "I don't know what age I was, but I hardly remember anything else about my mother; even what she looked like."

" 'That was all he said about her, and we talked about other things. It was such a warm, soft day. Arthur lay back in the grass, looking up at the sky, and we two sat to either side of him. I think I did most of the talking. But Mina was quieter than usual, I remember that well.

" 'I remember almost everything about that day like as if it was a painting, and I was outside it, instead of in it. I remember a man with an ass and cart came down to the bank of the stream where we were sitting, with a big barrel to fill for the cattle grazing inside the ramparts. Well, I suppose anyone would remember a thing like that, but I remember every detail of it, and how when the barrel was filled, and he was leading the ass up from the stream, the wheels of the cart rocked, and little silver drops of water were tossed up into the air, and they seemed to hang in the air for a minute, like a spray of tremble-grass, before they fell back into the barrel. Fancy remembering that all those years! And I remember, just close to Arthur's face once, where he was lying back in the grass, a little black insect — at least it must have been black, but it glinted green and gold and every color in the sun — a little insect you'd hardly see, it was so small, started to climb up a blade of grass, a thin green blade, and then, just when it was near the tip, the blade bent in the middle and down it splashed into the meadow again.

" ' "Oh dear," I exclaimed, and the others looked at me.

" ' "It was only an insect," I said.

" 'Arthur shook his head. "I hope he doesn't crawl into my ear," he said, but he wasn't greatly worried, and he threw back his arms over his head, palm-side upwards.

" 'Perhaps it was the way his palms were upwards that put it into Mina's head to do what she did. Perhaps it was me talking about the insect that made Arthur start and sit up. But anyway, all of a sudden he sat up, and began to rub his wrist.

" ' "Something stung me," he said crossly.

" 'Mina laughed.

" ' "It was only me," she said, and she leaned over him. "I only did this," she said, and she dabbled her fingers in the air over his wrist, not even touching him at all this time. "I was doing the mouse," she said.

" 'And that was a Saturday. We all walked home soon afterwards, and the following Monday they ran away, Arthur and Mina. And I never mentioned their names again to anyone, till now. I never told anyone about the mouse, because I don't see what it had to do with their running away, do you? And yet, it must have had something to do with it.' "

My mother stopped talking suddenly and looked at me.

"Did you ever hear such a rigmarole?" she said. "Could her mind be affected; that's what I want to know! Or can *you* make anything out of a story like that?"

THE LIVING

"How many dead people do you know?" said Mickser suddenly.
Immediately, painfully, I felt my answer would show me once
more his inferior.

"Do you mean ghosts?" I said slowly, to gain time.

"No," said Mickser, "I mean corpses."

"But don't they get buried?" I cried.

"They're not buried for three days," said Mickser, scathingly.
"They have to be scrubbed and laid out and waked. You're not allowed to keep them any longer than that, though, because their
eyes go like this," and he put up his hands to his eyes and drew
down the lower lids to show the inner lids swimming with watery
blood. "They rot," he explained, succinctly.

"Mind would you fall!" said I, hastily, thinking he might let go his
eyelids if he had to steady himself on the gate post.

We were sitting one on each pier of the big gate posts at the
schoolhouse that was down on the main road. We were supposed
to be sitting there watching the cars coming home from the Carlow
and Kerry football finals. But it wasn't much fun. As Mickser said,
it was only the family man that came home straight after a match.
The real followers, by which he meant the enthusiasts, didn't come
home till near night; or near morning, maybe! And they were the
only ones it was any sport to watch.

"Those ones have no drink taken," said Mickser, contemptuously,
of the cars that were going past at the time. "It's great sport when
the drunks are coming home. Passing each other out on the roads;

on the corners, mind! But your mammy wouldn't let you stay out long enough for that."

It was only too true. It was a wonder she let me down to the road at all. You'd think she knew there'd be no fun in it. She had a terrible dread of fun, my mammy. She always saw danger in it.

"You can go down to the schoolhouse and look at the cars coming home if you're careful. And mind yourself!" she said to me. "Keep well in from the road! And wait a minute. Don't sit up on that high wall the way I saw you doing once."

· That was why we were up on the gate posts, although they were much higher than the wall.

"Gate posts isn't walls," said Mickser, definitely.

That was Mickser all over. You could count on him to get you out of anything. But he could get you into anything too! You never knew where a word would lead you with him. This talk about dead people seemed safe enough though.

"How many do you know, Mickser?" I asked, fearful, but fascinated.

"Oh, I couldn't count them," said Mickser, loftily. "I bet you don't know any at all."

"My grandfather's dead."

"How long is he dead?"

"He died the year I was born," I said. "On the very day after," I added, importantly, having heard it told by my mother to many people.

"Bah!" said Mickser. "You can't count him. If you could, then you could count your great-grandfather and your great-great-grandfather and your great-great-great-grandfather and — " but he stopped enumerating them suddenly as a more vivid denunciation of my foolishness occurred to him. "Isn't the ground full of dead people that nobody knew?" He pointed down below us to where, through the nettles, the clay under the wall showed black and sour. "If you took up a spade this minute," he said, "and began digging down there, or anywhere you liked, you'd be no time digging till you'd come on bones; somebody's bones! Oh no!" He shook his head. "You can't count people you didn't *see* dead, like my Uncle Bat, that was sitting up eating a boiled egg one minute, and lying back dead the next minute. He's the best one on my list though," he added, magnanimously. "I saw him alive *and* dead. But most of them I only saw dead, like my two aunts that died within a week of each other. Everyone said it was a pity if they had to go it couldn't have been closer together, so we could have made the one wake of it. But if they did I might have to count them as one. What do you think?" He didn't wait for an answer. "How many is that?" he asked. "How many have I now?"

"Only three," I said, and my heart rose. He mightn't be able to think of any more.

Not a chance of it. He looked at me severely. He was a bit of a mind reader as well as everything else. "I want to pick out the good ones for first," he said.

That overwhelmed me altogether.

"Ah sure, Mickser," I said, frankly and fairly, "you needn't strain yourself thinking of good ones for me, because I never saw one at all. One of my aunts died a year ago all right, and they had to take me to the funeral because they had no one to leave me with, but they wouldn't let me into the house till the funeral was ready to move off. They took it in turns to sit out in the car with me."

"And what was that for?" said Mickser, looking blankly at me.

"I don't know," I said, in a grieved voice, but after a bit, in fairness to my mother and father, I felt obliged to hazard a reason for their behavior. Maybe they thought I'd be dreaming of it in my sleep!

"Not that it did much good keeping me outside," I said, "because I dreamt about it all the same. I kept them up till morning, night-maring about coffins and hearses!"

"Did you?" said Mickser, genuinely interested, but baffled too, I could see. "Coffins and hearses," he reflected. "What was there about them to have you nightmaring? It's corpses that give people the creeps." He looked at me with further interest, with curiosity. "I wonder what way you'd take on if you saw a corpse!" he said. And then suddenly he snapped his fingers together. "I have it!" he said. "There's a wake in a cottage the other side of the town."

"Mind would you fall," I cried, urgently this time, because there looked to be every danger of it with the way he was hopping about with excitement.

"Do you know the cottage I mean? It's at the level crossing. Do you know the woman in it, the one that opens and shuts the railway gates? Well, her son is dead. Did you know that? Did you ever see him?"

"A big fellow with red hair, is it?"

"That's the one," he cried. "She used to have him sitting outside the cottage most days on a chair in the sun. He was a class of delicate" — deftly Mickser tapped his own pate. "Up here," he said. "Did you know that? Well, he's dead now anyway. He died this morning. Isn't it a bit of luck I was put in mind of it?'

"This is your chance of having one corpse, anyway, for your list. But we'd want to get there quick," he said, taking one jump down off the gate-pier, into the nettles and all without minding them any more than if he were a dog. "We'll have to get down there before the crowds. They'll be lad to see us not matter who we are, if we're the first to come. They're always glad to see the first signs of people arriving, after the cleaning and scrubbing they've been at all night. And they love to see children above all — at first, that is to say. 'Look who we have here,' they say," he mimicked, in a voice that nearly made myself fall off the pier. " 'Bless their little hearts,' " he went on. " 'Come in, child,' they say, and they lead you inside, telling each other that there's no prayers like the prayers of a child. Up they bring you straight to the bed, and down they put you kneeling beside it where you can get a good gawk at everything. Oh, but it's a different story altogether, I can tell you, if you leave it till late in the evening. They've got wise to things by then, and you haven't a chance of getting inside the door. 'Out of this with you, you little brats.' That's all you'd hear then. 'This is no place for children — out of it, quick!' They'd take the yard brush to you if you didn't get yourself out of sight double quick. So we'd better go up there immediately. What are you waiting for?"

I was hanging back for more reasons than one.

"I was told to stay here," I said.

"You were told not to be climbing too," said Mickser, as keen as a lawyer. "So you can't say you were doing what you were told, anyway. Not but that it's doing all you're told to do that has you the way you are this day, knowing nothing about anything. Come on out of that, and I'll show you a bit of what's going on round you, or if you don't, I'd dread to think how you'll end up in the finish. Sure fathers and mothers are the worst people in the world to depend on for finding out the least thing. They're all out for keeping us back. I've proved that many a time with my own ones. And there's yourself!" he cried. "To think they wouldn't let you see your own aunt laid out! I know it wouldn't be me that would be done out of a thing like that. And what's more, you oughtn't to put up with it either. You ought to tell them there'd be no nightmaring or carrying on about corpses if you were let get used to them like me. Are you coming, or are you not?"

It was a sweet, mild afternoon as we set out for the edge of the town to where the level crossing was, and the small slated house to one side of it. It was very familiar to me when I was a bit smaller and my mother used to take me for a walk out of the town into the country air. We often had to wait for the gates to be opened for us, although the train would have thundered past.

"What is the delay?" my mother would ask impatiently.

"I have to wait for the signals, ma'am," the woman in charge would say. "You can pass through the wicket gate if you like, ma'am, but that's none of my responsibility."

"Oh, we're in no hurry," my mother would say hastily, no doubt to give me good example.

But there was no need. I had heard Mickser say he put a halfpenny on the line one day and the train made a penny out of it. I had no fancy for being flattened out to the size of a man. And anyway, I used to be very curious about the big, white-faced boy that used to be sitting in the little bit of garden outside the house on a chair; a chair brought out of the parlor, not one you'd leave outside like we had in the garden at home.

"Does she take it in at night?" I asked.

"Of course she does," said my mother, in a shocked voice, but she must have thought I meant the boy. "Please don't stare," she'd say to me. "Why do I always have to tell you the same thing fifty times?"

Only when the gates were opened, and we were crossing over the rails, would she let on to see him for her part. It was always the same.

"How is he today?" she'd ask the woman.

And the woman's answer was always the same too.

"Poorly." At times, but rarely, she'd add a few words. "It's a great cross to me, but I suppose God knows what He's doing."

"We must hope so anyway," my mother would say hastily, and she'd step over the rails more quickly till we were on the other side. "How is it," she'd say testily to me, "those gates are always shut no matter what time of the day we want to pass?"

And now here, today, for the first time in my life, the railway gates were wide open.

"Do you think they might have forgot to close them on account of the wake?" I said, hanging back nervously as Mickser dashed over the shining tracks.

He stood in the middle of the line and looked back at me.

"God knows it's high time someone took you in hand," he said. "You're nothing but an old babby. What harm would it be if they did forget? Haven't you eyes? Haven't you ears? And if it comes to that, haven't you legs? Come on out of that!" But he slowed down himself and looked up and down the line.

"We're the first here," he said, when we got to the cottage. "They're not finished yet," he said, expertly sizing up the look of the little house.

To me it was like as if it had been washed down from top to bottom like I was washed down myself every Saturday night, and not only the house, but the bit of garden outside it was the same, neatened and tidied, and the big stones that I used to remark around the flower beds keeping back the clay from the grass, were whitewashed every one of them! It was a treat: the stones bright white and the clay bright black with not one weed to be seen out of all the weeds there used to be everywhere. But the chair wasn't out!

"We're too early, maybe." Suddenly Mickser sidestepped over to the window that was to the left of the door. I couldn't see near so well as him, being behind him, but I saw enough to open my mouth. Between white counterpanes and white tablecloths and white mantlecloths and white doilies, the place was got up like the chapel at Lady Day. And, in the middle of it all, like the high altar, was a big bed with a counterpane as white and glossy as marble and —

But Mickser didn't let me see any more. He pulled me away.

"I don't think they're ready yet," he said. He seemed to be losing courage just as I was getting mine. He put his hands in his pockets and sauntered toward the door.

"There now, what did I tell you," he cried, as we only missed getting drenched to the skin by a big basin of slops that was sloshed out the door at that minute. "Did you ever go down the line?" he asked suddenly. And I knew he'd let up altogether on going to the wake.

"I'm not allowed walk on the line," I said. Anyway, I was bent on seeing the bed better, and what was on it. "Let me get a look in the window anyway." I skipped back over the flower bed and pasted my face to the glass.

What did I expect to see? I don't know. Not the full-grown man that was carved out on the bed, hard as stone, all but his red hair. The hair was real looking, like the hair on a doll.

"Eh Mickser. Could you give me a leg-up on the window sill?" I cried, getting more and more curious and excited.

"Are you pots?" said Mickser. "If they came out and caught you up on that windowsill you'd be clouted out of here with one of those stones," and he kicked at one of the big white stones, leaving the black track of his boot on it.

"A true word if ever there was one!" said a voice at that moment, and a thin bit of a woman in black came round the gable end with her sleeves rolled up and no smile on her, I can tell you. "Out of here with you!" she shouted. "This is no place for you!" Just the very thing Mickser said wouldn't be said to us.

But before we had time to get out of the flower bed, another woman came running out of the front door — the woman herself that used to have charge of the crossing gates.

"It's not right to send anyone from the door of a dead-house," she said, dully.

"Hush now; they're only gossoons," said the other one.

"He was only a gossoon too," said our woman. "Only a child. That's what the priest said to me many a time. Not that he ever had any childhood, any real childhood." She lost the dull look for a minute; a lively look came into her face. "Isn't that strange," she said, "I never thought of it before, but he was like an old man when he ought to have been a babby; and he was nothing but a babby when he ought to have been a man. I did my best, but it was no use. And you can't do everything, isn't that true? He'd have liked to have other children to keep him company, but they wouldn't understand."

We weren't sure if it was to us or the other woman she was talking. I wanted to say that I'd have kept him company, but that I didn't know if my mother would allow me. And as that didn't sound very polite, I said nothing. It was good I did, because I think it was to the other woman she was talking.

"There now! there now!" said the other one. "Isn't it better God took him before yourself anyway?"

"I used to pray He would," said the woman, "but now I'm not so sure. Wasn't it the unnatural thing to have to pray for anyway? Don't all women pray for the opposite; to die before them and not be a burden on them, and wasn't it a hard thing to have to bring them into the world only to pray for them to be taken out of it? Oh, it's little you know about it, and if there was a woman standing here in front of me, and she had the same story, I'd say the same thing to her. Isn't it little anyone knows about what goes on inside another person?"

She was getting a bit wild looking, and the other woman began dragging at her to get her back into the house. "Hush now, you'll feel different when time goes on."

"Will I?" said the mother, looking wonderingly at the other one. "That's what's said to everyone, but is it true? I'll feel different, maybe, sometimes when I look at the clock and have to pull off my apron and run out to throw back the gates. I'll feel different, maybe, when some woman stops to have a word with me, or when I have to take the jug and go down the road for a sup of milk. But in the middle of the night, or first thing when the jackdaws start talking in the chimney and wake me out of my sleep, will I feel different then? And what if I do forget?" she cried, suddenly pulling her arm free from the other woman. "I'll have nothing at all then! It will be like as if I never had him at all." She put her hand up to her head at that and began brushing her hair back from her forehead.

Stepping behind her back, the woman that wanted to be rid of us, started making signs at us to make off with ourselves, but it was too late. The dead man's mother started forward and caught us by the hands.

"We must make the most of every minute we have him," she cried. "Come inside and see him." She pushed us in the doorway. "Kneel down and say a prayer for him," she commanded, pushing us down on our knees, but her voice was wonderfully gentle now where it had been wild. "He was never able to pray for himself," she said, softly, "but God must listen to the prayers of children if He listens to nothing else. I used to long for him to be able to say one little prayer, and I was always trying to teach him, but he couldn't learn. When he'd be sitting out in the sun on his chair, I used to show him the flowers and tell him God made them. And do you know all he'd say?" — she gave a little laugh before she told us — " 'Who's that fellow?' he'd say! And he'd look round to see if He was behind him! But the priest said God wouldn't heed him; he said he'd make allowances for him. I sometimes think God must have a lot to put up with no more than ourselves. That's why we've no right to complain against Him."

But I wasn't listening. When she put us kneeling down, I put up my hands to my face and I started to say my prayers, but after a minute or two I opened my fingers and took a look out through them at the man on the bed. I was a bit confused. Why was she saying he was a child? He was a man if ever I saw one! Just then the woman swooped down on me. She saw me looking at him. I thought she might be mad with me, but it was the opposite.

"If only he could see you here now beside him," she said. She leaned across me and began to stroke his hands. And she began to talk to him, instead of to us. "Here's two nice little boys come to see you!" she said, and then her eyes got very bright and wild again. "He never had another child come into the house to see him in all his life. He never had another child as much as put out a hand and touch him, isn't that a lonely thing to think?"

It was indeed, I thought. I wonder would it be any use me shaking hands with him now, I thought. And it might be she saw the thought in my eyes.

"Would it be asking too much of you to stroke his hand?" she said, and then, as if she settled it in her own mind that it wouldn't be asking much at all, she got very excited. "Stand up like good boys," she said, "and stroke his hands. Then I won't feel he's going down into his grave so altogether unnatural. No; wait a minute," she cried, and she got another idea, and she delved her hand into her pocket. "How would you like to comb his hair?" she cried.

I was nearer to the head of the bed than Mickser, but Mickser was nearer to her than me, and I couldn't be sure which of us she meant. I wanted above all to be polite, but for that again I didn't want to put myself forward in any way. I stood up in any case so as to be ready if it was me she meant. She was taking a few big red hairs off the comb. Mickser stood up too, but it was only to give me a shove out of his way.

"Let me out of here!" he shouted, and pushing the woman and me to either side of him, he bolted for the door. The next minute he was flying across the lines.

And me after him. I told you I wanted to be polite to the people; the dead one included, but after all it was Mickser brought me, and it wouldn't be very polite to him to stay on after him. Not that he showed any appreciation, but I thought maybe there was something wrong with him: he was very white in the face when I caught up with him.

I was full of talk.

"Well! I have one for my list anyway, now," I said, cheerfully.

"I suppose you have," he said, kind of grudgingly, I thought, and then he nearly spoiled it all on me. "That one oughtn't to count by rights," he said. "He's wasn't all in it when he was alive; he was sort of dead all along!" He tapped his pate again like he did the first time. "Up here!" he added.

I thought about that for a minute. "He looked all in it there on the bed!" I said.

But Mickser didn't seem to take well to talking about him at all. "I've had enough of corpses."

You don't know how sorry I was to hear that, and I wondering when we'd get a chance to go to another wake.

"You're not done with them altogether, are you, Mickser?"

"I am," said Mickser, flatly. "Come on back to the main road. The cars are coming along good-o now. Can't you hear them? Some of

those boyos have a few jars in them, I'd say, in spite of the wives."
He looked expertly into the sky. "There'll maybe be a fog later on,
and in that case the lot will be coming home early; the drunks and
all! Come on!"

"Ah, you can go and watch them yourself," I said. "I'm going
home."

The truth was I was too excited to sit on any wall for long.
I wanted to go home because there were a few things I'd like to find
out from my mother, if I could bring the talk around to the topic of
corpses without letting on where I got the information I had already.

As I ran off from Mickser across the fields for home, I felt that I
was a new man. The next time there was a funeral I felt sure there
would be no need to leave me sitting out in a car. I felt sure they
would all notice a change in me when I went into the house.

"Wipe your feet, son," my mother cried out to me through the
open door of the kitchen, the minute I came in sight. She was often
scrubbing the floor. "Not that you'd be the only one to put tracks
all over the place," she said, and I could see what she meant, because
there, in the middle of the floor, was my brother's old bike, up-
ended, with the wheels in the air, resting on its saddle, and he busy
mending a puncture. Or was it my father she meant? Because he
was sitting the other side of the fire with his feet in a basin of water.

It must have been my father she meant, because she lit on him just
then. "This is no place for washing your feet," she said. "There's a
fire inside in the parlor. Why don't you go in there and wash them?
I haven't got room to turn around with you all."

"The parlor is no place for washing feet," said my father, quietly, and he pointed to the bike in the middle of the floor. "When
that fellow's done with that bike you'll be glad to have a bit of water
on the floor to swish out the mess he'll have made. Why don't you
make him take it out in the yard?"

My mother sighed. She was always sighing, but they weren't the
kind of sighs you'd heed. They were caused by something we'd
done on her, all right, but they were sighs of patience, if you know
what I mean, and not complaint.

"It's a bit cold outside," she said. But she turned to me. "Here, you, son," she said, and she picked up my satchel and shoved it under my arm. "Let you set a good example and go into the parlor and do your homework there by the nice fire."

But I wasn't going into the empty parlor.

"Dear *knows!*" she said. "I don't know why I waste my time lighting that fire every day and none of you ever set foot in there until it's nearly night. I only wish I could go in and sit by it. Then I'd leave you the kitchen and welcome."

But I think she knew well that if she was to go in there that minute, it wouldn't be many minutes more till we'd all be in there along with her, myself and my satchel, and my father with his feet in the basin, and the old bike as well if it could be squeezed in at all between the piano and the chiffonier and those other big useless pieces of furniture that were kept in there out of the way.

"Ah sure, aren't we all right here," said my father, "where we can be looking at you?"

"You must have very little worth looking at if you want to be looking at me," said my mother, in a sort of voice I knew well that sounded cross but couldn't be, because she always stretched up when she spoke like that, so she'd see into the little mirror on the mantel shelf and she always smiled at what she saw in the glass. And well she might. She always looked pretty, my mother, but she used to look best of all when we were all around her in the kitchen, annoying her and making her cheeks red with the fuss of keeping us in order.

"Mind would you catch your finger in the spokes of that wheel!" she cried just then to my brother.

"Mind would you catch your hair in it, my girl," said Father, because as the kettle boiled and the little kitchen got full of steam, her hair used to loosen and lop around her face like a young girl's. And he caught a hold of her as if to pull her back from the bike.

"Let go of me," she cried. "Will you never get sense?"

"I hope not," said my father, "and what is more, I don't want you to get too much either."

"Oh, go on with you and your old talk, before the boys and all," she cried, and then she tried harder to drag herself free.

"She's not as strong as her tongue would have us believe, boys," said my father, tightening his hold. And then he laughed. "You'll never be the man I am!" he said, and this time it was my mother herself that giggled, although I didn't see anything specially funny in it.

And that very minute, in the middle of tricking and laughing, my father's face changed and it was like as if he wasn't holding her for fun at all, but the way he'd hold us if he had something against us.

"You're feeling all right these days, aren't you?" he cried. "You'd tell me if you weren't, wouldn't you?" And then, suddenly, he let her go, and put his hands up to his head. "Oh, my God, what would I do if anything happened to you!" he said.

"Such talk!" said my mother again, but her voice sounded different too, and although she was free she didn't ask to move away, but stood there beside him, with such a sad look on her face I suddenly wanted to cry.

And all I had wanted to ask her about the poor fellow at the level crossing came back into my mind. But I didn't feel like asking her then at all. And do you know what came into my mind? It was the words of the prayers we said every night.

". . . the living and the dead . . ." Over and over we'd said them, night after night, and I never paid any heed. But I suddenly felt that they were terrible, terrible words, and if we were to be kneeling down at that moment saying them, I couldn't bear it: I'd start nightmaring, there and then, in the middle of them all, with the lamps lit, and it not dark.

But the kettle began to spit on the range, and my mother ran over and lifted it back from the blaze.

"How about us taking our tea in the parlor?" she cried. "All of us. The kitchen is no fitter than the backyard with you!"

And in the excitement, I forgot all about the living and the dead. For a time.

IN THE MIDDLE OF THE FIELDS

LIKE A ROCK in the sea, she was islanded by fields, the heavy grass washing about the house, and the cattle wading in it as in water. Even their gentle stirrings were a loss when they moved away at evening to the shelter of the woods. A rainy day might strike a wet flash from a hay barn on the far side of the river — not even a habitation! And yet she was less lonely for him here in Meath than elsewhere. Anxieties by day, and cares, and at night vague, nameless fears — these were the stones across the mouth of the tomb. But who understood that? People thought she hugged tight every memory she had of him. What did they know about memory? What was it but another name for dry love and barren longing? They even tried to unload upon her their own small purposeless memories. "I imagine I see him every time I look out there," they would say as they glanced nervously over the darkening fields when they were leaving. "I think I ought to see him coming through the trees." Oh, for God's sake! she'd think. I'd forgotten him for a minute!

It wasn't him *she* saw when she looked out at the fields. It was the ugly tufts of tow and scutch that whitened the tops of the grass and gave it the look of a sea in storm, spattered with broken foam. That grass would have to be topped. And how much would it cost?

At least Ned, the old herd, knew the man to do it for her. "Bartley Crossen is your man, ma'am. Your husband knew him well."

She couldn't place him at first. Then she remembered. "Oh, yes — that's his hay barn we see, isn't it? Why, of course! I know him well — by sight, I mean." And so she did — splashing past on the road in a big muddy car, the wheels always caked with clay, and the wife in the front seat beside him.

"I'll get him to call around and have a word with you, ma'am," said the herd.

"Before dark!" she cautioned.

But there was no need to tell him. The old man knew how she always tried to be upstairs before it got dark, locking herself into her room, which opened off the room where the children slept, praying devoutly that she wouldn't have to come down again for anything — above all, not to answer the door. That was what in particular she dreaded: a knock after dark.

"Ah, sure, who'd come near you, ma'am, knowing you're a woman alone with small children that might be wakened and set crying? And, for that matter, where could you be safer than in the middle of the fields, with the innocent beasts asleep around you?"

If he himself had to come to the house late at night for any reason — to get hot water to stoup the foot of a beast, or to call the vet — he took care to shout out long before he got to the gable. "It's me, ma'am!" he'd shout. "Coming! Coming!" she'd cry, gratefully, as quick on his words as their echo. Unlocking her door, she'd run down and throw open the hall door. No matter what the hour! No matter how black the night! "Go back to your bed now, you, ma'am," he'd say from the darkness, where she could see the swinging yard lamp coming nearer and nearer like the light of a little boat drawing near to a jetty. "I'll put out the lights and let myself out." Relaxed by the thought that there was someone in the house, she would indeed scuttle back into bed, and, what was more, she'd be nearly asleep before she'd hear the door slam. It used to sound like the slam of a door a million miles away.

There was no need to worry. He'd see that Crossen came early.

It was well before dark when Crossen did drive up to the door. The wife was with him, as usual, sitting up in the front seat the way people sat up in the well of little tub traps long ago, their knees pressed together, allowing no slump. The herd had come with them, but only he and Crossen got out.

"Won't your wife come inside and wait, Mr. Crossen?" she asked.

"Oh, not at all, ma'am. She likes sitting in the car. Now, where's this grass that's to be cut? Are there any stones lying about that would blunt the blade?" Going around the gable of the house, he looked out over the land.

"There's not a stone or a stump in it," Ned said. "You'd run your blade over the whole of it while you'd be whetting it twenty times in another place!"

"I can see that," said Bartley Crossen, but absently, she thought. He had walked across the lawn to the rickety wooden gate that led into the pasture, and leaned on it. He didn't seem to be looking at the fields at all, though, but at the small string of stunted thorns that grew along the riverbank, their branches leaning so heavily out over the water that their roots were almost dragged clear of the clay.

Suddenly he turned around and gave a sigh. "Ah, sure, I didn't need to look! I know it well!" As she showed surprise, he gave a little laugh, like a young man. "I courted a girl down there when I was a lad," he said. "That's a queer length of time ago now, I can tell you!" He turned to the old man. "You might remember it." Then he looked back at her. "I don't suppose you were thought of at all in those days, ma'am," he said, and there was something kindly in his look and in his words. "You'd like the mowing done soon, I suppose? How about first thing in the morning?"

Her face lit up. But there was the price to settle. "It won't be as dear as cutting meadow, will it?"

"Ah, I won't be too hard on you, ma'am," he said. "I can promise you that!"

"That's very kind of you," she said, but a little doubtfully.

Behind Crossen's back, Ned nodded his head in approval. "Let it go at that, ma'am," he whispered as they walked back toward the car. "He's a man you can trust."

And when Crossen and the wife had driven away, he reassured her again. "A decent man," he said. Then he gave a laugh — it, too, was a young kind of laugh for a man of his age; it was like a nudge. "Did you hear what he said, though — about the girl he courted down there? Do you know who that was? It was his first wife! You know he was twice married? Ah, well, it's so long ago I wouldn't wonder if you never heard it. Look at the way he spoke about her himself, as if she was some girl he'd all but forgotten! The thorn trees brought her to his mind! That's where they used to meet, being only youngsters, when they first took up with each other.

"Poor Bridie Logan — she was as wild as a hare. And she was mad with love, young as she was! They were company-keeping while they were still going to school. Only nobody took it seriously — him least of all, maybe — till the winter he went away to the agricultural college in Athenry. She started writing to him then. I used to see her running up to the postbox at the crossroads every other evening. And sure, the whole village knew where the letter was going. His people were fit to be tied when he came home in the summer and said he wasn't going back, but was going to marry Bridie. All the same, his father set them up in a cottage on his own land. It's the cottage that's used now for stall-feds — it's back of the new house. Oh, but you can't judge it now for what it was then! Giddy and all as she was — as lightheaded as a thistle — you should have seen the way she kept that cottage. She'd have had it scrubbed away if she didn't start having a baby. He wouldn't let her take the scrubbing brush into her hands after that!"

"But she wasn't delicate, was she?"

"Bridie? She was as strong as a kid goat, that one! But I told you she was mad about him, didn't I? Well, after she was married to him she was no better — worse, you'd say. She couldn't do enough for him! It was like as if she was driven on by some kind of a fever. You'd only to look in her eyes to see it. Do you know! From that day to this, I don't believe I ever saw a woman so full of going as that one! Did you ever happen to see little birds flying about in the air like they were flying for the divilment of it and nothing else? And did you ever see the way they give a sort of a little leap in the air, like they were forcing themselves to go a bit higher still — higher than they ought? Well, it struck me that was the way Bridie was acting, as she rushed about that cottage doing this and doing that to make him prouder and prouder of her. As if he could be any prouder than he was already and the child getting noticeable!"

"She didn't die in childbed?"

"No. Not in a manner of speaking, anyway. She had the child, nice and easy, and in their own cottage, too, only costing him a few shillings for one of the women that went in for that kind of job long ago. And all went well. It was no time till she was let up on her feet again. I was there the first morning she had the place to herself! She was up and dressed when I got there, just as he was going out to milk.

" 'Oh, it's great to be able to go out again,' she said, taking a great breath of the morning air as she stood at the door looking after him. 'Wait! Why don't I come with you to milk!' she called suddenly. Then she threw a glance back at the baby asleep in its crib by the window.

" 'Oh, it's too far for you, Bridie!" he cried. The cows were down in the little field by the river — you know the field, alongside the road at the foot of the hill on this side of the village. And knowing she'd start coaxing him, he made out of the gate with the cans.

" 'Good man!' I said to myself. But the next thing I knew, she'd darted across the yard.

" 'I can go on the bike if it's too far to walk!' she said. And up she got on her old bike, and out she pedaled through the gate.

" 'Bridie, are you out of your mind?' he shouted as she whizzed past him.

" 'Arrah, what harm can it do me?' she shouted back.

"I went stiff with fright looking after her. And I thought it was the same with him, when he threw down the cans and started down the hill after her. But looking back on it, I think it was the same fever as always was raging in her that started raging in him, too. Mad with love, that's what they were, both of them — she only wanting to draw him on, and he only too willing!

" 'Wait for me!' he shouted, but before she'd even got to the bottom she started to brake the bike, putting down her foot like you'd see a youngster do, and raising up such a cloud of dust we could hardly see her."

"She braked too hard!"

"Not her! In the twinkle of an eye she'd stopped the bike, jumped off, turned it round, and was pedaling madly up the hill again, her head down on the handlebars like a racing cyclist. But that was the finish of her!"

"Oh, no! What happened?"

"She stopped pedaling all of a sudden, and the bike half stopped, and then it started to go back down the hill a bit, as if it skidded on the loose gravel at the side of the road. That's what I thought happened, and him, too, I suppose, because we both began to run down the hill. She didn't get time to fall before we got to her. But what use was that? It was some kind of internal bleeding that took her. We got her into the bed, and the neighbors came running, but she was gone before the night."

"Oh, such a thing to happen! And the baby?"

"Well, it was a strong child! And it grew into a fine lump of a lad. That's the fellow that drives the tractor for him now — the oldest son, Bartley."

"Well, I suppose his second marriage had more to it, when all was said and done."

"That's it. And she's a good woman — the second one. The way she brought up that child of Bridie's! And filled the cradle, year after year, with sons of her own. Ah sure, things always work out for the best in the end, no matter what!" he said, and he started to walk away.

"Wait a minute, Ned," she said urgently. "Do you really think he forgot about her — for years, I mean?"

"I'd swear it," said the old man. And then he looked hard at her. "It will be the same with you, too," he added kindly. "Take my word for it. Everything passes in time and is forgotten."

As she shook her head doubtfully, he nodded emphatically. "When the tree falls, how can the shadow stand?" he said. And he walked away.

I wonder! she thought as she walked back to the house, and she envied the practical country way that made good the defaults of nature as readily as the broken sod knits back into the sward.

Again that night, when she went up to her room, she looked down toward the river and she thought of Crossen. Had he really forgotten? It was hard for her to believe, and with a sigh she picked up her hairbrush and pulled it through her hair. Like everything else about her lately, her hair was sluggish and hung heavily down, but after a few minutes under the quickening strokes of the brush, it lightened and lifted, and soon it flew about her face like the spray above a weir. It had always been the same, even when she was a child. She had only to suffer the first painful drag of the bristles when her mother would cry out, "Look! Look! That's electricity!" and a blue spark would shine for an instant like a star in the gray depths of the mirror.

That was all they knew of electricity in those dim-lit days when valleys of shadow lay deep between one piece of furniture and another. Was it because rooms were so badly lit then that they saw it so often, that little blue star? Suddenly she was overcome by longing to see it again, and, standing up impetuously, she switched off the light.

It was just then that, down below, the iron fist of the knocker was lifted and, with a loud, confident stroke, brought down on the door.

It wasn't a furtive knock. She admitted that even as she sat stark with fright in the darkness. And then a voice that was vaguely familiar called out — and confidently — from below.

"It's me, ma'am! I hope I'm not disturbing you!"

"Oh, Mr. Crossen!" she cried out with relief, and, unlocking her door, she ran across the landing and threw up a window on that side of the house. "I'll be right down!" she called.

"Don't come down, ma'am!" he shouted. "I only want one word with you."

"But of course I'll come down!" She went back to get her dressing gown and pin up her hair, but as she did she heard him stomping his feet on the gravel. It had been a mild day, but with night a chill had come in the air, and, for all that it was late spring, there was a cutting east wind coming across the river. "I'll run down and let you in from the cold," she called, and, twisting up her hair, she held it against her head with her hand without waiting to pin it, and she ran down the stairs in her bare feet to unbolt the door.

"You were going to bed, ma'am!" he said accusingly the minute she opened the door. And where he had been so impatient a minute beforehand, he stood stock-still in the open doorway. "I saw the lights were out downstairs when I was coming up the drive," he said contritely. "But I didn't think you'd gone up for the night!"

"Neither had I!" she said lyingly, to put him at his ease. "I was just upstairs brushing my hair. You must excuse me!" she added, because a breeze from the door was blowing her dressing gown from her knees, and to pull it across she had to take her hand from her hair, so that the hair fell down about her shoulders. "Would you mind closing the door for me?" she said, with some embarrassment, and she began to back up the stairs. "Please go inside to the sitting room, won't you?" she said, nodding toward the door of the small room off the hall. "Put on the light. I'll be down in a minute."

But although he had obediently stepped inside the door and closed it, he stood stoutly in the middle of the hall. "I shouldn't have come in at all," he said. "I know you were going to bed! Look at you!" he cried again in the same accusing voice, as if he dared her this time to deny it. He was looking at her hair. "Excuse my saying so, ma'am, but I never saw such a fine head of hair. God bless it!" he said quickly, as if afraid he had been rude. "Doesn't a small thing make a big differ," he said impulsively. "You look like a young girl!"

In spite of herself, she smiled with pleasure. She wanted no more of it, all the same. "Well, I don't feel like one!" she said sharply.

What was meant for a quite opposite effect, however, seemed to delight him and put him wonderfully at ease. "Ah sure, you're a sensible woman! I can see that," he said, and, coming to the foot of the stairs, he leaned comfortably across the newel post. "Let you stay the way you are, ma'am," he said. "I've only a word to say to you, and it's not worth your while going up them stairs. Let me have my say here and now and be off about by business! The wife will be waiting up for me, and I don't want that!"

She hesitated. Was the reference to his wife meant to put her at *her* ease? "I think I ought to get my slippers," she said cautiously. Her feet were cold.

"Oh, yes, put something on your feet!" he cried, only then seeing that she was in her bare feet. "But as to the rest, I'm long gone beyond taking any account of what a woman has on her. I'm gone beyond taking notice of women at all."

But she had seen something to put on her feet. Under the table in the hall was a pair of old boots belonging to Richard, with fleece lining in them. She hadn't been able to make up her mind to give them away with the rest of his clothes, and although they were big and clumsy on her, she often stuck her feet into them when she came in from the fields with mud on her shoes. "Well, come in where it's warm, so," she said. She came back down the few steps and stuck her feet into the boots, and then she opened the door of the sitting room.

She was glad she'd come down. He'd never have been able to put on the light. "There's something wrong with the center light," she said as she groped along the wainscot to find the socket for the reading lamp. It was in an awkward place, behind the desk. She had to go down on her knees.

"What's wrong with it?" he asked, as, with a countryman's interest in practicalities, he clicked the switch up and down to no effect.

"Oh, nothing much, I'm sure," she said absently. "There!" She had found the socket. The room was lit up with a bright white glow.

"Why don't you leave the plug in the socket, anyway?" he asked critically.

"I don't know," she said. "I think someone told me it's safer, with reading lamps, to pull them out at night. There might be a short circuit, or mice might nibble at the cord, or something — I forget what I was told. I got into the habit of doing it, and now I keep on." She felt a bit silly.

But he was concerned about it. "I don't think any harm could be done," he said gravely. Then he turned away from the problem. "About tomorrow, ma'am," he said, somewhat offhandedly, she thought. "I was determined I'd see you tonight, because I'm not a man to break my word — above all, to a woman."

What was he getting at?

"Let me put it this way," he said quickly. "You'll understand, ma'am, that as far as I am concerned, topping land is the same as cutting hay. The same time. The same labor cost. And the same wear and tear on the blade. You understand that?"

On her guard, she nodded.

"Well now, ma'am, I'd be the first to admit that it's not quite the same for you. For you, topping doesn't give the immediate return you'd get from hay — "

"There's no return from it!" she exclaimed crossly.

"Oh, come now, ma'am, come! Good grassland pays as well as anything — you know you won't get nice sweet pickings for your beasts from neglected land, but only dirty old tow grass knotting under their feet. It's just that it's not a quick return, and so — as you know — I made a special price for you."

"I do know!" she said impatiently. "But I thought that part of it was settled and done."

"Oh, I'm not going back on it, if that's what you think," he said affably. "I'm glad to do what I can for you, ma'am, the more so seeing you have no man to attend to these things for you but only yourself alone."

"Oh, I'm well able to look after myself," she said, raising her voice.

Once again her words had an opposite effect to what she intended. He laughed good-humoredly. "That's what all women like to think!" he said. "Well, now," he said in a different tone of voice, and it annoyed her to see he seemed to think something had been settled between them, "it would suit me — and I'm sure it's all the same with you — if we could leave your little job till later in the week, say till nearer to the time of the haymaking generally. Because by then I'd have the cutting bar in good order, sharpened and ready for use. Whereas now, while there's still a bit of ploughing to be done here and there, I'll have to be chopping and changing, between the plough and the mower, putting one on one minute and the other the next!"

"As if anyone is still ploughing this time of the year!" Her eyes hardened.

"Harrowing then," he conceded.

"Who are you putting before me?" she demanded.

"Now, take it easy, Ma'am. No one. Leastways, not without getting leave first from you."

"Without telling me you're not coming, you mean!"

"Oh, now, ma'am, don't get cross. I'm only trying to make matters easy for everyone."

But she was very angry now. "It's always the same story. I thought you'd treat me differently! I'm to wait till after this one, and after that one, and in the end my fields will go wild!"

He looked a bit shamefaced. "Ah now, ma'am, that's not going to be the case at all. Although, mind you, some people don't hold with topping, you know."

"I hold with it."

"Oh, I suppose there's something in it," he said reluctantly. "But the way I look at it, cutting the weeds in July is a kind of a topping."

"Grass cut before it goes to seed gets so thick at the roots no weeds can come up!" she cried, so angry she didn't realize how authoritative she sounded.

"Faith, I never knew you were so well up, ma'am," he said, looking at her admiringly, but she saw he wasn't going to be put down by her. "All the same now, ma'am, you can't say a few days here or there could make any difference?"

"A few days could make all the difference! This farm has a gravely bottom to it, for all it's so lush. A few days of drought could burn it to the butt. And how could I mow it then? What cover would there be for the 'nice sweet pickings' you were talking about a minute ago?" Angrily, she mimicked his own accent without thinking.

He threw up his hands. "Ah well, I suppose a man may as well admit when he's bested," he said. "Even by a woman. And you can't say I broke my promise."

"I can't say but you tried hard enough," she said grudgingly, although she was mollified that she was getting her way. "Can I offer you anything?" she said then, anxious to convey an air of finality to their discussion.

"Oh, not at all, ma'am! Nothing, thank you! I'll have to be getting home." He stood up.

She stood up, too.

"I hope you won't think I was trying to take advantage of you," he said as they went toward the door. "It's just that we must all make out as best we can for ourselves — isn't that so? Not but you're well able to look after yourself, I must say. No one ever thought you'd stay on here after your husband died. I suppose it's for the children you did it?" He looked up the well of the stairs. "Are they asleep?"

"Oh, long ago," she said indifferently. She opened the hall door.

The night air swept in immediately, as it had earlier. But this time, from far away, it bore along on it the faint scent of new-mown hay. "There's hay cut somewhere already!" she exclaimed in surprise. And she lifted her face to the sweetness of it.

For a minute, Crossen looked past her out into the darkness, then he looked back. "Aren't you ever lonely here at night?" he asked suddenly.

"You mean frightened?" she corrected quickly and coldly.

"Yes! Yes, that's what I meant," he said, taken aback. "Ah, but why would you be frightened! What safer place could you be under the sky than right here with your own fields all about you!"

What he said was so true, and he himself as he stood there, with his hat in his hand, so normal and natural it was indeed absurd to think that he would no sooner have gone out the door than she would be scurrying up the stairs like a child. "You may not believe it," she said, "but I am scared to death sometimes! I nearly died when I heard your knock on the door tonight. It's because I was scared that I was upstairs," she said, in a further burst of confidence. "I always go up the minute it gets dark. I don't feel so frightened up in my room."

"Isn't that strange now?" he said, and she could see he found it an incomprehensibly womanly thing to do. He was sympathetic all the same. "You shouldn't be alone! That's the truth of the matter," he said. "It's a shame!"

"Oh, it can't be helped," she said. There was something she wanted to shrug off in his sympathy, while at the same time there was something in it she wanted to take. "Would you like to do something for me?" she asked impulsively. "Would you wait and put out the lights down here and let me get back upstairs before you go?"

After she had spoken, for a minute she felt foolish, but she saw at once that, if anything, he thought it only too little to do for her. He was genuinely troubled about her. And it wasn't only the present moment that concerned him; he seemed to be considering the whole problem of her isolation and loneliness. "Is there nobody could stay here with you — at night even? It would have to be another woman, of course," he added quickly, and her heart was warmed by the way — without a word from her — he rejected that solution out of hand. "You don't want a woman about the place," he said flatly.

"Oh, I'm all right, really. I'll get used to it," she said.

"It's a shame, all the same," he said. He said it helplessly, though, and he motioned her toward the stairs. "You'll be all right for to-night, anyway," he said. "Go on up the stairs now, and I'll put out the lights." He had already turned around to go back into the sitting room.

Yet it wasn't quite as she intended for some reason, and it was somewhat reluctantly that she started up the stairs.

"Wait a minute! How do I put out this one?" he called from the sitting room door before she was halfway up the stairs.

"Oh, I'd better put out that one myself," she said, thinking of the awkward position of the socket. She ran down again, and, going past him into the little room, she knelt and pulled at the cord. Instantly the room was deluged in darkness. And instantly she felt that she had done something stupid. It was not like turning out a light by a switch at the door and being able to step back at once into the lighted hall. She got to her feet as quickly as she could, but as she did, she saw that Crossen was still in the doorway. His bulk was blocked out against the light beyond. "I'll leave the rest to you," she said, in order to break the peculiar silence that had come down on the house.

But he didn't move. He stood there, the full of the doorway.

"The other switches are over there by the hall door," she said, unwilling to brush past him. Why didn't he move? "Over there," she repeated, stretching out her arm and pointing, but instead of moving he caught at her outstretched arm, and, putting out his other hand, he pressed his palm against the door jamb, barring the way.

"Tell me," he whispered, his words falling over each other, "are you never lonely — at all?"

"What did you say?" she said in a clear voice, because the thickness of his voice sickened her. She had hardly heard what he said. Her one thought was to get past him.

He leaned forward. "What about a little kiss?" he whispered, and to get a better hold on her he let go the hand he had pressed against the wall, but before he caught at her with both hands she had wrenched her arm free of him, and, ignominiously ducking under his armpit, she was out next minute in the lighted hall.

Out there — because light was all the protection she needed from him, the old fool — she began to laugh. She had only to wait for him to come sheepishly out.

But there was something she hadn't counted on; she hadn't counted on there being anything pathetic in his sheepishness. There was something pitiful in the way he shambled into the light, not raising his eyes. And she was so surprisingly touched by him that before he had time to utter a word she put out her hand. "Don't feel too bad," she said. "I didn't mind."

Even then, he didn't look at her. He just took her hand and pressed it gratefully, his face still turned away. And to her dismay she saw that his nose was running water. Like a small boy, he wiped it with the back of his fist, streaking his face. "I don't know what came over me," he said slowly. "I'm getting on to be an old man now. I thought I was beyond all that." He wiped his face again. "Beyond letting myself go, anyway," he amended miserably.

"Oh, it was nothing," she said.

He shook his head. "It wasn't as if I had cause for what I did."

"But you did nothing," she protested.

"It wasn't nothing to me," he said dejectedly.

For a minute, they stood there silent. The hall door was still ajar, but she didn't dare to close it. What am I going to do with him now, she thought. I'll have him here all night if I'm not careful. What time was it, anyway? All scale and proportion seemed to have gone from the night. "Well, I'll see you in the morning, Mr. Crossen," she said, as matter-of-factly as possible.

He nodded, but made no move. "You know I meant no disrespect to you, ma'am, don't you?" he said then, looking imploringly at her. "I always had a great regard for you. And for your husband, too. I was thinking of him this very night when I was coming up to the house. And I thought of him again when you came to the door looking like a young girl. I thought what a pity it was him to be taken from you, and you both so young! Oh, what came over me at all? And what would Mona say if she knew?"

"But you wouldn't tell her, I hope!" she cried. What sort of a figure would she cut if he told about her coming down in her bare feet with her hair down her back? "Take care would you tell her!" she warned.

"I don't suppose I ought," he said, but he said it uncertainly and morosely, and he leaned back against the wall. "She's been a good woman, Mona. I wouldn't want anyone to think different. Even the boys could tell you. She's been a good mother to them all these years. She never made a bit of difference between them. Some say she was better to Bartley than to any of them! She reared him from a week old. She was living next door to us, you see, at the time" — he hesitated — "At the time I was left with him," he finished in a flat voice. "She came in that first night and took him home to her own bed — and, mind you, that wasn't a small thing for a woman who knew nothing about children, not being what you'd call a young girl at the time, in spite of the big family she gave me afterwards. She took him home that night, and she looked after him. It isn't every woman would care to be responsible for a newborn baby. That's a thing a man doesn't forget easy! There's many I know would say that if she hadn't taken him someone else would have, but no one only her would have done it the way she did.

"She used to have him all day in her own cottage, feeding him and the rest of it. But at night, when I'd be back from the fields, she'd bring him home and leave him down in his little crib by the fire alongside of me. She used to let on she had things to do in her own place, and she'd slip away and leave us alone, but that wasn't her real reason for leaving him. She knew the way I'd be sitting looking into the fire, wondering how I'd face the long years ahead, and she left the child there with me to break my thoughts. And she was right. I never got long to brood. The child would give a cry, or a whinge, and I'd have to run out and fetch her to him. Or else she'd hear him herself maybe, and run in without me having to call her at all. I used often think she must have kept every window and door in her place open, for fear she'd lose a sound from either of us. And so, bit by bit, I was knit back into a living man. I often wondered what would have become of me if it wasn't for her. There are men and when the bright way closes to them there's no knowing but they'll take a dark way. And I was that class of man.

"I told you she used to take the little fellow away in the day and bring him back at night? Well, of course, she used to take him away again coming on to the real dark of night. She'd take him away to her own bed. But as the months went on and he got bigger, I could see she hated taking him away from me at all. He was beginning to smile and play with his fists and be real company. 'I wonder ought I leave him with you tonight?' she'd say then, night after night. And sometimes she'd run in and dump him down in the middle of the big double bed in the room off the kitchen, but the next minute she'd snatch him up again. 'I'd be afraid you'd overlie him! You might only smother him, God between us and all harm!' 'You'd better take him,' I'd say. I used to hate to see him go myself by this time. All the same, I was afraid he'd start crying in the night, and what would I do then? If I had to go out for her in the middle of the night, it could cause a lot of talk. There was talk enough as things were, I can tell you, although there was no grounds for it. I had no more notion of her than if she wasn't a woman at all — would you believe that? But one night when she took him up and put him down, and put him down and took him up, and went on and went on about leaving him or taking him, I had to laugh. 'It's a pity you can't stay along with him, and that would settle all,' I said. I was only joking her, but she got as red as fire, and next thing she burst out crying! But not before she'd caught up the child and wrapped her coat around him. Then, after giving me a terrible look, she ran out of the door with him.

"Well, that was the beginning of it. I'd no idea she had any feelings for me. I thought it was only for the child. But men are fools, as women well know, and she knew before me what was right and proper for us both. And for the child, too. Some women have great insight into these things! And God opened my own eyes then to the woman I had in her, and I saw it was better I took her than wasted away after the one that was gone. And wasn't I right?"

"Of course you were right," she said quickly.

But he slumped back against the wall, and the abject look came back into his eyes.

I'll never get rid of him, she thought desperately. "Ah, what ails you!" she cried impatiently. "Forget it, can't you?"

"I can't," he said simply. "And it's not only me — it's the wife I'm thinking about. I've shamed her!"

"Ah, for heaven's sake. It's nothing got to do with her at all."

Surprised, he looked up at her. "You're not blaming yourself, surely?" he asked.

She'd have laughed at that if she hadn't seen she was making headway. Another stroke and she'd be rid of him. "Arrah, what are you blaming any of us for!" she cried. "It's got nothing to do with any of us — with you, or me, or the woman at home waiting for you. It was the other one! That girl — your first wife — Bridie! It was her! Blame her! She's the one did it!" The words had broken from her. For a moment, she thought she was hysterical and that she could not stop. "You thought you could forget her," she said, "but see what she did to you when she got the chance!" She stopped and looked at him.

He was standing at the open door. He didn't look back. "God rest her soul," he said, and he stepped into the night.

THE CUCKOO-SPIT

DRENCHED with light under the midsummer moon, the fields were as large as the fields of the sky. Hedges and ditches dissolved in mist, and down by the river the thorn bushes floated loose like severed branches. Tall trees in the middle of the fields streamed on the air, rooted by long, dragging shadows.

It was such a beautiful night Vera ventured a few steps out on to the gravel terrace but there came to a stand and looked around. It was a strange night. All that was real and erect had become unreal. The unreal alone had shape. And when in the long grass of the paddock a beast stirred, it was only for its shadow she could see where it lay. Unnerved, she turned back to the house. The house, too, had an insubstantial air, its white gable merging in the white of the sky. But on the bright ground its shadow fell black as iron.

It was when she reached the edge of this shadow that the young man stepped out and startled her.

"I thought you saw me," he said defensively. "The night is so bright. *I* saw *you*." Then his voice changed. "Are you all right?" he asked anxiously.

"Oh, yes," she said. His concern had already made nonsense of her fright. And in the strong light pouring down she could see him as plain as day — a young man with a kind face, his thin cheekbones splattered with large, flaky freckles. Their eyes met, and they smiled at each other, surprised and happy. "I ought to know you, I am sure," she said, since it was late and he wore no coat.

"I don't think so," he said. "I'm only down here sometimes in summer. I come to stay with an uncle of mine who lives across the river."

"Oh, I know him! Tim Hynes? At least, I know him by name. I never actually met him, but I'd very much like to. My husband used to talk a lot about him."

"I know," said the young man. "Tim was very upset by his death. So, of course, was everyone," he added hastily.

"Your uncle more than most, though. I was told he took it very badly. There was something, wasn't there, about his losing interest in the election — not voting at all?"

"That's right. He more or less gave up politics after that."

"I remember I got a wonderful letter from him at the time."

"Tim?" He raised his eyebrows, and, remembering the old man's spelling, she herself laughed.

"It was something he said. I never forgot it. He said it might have been hard — even for a man like Richard — to save his soul in Dail Eireann!"

"That's like a thing he'd say, all right, but I think it could have been to comfort you. Tim had no doubt whatever about the stature of the man we'd lost in your husband."

The plural pronoun caught her attention. "Are you interested in politics, too?" she asked, but she was hardly heeding his reply, she was so surprised at the sudden lessening of her interest in him. All the same, I ought to ask him into the house, she thought, if only for his uncle's sake. Or was it too late?

"Oh, it's far too late," he said. "I didn't intend to call. I was out for a walk, and I'd crossed over the bridge in the village and was going along the bank of the river below here when I saw that the windows were all lighted. To tell you the truth, I came up closer just out of curiosity. I was always fascinated by this house. Then I saw the door open. Somehow or other, I got a strange feeling that the house was empty. So I came up and knocked. It was when I got no answer I realized the odd situation I had got myself into, and I didn't know what to do. I was just standing there when I saw you coming. Do you do that often — go out and leave the door open?"

She turned and looked over her shoulder to where the open door let out a stream of golden light that cut its own shape on the shape of the shadow. "I wasn't far away," she said vaguely.

"That's true," he said. "And it was a lovely night for a walk!"

It annoyed her that, having been worried at the start, he was so easily satisfied about her safety. "I shouldn't have left it open all the same," she said, "but I only meant to walk a little way, just up and down outside the door."

"I know," he said. "The usual thing. You were tempted to go further."

Again she was irritated by his readiness to provide his own interpretation of the situation. "As a matter of fact, there was nothing usual about it," she said. "This is the first time since my husband died that I've set foot outside the house after dark alone. Except in the car, of course."

"I don't understand," he said quietly. "What could there possibly be to fear in the heart of the country?"

"That was what Richard used to say. But I wasn't brought up in the country, and that makes a difference. Even when he was alive, I was nervous out-of-doors after dark." She laughed. "I'll tell you something that happened one night. We kept a few hens. They were supposed to be my affair. The henhouse was over there." She pointed to a small triangular field behind the house, a small field bounded on three sides by a wood. "I was always forgetting to shut them up at night, and we often had to go out late and do it, but once it was the middle of the night when I woke up and thought of them, and I had to wake Richard, and we had to put on our coats and go out to them — in the very middle of the night!"

"Couldn't he have gone alone?"

"Of course not. They were *my* hens. It wouldn't have been fair to let him go alone."

He shook his head. "He must have been a very patient man."

"But it was a night just like this!" she cried.

Immediately, with her words the night seemed to press closer, lapping them round, not just with its mist and moonlight but with its summer smells of new-mown hay and sweet white clover. "We didn't go back to the house at all," she said, remembering that other night with quick and vivid pain. "We stayed out . . ." But she didn't finish the sentence, because suddenly she had an uneasy feeling that she was giving something away about that night, or about herself, or Richard. She finished it differently. "For ages," she said.

There was a little silence.

"Is he long dead?"

"Four years this summer," she said, and turned her face away coldly, but she felt his sympathy would not be so easily stemmed.

"You must miss him very much," he said. "I was thinking that as I watched you coming toward me. I was wondering how you were able to go on living here without him." But he must have felt tactless, or impertinent, because he looked away from her, out over the fields. "It's very beautiful here, of course," he added quickly.

"Tonight — yes!" she granted, but she gave a cold glance over the moonlit stretches of which he spoke with such unconcern. Did he not know that there were other nights, when those fields could wear a different aspect? "This is a night in a thousand!" she cried.

He missed the note of disparagement in her voice and turned back to her. "I suppose the more beautiful it is, the more lonely it must be for you."

She looked into his face. "I got over the worst of it long ago," she said harshly. "Do you know what *I* was thinking when I was coming across the fields? I was thinking that there is, after all, a kind of peace at last when you face up to life's defeats. It's not a question of getting stronger, as people think, or being better able to bear things; it's that you get weaker and stop trying. I think I couldn't bear anything now — even happiness." She paused. That was true, she thought, and yet she felt she had expressed herself inadequately. "It's just that I've got old, I suppose," she said more simply.

"Nonsense," he said lightly.

She sighed. "All the same," she said stubbornly, "there is a strange peace about knowing that the best in life is gone forever."

"You mean love?"

She nodded. "And youth," she said, but she thought she saw doubt in his eyes. "Aren't they the one thing?"

She was startled by the haggard look that came over his face. "I don't know," he said. "I hope not. God knows I've never had much of either."

"What do you mean? What age are you, anyway?" But before he could answer she realized that she didn't even know his name. "You didn't tell me your name, either."

"Fergus," he said, giving no surname.

He must be Tim's brother's child, she thought, and again at the thought of her old neighbor across the river she felt she ought to insist on his coming inside, no matter the hour.

"Oh, no, no," he said, actually beginning to move away. "I'm afraid to think how late it must be now."

"Well, perhaps you'll come again," she said formally, but she knew that in this matter generosity was not on her side. It was nice to see that he thought otherwise.

"That's very kind of you, Mrs. Traske," he said warmly. "I'd like very much to come." His pleasure was so genuine it added to hers, but all the same a ridiculous ache had gone through her when he used her surname, although anything else would have been unthinkable. A strange young man — years younger than her! Even if they got to know each other well, and he were to call again — and again — she could not imagine that he would call her Vera, ever. It was a name she had never liked. And lately she'd liked it less. At this moment, it seemed utterly unsuitable to her: a name for a young girl. It even seemed to have a strangely venal quality. But he was saying something, and she had to listen.

"I was only saying that I don't suppose you approve of calling people by their first names on a first meeting," he said.

Taken aback by the way their minds had run so near together, she hesitated. "Well, it doesn't give much chance for measuring one's progress with people, does it?"

"I never thought of that," he cried, and he looked at her, delighted. "I must remember that." Again he seemed about to go, but again he stopped. "I correct examination papers at this time of year. I may get word any day from my landlady in Dublin to say that they have arrived. I'll have to go back at once then. Would it matter — would you mind — if I came fairly soon? Very soon perhaps?"

"Whenever you like. I'm always here," she said, and then they said good night, and he walked away.

As she went into the house, she wondered if he would come again. She hoped he would; it was a pleasant encounter. And she kept on thinking about it as she went around the house, fastening the windows and locking the door. Even when she went upstairs, she stood for a while at the open window, looking out and going over scraps of their conversation. Some of the things she had said now seemed affected. Had she lost the knack of small talk? In particular, she thought of what she had said about happiness, and not being able now to bear it. That was so absurd, but surely he understood that she meant a certain kind of happiness, possible only to the young. Indeed, it might well be that it was when one let go all hope of ever knowing that again the heart was emptied and ready for the simpler relationships — those without tie, without pain. But when she put out the light and turned back the white counterpane, breaking the skin of light on it, she felt vaguely depressed. Would there not always be something purposeless in such attachments?

Did she expect him to come again? Certainly not the very next evening. And so early! Only a short time before, she was in the garden, weeding and staking plants — working away, without knowing the day had ended. It was by the light of a big yellow moon that she was trying to see what she was doing. It was so low a moon, so close to the ground, and it shed so gold a light that, like the sun, it gilded everything. Unlike the moon of late night, it did not take all color from the earth but left a flush of purple in the big roses and peonies, and a glow of yellow in their glossy stamens. Yet it was night. The birds were silent; a stillness had settled over the farm. Nervously, she gathered together the rake and the spade, and, hardly waiting to put them away, she hurried toward the house. But in the doorway she delayed. There was a peculiar quality abroad. Was it expectancy? It's in the night, though, and not in me, she thought — but just then, like a high wind falling, the expectancy died down as a step sounded on the gravel.

"You didn't think I'd come so soon, did you?" he said, smiling. "It's even more marvelous than last night, though, and I thought of you not liking to go out at night alone. But you were going out?"

"No. Going in!" she said.

"Good. I'm glad I came. Get something to put over your shoulders. But hurry!"

In spite of her surprise, she didn't hesitate. "I won't be a minute," she said. "Won't you come in while you're waiting?"

He shook his head. "Houses weren't built for nights like this."

When she came out, he was standing clear of the shadows of the house, in the full light. "I was telling my uncle about you," he said when she joined him. "He wasn't in bed when I got back last night. He sent you his regards. In fact, he sent you several messages — so many I'm sure I've forgotten the half of them." He smiled at her. "No matter! You can take them as given; they were all compliments and good wishes. And now," he said, surveying the view and taking her arm casually, "which way will we go? Down by the river? Or is the grass too high?"

"We can follow the cowpaths."

"Oh, but the cattle go in single file, and we want to talk," he said, and he linked her more closely. It made her uncomfortable, but she knew that when they crossed over the wooden fence around the house and went into the field in front of it, they would have to unlink. He realized it, too, after a few steps. "It's like wading through water, isn't it?" he said, amazed, as the high grass weighted down their feet. "Does it never get eaten down? The place seemed heavily stocked to me as I came along here."

"It would take all the cattle in Ireland to graze it down at this time of year," she said carelessly.

He turned to her with an earnestness that was touching. "You had courage to keep it when you are so nervous here," he said. "Any other woman would have sold it and gone back to the city."

"That never once entered my mind," she said, remembering how from the first she was aware of the security she drew from this piece of ground. But she saw by his face that he thought she had kept it for the sake of the past.

"I must tell you something," he said. "I nearly wrote you a letter last night after I went away from here. Would you have thought it very odd? The only reason I did not was because I'd have had to come back with it, and I thought that a footstep during the night might frighten you."

"It would have frightened the wits out of me," she said quickly. She did not ask what he would have said in the letter.

"I knew it would," he said. "I'm glad I didn't do it. Anyway, I think you knew without my saying it how much it meant to me — meeting you."

"It was nice for me to meet you, too," she said lightly. But he was deadly serious.

"There is nothing rarer in the world than happiness," he said.

"Happiness?" she said sharply.

"I know what you're thinking, but there is a kind of happiness that is indestructible; it lives on no matter what comes after. At least, that was how it seemed to me listening to you talking last evening."

"But we were only talking for such a little while," she protested.

"No matter!" he said. "And anyway, last night was not the first time I'd seen you. I used to study down by the river long ago — on our side — and I used to see you and your husband walking together in the fields. You used to go with him to count the cattle, didn't you?"

"Yes. I always went with him," she said absently, because her mind was going back over the previous evening.

"How I used to envy your companionship," he said. They had reached the riverbank and they had to walk slowly, because the ground was dented and uneven from where the cattle in wet weather had cut up the sod, which now was hard as rock. "Not that I have much experience," he went on, "but of the marriages I've seen at close quarters, not many were like yours. They weren't failures, either; I suppose they were happy enough in a way, only . . ." He hesitated. "Only it wouldn't be my way," he said flatly.

"And what," she said laughingly, "would be your way?"

"Well, that's just it," he said. "That's what I wanted to try to tell you in the letter. You see, I didn't have any clear idea of what I would want from marriage — I only knew what I wouldn't want — until last night, listening to you."

"I don't understand!" she cried nervously, but she did remember that at one moment the night before she had felt uneasy. Had he formed some impression of his own at that moment? If so, she would probably be powerless now to alter it. Distantly, she turned away and looked down into the river. "Supposing the impression I gave you was wrong," she said. "Supposing I falsified it." When he said nothing, she turned and looked at him and she saw he was bewildered. Filled with remorse, she put out her hand to him. "It wasn't false," she said quickly, "but that was one of the things I used to dread after his death — that the past would become altered in my mind, and that he would be made into something that he wasn't."

"Not by you, though?"

"No. By others, but it might have come to the same thing in the end. You cannot imagine how awful it was in those first months, having to listen to people talking about him, going on and on about him — mostly his family, of course, but my own people were nearly as bad, and friends and neighbors. Everybody. And all the time they were getting him more and more out of focus for me. He was — but you've heard your uncle talk about him, so you'll know what I'm going to say — he *was* nearly perfect, guileless. He knew only candor — the kind of person who'd make you doubt the doctrine of original sin! But to listen to his family you'd think he was a man of marble. They diminished him. Instead of adding to him, they diminished him. Can you understand that? I used to think, immediately, that that was the way they would speak of him whatever he'd been; the dead are always whitewashed. And he didn't need it. In the end, instead of listening to them, I used to sit trying to think of *something* about him that I didn't like!"

"Did you?"

"Well, we used to quarrel when we were first married, but in all fairness to him it was usually my fault. There was one thing, though — it always ended with his taking the blame. Not to be noble or anything like that, but just to stop arguing, which he hated; to get us back to being happy again. He used to say it didn't matter what happened, I'd always blame him for it anyway, so it might as well be first as last. Well, one evening a few weeks after his death, I was visiting his people and listening to the same old rigmarole about him, and I got into a kind of a panic. Soon I wouldn't be properly able to remember him at all; I thought I'd lose hold of what he was really like. I was so unhappy. And when I got up and went out to the car, it was a miserable evening outside. It was raining, for one thing, and the canvas roof of the car was leaking. I wouldn't have minded that, only just at the loneliest and darkest part of the road I got a puncture. Well! I got out and I stood there in the rain and it seemed the last straw. But suddenly, instead of pitying myself, I felt the most violent rage sweep over me. Toward him — Richard. If only I could have confronted him at that moment, there'd be no doubt of what I'd have said. 'Why did you die, anyway?' I'd have shouted. 'Why didn't you take better care of yourself and not leave me in this mess?' And then — "

But Fergus interrupted. "Don't tell me! I know what happened next," he said. "You had him back again — just as he always was — unchanged, amused at you."

"Yes. And I began to laugh, there in the rain."

There was silence for a few minutes. "Tell me," he said then. "What did you do about the puncture?"

"Oh, that!" She shrugged. "I forget. What with one thing or another, in those days I was nearly always in that sort of situation. Such things were the commonplaces of my existence. I suppose another car came along, or I called at some cottage, or perhaps I walked to the nearest village. I can't remember."

"Things must have been hard for you in the beginning," he said gently. "But you managed very well."

"Oh, I don't know," she said deprecatingly. "Some things were hard in the beginning, but other things only got hard long afterwards. I'll tell you a strange thing, though, if you're interested. I don't think I fully realized until recently, but in my heart I *did* blame Richard all along — not for dying, but for being what he was, for leaving a void that no one less than him could fill."

They walked along a few more paces. "Is that why you didn't marry again?" he said. "It seems such a pity."

"For me?"

"Well, for you, too, of course, but I wasn't thinking of you. I was thinking of how much you have to give." But as he spoke he seemed to lose confidence in what he was saying. "I suppose giving isn't enough, though," he finished uncertainly.

Sadly, she shook her head. "And yet it was a poor kind of faithfulness really, wasn't it?"

"It's the only kind there is, I think," he said. "Do you know something?" he added impetuously. "When I was walking home last night, I was thinking about your husband, and I envied him."

"A dead man!"

"It's not as absurd as it may seem. I feel certain that I'll never have one quarter of the happiness he had."

"But you're so young!" she cried. "How can you tell what's ahead?"

He looked away. "It isn't a question of age — you know that. It's temperament perhaps, or maybe it's merely chance." He looked back at her. "It's not that I haven't a normal capacity for love, either. The truth is that I have to be crazily involved or not at all. And I've never seen that kind of thing last for long. That was why, knowing what companions you were, it meant so much to me, last night, to see that you'd never lost that other quality, either. Do you know when I knew?" he asked. He faltered before the cold look she gave, but he rushed on. "When you told me about staying out all night!"

"Except that I didn't say that," she said, and her voice, too, was deadly cold.

"I know!" he cried. "But you did stay out all night, didn't you? That was what you were going to say? It was when you didn't say it I knew for certain what it was like — that night. I didn't really think love could go on like that, unless" — he faltered again — "unless illicit love," he said simply.

Uncomfortable, she walked a little faster, so that she outdistanced him by a few steps.

"I was right, wasn't I?" he called softly.

"Yes," she said at last. What was the use, now, of denying those dead hours? She sighed and waited for him. "I suppose you'd like to be married," she said, surprising herself by her words.

He answered more lightheartedly than she expected. "To the right person. You'd have been just right for me!"

It was because he said it so lightly and because she was oppressed by what had gone before that she, too, spoke lightheartedly. "Oh, don't relegate me to the past like that! Why not say I'm a premonition of someone to come."

But his face clouded. "I wouldn't say there'd be two of you in the one lifetime!" There was a note in his voice that was new and harsh, and, frightened by it, she was about to suggest that they turn back, when, wheeling around, he himself suggested it. "We'd better go back. Anyway, the moon has gone behind a cloud."

"Has it?" Her eyes had been upon a small field of old meadow, along which they were passing. It was so neglected that the big white daisies in it met head to head and gave it an unbroken sheen of white that in the dark was like the luster of the moon.

"Oh, look at those daisies!" she cried, pointing to them. "The place is getting so neglected. I'll have to plough up that piece of ground and lay it down to new grass. There is so much that is neglected."

"Nonsense. I never noticed any neglect," he said so aggressively that, in order not to be annoyed, she had to tell herself that he was speaking, after all, in her defense.

"You haven't seen the place by day," she said quietly.

"I see it every day," he said. "There isn't a bit of it I can't see from the other bank of the river. I saw *you* outside this morning, didn't I?"

"Did you?" It confused her to think of being seen without knowing it — by anyone. She was glad that they were nearly back. They had been walking faster on the return than when they set out, and already they had reached the wooden paling in front of the house. "You'll come inside this time, I hope," she said, "and have some coffee?"

"We'd better see what time it is first," he said. "Tim was horrified at how late I stayed last night." Raising his arm, he was trying to see his watch, as if — she thought irrelevantly — as if with that upraised arm he was trying to ward off a blow.

"Wait! There's a light in the porch," she cried. "It can be switched on from outside." But the switch was almost impossible to find among the tangled and overgrown creepers. "There's neglect for you!" she said as she plunged her arm deep into the leaves. "The roses are almost smothered," she said sadly.

Yet when she found the switch and the light went on, the big white roses lolloped outward toward them. On long, neglected stems, blown and beautiful, they hung face down. Impulsively, he reached out and took one between the palms of his hands, tenderly, as if it were the body of a small bird.

"Would you like one?" she cried, and she tried to break a stem, but she had difficulty before the sappy fibers frayed and severed.

He took it from her, pleased. And then he gave an exclamation. "Oh, look at what's on it! A cuckoo-spit."

"How disgusting. Throw it away," she said. "I'll get you another one."

But he put his hand protectively about it. "Why did you say that?" he asked. "I was only amazed that a cuckoo should come so close to the house — " He saw her face before he went any further. "I forgot," he cried, embarrassed. "They *never* do, isn't that so?"

"Never!" She smiled. "They're never seen at all! At least I've never met anyone who saw one."

"That's right. I should have known," he said.

She saw at once that he was humiliated by his mistake, and she wanted desperately to make him feel better. "When I was a child," she said quickly, "I thought it wasn't a bird at all, but a sound, like an echo."

But he didn't smile and he looked down at the rose. On the stem, in the cleft between it and the axle of the leaf, there was a white blob, as if of spittle. "What is it, anyway?" he asked. "I've often seen it before."

"Give it to me," she said quietly, stretching out her hand. With the tip of her finger, she flicked the blob of white stuff onto the back of her other hand. "Look," she said, as the frothy secretion began to thin away, the beads of moisture winking out, one by one, until, slowly and weakly on its unformed legs, a pale sickly-yellow aphis crawled out across her skin. "That's what it is!" she said, but at the feel of it on her flesh she shuddered, and shook it violently from her.

"You shouldn't have touched it." Throwing down the rose, he pulled out a handkerchief and took her hand, and began carefully to wipe it all over. "It always seemed so beautiful," he said regretfully, "a sign of summer."

"Ah, well, it *is* a sign of summer," she said, but her mind was not really on what she was saying, because although he'd wiped away all trace of the spit from her hand, he still held it carelessly in his own. Unused for so long to the feel of another's flesh, she was affected almost as strongly as by the feel of the plant louse. Shuddering again, she drew her hand away.

"You're cold?" he said.

Cold? Was it possible you could be so near to another and so unaware of what went on within them? "You must be cold, too," she said. "Come in and we'll have a hot drink."

"I've already stayed too long," he said, bending down and picking up his rose. "Next time we must manage better."

There was evidently no question of his not calling again.

"I hope you enjoyed the walk," he said easily, and then, before he turned away, he looked directly at her. "Good night, Vera," he said.

She looked after him. Why had she enjoyed it so intensely? *That* was the question.

When she went inside, she attended absently to what had to be done before going upstairs for the night. Then, upstairs at last, she again went to the window and looked out. The moon, free of clouds once more, cast its luster over everything. And, standing there, looking out, she remembered the times as a girl, before she was married, when she stood at an open window on a night like this, her heart torn by a longing to share the feelings that welled up in her. Yet later, when she had Richard, there was not a single night that she had gone to the window for as much as a glance at what was outside. Always, no matter what the day or the night, there was him blocking out all else. And this view before her now — she'd only really seen it after his death. But now, oh now again its insistent beauty tormented her. But wait — not with the same kind of longing! And then she thought of something Fergus had said. He was wrong; a time came when giving *was* enough. She stared over the moonlit fields and the high cobbled sky. And she knew what she wanted. She wanted to reach out and gather it all up and shove it into his arms. To give it and be done with it, she thought. And afterwards not ever to have to look out at it again.

Next morning, she wakened late. Downstairs there was a loud knocking on the door. It was a gray day with a mist over the river, and in the fields cattle loomed dark, as if they swam in the waters of a fabulous sea. The knocking came again, more urgently and she sprang out of bed and went to the window. Below, standing back from the door, she saw him just under her window, looking up. "Oh, just a minute. I'll come right down!" she cried, pulling back instinctively.

"Don't come down!" he called up. "I can't wait. I haven't a minute."

"You have to go back?" In spite of the cold glare of day, she leaned out.

"The exam papers came!" he said. "When I went back to Tim's place last night, there was a message saying they'd arrived. I have to get back. To get them finished in time. I have to start on them at once." Suddenly he turned his head as if to listen. "Is that the bus?" he cried, dismayed. "I shouldn't have come. I'll miss it. But I wanted to tell you I was going in case you'd be looking out for me tonight."

That he had any notion of coming that night — the third night in a row — took her by surprise. That he could have thought she might have been expecting him left her speechless.

"I'll have to go!" he cried, but he put his hand to his ear. "It's not the bus!" he said, and he relaxed. "I didn't think they'd come for a few days more — the papers. The exam was only last week. But the sooner they come, the sooner I'll get paid!"

Depressed already by the day and by its cold light upon her unprepared face, and, of course, by his going, this glimpse of his unknown life was too much to endure. There was something so altogether offhand about this, their last conversation, that when in the distance she did hear the bus, she was not sorry. "Listen!" she said. "This is it — the bus."

"It can't be." He listened intently. It was. At once all his off-handedness left him. "What I really wanted to ask is if you ever come up to Dublin?" The sound of the bus was louder and nearer. "If you ever do come, and if you could spare the time, I needn't tell you I'd love to meet you. Perhaps you'd let me give you a cup of tea somewhere . . ." His words tailed off, as he looked over his shoulder.

As for her, there was no time to dissimulate her pleasure. "I often go!" she cried. "And I'd be pleased to meet you." But just then she thought of a way in which she could trim the truth a little. "I was only thinking last night, after you'd gone, that I ought perhaps to give you the names of a few people in Dublin — friends of my husband's on whom you might call . . ." She faltered there. "People with some political influence, I mean," she said. "If you are serious . . ."

"I am!" he cried. "Write out a list and bring it with you. That's great." Satisfied that she was coming, he hardly saw the necessity of fixing a day, and was turning away when he realized the need. "When?" he cried.

"And where?" she cried, leaning out across the sill.

"How about Tuesday next? Or is that too soon?"

There was no time to think. "Tuesday!" she agreed.

"But where?" she cried. "How about meeting in Stephen's Green? We can decide afterward where to go." It was settled.

Or was it?

"What will happen if it isn't a fine day?" he cried.

"Oh, it will be fine!" she cried recklessly. "You'll see!"

It rained, after all, on Tuesday. At first, she wasn't going to go to Dublin at all, but she was too unsettled to stay at home. She'd go up for a few hours anyway, she decided. And then, shortly before four o'clock, unexpectedly the rain cleared. As she parked her car on the side of the Green, she could see through the railings that the park was almost deserted. Uncertainly, she went in through a side gate. She felt better when she saw the paths were already drying out and from the wet branches overhead small birds, plump and round, were everywhere dropping to the ground like apples. On the grass, starlings and sparrows ran about like children, as if for once the earth was sweeter than the sky. Would he come? Would he think it too wet? Dispirited, she walked along the vacant paths till she came to the shallow lake in the center. And there, by the lakeside, standing under a tree, she saw him.

It was, she thought, the suddenness of seeing him that made her heart leap; only that. The next moment, a line from an old mortuary card came involuntarily to her mind. The card had been given to her by an old nun at the time of Richard's death, and her pallid belief in a life beyond the grave had been quenched entirely by its facile promise: *Oh, the joy to see you come.* But now the words rushed back to her, ready and apt. *I shouldn't have come,* she thought with terror. It was too late, though. He had seen her.

"You came?" he cried.

"Didn't you know I would?"

"It was raining!"

"It stopped, though." They began to walk along the side of the shallow cemented lake. "You must have known I'd come when you yourself came," she said.

"I only hoped! Can we ever be sure of anything?"

"Of some things, surely," she said, to gain time and think what she should do. There must be no more of these meetings. That was certain. But surely she could at least enjoy this afternoon? What harm could there be in it, except for her? And then only if she gave way to barren longings that might set the past at naught. She gave a sidelong look at him. He seemed so happy. What did it matter what she felt, as long as no one knew. As long as *he* didn't know! And he was concerned with the trivia of their conversation.

"I suppose you mean friendship?" he said. "But can there be friendship between a man and a woman?"

It was such a *young* question, it endeared him still more to her. She and Richard used to talk like that long ago. "I don't know," she said, "but I remember reading somewhere that there are only two valid relationships — blood and passion."

He was staring down at the cinder path under their feet as they paced along. "It's an interesting thought, isn't it?" he said. Then he looked up at her. "What about us, though?"

Disconcerted, she gave a shrug. "Oh, we don't come into any category at all," she said, "except . . . Wait a minute. I have something for you — I'd forgotten. It justifies our association." Opening her handbag, she took out the piece of paper on which she had written a list of names. "Here are the people on whom I thought you should call."

"Oh, thanks," he said, but he took it from her absently, and without looking at it he shoved it carelessly into the outer pocket of his jacket.

"Hadn't you better put it in your wallet? I went to a lot of trouble looking up some of the addresses. And, by the way, I put a mark beside the names of a few people to whom I thought I ought to introduce you personally."

"You mean go with me?" He put his hand in his pocket and pulled out the paper again, smoothing it and looking at it this time with interest. "That's different," he said enthusiastically, but to her dismay the next minute he rolled it into a ball and tossed it into a wire basket that was fastened to a tree. "That means you'll have to come up to town again. For the whole day next time." He smiled happily. "Let's go up this way," he said, pointing to a narrow path that ran over a humped bridge, low and covered with ivy. It was a little more than a decoration, for under it the water was utterly still. "Go on with what you were saying," he said. They had stopped and were looking over the parapet.

"Look, the water isn't flowing at all," she said. It was dusty and stippled with pollen from an overhanging lime.

But he didn't look. "What do you mean by saying we don't come into any category?" he asked. "Is that an obscure reference to my age?"

"No. To mine," she said, and when he laughed she thought she had distracted him.

She hadn't. "I knew that was what you meant," he said. And with a stony expression he looked down into the water. "Vera," he said quietly, "listen to me. Never once since the first night I met you have I ever felt you were a day older than me."

"That's nothing," she said sadly. "I never felt you were a day younger than me! But facts are facts." She straightened up and spoke flatly. "I always seem to be more attracted to people younger than me than to my own contemporaries — at least since Richard died. I was beginning to think that my heart was like a clock that had stopped at the age he was when he died, and that it was him I was looking for, over and over again, wherever I went — whenever I went into a strange place, or met new people."

"And wasn't it?"

"I don't think so. I think it was myself I was trying to find — the person I was before I married him. When he died I knew I had to get back to being that other person again, just as he, when he was dying, had to get back to being the kind of person he was before he met me. Standing beside him in those last few minutes, I felt he was trying to drag himself free of me. Can you understand that? Does it make any sense to you?"

"I think so," he said gravely. "And it would explain what I said — that from the first you seemed so young to me. It was because you were making a new beginning. I felt it at once, although I knew you must be older than me — in years, I mean."

"Not years," she said. "Decades."

"Oh, Vera!" he said, exasperated. "Don't exaggerate."

But she wasn't going to concede anything. "It might as well be centuries," she said bitterly.

He turned and faced her. "No," he said gravely. "Two people reaching out improbably toward each other; not impossibly." He took her hand. "Vera, what are we going to do?"

The first thing to do, she knew, was snatch back her hand, but someone was passing, and she could not let them be seen struggling. Instead, she looked down at her hand in his. This is the closest we'll ever be to each other, she thought. Then, the person past, she pulled her hand free.

"This is crazy!" she cried. "What are we saying? I thought it was bad enough that I — " Realizing what she was admitting, she turned away abruptly. "It's just crazy, that's all. I shouldn't have come!" she said childishly. "I knew it the minute I saw you. I was going to turn and run back to the car, only you looked up and saw me and it was too late."

"Yes, it was too late," he said. "It was too late the first night of all."

"Oh, no!" she cried. "Not from the beginning!" It was essential she be able to blame herself, to claim complicity in letting it go on, for the course it took, for the walks, the late hours, the intimacy of their conversation. Otherwise, there would be an inevitability impiled, and that she could not face. There would be helplessness as well as hopelessness. The tears rushed into her eyes.

"Vera!" he cried in distress. "Don't be upset. This may be unlooked for, but you must know it's not unprecedented?"

"I know nothing!" She dried her eyes. "I've heard things, of course. I've read things! Elderly housemaids jumping out of closets at little boys!"

"Vera!" He raised his hand and she thought he was going to hit her. "Shut up. Do you hear me!" he cried. "Shut up. The question is, what are we going to do?"

"We must put an end to it, that's all!"

"An end? At the beginning? You can't mean that?"

"What else can we do?"

"I don't know, not at this moment," he said, "but surely to God, whatever we've found in each other — something we both know is rare — surely that's not to be thrown away." He paused. "Before we've got anything out of it," he said, almost pettishly.

"What is there to be got out of it, only pain and heartache?"

"For which of us?" There was a pathetic eagerness in his voice. But she shook her head. "Does that matter?"

"I suppose not," he agreed miserably, and yet instead of resignation he had a stubborn look, and he caught at her hand again. "Isn't pain the price of most things?" he cried. "You're too ready to give up, Vera. I meant what I said a while ago — there are precedents for this. We aren't the first people in the world to be in this particular plight. I've heard of this kind of thing, and read about it. It always seemed — "

She interrupted him. "What it was — unnatural!"

"Oh, Vera," he said wearily. "Why are you so bitter? I was only trying to say that it was something altogether outside my experience."

"And mine!"

"All right," he said, "but isn't everything outside our experience until it comes into it? Wait a minute. There was a friend of my

own — I don't know how I forgot that — a close friend, too, in
my first year in college! He was in love with a woman years older
than him — fourteen years, I think! They did their best to break
away from each other, but in the end they got married and — "

She pulled away from him roughly. "Married!" she repeated
hysterically. "And anyway," she cried callously, "what is fourteen
years!"

He was arrested by that. "What age are you anyway, Vera?"

"What age are you?" she demanded, but she didn't really want
to know. "Don't tell me," she cried, taking her hand away. She
knew it was worse than she'd thought. "It doesn't matter," she said
hopelessly. "Let's leave things as they are, and not show them up
to be altogether farcical."

He said nothing, but she saw him wince. He reached out idly
and picked an ivy leaf from the parapet and dropped it into the pond
below, where it lay flat on the stagnant water.

It seemed a chance for her to say what had to be said. "We must
stop seeing each other. At least by design," she added, having
caught sight of his face.

"I see," he said. He stood up. "And you dismissed friendship, as
far as I remember, didn't you?" he said.

She shrugged. "This isn't friendship!" She glanced at the sky.
"It's going to rain again," she said dully.

As she spoke, a drop of rain fell singly and heavily onto the sleeve
of her blouse, and as the stroke of the hammer brings a spark to
iron, the heavy drop brought her flesh to the linen. She looked
down, and then she saw that he was staring, too. Without a word
said, the air began to throb, and it was with love — no less. Her
eyes filled with tears. "It may be rare — love, I mean," she said,
turning aside, unable to look at him anymore, "but where it is,
everything is easy. Friendship is so exacting. Perhaps that's why
they can never exist together at the same time. And why they
never" — she turned back and looked into his face — "can be sub-
stituted for each other. Let me tell you something," she said
quickly and urgently, although as she said them the words seemed
to echo in her mind and she remembered the disastrous effect of the
other incident she'd told him on the first night of all. But she went
on. "It was one evening last summer, and I was staying with friends

in Howth. After dinner, we went out on the cliff, and I asked something I'd always wanted to know — why the lights across the bay were always twinkling. But they weren't twinkling; they were steady. It was the level of the air in between that was uneven. Do you see?" she said sadly. "It's the same with us."

"I see," he said for the second time, and he threw down another leaf onto the water. Then he straightened up. For a moment, she thought everything was ended. "Where is your car?" he asked. But nothing was ended. "We can't settle this here," he said. "I'm coming down to the farm with you. We'll have to have a long talk." He paused. "Unless you could stay the night in town?"

"Oh, I couldn't possibly!" she cried.

"Well then, I'll come down," he said.

"And stay with Tim?" She was distractedly looking in her pockets for the keys of the car. They were going out of the park gates into the street. But when she looked at him, she saw that he was staring strangely at her.

"Where else?" he asked.

"Oh, I know there *is* nowhere else," she said, but she felt the ground was slipping from under her as if she were the one who was young and inexperienced — even endangered. But it was only that she was out of practice in a game where every word, every gesture counted for ten. "I only meant that your uncle might think it odd for you to go down unexpectedly."

"I never go any other way," he said. "Are you sure that's what you meant?"

"And if it wasn't!" she said, startled at the chancy note in her voice. "What would be the gain?"

"If we got rid of the tension that has built up between us, we might salvage something," he said, but there was a trace of despondency in his voice again.

"There might be nothing to salvage," she said. "And supposing the bonds only tightened?"

"Would you care?" he asked.

"Not then. But I care *now*, while I'm still able to care."

"Tell me one thing. For whose sake would you care — your own or mine?"

She looked away from him, over the street into which they had entered. "Not for either of our sakes, I think," she said. She nodded at the people hurrying by in all directions. "For them, perhaps."

"Don't be nonsensical," he said, and as they reached the car he caught the handle of the door. "I'll come down. And you must let me stay the night, Vera. Just to talk." He looked at his watch. "It's a bit bright to go down yet, though, isn't it? We ought to wait till it's darker, in case it would get about that I was down."

"And stayed with me?"

He nodded.

For a minute, she let herself dwell on the thought of having him in the house with her, under the same roof, however separate in all else. "I'd have to drive you up again very early before it was light, wouldn't I?"

"You could go to bed for a while," he said. "I'd call you."

She knew then that they fully understood each other. They got into the car.

"There's just one thing I have to do before I can go," he said. "I have to call at Hume Street to collect another lot of exam papers. Can we stop there? I won't keep you a minute."

She started the car.

"You didn't really think that you could walk out of my life like that?" he asked as she drove along. "I feel certain that no matter what happens you'll never altogether leave it."

She said nothing, and in a few minutes they had reached Hume Street. Before he got out of the car, he looked at her. "There's something I want to say now, before we go any further," he said. "No matter what happens, I want you to promise me that if you ever want me for anything, you'll tell me. Will you promise that?"

"Why do you want me to promise now?" she asked, but she leaned across him and opened the door. "Never mind. I promise," she said quickly. Then, knowing he must have guessed what she had in mind to do, she waited till he went up the steps and she drove away.

It was nearly a year later. She had not seen him in the time be-tween, nor did she expect to, when one evening there was the sound of a car at the door. "Well?" she said weakly when she opened it and saw him standing there.

Like the first time of all, they looked at each other, and this time, too, the look was one of surprise — but not of happiness.

"How are you?" he asked. There was a keen edge to his voice. "I don't need to ask," he said quickly.

"And you?" she asked. He looked well.

"I wasn't going to call at all," he said then. "But — " he paused — "I have a car now . . ."

It saddened her to see him ill at ease, standing so stiffly. Why did he come, she wondered. "You were anxious? Is that it?" she asked laughingly, thinking that by making light of it she would dispel the shadow of what had been between them. But she saw at once she had only brought it back. In a moment, the old atmosphere of intimacy was recreated — and yet it was not the same, or anything like the same.

"It was because of the old man I called," he said dully. "He thought it odd that I hadn't come to see you — I've been down here for two weeks."

"Ah, well," she said, "he didn't understand."

He looked at her intently. "I'm not so sure about that," he said. "I didn't tell you something he said last year — one of the nights I went back late. He gave me a queer look. 'If you were better favored,' he said, 'I'd be thinking things.' "

"He was only joking, of course."

"I'm not so sure." They were still standing in the doorway. "May I stay awhile?" he said suddenly.

Almost imperceptibly, she hesitated, but he noticed it. "You're not going out, are you?" he asked.

"I was going out," she said reluctantly.

"Must you?"

"I'm afraid I must."

He seemed really surprised. "Will you be long? Could I come back later? As a matter of fact, I have to go to Dublin this evening. I only intended calling for a minute." He looked at his watch. "I could be back in two and a half hours. Where are you going, anyway?"

"Today," she said, still more reluctantly, "today is Richard's anniversary. I was going to the cemetery. Normally, I never go near it, but I got word to say the headstone has slipped, and that it must be seen to at once — in case it falls altogether. It could break, or do damage to other graves. I have to go and see what is to be done, and make arrangements about it."

"Oh, I see," he said. "It can't be all that urgent, surely. Isn't this a bad day to go in any case? Or do you usually go on his anniversary?"

"I told you I never go. Never, never! This is purely a coincidence."

"Well, then. You certainly shouldn't go today. It's getting late, too. Put it off to another day!"

"I think I ought to go this evening," she said. "I don't mind, really." But suddenly an idea struck her. "It would make it a lot easier if there was someone with me. I don't suppose . . ." She paused, and for a minute she thought he had not seen any connection between him and her unfinished sentence.

But he had. "Of course! There should be someone with you. You certainly should not go alone! Don't think of it! Leave it till tomorrow or the next day, and *I'll* go with you. Better still, I'll go without you and see what's to be done. It's not a job for a woman anyway! Where is he buried, by the way?"

"Kildare."

"So far?"

"It's not so far, only a few miles."

"I'd probably be going from Dublin, but no matter. Put it out of your head now, and I'll take care of it."

"You couldn't come this evening?"

"With you?"

"With me, of course. I know it must sound superstitious, but I hate to think of getting word about it today of all days, and not going — not wanting to go."

"Rubbish!" he said easily. "Anyway, it's my affair now."

"You couldn't possibly come this evening?" she persisted. "Why do you have to go back to Dublin? Is it urgent?"

"Oh, it's not exactly urgent, but I'd like to go. I've arranged to give a driving lesson to someone. It need only take half an hour, but I promised to do it. A half an hour would be plenty; that's why I said I'd come back if you agreed to it, but of course the light would be gone by then — for the other job, I mean."

She was listening very attentively. "Is it a girl?" she asked quietly.

"You know it's not a girl."

"Why not? I only asked because if it was a girl I'd know you couldn't possibly break your word."

He stared. "You wouldn't mind?"

"It would be natural," she said.

"Was that your remedy?"

She didn't bother to reply to that. "Well, if it's not a girl, who is it?" she asked flatly.

"It's just a fellow who works in the Department of Education. It's through him I get the exam papers to correct."

"Couldn't you get in touch with him?"

"He's not on the phone."

She pondered this. "You could send him a telegram."

"He wouldn't get it in time."

"He'd get it afterwards, and he'd understand, surely?"

"I don't know if he would. And anyway, I couldn't leave him up there in the park, hanging around waiting for me, thinking every minute I was coming and afraid to go away."

She gave a short laugh.

"I suppose," he said, "you think that if it was last summer I'd have gone with you no matter what!"

"Oh, no!" she cried. "Last summer I wouldn't have let you come. I wouldn't have *needed* you. It would have been enough to know you'd have come if you could." Her coat was lying across the hall table. She took it up. "I must go," she said simply.

"So you were right," he said, blocking her way. "We salvaged nothing."

She put on her coat. Then she looked into his face. "Don't blame me for being right," she said. "I sometimes think love has nothing to do with people at all." Her voice was tired. "It's like the weather!" Suddenly she turned to face him. "But isn't it strange that a love that was unrealized should have — "

"Given such joy?" he said quietly.

"Yes, yes," she said gratefully. Then she closed the door behind them. "And such pain."

"Oh, Vera, Vera," he said.

"Goodbye," she said.

Goodbye.

HAPPINESS

MOTHER had a lot to say. This does not mean she was always talking but that we children felt the wells she drew upon were deep, deep, deep. Her theme was happiness: what it was, what it was not; where we might find it, where not; and how, if found, it must be guarded. Never must we confound it with pleasure. Nor think sorrow its exact opposite.

"Take Father Hugh." Mother's eyes flashed as she looked at him. "According to him, sorrow is an ingredient of happiness — a *necessary* ingredient, if you please!" And when he tried to protest she put up her hand. "There may be a freakish truth in the theory — for some people. But not for me. And not, I hope, for my children." She looked severely at us three girls. We laughed. None of us had had much experience with sorrow. Bea and I were children and Linda only a year old when our father died suddenly after a short illness that had not at first seemed serious. "I've known people to make sorrow a *substitute* for happiness," Mother said.

Father Hugh protested again. "You're not putting me in that class, I hope?"

Father Hugh, ever since our father died, had been the closest of anyone to us as a family, without being close to any one of us in particular — even to Mother. He lived in a monastery near our farm in County Meath, and he had been one of the celebrants at the Requiem High Mass our father's political importance had demanded. He met us that day for the first time, but he took to dropping in to see us, with the idea of filling the crater of loneliness left

at our center. He did not know that there was a cavity in his own
life, much less that we would fill it. He and Mother were both
young in those days, and perhaps it gave scandal to some that he was
so often in our house, staying till late into the night and, indeed,
thinking nothing of stopping all night if there was any special reason, such as one of us being sick. He had even on occasion slept
there if the night was too wet for tramping home across the fields.

When we girls were young, we were so used to having Father
Hugh around that we never stood on ceremony with him but in his
presence dried our hair and pared our nails and never minded what
garments were strewn about. As for Mother — she thought nothing
of running out of the bathroom in her slip, brushing her teeth or
combing her hair, if she wanted to tell him something she might
otherwise forget. And she brooked no criticism of her behavior.
"Celibacy was never meant to take all the warmth and homeliness
out of their lives," she said.

On this point, too, Bea was adamant. Bea, the middle sister, was
our oracle. "I'm so glad he *has* Mother," she said, "as well as her
having him, because it must be awful the way most women treat
them — priests, I mean — as if they were pariahs. Mother treats
him like a human being — that's all!"

And when it came to Mother's ears that there had been gossip
about her making free with Father Hugh, she opened her eyes wide
in astonishment. "But he's only a priest!" she said.

Bea giggled. "It's a good job he didn't hear *that*," she said to me
afterwards. "It would undo the good she's done him. You'd think
he was a eunuch."

"Bea!" I said. "Do you think he's in love with her?"

"If so, he doesn't know it," Bea said firmly. "It's her soul he's
after! Maybe he wants to make sure of her in the next world!"

But thoughts of the world to come never troubled Mother. "If
anything ever happens to me, children," she said, "suddenly, I mean,
or when you are not near me, or I cannot speak to you, I want you
to promise you won't feel bad. There's no need! Just remember
that I had a happy life — and that if I had to choose my kind of
heaven I'd take it on this earth with you again, no matter how much
you might annoy me!"

You see, annoyance and fatigue, according to Mother, and even illness and pain, could coexist with happiness. She had a habit of asking people if they were happy at times and in places that — to say the least of it — seemed to us inappropriate. "But are you happy?" she'd probe, as one lay sick and bathed in sweat, or in the throes of a jumping toothache. And once in our presence she made the inquiry of an old friend as he lay upon his deathbed.

"Why not?" she said when we took her to task for it later. "Isn't it more important than ever to be happy when you're dying? Take my own father! You know what he said in his last moments? On his deathbed, he defied me to name a man who had enjoyed a better life. In spite of dreadful pain, his face *radiated* happiness!" Mother nodded her head comfortably. "Happiness drives out pain, as fire burns out fire."

Having no knowledge of our own to pit against hers, we thirstily drank in her rhetoric. Only Bea was skeptical. "Perhaps you *got* it from him, Mother, like spots, or fever," she said. "Or something that could at least be slipped from hand to hand."

"Do you think I'd have taken it if that were the case!" Mother cried. "Then, when he needed it most?"

"Not there and then!" Bea said stubbornly. "I meant as a sort of legacy."

"Don't you think in *that* case," Mother said, exasperated, "he would have felt obliged to leave it to your grandmother?"

Certainly we knew that in spite of his lavish heart our grandfather had failed to provide our grandmother with enduring happiness. He had passed that job on to Mother. And Mother had not made too good a fist of it, even when our own father was living and she had him — and, later, us children — to help.

As for Father Hugh, he had given our grandmother up early in the game. "God Almighty couldn't make that woman happy," he said one day, seeing Mother's face, drawn and pale with fatigue, preparing for the nightly run over to her own mother's flat that would exhaust her utterly.

There were evenings after she came home from the library where she worked when we saw her stand with the car keys in her hand, trying to think which would be worse — to slog over there on foot, or take out the car again. And yet the distance was short. It was Mother's day that had been too long.

"Weren't you over to see her this morning?" Father Hugh would demand.

"No matter!" Mother would no doubt be thinking of the forlorn face our grandmother always put on when she was leaving. ("Don't say good night, Vera," Grandmother would plead. "It makes me feel too lonely. And you never can tell — you might slip over again before you go to bed!")

"Do you know the time?" Bea would say impatiently, if she happened to be with Mother. Not indeed that the lateness of the hour counted for anything, because in all likelihood Mother *would* go back, if only to pass by under the window and see that the lights were out, or stand and listen and make sure that as far as she could tell all was well.

"I wouldn't mind if she was happy," Mother said.

"And how do you know she's not?" we'd ask.

"When people are happy, I can feel it. Can't you?"

We were not sure. Most people thought our grandmother was a gay creature, a small birdy being who even at a great age laughed like a girl, and — more remarkably — sang like one, as she went about her day. But beak and claw were of steel. She'd think nothing of sending Mother back to a shop three times if her errands were not exactly right. "Not sugar like that — that's *too* fine; it's not castor sugar I want. But *not* as coarse as *that*, either. I want an in-between kind."

Provoked one day, my youngest sister, Linda, turned and gave battle. "You're mean!" she cried. "You love ordering people about!"

Grandmother preened, as if Linda had acclaimed an attribute. "I was always hard to please," she said. "As a girl, I used to be called Miss Imperious."

And Miss Imperious she remained as long as she lived, even when she was a great age. Her orders were then given a wry twist by the fact that as she advanced in age she took to calling her daughter Mother, as we did.

There was one great phrase with which our grandmother opened every sentence: "if only." "If only," she'd say, when we came to visit her — "if only you'd come earlier, before I was worn out expecting you!" Or if we were early, then if only it was later, after she'd had a rest and could enjoy us, be *able* for us. And if we brought her flowers, she'd sigh to think that if only we'd brought them the previous day she'd have had a visitor to appreciate them, or say it was a pity the stems weren't longer. If only we'd picked a few green leaves, or included some buds, because, she'd say disparagingly, the poor flowers we'd brought were already wilting. We might just as well not have brought them! As the years went on, Grandmother had a new bead to add to her rosary: if only her friends were not all dead! By their absence, they reduced to nil all *real* enjoyment in anything. Our own father — her son-in-law — was the one person who had ever gone close to pleasing her. But even here there had been a snag. "If only he was my real son!" she used to say, with a sigh.

Mother's mother lived on through our childhood and into our early maturity (though she outlived the money our grandfather left her), and in our minds she was a complicated mixture of valiance and defeat. Courageous and generous within the limits of her own life, her simplest demand was yet enormous in the larger frame of Mother's life, and so we never could see her with the same clarity of vision with which we saw our grandfather, or our own father. Them we saw only through Mother's eyes.

"Take your grandfather!" she'd cry, and instantly we'd see him, his eyes burning upon us — yes, upon *us*, although in his day only one of us had been born: me. At another time, Mother would cry, "Take your own father!" and instantly we'd see *him* — tall, handsome, young, and much more suited to marry one of us than poor bedraggled Mother.

Most fascinating of all were the times Mother would say "Take me!" By magic then, staring down the years, we'd see blazingly clear a small girl with black hair and buttoned boots, who, though plain and pouting, burned bright, like a star. "I was happy, you see," Mother said. And we'd strain hard to try and understand the mystery of the light that radiated from her. "I used to lean along a tree that grew out over the river," she said, "and look down through the gray leaves at the water flowing past below, and I used to think it was not the stream that flowed but me, spread-eagled over it, who flew through the air! Like a bird! That I'd found the secret!" She made it seem there might *be* such a secret, just waiting to be found. Another time she'd dream that she'd be a great singer.

"We didn't know you sang, Mother!"

She had to laugh. "Like a crow," she said.

Sometimes she used to think she'd swim the Channel.

"Did you swim *that* well, Mother?"

"Oh, not really — just the breast stroke," she said. "And then only by the aid of two pig bladders blown up by my father and tied around my middle. But I used to throb — yes, throb — with happiness."

Behind Mother's back, Bea raised her eyebrows.

What was it, we used to ask ourselves — that quality that she, we felt sure, misnamed? Was it courage? Was it strength? Health? Or high spirits? Something you could not give or take — a conundrum? A game of catch-as-catch-can?

"I know," cried Bea. "A sham!"

Whatever it was, we knew that Mother would let no wind of violence from within or without tear it from her. Although, one evening when Father Hugh was with us, our astonished ears heard her proclaim that there might be a time when one had to slacken hold on it — let go — to catch at it again with a surer hand. In the way, we supposed, that the high-wire walker up among the painted stars of his canvas sky must wait to fling himself through the air until the bar he catches at has started to sway perversely from him. Oh no, no! That downward drag at our innards we could not bear, the belly swelling to the shape of a pear. Let happiness go by the board. "After all, lots of people seem to make out without it," Bea cried. It was too tricky a business. And might it not be that one had to be born with a flair for it?

"A flair would not be enough," Mother answered. "Take Father Hugh. He, if anyone, had a flair for it — a natural capacity! You've only to look at him when he's off guard, with you children, or helping me in the garden. But he rejects happiness! He casts it from him."

"That is simply not true, Vera," cried Father Hugh, overhearing her. "It's just that I don't place an inordinate value on it like you. I don't think it's enough to carry one all the way. To the end, I mean — and after."

"Oh, don't talk about the end when we're only in the middle," cried Mother. And, indeed, at that moment her own face shone with such happiness it was hard to believe that her earth was not her heaven. Certainly it was her constant contention that of happiness she had had a lion's share. This, however, we, in private, doubted. Perhaps there were times when she had had a surplus of it — when she was young, say, with her redoubtable father, whose love blazed circles around her, making winter into summer and ice into fire. Perhaps she did have a brimming measure in her early married years. By straining hard, we could find traces left in our minds from those days of milk and honey. Our father, while he lived, had cast a magic over everything, for us as well as for her. He held his love up over us like an umbrella and kept off the troubles that afterwards came down on us, pouring cats and dogs!

But if she did have more than the common lot of happiness in those early days, what use was that when we could remember so clearly how our father's death had ravaged her? And how could we forget the distress it brought on us when, afraid to let her out of our sight, Bea and I stumbled after her everywhere, through the woods and along the bank of the river, where, in the weeks that followed, she tried vainly to find peace.

The summer after Father died, we were invited to France to stay with friends, and when she went walking on the cliffs at Fecamp our fears for her grew frenzied, so that we hung on to her arm and dragged at her skirt, hoping that like leaded weights we'd pin her down if she went too near to the edge. But at night we had to abandon our watch, being forced to follow the conventions of a family still whole — a home still intact — and go to bed at the same time as the other children. It was at that hour, when the coast guard was gone from his rowing boat offshore and the sand was as cold and gray as the sea, that Mother liked to swim. And when she had washed, kissed, and left us, our hearts almost died inside us and we'd creep out of bed again to stand in our bare feet at the mansard and watch as she ran down the shingle, striking out when she reached the water where, far out, wave and sky and mist were one, and the grayness closed over her. If we took our eyes off her for an instant, it was impossible to find her again.

"Oh, make her turn back, God, please!" I prayed out loud one night.

Startled, Bea turned away from the window. "She'll *have* to turn back sometime, won't she? Unless . . . ?"

Locking our damp hands together, we stared out again. "She wouldn't!" I whispered. "It would be a sin!"

Secure in the deterring power of sin, we let out our breath. Then Bea caught her breath again. "What if she went out so far she used up all her strength and she couldn't swim back? It wouldn't be a sin then."

"It's the intention that counts," I whispered.

A second later, we could see an arm lift heavily up and wearily cleave down, and Mother would be in the shallows, wading back to shore.

"Don't let her see us!" cried Bea. As if our chattering teeth would not give us away when she looked in at us before she went to her own room on the other side of the corridor, where, later in the night, sometimes the sound of crying would reach us.

What was it worth — a happiness bought that dearly?

Mother had never questioned it. And once she told us how on a wintry day she had brought her own mother a snowdrop. It was the first one of the year — a bleak bud that had come up stunted before its time. "I meant it for a sign. But do you know what your grandmother said? 'What good are snowdrops to me now?' Such a thing to say! What good is a snowdrop at all if it doesn't hold its value always, and never lose it! Isn't that the whole point of a snowdrop? And that is the whole point of happiness, too! What good would it be if it could be erased without trace? Take me and those daffodils!" Stooping, she buried her face in a bunch that lay on the table waiting to be put in vases. "If they didn't hold their beauty absolute and inviolable, do you think I could bear the sight of them after what happened when your father was in the hospital?"

It was a fair question. When Father went to hospital, Mother went with him and stayed in a small hotel across the street so she could be with him all day from early to late. "Because it was so awful for him — being in Dublin!" she said. "You have no idea how he hated it."

That he was dying neither of them realized. How could they know, as it rushed through the sky, that their star was a falling star! But one evening when she'd left him asleep Mother came home for a few hours to see how we were faring, and it broke her heart to see the daffodils out all over the place — in the woods, under the trees, and along the sides of the avenue. There had never been so many, and she thought how awful it was that Father was missing them. "You sent up little bunches to him, you poor dears!" she said. Sweet little bunches, too — squeezed tight as posies by your little fists! But stuffed into vases they couldn't really make up to him for not being able to see them growing!"

So on the way back to the hospital she stopped her car and pulled a great bunch — the full of her arms. "They took up the whole back seat," she said, "and I was so excited at the thought of walking into his room and dumping them on his bed — you know — just plomping them down so he could smell them, and feel them, and look and look! I didn't mean them to be put in vases, or anything ridiculous like that — it would have taken a rainwater barrel to hold them. Why, I could hardly see over them as I came up the steps; I kept tripping. But when I came into the hall, that nun — I told you about her — that nun came up to me, sprang out of nowhere it seemed, although I know now that she was waiting for me, knowing that somebody had to bring me to my senses. But the way she did it! Reached out and grabbed the flowers, letting lots of them fall — I remember them getting stood on. 'Where are you going with those foolish flowers, you foolish woman?' she said. 'Don't you know your husband is dying? Your prayers are all you can give him now!'

"She was right. I *was* foolish. But I wasn't cured. Afterwards, it was nothing but foolishness the way I dragged you children after me all over Europe. As if any one place was going to be different from another, any better, any less desolate. But there was great satisfaction in bringing you places your father and I had planned to bring

you — although in fairness to him I must say that he would not perhaps have brought you so young. And he would not have had an
ulterior motive. But above all, he would not have attempted those
trips in such a dilapidated car."

Oh, that car! It was a battered and dilapidated red sports car, so
depleted of accessories that when, eventually, we got a new car
Mother still stuck out her hand on bends, and in wet weather jumped
out to wipe the windscreen with her sleeve. And if fussed, she'd
let down the window and shout at people, forgetting she now had a
horn. How we had ever fitted into it with all our luggage was a
miracle.

"You were never lumpish — any of you!" Mother said proudly.
"But you were very healthy and very strong." She turned to me.
"Think of how you got that car up the hill in Switzerland!"

"The Alps are not hills, Mother!" I pointed out coldly, as I had
done at the time, when, as actually happened, the car failed to make
it on one of the inclines. Mother let it run back until it wedged
against the rock face, and I had to get out and push till she got going
again in first gear. But when it got started it couldn't be stopped to
pick me up until it got to the top, where they had to wait for me, and
for a very long time.

"Ah, well," she said, sighing wistfully at the thought of those
trips. "You got something out of them, I hope. All that traveling
must have helped you with your geography and your history."

We looked at each other and smiled, and then Mother herself
laughed. "Remember the time," she said, "when we were in Italy,
and it was Easter, and all the shops were chock-full of food? The
butchers' shops had poultry and game hanging up outside the doors,
fully feathered, and with their poor heads dripping blood, and in the
windows they had poor little lambs and suckling pigs and young
goats, all skinned and hanging by their hind feet." Mother shuddered. "They think so much about food. I found it revolting. I had
to hurry past. But Linda, who must have been only four then,
dragged at me and stared and stared. You know how children are at
that age; they have a morbid fascination for what is cruel and bloody.
Her face was flushed and her eyes were wide. I hurried her back to
the hotel. But next morning she crept into my room. She crept up

to me and pressed against me. 'Can't we go back, just once, and look again at that shop?' she whispered. 'The shop where they have the little children hanging up for Easter!' It was the young goats, of course, but I'd said 'kids,' I suppose. How we laughed." But her face was grave. "You were *so* good on those trips, all of you," she said. "You were really very good children in general. Otherwise I would never have put so much effort into rearing you, because I wasn't a bit maternal. You brought out the best in me! I put an unnatural effort into you, of course, because I was taking my standards from your father, forgetting that his might not have remained so inflexible if he had lived to middle age and was beset by life, like other parents."

"Well, the job is nearly over now, Vera," said Father Hugh. "And you didn't do so badly."

"That's right, Hugh," Mother said, and she straightened up, and put her hand to her back the way she sometimes did in the garden when she got up from her knees after weeding. "I didn't go over to the enemy anyway! We survived!" Then a flash of defiance came into her eyes. "And we were happy. That's the main thing!"

Father Hugh frowned. "There you go again!" he said.

Mother turned on him. "I don't think you realize the onslaughts that were made upon our happiness! The minute Robert died, they came down on me — cohorts of relatives, friends, even strangers, all draped in black, opening their arms like bats to let me pass into their company. 'Life is a vale of tears,' they said. 'You are privileged to find it out so young!' Ugh! After I staggered onto my feet and began to take hold of life once more, they fell back defeated. And the first day I gave a laugh — puff, they were blown out like candles. They weren't living in a real world at all; they belonged to a ghostly world where life was easy: all one had to do was sit and weep. It takes effort to push back the stone from the mouth of the tomb and walk out."

Effort. Effort. Ah, but that strange-sounding word could invoke little sympathy from those who had not learned yet what it meant. Life must have been hardest for Mother in those years when we older ones were at college — no longer children, and still dependent on her. Indeed, we made more demands on her than ever then, having moved into new areas of activity and emotion. And our friends! Our friends came and went as freely as we did ourselves, so that the house was often like a café — and one where pets were not prohibited but took their places on the chairs and beds, as regardless as the people. And anyway it was hard to have sympathy for someone who got things into such a state as Mother. All over the house there was clutter. Her study was like the returned-letter department of a post office, with stacks of paper everywhere, bills paid and unpaid, letters answered and unanswered, tax returns, pamphlets, leaflets. If by mistake we left the door open on a windy day, we came back to find papers flapping through the air like frightened birds. Efficient only in that she managed eventually to conclude every task she began, it never seemed possible to outsiders that by Mother's methods anything whatever could be accomplished. In an attempt to keep order elsewhere, she made her own room the clearinghouse into which the rest of us put everything: things to be given away, things to be mended, things to be stored, things to be treasured, things to be returned — even things to be thrown out! By the end of the year, the room resembled an obsolescence dump. And no one could help her; the chaos of her life was as personal as an act of creation — one might as well try to finish another person's poem.

As the years passed, Mother rushed around more hectically. And although Bea and I had married and were not at home anymore, except at holiday time and for occasional weekends, Linda was noisier than the two of us put together, and for every follower that we had brought home she brought twenty. The house was never still. Now that we were reduced to being visitors, we watched Mother's tension mount to vertigo, knowing that, like a spinning top, she could not rest till she fell. But now at the smallest pretext Father Hugh would call in the doctor and Mother would be put on the mail boat and dispatched for London. For it was essential that she get far enough away to make phoning home every night prohibitively costly.

Unfortunately, the thought of departure often drove a spur into her and she redoubled her effort to achieve order in her affairs. She would be up until the early hours ransacking her desk. To her, as always, the shortest parting entailed a preparation as for death. And as if indeed it were her end that was at hand, we would all be summoned, although she had no time to speak a word to us, because five minutes before departure she would still be attempting to reply to letters that were the accumulation of weeks and would have taken whole days to dispatch.

"Don't you know the taxi is at the door, Vera?" Father Hugh would say, running his hand through his gray hair and looking very disheveled himself. She had him at times as distracted as herself. "You can't do any more. You'll have to leave the rest till you come back."

"I can't, I can't!" Mother would cry. "I'll have to cancel my plans."

One day, Father Hugh opened the lid of her case, which was strapped up in the hall, and with a swipe of his arm he cleared all the papers on the top of the desk pell-mell into the suitcase. "You can sort them on the boat," he said, "or the train to London!"

Thereafter, Mother's luggage always included an empty case to hold the unfinished papers on her desk. And years afterwards a steward on the Irish Mail told us she was a familiar figure, working away at letters and bills nearly all the way from Holyhead to Euston. "She gave it up about Rugby or Crewe," he said. "She'd get talking to someone in the compartment." He smiled. "There was one time coming down the train I was just in time to see her close up the window with a guilty look. I didn't say anything, but I think she'd emptied those papers of hers out the window!"

Quite likely. When we were children, even a few hours away from us gave her composure. And in two weeks or less, when she'd come home, the well of her spirit would be freshened. We'd hardly know her — her step so light, her eye so bright, and her love and patience once more freely flowing. But in no time at all the house would fill up again with the noise and confusion of too many people and too many animals, and again we'd be fighting our corner with cats and dogs, bats, mice, bees and even wasps. "Don't kill it!" Mother would cry if we raised a hand to an angry wasp. "Just catch it, dear, and put it outside. Open the window and let it fly away!" But even this treatment could at times be deemed too harsh. "Wait a minute. Close the window!" she'd cry. "It's too cold outside. It will die. That's why it came in, I suppose! Oh dear, what will we do?" Life would be going full blast again.

There was only one place Mother found rest. When she was at breaking point and fit to fall, she'd go out into the garden — not to sit or stroll around but to dig, to drag up weeds, to move great clumps of corms or rhizomes, or indeed quite frequently to haul huge rocks from one place to another. She was always laying down a path, building a dry wall, or making compost heaps as high as hills. However jaded she might be going out, when dark forced her in at last her step had the spring of a daisy. So if she did not succeed in defining happiness to our understanding, we could see that whatever it was, she possessed it to the full when she was in her garden.

Bea said as much one Sunday when she and I had dropped around for the afternoon. Father Hugh was with us again. "It's an unthinking happiness, though," he caviled. We were standing at the drawing room window, looking out to where in the fading light we could see Mother on her knees weeding, in the long border that stretched from the house right down to the woods. "I wonder how she'd take it if she were stricken down and had to give up that heavy work!" he said. Was he perhaps a little jealous of how she could stoop and bend? He himself had begun to use a stick. I was often a little jealous of her myself, because although I was married and had children of my own, I had married young and felt the weight of living as heavy as a weight of years. "She doesn't take enough care of herself," Father Hugh said sadly. "Look at her out there with nothing under her knees to protect her from the damp ground." It was almost too dim for us to see her, but even in the drawing room it was chilly. "She should not be let stay out there after the sun goes down."

"Just you try to get her in then!" said Linda, who had come into the room in time to hear him. "Anyway, don't you know by now that what would kill another person only seems to make Mother thrive?"

Father Hugh shook his head again. "You seem to forget it's not younger she's getting!" He fidgeted and fussed, and several times went to the window to stare out apprehensively. He was really getting quite elderly.

"Come and sit down, Father Hugh," Bea said, and to take his mind off Mother she turned on the light and blotted out the garden. Instead of seeing through the window, we saw into it as into a mirror, and there between the flower-laden tables and the lamps it was ourselves we saw moving vaguely. Like Father Hugh, we, too, were waiting for her to come in before we called an end to the day.

"Oh, this is ridiculous!" Father Hugh cried at last. "She'll have to listen to reason." And going back to the window he threw it open. "Vera!" he called sternly — "Vera" — so sternly that, more intimate than an endearment, his tone shocked us. "She didn't hear me," he said, turning back blinking at us in the lighted room. "I'm going out to get her." And in a minute he was gone from the room. As he ran down the garden path, we stared at each other, astonished; his step, like his voice, was the step of a lover. "I'm coming, Vera!" he cried.

Although she was never stubborn except in things that mattered, Mother had not moved. In the wholehearted way she did everything, she was bent down close to the ground. It wasn't the light only that was dimming; her eyesight also was failing, I thought, as instinctively I followed Father Hugh.

But halfway down the path I stopped. I had seen something he had not: Mother's hand that appeared to support itself in a forked branch of an old tree peony she had planted as a bride was not in fact gripping it but impaled upon it. And the hand that appeared to be grubbing in the clay was in fact sunk into the soft mold. "Mother!" I screamed, and I ran forward, but when I reached her I covered my face with my hands. "Oh, Father Hugh!" I cried. "Is she dead?"

It was Bea who answered, hysterical. "She is! She is!" she cried, and she began to pound Father Hugh on the back with her fists, as if his pessimistic words had made this happen.

But Mother was not dead. And at first the doctor even offered hope of her pulling through. But from the moment Father Hugh lifted her up to carry her into the house we ourselves had no hope, seeing how effortlessly he, who was not strong, could carry her.

When he put her down on her bed, her head hardly creased the pillow. Mother lived for four more hours.

Like the days of her life, those four hours that Mother lived were packed tight with concern and anxiety. Partly conscious, partly delirious, she seemed to think the counterpane was her desk, and she scrabbled her fingers upon it as if trying to sort out a muddle of bills and correspondence. No longer indifferent now, we listened, anguished, to the distracted cries that had for all our lifetime been so familiar to us. "Oh, where is it? Where is it? I had it a minute ago! Where on earth did I put it?"

"Vera, Vera, stop worrying," Father Hugh pleaded, but she waved him away and went on sifting through the sheets as if they were sheets of paper. "Oh, Vera!" he begged. "Listen to me. Do you not know — "

Bea pushed between them. "You're not to tell her!" she commanded. "Why frighten her?"

"But it ought not to frighten her," said Father Hugh. "This is what I was always afraid would happen — that she'd be frightened when it came to the end."

At that moment, as if to vindicate him, Mother's hands fell idle on the coverlet, palm upward and empty. And turning her head she stared at each of us in turn, beseechingly. "I cannot face it," she whispered. "I can't! I can't! I can't!"

"Oh, my God!" Bea said, and she started to cry.

"Vera. For God's sake, listen to me," Father Hugh cried, and pressing his face to hers, as close as a kiss, he kept whispering to her, trying to cast into the dark tunnel before her the light of his own faith.

But it seemed to us that Mother must already be looking into God's exigent eyes. "I can't!" she cried. "I can't!"

Then her mind came back from the stark world of the spirit to the world where her body was still detained, but even that world was now a whirling kaleidoscope of things which only she could see. Suddenly her eyes focused, and, catching at Father Hugh, she pulled herself up a little and pointed to something we could not see. "What will be done with them?" Her voice was anxious. "They ought to be put in water anyway," she said, and, leaning over the edge of the bed, she pointed to the floor. "Don't step on that one!" she said sharply. Then, more sharply still, she addressed us all. "Have them sent to the public ward," she said peremptorily. "Don't let that nun take them; she'll only put them on the altar. And God doesn't want them! He made them for *us* — not for Himself!"

It was the familiar rhetoric that all her life had characterized her utterances. For a moment we were mystified. Then Bea gasped. "The daffodils!" she cried. "The day Father died!" And over her face came the light that had so often blazed over Mother's. Leaning across the bed, she pushed Father Hugh aside. And, putting out her hands, she held Mother's face between her palms as tenderly as if it were the face of a child. "It's all right, Mother. You don't *have* to face it! It's over!" Then she who had so fiercely forbade Father Hugh to do so blurted out the truth. "You've finished with this world, Mother," she said, and, confident that her tidings were joyous, her voice was strong.

Mother made the last effort of her life and grasped at Bea's meaning. She let out a sigh, and, closing her eyes, she sank back, and this time her head sank so deep into the pillow that it would have been dented had it been a pillow of stone.

THE NEW GARDENER

CLEM was the man for us. "No matter. I'll get it to rights," he said blithely, when he saw the state of the garden. Five weeks of early spring with no man in it, and a wet season at that, it was a fright. "And now where's the cottage?" he asked.

He had crossed over from Holyhead on the night boat, come down to Bective on the bus and walked up from the crossroads. "I left the family in Dublin," he said. "I want to get the cottage fixed up before they see it. It was a rough crossing, and Pearl got a little sick."

Which was Pearl? The snapshots he'd sent in lieu of an interview had shown him surrounded by a nice-sized family for so young a man. Holding on to one arm was a woman, presumably his wife, but she must have stirred as the snap was being taken, because she was a bit blurred. Her dark hair was cloudy anyway and it partly hid her face. In spite of the blurring, her features looked sharp though, but this was of small moment as long as she could take care of the small children that clung about Clem, especially the baby girl, who snuggled in his arms.

"They're coming down on the evening bus," he explained. "Where can I get a horse and cart? I want to pick up a few sticks of furniture for the place. I suppose I'll get one in the farmyard?"

In a few minutes he was rattling off in the farm cart, standing with his legs apart, his yellow hair lifting in the breeze of his departure, and the white tennis shoes — which he had worn also in the snap — looking, to the last glimpse, magnificently unsuitable. In less than an hour he was back with a load of fat mattresses, bulging pillows and bedding, the lot barricaded into the cart by a palisade of table legs and up-ended chairs.

"Another run and the job is done," he cried, as he toppled it all out on the grass patch in front of the cottage, and galloped off to town once more.

The second time he could be heard coming a mile away with a load of ewers and basins, pots and pans, washhand stands, an oil cooker and several tin cans, that clattered together on the cart behind him. "These must be got into the house at once," he said solicitously to a young lad sent up from the yard to help him. "There's damp in the air, and I don't want them rusted. Don't stand there gawking, boy," he added, as Jimmy stared at the bedding already beaded with mist. "Bedding is easy aired. Rust is a serious matter. Learn to distinguish!"

Then there began such a fury of lifting and carrying, pushing and pulling, such banging of nails and bringing down of plaster, but above all, such running in and out of the cottage that Clem's shoes came at last into their own. They were so apt for the job on foot.

By evening every picture was hung, every plate in place, the tables and chairs were right side up and the oil cooker lit and giving off its perfume. The bedding was still outdoors.

"No matter. Food comes first. Learn to distinguish!" cried Clem again, as he held a plate under a brown-paper bag and let plop out a mess of cream buns. "They'll be starving," he said. "Pearl isn't much of a feeder," he added sadly, "but the others have powerful appetites."

He still hadn't said which was Pearl, but it wasn't the wife anyway, because when Jimmy saw them trudging up the drive a while later, there was no wife, there was only Clem with the two small boys, the bigger girl, and the little one in his arms snuggled close to him, just as in the snap, with only her curls to be seen. Yet when Clem let down the child, Jimmy wondered no more, for she was the dead spit of a pearl.

"Did you ever see the like of her?" cried Clem delightedly, as he saw Jimmy looking at her. "She puts me in mind of apple blossom! That's what I should have called her — Blossom," he said sadly, "but no matter. I don't like fancy names anyway. Come now, Moll!" he said, turning to the bigger girl, "let's get her to bed. She's dog-tired." Planting Pearl in Moll's arms, he ran out and pulled in one of the mattresses. "It's a bit damp all right," he said, in surprise. But, undismayed, he dashed into the garden and came back with three large rhubarb leaves. "Put them under the sheet," he said. "Leaves are waterproof. Trust nature every time." Then as Moll was about to stagger away with Pearl in her arms, he ran after them and gave Moll a hug. "She's the best little mother in the world," he said. "I don't know what I'd do without her."

It was the first and last reference, oblique as it was, to the absence of Mrs. Clem.

As the days went on, however, the absence of Mrs. Clem was seldom felt, for if Clem was a good father, he was a still better mother. True, he sometimes had to knock off work in the garden to cook a hot meal for them, to fetch them from school, or oftenest of all to wash Pearl's hair, but he still did more work in one day than another man would in six. And it wasn't just hard work: Clem had a green hand if ever man had.

On the first morning of all, he made his only complaint. "There isn't enough shelter in this garden," he said. "Living things are very tender." And disregarding the fact that he'd just whitened his tennis shoes, he leaped into the soft black clay of the border and broke off branches recklessly from syringa, philadelphus and daphne. Then he rushed around sticking the twigs into the ground, here, there and everywhere.

He must be marking the places where he's going to plant things, thought Jimmy. But before a week was out, the twigs that had wilted and lost their leaves stiffened into life again and put forth new shoots. A green hand? When Clem stuck a spade into the ground at the end of a day, Jimmy half-expected to see it sprouting leaves by morning. There was nothing Clem couldn't do with a plant. In any weather he'd put down a seed. In any weather he'd take up a seedling. "It'll be all right if you handle it lightly," he'd say gaily, planting seeds with the rain falling so heavily on the wet clay that it splashed back into his face and spattered it all over. And when the sun did shine, as often as not he'd be down on his knees with his box of seedlings, pricking them out.

"Won't they die in the sun?" Jimmy asked.

"Why would they die?" Clem looked surprised. "Like all living things, they only ask to be handled gently."

To see Clem handle a young plant, you'd think it was some small animal that he held in his hands. Even the seeds got their full share of his love and care, every single one, no matter how many to a packet. Once he nearly made Jimmy scratch up a whole cement floor in the potting shed where he'd let one seed fall.

"We can't leave it there with no food and no drink and no light and no covering," he cried, as he lit a match to help in the search.

Jimmy felt a bit put upon. "What about all the packets of seeds that are up there on the shelf?" he protested. "The last fellow forgot to sow them until it was too late!"

"But it's never too late!" cried Clem. "Where are they?" And the next minute he had rummaged out the old seeds in their discolored paper packets with their faded flower prints. "Everything should get its chance," he cried, and he gathered up every flower pot in sight and, filling them with the finest of sieved clay, he poked a seed into each one. "If there's life in those seeds, they'll take flight before the end of the week!" he told Jimmy. And in less than a week, over each pot there hovered two frail green wings. Yet, for all the energy he spent on plants and chores, Clem still had energy to spare.

"How is the fishing around here?" he asked one evening, a few weeks after his arrival. "I'd like to take the children fishing. Wouldn't you like to go fishing, Pearl?" he asked, turning to her. She was a good little thing, and she never gave any trouble. All the minding she got was following Clem around the place. Now and again he'd tell her to get up off a cold stone, or to mind would a wasp sting her. There was one thing he was very particular about though, and that was that she should not take off the little woolly coat she always wore.

"Pearly hot!" Pearl would say. No matter! He made her keep the coat on. It was, however, very hot indeed that afternoon in May, and when Clem bent down to dibble in a few colchicums for the autumn, Pearl stamped her foot.

"Pearly hot," she said, defiantly, and off she took the yellow woolly coat and down she threw it on the ground. Jimmy bent down to pick it up. When he looked up, he was astonished to see Clem's eyes filled with tears. "I hate anyone to see it," said Clem. "I can't bear to look at it myself! But I knew it couldn't be covered forever!"

On the inner, softer side of Pearl's arm was a long, sickle-shaped scar. It was healed. It wasn't really very noticeable. Many a child had a scab twice as big on its knee, or on its elbow, or even it's nose! But all the same, Pearl's scar made Jimmy shudder. Perhaps because it was on the soft underflesh, perhaps because of the look it had brought to Clem's eyes, this scar of Pearl's seemed to have a terrible importance.

"Was it an accident, Clem?"

"No," said Clem shortly.

Could Clem . . . ? But no, no! She was his seedling, his fledgling, his little plant that, if he could, he would cup between his hands, and breathe upon, press close and hold against him forever. As it was, he put his arms around her. "Wouldn't you like to catch a little fish, Pearl?" he was asking her. "I'll get a sally wand for you, and I'll peel it white! You'll catch a great big salmon maybe!"

His own ambition was more humble. He turned abruptly to Jimmy. "I suppose there's plenty of pike?" he asked. "Can we get a frog, do you think? Frogs are the only bait for pike. Get hold of a good frog, Jimmy, and we'll meet you down at Cletty Bridge in ten minutes."

To get a frog on a May evening in Meath! On a wet day, yes — the roads were plastered with them, sprawled out where cars had gone over them. But this evening Clem and the children must have been a full hour down by Cletty pool before Jimmy came running to them, his hand over his pocket.

The children were all calling to each other and laughing, and Clem was shouting excitedly, but it was Pearl's small voice that caught the ear, babbling as joyously to Clem as the pebbles to the stream. There was joy and excitement in the air, and joy welled up in Jimmy's heart, too, as he scrambled over the wall and tumbled happily down the bank, filling the air with the bittersweet smell of elder leaves as he caught at a branch to save himself from falling.

"Good man! You've got the bait!" cried Clem, his expert eye

picking out the bulge in Jimmy's pocket. He was helping Pearl to cast her line. It was a peeled willow wand and dangling from it was a big black hairpin bent into a hook. As Jimmy took the frog out of his pocket, however, Clem reached for his own rod which, to have out of harm's way, he had placed crosswise in the cleft of an elder bush that hung over the stream. As he took it down, the taut gut slashed through tender young leaves and, once again, their bitter scent was let out upon the air.

"Here, Jimmy! Here's the hook!" he cried. "Put on the frog!" Taking a tobacco tin out of his pocket, Clem selected a hook and, fingering it gently free of the other hooks and flies, he laid it in Jimmy's palm. Then he began to unwind his reel. For a few minutes the sound of the winding reel asserted itself over all the other sounds in the glade, until gradually it was absorbed into the general pattern of sound.

Suddenly there was another sound; a horrible sound: A screech. It split the air. It turned every other sound into silence. It was the frog. There was nothing human in that screech, but every human ear in that green place knew what the screech held — it held pain — and pain as humans know it.

"What did you do to him?" yelled Clem, and his face went black with rage. Throwing down the line, he caught hold of the screeching frog. Quick as thought, he pulled out the hook that had only gone a small way into the bulging belly, but had brought out a bubble of its bile-like blood. Then, throwing down the hook and stamping on it, he held the little slimy creature between his two hands.

"You are all right now," he told it, looking into its bulbous eyes, as if he'd force it to cast out fear. Then he turned to Jimmy again. "You didn't know any better," he said sadly. "You're only a child yourself. But let this be a lesson to you. Never in your life hurt or harm a defenseless thing! Or if you do, then don't let me see you do it! Because I could not stand it. I could not stand it," he repeated, less gently. "I never did a cruel thing in my life. I couldn't do one if I tried and — by God's blood — I could not see one done either! I only saw a cruel deed done in my presence once." Then he lowered his voice so only Jimmy could hear, "and once was enough! I couldn't stand it!" he cried. "I couldn't stand it." And he closed his eyes as if he saw it all again. When, after a minute, he opened his eyes again, he had a dazed look. It was as if he was astonished to find himself there, where he was, on the sunlit bank. More than that — he looked amazed that the sun could shine, amazed that the birds could sing.

"Are you feeling all right?" Jimmy asked.

Clem looked at him still dazed. Then it was as if he took a plunge back into the happiness around him.

"Here, give me a hook!" he cried, rooting around in the box. "This is the way it's done!" Deftly tucking up the legs of the frog so it fitted snugly into one hand, he nicked its back with the point of the barb, and then passed the hook under the skin, bringing it out again slowly and gently as if it were a needle and thread and he had just taken a long, leisurely stitch. "There! You see! It didn't feel a thing," he said, and hastily fixing the hook to the end of the line he reeled out a few yards of it and let the frog hang down.

Delightedly he gazed at it for a minute, as it moved its legs rhythmically outward and inward in a swimming motion. "Wait till we let him into the water!" he cried then, and he ran to the edge of the pool, scattering the children to either side and throwing the line out over of the pool. Suspended in the air the frog hung down, as still as the lead on the end of a plumb line, its image given back by the clear water that gave back also the blue sky and the white clouds as if they were under, not over, the pebbles and stones. Then Clem began to unwind the reel, and the frog in the air and the frog in the pool began to draw close to each other, till the real frog hit the water with a smack. Once there, its legs began to work again.

"Swim away, son," said Clem indulgently, and he unwound more of the line. "You'd think it was taking swimming lessons, wouldn't you?" he said, watching it amiably.

"But won't the pike eat him?" said Jimmy. "Isn't that worse than getting the hook stuck in him?"

Clem turned around. "Nonsense!" he cried. "Death and pain are two different things. Learn to distinguish, boy!" And he called to Pearl. "Would you like to hold the line for a while, Pearl?"

But Pearl was not looking at the frog. Something behind them had caught her attention.

"Who are those men, Daddy?" she asked, as two big men in dust coats, who had been watching the scene for some time from the causeway, began to get over the wall and slide down the bank toward them.

Clem looked back. "Here, Jimmy," he said. That was all and he handed him the line.

"You know why we're here?" asked one of the detectives. Clem simply answered their question with a question of his own. "What about the children?" he asked.

Never would Jimmy have thought that detectives could be so gentlelike and kind. "The children will be well treated, Clem," said one. The other addressed Jimmy. "Stay here with them, you Jimmy, and keep them amused. We've got a woman in the car up on the drive, and she'll come down to you in a minute and see what's to be done." They turned to Clem. "We'll have to ask you to come with us, I'm afraid."

Clem nodded briefly. Then he turned to Jimmy. "Here, give me the line again for a minute," he said, and as Pearl had snuggled close to him, her two arms around one leg as if it was a pillar, he freed her grasp and put the rod into her hand.

"You can have the first turn, Pearly," he said. "Then Moll. Then the others. After that it will be turn and turn about for you all!" His voice was authoritative, even stern. Then he nodded to the men, and finding it slippery to walk in the dirty tennis shoes, he caught at some of the elder branches, and by their help scrambled up the bank alongside the men.